Unk' Zeke's Pond

Rico Chamblain

Unk' Zeke's Pond

Published by Wheatmark®
2030 East Speedway Boulevard, Suite 106
Tucson, Arizona 85719 USA
www.wheatmark.com

ISBN: 979-8-88747-073-3
LCCN: 2023906646

Bulk ordering discounts are available through Wheatmark, Inc. For more information, email orders@wheatmark.com or call 1-888-934-0888.

Chapter 1

Jo' tis yo' boy, *Word-up* taints nuttin liked the beautifully funky-fresh git-mo aroma *ja' can smell da' honey dripping* albeit an al-natural afro chic hip-swinging bodacious *She* be one sophisticated lady done stepped-it to the visitor's podium arrival planet earth straight-up outta the primordial dust a cinnamon nutmeg brown-eyed babe not to be in-waiting cause that She be *Mother Nature*! She be of the original W*ho'dat* cosmic order everyting dat be anyting this world! Mother Nature be an elegant basket-case of the *P-funk*, She be a colorful cornucopia of the greatest all tings earthly aromatic to done burst-it loose a'many hungry man's nose wide the *Holy shits Batman* open! Yowls Sir, an al-naturelle bare-arsed buck-wild naked *Who'dat* done burst forth unto this world from amongst the Cosmos! She be the live livid entity all tings unto this world She be the real truth, Ruth! Ma' Nature be the green multi-colored flora embedded in the earth, She be all dems soaring wing-tips dems black birds a'chasing after swarming bumble bees whilst droppings little love *Harold Melvin and the Blue Notes* offerings onto the windshields of mankind's just hand-washed hand-waxed bucket a colorful speckled vivid *solid my brotha* reminder dat all the birds and alls the bees just liked Ma' Nature can be when theys wannabe a bitch!

Ma' Nature be founded in and within all tings bug-eyed crawling even flying pestering insects like dems needle-nosed fo' *Medgar Evers* poised to strike a bite thems bloodthirsty pesky skeeters as swell dems red covered black polka-dots just aints fancy dressings fo' a lady bugs justa itching to be done crawled-it all over one's bare unpampered gingerbread buttermilk brown bottom little-*whinny da' pooh*-butts Ma' Nature be founded in the rich loam paradise of a mill-less pond outposted the city limits of a *We bees onliest po' Blacks dat comes-it up P-funk filthy fresh outta the deep fiddle-dee-dee south* black country folk to arrive the Awe, the inspired *Stevie Wonder* of a Blessed peace dat be inside an immaculate outsourced Earthly jump-off knowed-it to the bestest of all mankind as Unk' Zeke's pond! *Good God All-Mighty!*

Big Guy In da Sky done did a darn good thang fo' us peoples of the *Who'dat* Nation Hisns fo'reallies on the personal chosen few! *Big Poppa* done did justa straight-up *do-wah-ditty* seed Unk' Zeke's pond gots justa little sump'tin of the sumptin for the every *I am Somebody* dat done dared to tread lightly upon its *not-so fast, little fella* Holy grounds! Unk Zeke's pond be that moment of Awe to alls thems seekers of theys freedom, the human cargo *give me liberty, youse can keep yo' death* passengers ridings steadfastly along *Sojourner's Truth's* underground railroad! Unk' Zeke's pond be da' spot to done enabled-it for the many amongst the darken and righteous *Who'dat Nation* pursuing deys God-given Universal Law to live freely theys inalienable right to the freedom to be human an unchained unbonded being of this world!

Unk' Zeke's pond be the spot, the exactamente paradise where a'many freedom seeking Blackfolk done copped a squat with freedom's one-way ticket held high in hand Black fisted-tight as theys done answered freedom's wonderous call *slipping into darkness* a justified stepped-it onward steadfastly path to the North. America done at its onset legally endorsed then brutally and inhumanely enforced a caste system of legalized slavery upon *We the Peoples* of a darker hue thus it must be truly stated America dat *give me Liberty* screaming bitch be no lady, harken not unto herns lying words for by her actions must she be judged a certified whoremonger pimping out herns owned darken beautiful *chillens* to the next *White male only* highest bidder!

Unk' Zeke's pond at a firstest glanced-it lookey-looked to be a little mill less pond sitting amid a vast army of worthless ashy white black spidery lined birch trees witch thems woebegone trees done had theys own-*sad sac*-selves been run amok by an army of the woebegone weeds yet Unk' Zeke's pond whence viewed from its mostest prolific, the goodie-stuff side swells unto thems the very luckiest folks theys woulda done fo'sho'nuff seed the magic, its beauty and the all encompassing purpose that be Unk' Zeke's pond! In-order to get to that peaceful spot theys onliest had to take a small-step backwards in theys mind's inner eye cause it be there that the understanding commenced inside the all seeing theys mind's inner unyielding personal universe the sweet fo' *Medgar Evers* flowing spot! These be the words of my Unk' Zeke "*dish here little pond bees the fo'reallies Enchanted Forest. Yes, Sir! Bobs-me-uncle there bees magicalness right here, everywhere n' Its there!*" Unk' Zeke for the moment would have voiced into existence hisns little earthen pond onto its rightful pedestal, a Peace unto all inhabitants of this little insignificant egotistical World and all Worlds beyond! *Citizens of the Universe, generational happiness has been sown in dis here little pond therefore come ye one, come ye all and reap the joy that be yourns! Peace be unto all that Be, my Brotha*! Unk' Zeke's pond done been placed upon this Earth to serve the supreme purpose of teaching all mankind to take a pause for the cause to trust the magic of a Soul cleansing funky little pond for all that was, be and for all that fo' *Medgar Evers* will be! It's our World to live so get a grip and *shake dat ass* Babycakes!

As a whinny-*da pooh*-butts justa Biggy-smalls bite-sized kiddie a wondering gingerbread cinnamon spiced nutmeg crusted babyboy child, I done knowed-it deep within my heart and Soul that there be just a little *sump-tin sumptin* special abouts dat little pond and there be no butter place on this green Earth to take in the Awe, a plausible moment before bare-arsed ripping-it to done running-it through Unk' Zeke's P-funk *may the mothership be with you* pond! I tried my bestest to done spent my every rug-rat crumbsnatching awaking moments perusing the *funky-stuff* dat be Unk' Zeke's pond! On the daily-double, a slow rolling-it white-misty fog witch done covered-it that pond and my nutmeg backside from big-*diaperless*-butt up to big *happy-nappy* head there be justa little on the slow white misty rolling fo' *Medgar Evers* up'town Baby! It be a P-funk misty dat little froggy soft cloudy white misting a cling-to-me *Baby, I'm for reals* foggy kinda thang dat done jumped-it to the goodie-stuff kinda thang done hugged its serene self minty-fresh flam-*Liberace*-buoyancy misty that truly be enchanted filled mostest parts human bumping-it up parts the unworldly witch peeps done called the *lost who'dats* caused the last known splinters of the windmills inside deys *gone fishing* mind bees all roiled-it up in what be the sparklings of dat fog yet theys black asses done left this world fo' a'nuttier realm!

Unk' Zeke's pond white misty be not jo' big-*scary*-butts weird London, England *death be on yo' ass* vampirish fog that London Bridge be falling down witch be the cover story for an eerily sub-human be *stalking yo' ass* evil assed-out fog, No way! Unk' Zeke's pond misty be Christened all kinda colors of the rainbow sparkled *Lucy in the sky* with emerald cut *Tiffany* diamonds sprinkled by little green fairy-tailed elves throughout the wee-bee hours of the stormy Black knights just so come the mornings broiled within the rising sun's *love-me love-me* beams to done brighten up the exact spot fo' swell a'many *happy-nappy* camper's summertimes daze! Unk' Zeke's pond on the reals just had to have been elfin magical! All tings Universal Law being copacetic, many a righteous *lucky charmed* mornings, I be liked dis *lil piggy done went to da market baby* bumping-it

Unk' Zeke's pond alive with the ritmo of the rainbow arched within its glittered misty of my youth the extraordinary beauty the true wizardry of Unk' Zeke's pond white misty be the all-naturelle bestest of the lastest of God's goodie-stuff!

Unk' Zeke's pond misty double dripped-it the sacred droplets seed the pristine solemn tears of fallen Angels be in its elegant waters. The Heavens *Lord have mercy* weepings done flowed-it downward the boles of all thems tall birch trees and thems Blessed Holy offerings done cascaded crystalized moistened manna to done etched into thems birch's boles theys unique design. It be a fat fact, Jack that each bole fo' *Medgar Evers* be engraved with the prayers of a'many *who'dat's* final moments on earth as theys done beseeched a God, any God to free theys Souls from the filthy imbecilic redneck deputized po-po on the prowl to be doing hisns pure unadulterated evilness. Unk' Zeke's pond be done gots Blessed big timey from all dat be Holy from the unaltered waters outta the eye-wells of weeping Angels thems blessed tear-drops be the what that done deep cleansed the filthy evil sip bottom waters

Unk' Zeke's pond be to my little poop-butt up-shoot and the posse's small-*thunder struck*-butts super-kool kiwi-lime *Kool-Aid* kool green and I justa loved it to drink in the flavor dat be the savor of all dat so-wild-to-be-soooo-much greenery not onliest fo' the eyeballing big-*beautiful*-butts also to done covered-it me backside seed that be a'nuttier duty fo' thems overly growed-it weeds and justa liked me theys big-*reedy*-butts be just so-so green! I'd done lived-it *Biggy-smalls* inside Unk' Zeke's pond to done scampered up a'many birch tree bole just to done sat-it deeply into the cradle of the inherent safety of that tree's spidery limbs witch be on the reals kid climber friendly with long tall limbs *stretched out unto the heavens* in memory of all the *who'dats* that done passed-it the way of the *gotta go* gone bye-bye!

I done knowed-it just witch one of thems skinny boles to done scaled-it with a cache of weapons be theys bb's and or rocks or to done hid behind to done saved my little backside when thems da' *Dirty-Dozens* be abouts and out on the prowl! Listen up folks cause I tell ya' God never fo' *Medgar Evers* done made a butter tree with a spidery black prayer lined bole just for po' black chillens to be ah climbing! I'm gonna tell ya' straight-up Unk' Zeke's pond onliest real truth, Ruth purpose in this walk of life be to be a lush green magical fun-filled mystical wonderland overflowed to be brimming with *ping-pow-zowie-Yowls-Sir-ping-ping—zing—*

oooooouch---Ratz—ass--zing—ping—ping---ouch---WTF *WhatTheFlick---Hell to all southern belles---What duh Bee-jeesus*!

Chapter 2

I HAD DONE JUMPED UPON my stick-horse to done runned-it and to done runned-it quick as swell I done managed to calm meself to a steady yet hurried beat. It had all been my owned fault, I hadda been slipping whilst day-tripping standing pooh-butts tall all out in the wide and open bump-in-it up in the fishbowl justa daydreaming and ego tripping the light fantastic. Idly waltzing through Unk' Zeke's pond gonna get a baby booster's hip-pockets pinged full of the *Little Daisey rifle* bb-gun lead from thems *Hells a'coming* da' *Dirty Dozens'* ambush! *Mz. Experience,* fav niece of *Father Time* done taught-it to always puts my trust in thems talled green bushy wild-weeds for cover: lesson one, *grasshopper*; never ever to stop at yo' first haven because thems darn da' *Dirty Dozens'* after theys done pinged-it yo' backside hip-pockets full of lead then theys would have stopped-it in theys young ruffians derelict tracks fo' an earful of any to all sounds of you hauling arse firstest outta the back door as swell be on the lookey-look fo' any unnatural movements of thems scraggly weeds. Heaven help the unhappy-nappy arse that done begun to whimpering after having had hisns little baby-bare bottom touched-up thens thems bad hombres would to done pepper-sprayed mo' bb-lead dat *Mommie Mommie Mommie* crying arse way! Lesson two: grasshopper never evers runs a'scared! You must at all cost befo' the loss be to done kept-it to calming jo'self all the whilst channeling thems fearful thoughts outta ya head as swell be on the *run-Blackie-boy*-run!

We be family and we be always together horsing around whilst watching all thems old timey Hollywood war and western movie reruns on the black and white then as soon as the next *Momma can we can go out to play* day done broke bright sunshiny light upon our black crusty behinds firstest tings first right after bursting a move into Unk' Zeke's pond the posse be done divvied-it up ourselves into the two groups: half the posse be thems good guys and dems a'nuttier knuckles be from the other side of the tracks bad-boys dems da' *Dirty Dozens'* just to imitate thems oater/war Tinsel-town re-runned-it movies. We all wanted-it to be GI Joe all-American war heroes instead of that sad in the sack clod-duster hero big-*wannabe*-butts we toted thems *Little Daisey* BB rifles so naturally we done loved-it ourselves nuttin butter than some *home on the range* oaters the reel truth, Ruth the western hero always had thems *fight* issues seed the oater be "*Uh, excuse me, Mr. Billy-bad-ass, Sir can it wait tills the end of this movie befo' I gives you this here arse whopping*"! Though physically, he a tall drink of water yet the oater be just empty calories in a meat-n-taters world full of root-beer floats! The clod-buster had to shoulder thems *aint itching to fights* feelings throughout mostest the whole darned movie *Emmett Till* comes the approach of the climatic end thens comes the *Hell a'floating tall waters* theres gonna be bubblegum and butt whuppings aplenty and that there oater hero be all outta the bubblegum!

In the Hollywood reel world, the all-American GI hero onliest had to fight to done killed-it off thems evil nazi Jew-boy killing mofos and thems bucktooth Pearl Harbor attacking nips the *rucky-rooseys* thens get back to the home front to done pucker-it up to done kissed the babe! We be the sevens going on nines therefo' the onliest ting dat we hadda done knowed-it fo' a fat fact, Jack about girls be theys Hollywood babes or be theys street urchins dat snit didn't matter *one wit the Devil's spit* cause to us's theys be from the one to the all the same just a bunch of big loud *I'm telling my momma thens I'ma gonna be going to yo' house and telling yo' momma* mouths and theys all had themselves a chunk of the cooties too boot!

We done cut out dems cootie kissings endings seed I didn't liked-it thems girlie-gurl kisses either not even from my Moms specially front street da' posse *hecks be Huckleberry*! Bad enough that all us's teenaged aunties and female cousins done alla time grabbed-it us by the naps a ting witch theys *coming of age* sassy butts done tagged *cabbage-patch'n* cause theys justa reached-it a strong savory brown hand inta the posse to done grabbed-it fo' themselves a head justa an any nappy-head then which *Medgar Evers* one of us big watermelon heads done surfaced outta the bunch it would be fo' dat unlucky camper *kiss-kiss-kiss*!

Chapter 3

I HADN'T WANTED-IT TO BE getting-it kissed by thems aunts nor to be kissing no girls especially thems tree honey brown bags of sugar coated cooties that I hadda done growed-it up with seed thems tree be justa trio of the worstest big-*tat-a-teller*-butts Thelma Mae Williamson, Geraldine

Louise Whitestone and Rosie Leigh Robinson thems tree *Sugar Babies* be the girls of my crumbsnatching through adolescent world, UGH! Geraldine gonna let me make-it out with her comes the prom night, she gonna be *"Aint no uneducated soon to be shit-house rat crazed assed-out Viet Nam nut-jobber gonna be popping my cherry!"* Geraldine on the afore hand done mentioned-it, quoted-it or indicated that little cautionary tale big-*teasing*-butts she done followed-it up with herns teenaged super sweet-n-sexy smile and a *"we can make-out, watch yo' hands, Zeke!"* Heck, I'd spent-it sooo much of my childhood in that pond of Unk' Zeke's that all the peeps hadda begun innocently e'nuff to just naturally done tooken-it to calling me *Zeke*! Growed-it up folks and all thems kiddie, youngster and the teenaged just all the peeps of the Chocolate City iffn theys hadda done asked-it to anywho as to where I might be on any given day at any given time then the natural *snapback* would've most likely be a "*he down et Zeke's pond*" then as times done shift-it and hadda slipped-it through the grains of sand iffn thems same peeps axed the same question swells theys all somehow to a'nuttier hadda managed-it to done slipped-it up just a wee-bee bit to have swallowed-it them words *he down et .... pond* seed thems same peeps would've done dropped-it off and or chopped-it off the descriptive words to done hollered-it "*et Zeke's*" and justa mighty bite and tab-shortly there afterwards thems two little left-it over distinguishing words *et Zeke's* hadda gotten theys grammatical selves and me morphed-it into the one just as iffn somehow me and Unk' Zeke's pond hadda gotten-it somehow sumptin sumpting mutated into the one thus for the all and to the every damn some-to-body even my Moms and my Dad done started-it to justa calling theys *git-along little doggie* gingerbread browned babyboy "*Zeke*" my Moms and Dad and justa everybody be liked "*Yo' Zeke, damn-it boy whacha be doings over there*" as natural as the day be long! As for me, I'd just loved-it seed everybody always be trying to hang a nick-named moniker unto a'nuttier sum-body else seed iffn the name be Robert theys gonna holla *Bob* iffn the name be Donald theys all gonna shout-out *Duck* evens iffn the name be Vincent or Manuel theys gonna shout-out *Gawd damned skeeze-ball greaser scum-bucket Vinny the fucking wop* or *Manny the fucking scuzz-ball Messycan*! I be justa happy-nappy *skin'in to be grin'in* because I just loved-it the nickname *Zeke* ting be dat backs then I done loved-it nuttin butter in the life than to be out fooling around et Unk' Zeke's pond then the second ting be liked the first day of the new school year and I be a'sport'n thems brand new *Converse* that nickname and thems JC-walk on water sneakers be the one and the same cause the name Zeke laced-me up to perfection!

Come Marine Corps boot camp everyone gonna be chicken scratching theys gal back home and I won't really have meself a sho'nuff *Shorty* to squibble back et so I gonna write Geraldine because us two hadda had a passionate bite earlier justa few weeks prior et that prom night we two be lovebirds seed me and brownsuga fine Geraldine done made-it out *Biggy-smalls* in the backseat of the bucket *tank God* fo' the make-out session herns super soft lips red-hot sweet caramelized *Sugar Babies* kisses made me one lucky ass man! The gorgeous teenaged 18-year old Geraldine done *rocked my world* herns hot sweet kisses be all the goodie-stuff left unto this world big-*dummy*-butts thems savored kisses done sho'nuff rearranged the silky cobwebs in my mind thus what I had not knowed-it dat lovely Black Knight in the backseat be that I done gotten myself onto third base on a foul *stinky-finger* tip! Harold, dat dumb-ass knuckle-head be Geraldine's older brother be the one to done *pissed on my cornflakes* dat dumb-ass gonna be done wrote me back and dat sick fool done sent-it hisns reply on a pink postcard to the USMC bootcamp witch the *mofo* on the backside of that card in big assed *Bic* black inked lettering done wrote-it that he *gonna stump a meat-hole in my dumb-ass* iffn I be to *Medgar Evers* write hisns baby-sista Geraldine ever a'gin-n-juicy Lucy thems two *she love me* big-*misinformed*-butts *she love not* notes gonna be the t-total extent of all my USMC bootcamp love letterings.

Chapter 4

STILL, WAR HEROES BE DA' *Shit'* because mainly theys always got the girl, my Geraldine incident aside. Never the less dat misconstrued-it life lesson be the major first class of my love-life relationships in that I'd done publicly learnt-it thems Hollywood reel truths be liked that damned public unschooling of the Negro only justa all that snit just be his-*Jew boy*-story justa chunk of broadcasted lies because the mostest of Hollywood *on the reels* heroes and would-it be heroes never even gots close to doing half the Hollywood *goodie-stuff* theys been accredited to be idealized on a gigantic guiled screen. All dat shit just be PR *philly rotten* attributes to Mr. Charlie Po'dunk and his-*white lies*-story an erroneous script about a po'dunk that never ever was thus could never evers be a fo'reallies war/

oater hero! The Hollywood reel hero be just a *caped crusader* plain vanilla wrapper decked to hisns white cotton balls with onliest minute bits and pieces of the real truth, Ruth! All thems straight-up dignified Blackfolk all thems *who'dats* done comes *up-gnawth* a'running to done be outta the *evil sip* delta basin caused theys very lives done depended on the Great *Git-a-way* swells all thems po'folks done unofficially loved-it theyselves nuttin butta than some *Honest Abe* Lincoln and John Fitzgerald Kennedy just you stepped-it the one or the two feet insides any of theys homes and the one iffn not the both of thems presidential whiteys done rode-it *high-n-tight* shotgun in plain eyeballing sight on theys paper thin drywalls alongside other kinfolk photos liked dems two po'dunk whitey woodchuck jackasses be family or sumptin-sumptin! My Moms done on a purpose kept ol' Abe in the kitchen *stove-pipe hat* mofo and JFK's big-*pasta*-butt ruled inside the dining room across from a *whiteboy long haired hippy-freak* dago-Roman Catholica approved iconic lying assed photograph of *a hands held in prayer* Jesus be all the crap! My Dad would alla time threaten to knock-down and or break all tree of thems funky-hunky pics *da holy trio of po'dunk peckerwoods* when he hadda jumped-it off and unto a *bad moon rising* kinda vibe then be the times my Moms done straight-up argued to my Dad and or to any-a-body in dat rising blood "*taint so much as to what theys didn't do or didn't done got did butz the how comes and thems whys of it all. Theys done tried to do the right thing and because theys tried then deys bees good peoples. It aints nonya theys fault dat the evilness of thems po'dunk white-trashy-folks done gone and killed them alls befo' theys had a chance to done finished up all the good things theys hadda done started! Gone now Git! Leave my pics be!*'"

In the hood, *Ol' Abe stove-pipe hat wearing mofo'* Lincoln be a consecrated publicly anointed Saint back in them daze cause he the one that done freed us Blackfolks. *Ol' Abe* done did free us outta the jaws of slavery all the times him a'looking liked he been beat hardily with the jawbone of an ass! Later in life, I done learnt-it dat Ol' Abe hadn't wanted-it to actually free the slaves seed dat long bearded, yeah he only slept *hey-hey Michael J* with men *just fo' da sleeping* cause backs then bedding be not so now-day cheap *wink-wink* hot-damn ya' ever sneaked-it a peek at that faithful little wifey of hisns fo' damned sho' she be not yo' *Good-Golly Miss Molly* hecks be *Huckleberry*, Word-up in any books beyond thems worthless his-*lying ass*-story books fo' the uneducation of the *Negro only* it be written dat sad faced presidential sad-eye hadda only wanted to keep all them States united comes the Hell or high *roll-*

Tide-roll waters! John-F*ricking brings me all thems blonde Hollywood starlets to my Whitehouse no-tell motel*-Kennedy didn't do Jack-shit big-*pimp'n*-butts to done jack-jumped hisns jackass pasty paddy crack across the drink to done stood tall po'dunk proud before the Berlin wall telling thems *soured-krauts* the f'n lie *"...as long as one man is enslaved, no man is free"* The po'dunk *bay-of-pigs* President *Spuds MacKennedy* be yakking total bull-shit Heck, he couldda not done forgotten-it all those *Whites only* toilets and *Colored* water fountains in hisns own damned *Whitehouse no-tell motel* big-*boney*-butts *good* Gawd All-Mighty! Say it with me, good Gawd All-Mighty! He did done gots hisns-*Pussi Galore*-self da' babe and not justa any bae that *Marilyn Monroe* be one most fine-assed world-class *Happy Birthday Mr. President* holla et ya' Boy cause that bae be a bonafide Hollywood beauty *hecks be Huckleberry*, the Mrs. President *Jackie K'* had it going-on in herns own damned rights living-it up the Camelot life! There be no good to come abouts speaking ill the sandal-footed long-haired hippie-freak Jew-boy commissioned martyr buy-buy thems greaseball dago Romans to be a world renowned demi-God!

The heroic coin gots two sides the one witch mostest too all thems *Baby, I'm for real* honest Injun genuine heroes never be properly mentioned nor *don't ya dare* publicly recognized by sad Hollywood *get dat paper* mongrels. President Lyndon Baines Johnson that ugly-arse been beat with a Presidential ugly stick mofo be *da' shit* sum dems LBJ presidential acts be 100% Superfly bumped-it hisns far *Too-Short* "what's my favorite word" daze atop the Whitehouse crapper! I didn't never done seed hisns boo-ugly hound-dog mug framed on nobody's *Home sweet Home* walls! LBJ be *da' Man, Baby* yet nobody and I means No fucking body to dis day done gave nor does theys wanna give LBJ, The *Presidential Man* hisns props! President Lyndon Baines Johnson did what both thems a'nuttier two a'scared assed whiteboy Presidential woodchucks should have done did seed firstest tings first be President LBJ protected, promoted then projected our Black be beautiful race from the inferior position of a second-classed citizenship big-*backward*-butts justa chunk of hobnobbers standing at the back of the *inner-city country school* bus scratching our nut-sacks straight-up and outta the *hoodee* to be first-class with rights to vote and be equal citizens amongst the powers that be plus *Happy Birthday to me* Mr. President Lyndon Baines Johnson done made that *locked-in-a-barrel* cross-dressing closeted homo non-sapien J. Edgar Hoo-*ever run da klan be hisns*-man and thems *Fat Bald Idiots* the Federal Bureau of Investigation to done stepped-it double-Dutch balls deep into the cornholes of all thems evil-assed *klu-less klutzing klaners* killing Black folks and white folk mostly Jewish folk *freedom riders* all across a 1960s *We shall over-come* a racist America! President Lyndon Baines Johnson be da' real *Shit* yet most peeps both thems dat be the uppity educated Blacks and especially thems Hollywood Jew-boys and the Whites only racist thems fools done taught-it just cause that all peoples to be done wrong learnt-it the American educational system bye-bye way of hisns-*lying assed*-story that LBJ be not remembered as *da' Shit* big-*hunky*-butts the real turd *they* used President LBJ very own words against him *"...I won't be sending little black and white American boys... off to fight...little yellow and brown Asian boys..."* far away yonders in thems there *let's rumble motherfucker lets rumble* killing rice fields of Viet-Nam just to save the *skank-hoe-frenchy-fry Pepe* DuPont in the guise of protecting the French economy. President LBJ be my *numero uno* fav US President though the brains of the operation gots a big-*crazed*-butts straight-up hard-on to the Corps love for one Mr. President William Jeffer-*Son, I did not have sexual relations with that woman*-Clinton, hecks-bee Huckleberry!

Chapter 5

***YES'UMS*, THAT BE THE GOODIE-STUFF** witch I be done learnt-it come big schooling big-*nerdy*-butts for the then the magic of Unk' Zeke's pond be that you could get-it all wrapped-it up just to be warped-it up in its beauty then start to be done day-tripping the *Big Eazy* way instead of taking care of the bees-wax liked that early morning when I be out strolling in the fishbowl and da' Dirty Dozens' done popped my tattered *hand me down* breeches full of BB-gun lead, hecks be Huckleberry! I was supposed to be on the scout-it out the looky-look fo' dems da' *Dirty Dozens* witch dat fated morn thems knuckles be led by my cousin *Junebug'* normally me and *Bug* hung tighter than fat-assed ticks on a bloodhound's big-*funky*-butts dat day Bug be my number one enemy and I'd bet ya' 10 tiger-eye marbles to a busted BB that *kiddy-o* be the one to done shot me in the keister even though Bug be past 7-years-old he still peed his pants, so hisns big-*piss soaked*-butt branched up in a wet birch's early morning dew wouldn't have been a problem. Bug gonna growed-it up to be an executive *Baby I'm fo' real* Superfly a straight-up pharmaceutical entrepreneur dat be butta knowed-it in the hood as *da' Pusherman* a street dealing eight-baller with a drive-it up to be stepped-it up branch marketed on every corner the CC! Bug gonna be the provocateur of thems sweet dreams as swell thems sociopathic nightmares to all them strung-out junkies, Babycakes!

Bug had fo' hisns 2nd-Louy, David *One-eyed Jack'* Johnson that boy could fo'reallies shoot and he done loved-it hisns-self nuttin more than to sit-it up high in a birch wet or dry justa waiting on some knucklehead with hisns mind in the clouds to passer bye-bye seed fo' *One-eyed Jack'* there be nuttin butter than ambushing a dumb-butt out strolling along with a wandering mind. *One-eyed Jack'* wasn't supposed to be out there making BB-gun war yet dat bad-butt be the bestest sharp-shooter of us all and he hadda done always come to play. The summer befo' unfortunately he had gotten hisns nappy-head pinged-it by a stray BB when he done gotten outta the hospital he done gots *Blessed* with the kiddy *Kool-Aid* summer punch koolest call-sign ever *One-eyed Jack*! Mostest times he done kept-it that marble in hisns front pocket witch he could snatch-out and throw-it at ya' then holla the shout-out "*yo' Blackie-boy, gonna hit ya' with my good eye!*" The Biggy-smalls ting be that hisns momma be mad at *dem damn hellish young fool who'dats gon and done cost my baby-only hisns good eye-sights* she would to be laid to her silk-lined box Marble city a'still a'fussing justa cussing us damned foolish fools! She be done fumed that madness fo' mo' than fo'dee years, talk about gripping a grudge big-*mad*-butts comes the future the peeps are gonna elect *One-eyed* Mayor to the CC then hisns momma gonna walk-it all over town proud as a peacock preening herns multi-colored feathers talking-it up her babyboy cause he the Honorable on the reals Mayor thus *One-eyed Jack* gonna become som'body he gonna be a *Baby, I'm for real* legit kinda fella unlike us' *up-to-no-good* heathenish crumbsnatchers that done cost *One-eyed* hisns onliest good eye-sights!

George *lemonhead* Carson, on a good day dat football head fool be a'nuttier dead-eye shooter! *GeorgieC* after bumping up aged 12, it be proof-positive that you done gots yo'self into one knocked-down dragged-out fight iffn ya' done hollered *lemonhead* hisns way big-*don't tag me*-butts he gonna be the onliest one of the posse to done growed-it up to buy Bug's *live the dream* wares seed nonya us knuckles hadn't a clue bouts hisns nightmarish clipped wings *hecks be*! Comes age 14 *GeorgieC* dat fool gonna be strung-out, hooked-it on the mo' than just phonics! *GeorgieC* gonna be ghetto crooking-it *wild thang* he gonna be snatching old lady purses rights offa theys old wrinkled and frail arms fo' to ride the white-crosstown horse, the white momma, Mrs. Heroin gonna put a solid chokehold on hisns big-*junkie*-butts by the 9th grade dat fool gonna be out on thems mean-assed streets strong-arm pistol-whipping grown asses! *GeorgieC* he gonna hit it Biggy-smalls them numbers! Dat fool done told-it us dat he'd done dreamt-it bouts One-eyed's funky-ass glass marble fo' many a daze *Lemonhead* said he couldn't get that glass eye outta hisns big nappy fo' over a month so he done looked-it up the tree numbers then went out and played thems numbers dat he'd gotten outta the lucky-dream book *Captain Redd's* sure-fire the last of this world luckyman's sho'nuff dream winning numbers! For the fortunate few who don't know *the numbers* swells a *Reader's Digest* snippet of the game be in that *the numbers* be an illegal ghetto bound tree-numbered lottery system run by dems damned dago mafioso chicken-shit mofos outta the Windy City. The numbers be ghetto fool's gold, the original hoodee residential idiot's tax that be played by po'assed-out folks way long before Mr. Charlie McWhitey done *flipped-da-scrip* on that dago bitch to the latter day Saintly bump'n all fiddy States *Mr. Powerball*!

The Washington twins Xiomar and António be barely 5 and theys onliest had pea-shooters for weapons all the times theys be a'waddling bouts us with theys narrow runny-nose smallish-*crying*-butts theys crusty assed-out good fo'nuttin daddy be the only colored cop in the CC so we hadda on a fo'reallies purpose done let thems too ugly shitty-diaper pooh-butts hang along the outskirts of camp. Thems two come-alongs tag-alongs with theys little homemade rubberband slingshots thems two-mirrored butt-uglies be our security blanket because peoples be a'far less than likeliest to be willing to beat our small-*pooh pudding*-butts iffn theys done peeked-it themselves an awful funky fresh eyeful thems two gawd-awful butt-ugly twins hanging-out! Dems chuckle-headed twins gonna follow a narrow hardline in theys potbelly daddy's extra-small footsteps and become city cops come theys done growed-it up ugly-assed selves. Xiomar gonna give me a speeding ticket even though I won't be speeding. He'll holler the ugly-ass lie *"Any dumb-fuck dumb enough to go to Nam' be stupid enough to pay a dumb-ass's speeding ticket"* when the ugly fool ass done hit me with thems red-blue flashing bubble-gums I'd done taught-it *orange you glad* Kool-Aid kool because I done seed it be hisns lumpy fat-ugly ass breaking sweat getting outta the po-po wagon that be *Emmett Till* he done handed-it me that damned fiddy-dollar ticket! I done knowed-it a fat fact, Jack dat hisns butt-ugly ass just be enviously jealous cause he sad *shit-sack* of a jelly donut eating cop-daddy hadn't done let hims nor hisns just as equally butt-ugly brother GI-up! Tony-T, that butt-head, he gonna tell it to everybody bouts the moon-lit Black knight when dat sneaky-Pete fool ass done catched-it me and Thelma in the back-seat of herns city councilman daddy's *duce-n-a-quarta* seed it be a summer-time knight the CC, it be African hot be why we had all the windows rolled down in dat bucket thus the butt-ugly bastard had done gotten hisnsself a real earful of how Thelma done cussed-it me *good-n-aplenty* for not finishing what I had done gone and done started-it in that damned torrid hot as all *Hell to southern belles* fake-leather bucket's backseat! That be my inner circle, the upper room the boon-coon boss'men outta my childhood da' posse' my main boo-coos' big-*war be Hell*-butts then justa an anytobody bumping-it a *Little Daisy BB Sharpshooter* be welcomed to rifle-up and come to play bb-gun war with us out in the magical Unk' Zeke's pond, Yes lawdy!

Chapter 6

I JUST LOVED-IT ME AND the posse be play acting dems Hollywood reel heroes big-*rifle*-butts it didn't take no Hollywood spin doctor to tell me who my real heroes be, I awoke to Dad and my Moms every morning. My Moms didn't take kindly to us playing in thems woods out to Unk' Zeke's pond, it be a good-n-plenty times my Moms done said dat there be rattle snakes and water moccasins out there big 'nuff to eat a grown man's naked ass so me and the posse done lookey-looked to done poked-it all over that sacred pond big-*dummy*-butts we never done found a'nuttin no bigger than a garter snake. On the reals, my Moms didn't liked-it a lot of the things we knuckleheaded tykes hadda done big-*waddle waddle*-butts that be onliest cause as Dad put it down my Moms used to be a girl, *Ugh*! Take the time I be about 4, I hadn't done started-it that unschooling for the Negro only bullshit! I be playing on the front porch with the posse and we all still had them its winter tight naps atop our heads thus it be an early pooh-butt springtimey daze. *"Dem boys needs theys hair on they heads to fight off dat Hawk"* Dad always challenged my Moms come early springtime so that me and my older brother Calvin could keep the naps a'covering our heads to fight off catching a cold or the flu. Now, *Mr. Hawkins* be that icy cold, brrrr-wind witch *to Hell with global warming* done blew across a frozen Lake Michigan come every wintertime the CC and that day everybody who be somebody on that front porch be jaw-jack'n *Bazooka Joe* bubblegum seed everyone big-*goofy*-butts me outside on dat closed-in porch be blowing dem big-time bright pink bubbles followed-it up with a loud bubble done got burst-it smack! I couldn't blow a bubblegum bubble to save my life so to stop the teasing I had chewed-it up a big wad of the gum to done strung-it out that wad of the pink *Bazooka Joe* into my hair that be when everybody done stopped-it theys kidding and the ribbing to done rolled-it theys winter fat-belly over with the laughter! I must have been some sight, black wooly afro 'cepting backs then there be no such ting as afros seed wooly hair atop a yardrat's head justa meant-it dat po' pic-a-ninnies' assed-out peeps couldn't afford a haircut we be on the cutting-edge dems times befo' *'fros* became chic! My Moms hadda tooken-it justa one look outta the bigroom window to done peeped-it just what be up with all the laughter and merriment big-*on the lookey look*-butts whence she done glanced-it my direction to done seed-it my black naps and all that pink bubblegum then she went nuts to done kicked the everybody dat be somebody offa dat front-porch befo' she dragged-it my not so happy pink bubblegum decorated nappy head inside the big room fo' the privacy then she'd done beat my backside with a *go fetch-it* tree branch of a switch. My Moms done phoned Dad the fo'-one-one so when he'd gotten home straight-offa jump avenue he done beat my butt, Mr. Griffin ran a *pig's hairy snout* outta hisns basement and when the gum got caught in hisns clippers swells right thens I hated to be there he done beat my dumb-*I did it for the laughs*-butts when he done charged double fo' the cut then I'd done gots me dumb-*giggles*-ass two more big-*dummy*-butt whuppings befo' the Black knight be over! To this day I don't chew nobody's f'n gum and I *Gillette* razor shave my own damn Ma' Nature's original bald no mo' nappy-ass head!

My Moms hadn't been all that bad et tall, truth be knowed-it, she really did break-out thems spoils fo' herns ginger brown #2 babyboy mostest times, liked iffn some growed-it up fool hadda done caught-it up to me pissing my pants then had tried whopping-it up on me, my Moms done on the quick *"Don't be ah foolin with my ginger bread brown bouncing babyboy, he gonna be a Do Right Man"* she'd always tossed-it just a little sump-tin sump-in a personal reference to the Queen, Aretha Franklin when *Medgar Evers* she could squeeze-it in herns shout-out *"my babyboy taint no link in the Chain of Fools, gone now, GIT!"* My Moms sang them downhome spoonfull loving blues on the daily-double seed my Moms done belted-out thems bluz with more than just a mere sense of pride because the mostest of thems moms around the CC be *gee-golly* churchfolk moms so theys done strutted theys *can'ts I sing* let the choir say *Amen* stuff front and centered thems kneebanging *get yo' Jesus freak-on* sessions. My Moms be nobody's fool seed my Moms didn't cater to any dat bible thumping nonsense, my Moms be not the fool decked to the nines standing thems Sunday-go-to-meetings and that be why iffn it be a winterized warm e'nuff day my Moms done opened-it all the windows in the whichever room she tending specially come the springy summertimes daze just sho' folks still be to done knowed-it the fat fact, Jack, the real truth, Ruth *who'dat* be the fo'reallies *Queen Bee* bumping arias the CC!

My Moms for having once been a girl be fo' sho'nuff kool Jamaica mon *Kool-Aid* royalty kool yet when I had started to age and hadda gotten justa a bite of a manly growl in the chest coupled-it up with the gleam in the eye swells then my Moms hadda problem to done come down hardtack against any *Shortie* witch I be attempting to make on the any given daily-double dat Shawtee my Shortie! Big-*man gotta have a Shorty*-butts the Shorty be Shawtee, I 'members my Moms coming-down hard-tack face to grille onto my firstest Shawtee fo' *Medgar Evers* because my Moms be *no love* fo' Shortie fine ass! My firstest very own *Shawtee* be one hip-swinging fine-assed young struttin Momma, dressed to kill, red apple-candied-be-dandy micro-mini and *Yes, Lawd iffns there be a Lawd hava Mercy* Shawtee's PHATT*PrettyHotAssTotallyTempting* bumpers swang *sweet low, sweet chariot* my Shawtee be a *Baby I'm for Real* itty-bitty-piece-o-leather big-*fine*-butts swell puts together, Shawtee be fine! When I hadda first peeped-it Shawtee bouncing uptown Fifth Avenue, my lovejones come down hard, it be heavy, Baby! Seed this ugly, God-awful ugly he done even made thems butt-ugly assholes twins look handsome be dat skinny-assed non-prime time ghetto pimp, sporting a cheap-assed polyester light-blue button-it up the front napped assed-out velour jumpsuit, white fake-pleather kicks, gold rings and gold teeth witch he'd done clinched-it *jawbone of an ass* tight around an old and stale *White Owl* cee-gar then all *Hell to the Nawl* that po'assed-out pimp he wassa trying hard to put thems pleather kicks to Shawtee's *baby, gotz back* plumpers plus thems grubby, grimy, knotted-up perverted ashy hands of hisns had hard rubbed-it along Shawtee's patootie allatime dat there punk-assed pimp a'thinkin-it he gonna trick the fine-assed Shawtee out to the next highest bidder! *Oh, Hell, to da' No*! I'd done gone berserk and braked-it the boat, right smack the middle of 5th Ave *Up'town, Baby* I hadda jumped outta the 67' *Goat* dat be my big bro Calvin's pony, he done left-it to me whilst he'd gone off to fight fo' LBJ, God, country and my Mom's greens-n-fatback with deep-dish crumbled peach cobbler-pie, I hadda done a full ragga-muffin up to be outta the Goat, I justa jiffy popped-it up then hardtack unto that punk-assed pimp's skinny crusty black ass! It be brutal, baby! I took Shawtee home and made her mines then to the I and she *hey-hey Michael J* gotz to be there fo' *Medgar Evers* and a daze, it be young love yet it be strong love and a Righteous love, Babycakes!

My Moms and my very firstest Shawtee straight-up fall-out day be bouts us tree slow dragging-it the streets of the CC cause the winter bouts to be done hauled ass caps over frozen teacups when we'z be rolling thems *McFilthy* slushy slimy streets of the Chocolate City, Baby! My Moms hadda been on the haunt justa do some Tri-City farmer's market *close yo' mouth skank it be me* shopping! My Moms had accepted-it herns beautiful moms-self an on the personal mission to strut herns moms stuffings front-street amongst all the other moms bouncing dat market place thus she be more than a bit mildly pissed at me cause I be running-it on the slow-hand, light tapping the gas and justa mite heavy on the brake *yo' ass* pedal sorta ting. Dat Sundae my Moms aints fo' having no late-late afternoon matinee cause my Moms be justa itching to strut-it into that Sundae soiree to done showed-it thems stank heifers just who da' *who'dat* be thus my Moms be hating hard on my Shawtee. My Moms wanted me to come down hardtack Shawtee big-*stomp dat ass*-butts I don't be abusing my Shawtee for nary an any-*not even iffn you bees my beautiful Moms*-body seed my Moms be thinking that I done treated my Shawtee sway too meek, mild and gentle-liked seed it be no inner-city top-secret bouts me and Shorty therefo' my Moms hadn't no need to squeezed the grapes to be done heard-it exactamente through the ghetto *say Whadd, No shit* grapevine as to how me and fine-assed Shawtee done hooked-it up, Babycakes!

My Moms be a'tinkering dat Shawtee be some little whorish-assed floozy, the swine's ear justa big-*trifling*-butt sista and my Moms thinking dat my dumb-*mannish*-butt be a'tinkering that I gots meself da' *Mona Lisa* a stolen treasure that be whys my Moms done talked trash up-front Shawtee's grille! *Medgar Evers* since I be knee high to a jack-legged grasshopper, my Moms hadda done always said-it "*If I can't say it to a face, I won't waste it on an ass*! Dat Sundae she done hollered-it mo' *Never thought*

I'd live the day, my babyboy be to kick me to the curb for some cheap assed trick! *Justa jay-bird naked assed streetwalker done been rejected from a lowlife house of ill repute*! *Why thisns little trifling tail-wagger can't cut cud in a whores pasture*! It be a fat fact, Jack dat my Moms hadn't been giving love nonya any kinda R-E-S-P-E-C-T to my Shawtee! My Moms hadda been squawk-boxing at me all the whilst Shawtee hating then just fo' the heck-of-it all my Moms done brung down the Heavens to done leveled-up a'nuttier notch she be adding a little *JC* to the mix and my Moms didn't even believe in the *Son of no-man* whom fo' us family be mo' liked dat hippie-freak Son of a *shut-yo' mouth* big-*worshipping*-butts whom the non-heathens thems that don't be pagan asses done tooken-it to call theys God, I'll be damned! My Moms be liked *Lord, Lawd, eyes done gone and raised me a fool, baby Jesus, I swear this Son, of mine, he trying to cotton-pick my last nerve*! My Moms be laying low the *Word-up* cutting thems heads n' justa cutting cards with da' Devil hisns owned evil-assed self dat day witch hadda so happened to have been one Hallelujah glorified the Sun-*gonna shine on me*-day and dat chocolate double-Dutch fudge Sundae hadda been served-it up with a double scoop the rocky-road and just liked my Shawtee dat day be t-totally fine!

Old Man Winter done winked hisns *ta-ta, Baby* and Mz. Spring be sprung! *Aunt Hannah* done shook-it off herns old musky rabbit fur coat then be beaming down upon *We the Peoples* a smile so bright, it done baked herns utmost favoritest chill'ums gingerbread brown! The melting winter snow be in the process of roiling itself into a slimy muddy slushy sorta slop witch be a mixture of rock salt and *what-the-Hell*! Thems potholes be filled with a raw sewage witch been self-perpetratedly formed by itself of itself to done created a nasty cocktail outta rock-salt, dirt, broken gravel, road kill and bits to pieces of broken-off road tar. Thems McFilthy potholes be thoroughly littered throughout all them mean assed CC streets every come the springtime seed the insides of them pot-holes be a'nuttin mo' than a cold-assed mess of *messings* justa slime icy sweltering bucket of rotting gruel knowed-it locally as *da' nasties*! I be justa easing it through *da' nasties* on the slow-poke liked so slow dat cars, buses and even thems CC yellow we *drive it slo to get mo' of yo' dough* taxi-cabs be justa whizzing *Right-on my Brother* a sweet kiss my patootie goodbye-bye and it hadda been thems a'whizzing bye-bye buses and cabs dat hadda set my Moms on the edge of herns seat cantered atop my last nerve!

My Moms be justa mite bit peeved cause I be a'creeping-it through a city with no speed limits.! Shawtee knowed-it for a *PHATT* fact, Jack dat she be fine and my Moms, swells my Moms be just liked all thems other womenfolks the CC that hadda done gone and peeped-it themselves a bountiful *you be welcomed* eyeful of the lookey-looks at my Shawtee then theys be and justa swell hadda a sho'nuff need to bleed jealousy green-eyed monster green, Lord knows, theys had good cause seed my Shawtee be a beast cause my Shortie be just fine! My Moms be sitting tight, wind caught in her cheeks, riding shotgun and dressed-it to the nines! My Moms be styling with a purpose, wearing her yellow Sundae *go-to-meeting* dress big-*aints I cute*-butts come the somehow she'd never quite made it to dat church-mousy meet-it up my Moms justa didn't to never ever be knowed-it to done set nary a foot in nobody's house of lies nor the First Bap-the-piss Church of Fables and Myths. My Moms be wearing one of herns pillbox hats and that little wannabe cropped at the knees fez be adorning her well coifed head liked it be some kinda *Queen for a day* tiara to done matched-it herns dress both hat and dress be a bright goofy deep dark autumn sunset yellow. My Moms, Bless her lil *dat boy done pissed me off* heart liked lots of older womenfolk of thems times, my Moms and theys just loved-it themselves some-o-dems church lady hats not those big assed tree-foot ghetto *sky-toppers* my Moms woulda went to church befo' being caught wearing one of those big-*floppy*-butts the chic women of them daze wore thems dainty little pillbox church lady hats that had been made Superfly fabulous and a worldwide fashion fad pinned famously unto *Jackie K'* when she be the *first lady* married to that jackass presidential whitey JFK. It hadda been super chic fo' the all proud Black be beautiful Soul-Sistas to done hauled attitude whilst theys be out a'sport'n and a'strut'n theys Sundae go to meeting dress sets always topped-it off with a matching pillbox come front-street Tri-City farmer's market justa show folks exactamently *who'dat* folks be!

The Sundae afternoon, Tri-City farmer's *Woman strut yo' stuff* market be as advertised the Sophisticated Soul-Sista's Sundae social! My Moms kept paying dat rent with them mild moms kinda chides waving them two one-dollar bills at me hollering bouts *Boy*! *I gots me some gas money, git on the good foot*! *This lil piggy gots to git to the market*! *Son, you drive like Mr. Lollipop, all-day sucka*! *Don't make me go Rudy Ray Mo' on yo' young ass*! Rudy Ray Mo', he da' *brotha* that had fo'reallies invented rap, way back in the *fo'dees* and dem *fiddies* Blackfolk usta done talked straight-up shout-out *cuss yo' ass* rhymes *Yeah, motherfucker I be cussing* shit dissing the one to a'nuttier then Rudy Ray Mo' done record albums recreating dems old-timey mofos rhyming of *the dozens* witch be talking about *Yo' Momma* with a string of curse words as verbs, nouns and adjectives dat kinda went a little sumptin sumpting *"Yo' momma bees a dirty little hoe born on a dirt street… dat filthy rotten lowdown bitch can't cook or clean but she'll suck the Hell outta dick-meat*! No! I had not then nor never done needed-it dat my Moms go Mr. Rudy Ray Mo' on my big-*dumb*-butts still me and my Shawtee be driving my Moms to market on the *slo' ya roll* and Shawtee she be just fine! The squawkbox be tuned to *KBLU*, my Moms loved-it them lowdown and dirty blues fo' Blackfolk the Blues bees family we'z gots our *Uncle* BB King strumming hisns *Sweet-16*, step-up young-fella *first-Cousin* ZZ Hill *Downhome bluz* and *sweet-Cuz* Etta James always a'wanting herns *Wang-dang doodled*! Dat Sundae afternoon my Moms be not warbling seed she be justa shucking-n-jiving my last ear of corn thus what hadda done happened on the *In-coming* onliest the good *Reverend Leroy* a character role played out by the Brother Flip Wilson performed on hisns own 70's TV sitcom *The Flip Wilson Show* seed it be onliest the great Reverend Leroy to done knowed-it *"the Devil, made me do it*!"

My Shawtee be fine yet she had onliest one major flaw and that be that Shawtee hadda herns fine-assed self a large gaping rusted-it out hole! Don't go there seed my *Shawtee* on the reals be a 65' Ford *Mustang Sally*, tight all over, except'n on the passenger-side justa few inches above where my Moms little moms feet done rested seed it be just mere inches topside my Moms *these lil piggies needs to get to dat farmer's market* be where that gapped hole in the passenger-side floorboard be and that hole on the *downlow* be hidden beneath a loose piece of red floor carpet covered by a'nuttier loose piece of the clear plastic floor mat. *Swells, Sir* under thems two cover-ups there be a long jagged-out some eight inches in length rusty hole from the thens to the now iffn you hadda done lifted that loosely tucked-it in place clear plastic mat and eased it backwards justa bite that carpet then undoubtedly you would have done seed it exactamently where *da' rubber meets the road*!

I be on the creep justa inch-by-inch driving my Moms when *the Devil be damned* I done peeped-it just ahead along the passenger-side of the roadway the chosen-frozen witch be one dems large potholes filled to the brim with what looked-it to be a bad-batch brewing the stinking *Lawd have mercy* awful CC *da' nasties* justa awaiting the unsuspecting *Surprise Surprize Surprise Sergeant Carters* of this world! I hadda on the spur donkey-punched my Shawtee real hard then Shawtee on cue done leapt-it forward with such a force to done caught my Moms completely unawares and too far away and off her royal guard! My Moms hadda done gottens hernself all into the flow of chewing-out my dumb-butt thus she be somewhere out there on the yonder such that my Mom's woman's intuition thing must have been placed discretely on hold, *Swells, Sir* instantaneously the force be with my Moms to done pushed her deep into the shotgun seat cushions. My Moms eyes had widened *bug-eyed* then she had went fish-mouth, my Moms left hand clutched-it hard onto the edge of her seat and her right hand done damn near ripped-it off the passenger-side door armrest! I hadda done seed my Moms had stiffened both of herns short *little mom* legs straight out to brace herself against the powerful *get' her Shawtee* forward launch! My Moms done let go with a barely audible big-*dummy*-butts me and my Shawtee done sho'nuff a'heard-it my Mom's not so silent truly justifiable "*oh, shit*" yet things were just beginning to unfurl the furious next up to the plate hadda been the force of all that icy cold slimy slush, a bad-assed batch of *da' nasties* witch just mere seconds earlier had been underfoot embedded in a pothole theys be as one on the fly as theys foul asses done flew-it through and pass the rusted-it out jagged hole in the floorboard, passed the loose red carpet, passed dat clear plastic mat theys done flown cause thems damned CC *da' nasties* it be on the *In-Coming*!

BLAM that loose clear plastic floormat hadda bitch slapped-it hardtack sumptin-sumptin that be an under part the dashboard as thems damned CC *nasties* hadda done a military precision flyby seed theys as one done came a'flying-it into Shawtee justa projectile of an icy smelly foul mess aimed straight towards my Moms beautiful *Surprise Surprize Surprise Sergeant Carter* Gomer Pyle of TV's 60's sit-com Gomer Pyle USMC gingerbread brown lovely face. My Moms musta gotten herns mom-self a matching set of dog ears coupled-it up with dog scents because in that nano of a split second befo' she be doused by all that McFilthy vollage seed my Moms had done clutched her little brown peepers super anti-water sealed with a kiss tight and for the first time that afternoon my Moms done voluntarily closed-it her mouth completely shut *tanks be to God* for small favors!

I done seed it all thems nasties light-it up my Moms with surround-sounds there be the loud *SPLAT* followed quickly and closely by a small series of the *plop-plops ploppity*-plops as all thems putrid down right rotten CC nasties hadda done slammed-it onto my Moms with a we be *da' nasties* veracity! Theys funky-asses be so bold as to done knocked that little pillbox right-offa its perch then that goofy yellow bow tied in the front-middle wannabe a fez done landed-it all slimy and brackishly splattered onto Shawtee's backseat! My Moms had been covered from herns head to herns little Mom feets in a series of the spreaded out black be slime-bucket muddy splatters of the *Welcomes to the springtime* CC, Baby! An official *da' nasties* welcome wagon had straight-up done stunk-it up the place! *Good Lawd,* briefly justa merely an insane moment, I hadda incredulously done thought-it the ludicrous about laughter being dat bestest form of all medicines big-*watch it boy*-butts the look that hadda crossed my Moms beautiful flawless yet CC nasties covered honey-butter sepia face be mo' than e'nuff to done put my dumb-*why the Hell did I do dat shit*-Mr. Smarty-pants in a complete and deeply profound check! My Shawtee be fine and Shawtee hadda justa done us proud to be the lioness of the concrete jungle whens my Shawtee's ass ripping roar done purred-it back to herns Sundae afternooner kitty-kat meow in a city sans speed limits, wordlessly, I hadda done flipped a bitch then slow dragged-it with my proud heroine backs home street! My Moms hadda done chilled-it on the jive talk *no mas* the tete-a-tete my Moms done looked straight ahead and it had all been quiet an eerily quiet kinda silence as the blocks wisped slowly on the *ta-ta* Tri-city, Baby *Jello* home sweet home! My Moms with all the dignity of a Queen hadda tooken-it out one of the many of herns emergency *got it right here* packages of the *Kleenex* and had done begun to daub, dap to dabble away at thems da' nasties *Good Lawd*, did it reek! KBLU blared the Queen of Soul singing an ode to a *Do right man* and I swears to God, that I hadda done heard-it my Shawtee when she done geared-it up herns fine-assed self one, Hell yes, my soul be to satisfied chuckle! I wouldn't lie to ya, Baby!

Chapter 7

Now Iffn my Moms be my heroine then Dad justa gotta be my hero and justa liked my Moms thens Dad didn't play no fool to nonya that crazy churchyfied *triple-cross yo' black ass* turkey stuffings and justa liked-it my Moms swells Dad done loved-it hisns-self thems downhome blues 'cepting *Lawd hav'a mercy* unliked my Moms my Dad justa couldn't hold a tune nor sing a lick yet dat one itty-bitty-titty detail done never to *Medgar*

Evers stopped Dad from trying! Dad be liked boy *I can holla cause the bluz be in me* then dems *who'dats* be in the done knowed-it woulda done hollered-it back *just let stay it inside ya'*! *Po'leesa Lord don't let him try'n sing*! Every so often there would be a *Git-nite, Git-rite* a dones got-it together, Fish-fry block party with all the family and neighbors it would be one come ya' all come justa *git yo' ass on over* here fo' the goodytimes! Thems womenfolks rolled-it in cornmeal then deep-fried all the *off the hook* fresh catfish caught by thems menfolks out to Unk' Zeke's pond, us kiddy-poos done whooped-it to done hollered-it up all over the place thens the menfolks dat done drank theys bootleg rye-whiskey, homemade wines and homemade brewskis then theys done cussed-it up a *Titanic* storm. Dem times be when Dad done copped to feeling da' good buzz then he justa hadda to done sang-it hisns one and the onliest song that I'd *Medgar Evers* done knowed-it fo' Dad to have tempted to caterwaul cause sho'nuff dem sounds from Dad's lips be an outright abuse to yo' ears, Dad singing be liken unrhythmic *Hell hounds on your tail* screech-screaming followed by a series of belched guttural grunts big-*no singing*-Dad done always attempted to sang hisns *tank God* just the one hisns onliest song *Rye Whiskey* as loud and as often as dem menfolks and womenfolks would allow fo' theys audio beatdown seed my Dad's swan song went kinda sumptin-sump'tin *"Rye whisk---key, rye whisk---key, rye whisk---key I crrrrryy iffn a tree don't fall on me--------I'll drink till I die...if an ocean were whisk---key and I were a duck... I'd swim to the bottom then drink my way up! Rye whisk---key, rye whisk---key, rye whisk---key I crrrrry..."* fo' sho'nuff Dad did be crying thems words of whiskey praise. Those nights be the bestest of Black knights cause whence all the foolishness witch always done followed-it a Fry-nite fish-fry and the lights be out then the party be over then my Moms usually made Dad sleep it off in the room with me and Calvin, my big bro on them knights Dad would tell us two, hisns childhood stories outta the *Lil Missy-sip-pee* delta basin to give us the fo'-one-one bouts the lousy South. Dad would tell me and Calvin bouts our grand-daddies and great grand-daddies, hisns brothers whom be our Unks and especially Unk' Zeke and theys growing-it up times and how theys all had done learnt-it to drive just to done runned-it dat Mr. Charlie's homemade whiskey-still *panther piss* from the *Lou-easy-Anna* always ups and into the cold-ass a witch's tit *Chi-town*! Those nites while telling thems tales Dad would lay me on hisns chest plus he'd hic-cup justa bits and bites of hisns Rye Whiskey song *Emmett Till* I done drifted off into the sweetest dreamland as I'd *Medgar*

Evers woulda gotten to done visited-it in my kiddie-folk mind intermixed versions of me and the posse, Unk' Zeke's pond with Dads childhood of da' lousy south! I had truly lived-it fo' my Moms home cooking whilst she done belted-it out a hefty serving of thems downhome blues, Dad moaning hisns one be onliest *Rye Whiskey* song, me and the posse rolling high-n-tight cause it be BB-gun war out Unk' Zeke's pond, hecks be, Huckleberry would it *Medgar Evers* get any butter than that?

Chapter 8

"GO AHEAD YOU DIM-WITTED FUCK! *Negro, you aint no damned Mexican*! *Go head'n gimme ya' best shot*!" Good Lawd, what da Hell, please tell me that I did *NOT* just say that? *Po'leease Lordy* just let it all be a great big mistaken part of my dumb-assed *it's a small world* imagination, I bees back to home the CC justa kiddie dreaming atop Dad's broad chest and thems words to never done slipped-it the fuck outta my mouth! *Triple B'* had been rollin' up hardtack and dat mad Devil-dawg be the one Mofo that I'd surely didn't want nor need-it hisns psycho ass to be on the receiving end of dat swiftly answered ill-fated knuckleheaded request! *Triple B'* the big-*dumb ass*-butts *Trips* for short *Baby Brother Brown,* a very dark skinned Mexican-American done stepped-it outta Palmdale, Cali-*fornicatin*-ya' that man be liked *John Wayne* toilet paper he didn't truck no shit off no *Injun* nor any-to-nobody else! Why the fuck had I trucked-it up with hisns crazed psycho ass? Fuck me! Trips hadda taken that *open invitational* to done fired-it at point-blank range a ball at dummy round into my dumb-ass from hisns Colt .45 *Hell no, Toto we aints no where Kansas* though the bullet only slightly done glazed-it to done grazed the very tippy-tip of my left shoulder big-*lucky*-butts at close quarter ranks dat worthless ball bullet messings done managed-it to stripped-it my skinny black assed shoulder wide-*the fuck*-open to the white-meat! Tank-*fuckin*-God, we'z be nowheres in some non-descript fucking jungle somewheres Colombia, South America where we done carried-it that worthless local powder ammo fo' when the use of *friendly fire* became a necessity cause we be *Skull Brothers'* hard to the Corps, twisted head-cases *Ja'renes* not them gyrenes big-*funky assed*-butts dumb, stupid jug-headed i.e. the *Baby, I'm for real* Mc-*fucking*-Coy jughead jarheaded Marines, dumb-assed marines who'd fight each other plus anywho and everybody though there be nuttin personal about it, just the way it be! Sump'tin ta sump'times, a man just gotta strap-on a pair! My clip-on balls be snapped in place frog pussy tight cause I be in it fo' the long haul!

What had happened, my husband, *Ritz* the dumb-ass richy-rich of the rich be one thems ugly assed pinky-faced sons of a two-percenter! Ritz be a tanned white cracker fuck-up and that fool had done just fucked-it up bad, fo'-*fucking*-reallies bad! That *gringo* whiteboy son-a-bitch undisciplined no honor lowdown dirty po-po douchebag had caused our main *Boo-Coo,* Priest, he'd only do Catholic girls, may he rest in Peace to be done liked the *potheads* of Company-G used to put it *"Bro Priest done stepped-it out to smoke on high*!" Ritz, sorry-assed mofo be one dems new boytoy federal pigs the newest chunk of assholes masquerading as po-po formed bye-bye good riddance theys fucked-it all up the first time around Ron-*Nancy, where am I*-Reagan administration that had empowered the sons of rich bitches dems GOP moneybags to be the then latest of the worstest crop of *angel-eyes* squealing federal pigs! Ron and the Bush-daddy dems two White Housed presidential *Whiteys only* GOP bastards had no longer trusted *Ollie* with justa few *Ja'renes* to done protected all-American homies from thems midget-sized drug lords, thems South America beaners dat be eating *filthy lucre* cocaine laced tacos whilst shitting-out the almighty *Benjamines*!

Bush-Reg done paid them Ivy league sons of the upper 2% big assed monies whilst thems pent-up bitches at the Pentagon, done pinned little tin medals and red, white and blue ribbons to our grunt ghost-turds severely underpaid asses liken we *Ja'renes* be justa a chunk of useless assassin trained fuckable boytoys, *FUCK dat shit* we be Marines not the fucking Army! Anywho Bush-Reg ordered us Ja'renes to teach dem DEA boys how to oversee them short-legged pygmy druglord fucks whom be justa chunk of useless beaner-bags crushing a Napoleonic Biggy-smalls complex thems damned-it to all diabolical gibberish speak puny *Hell to all southern belles* ball-sack suckers used ta' be Aztec gibberish speak legs no longer than a whiteboy dick piss-midgets be thems cocaine druglords a'sway down yonkers in thems *rumble lets fucking rumble* fine-assed nene *nay-nay* loaded jungle-gyms of the South and Central Americas! Bush-Reg done unofficially ordered-it our little specialized military tactical unit away from thems *you nemba-one GI, me boom-boom long time* upside-downside split pineapple sweet-ass LBFM*LittleBrownFuckingMachines* working the shorelines of the Philippines, Malaysia, Thailand, Nam, Japan and all kinda other such similar enterprising Pacific rim-job countries of the far fetching crotch grabbing *me boom-boom good-time Baby* far-eastern world just to go teach them newest rookie fuck-ups federal po-po just how it be to done did the proper curtsey-to and dossey-doe in them wetland jungles of thems South Americas because of the slightest possibility that all thems po'dunks living the *American dream* coke fiends couldn't nor wouldn't *Just say NO to Drugs*! The *Nancy* pants!

Those newest po'dunk po-po fools hadda went directly from theys Colored nannies tit straight to the cocoa-nut shit and thems dip-shit sons of rich white bitches didn't have a fuckin' numb-nut's clue as to the WTF witch way be up! DEA*DumbEagerAssholes* be justa a bunch of the richy-rich dat done kept us ja'renes supplied with a'plenty of post Nam trigger-action and *Good Lord,* Heaven helps the ones that helps themselves to dems tight pussy fine-assed batches of thems the *good be a'plenty* sexy South American Senorita poontang yet still the DEA be just a bunch of undisciplined *Clorox* bleached-it screaming assholes from theys receding and quickly balding pates to theys cottony soft-pink bottoms-up asses!

TOP our unit Commander done all too happily, fuck joyously be the *Word-up* be he to done wed me to my second DEA husband that po'dunk mofo Ritz *"beans to weenies, Mofo' and you will honor thy husband"* TOP done roared-it my way during the ceremony *"Square yo' ass, jigger-boo*!*"* That tanned rich-assed cracker-motherfucker Ritz had done proven-it to be a very unfaithful assed-out screw-ball man-gynna bitch-ass *get-the-fuck-outta-my-way skank*-hoe husband just earlier that morning, it had all been the simple, an easy-squeezy, a simplistic dog and pony show just a plain-ass vanilla *ranchito* raid big-*dumbfuck*-butts that fuck-up lousy white lazy assed cunt bastard chicken-shit piggly-wiggly fed po-po done turned what had been an ordinary nuttin special vanilla bean fart stroll down *Main Street Disney* into a WTF *Rocky-road Horror Picture Show* the cunt bastard whore be a skank-ass motherfucker!

After all the shit of that early morning raid done gone wrong bad-fucking-bad too the fucking wrong once all dat bullshit done been cleared-it then that sway too black to be a fucking Messykin bastard the HNIC*HeadNiggerInCharge* 2nd in-Command, Master Gunnery Sergeant Brown hadda been about to make dat rich-bastard two-percenter *Punky Brewster* pink-ass Ritz cracker suck hisns wife's hairy big black dick! *Swells, Sir* I justa hadda had to done *stand by my man* and that be the when that I had done jumped-it my dumb black ass between dat fake Messykin wannabe beaner big-*fuck head*-butts on the reals a fucking unhinged combat trained psycho mofo and hisns bone thus my dumb-ass getting all ballsy stepping-it up betwixt the psycho and dat flakey flunky white hunky just plain assed simply put be *Not Good* t'was *Not* a good fucking ting to be done *sheesk* not fucking good a'tall!

The bestest thing about hindsight be and fo' *Medgar Evers* will always be thems 20/20 rear-sights never to never ever done needed-it the nonya a readjustment, never a pair of corrective lenses nor collective guesses hence in hindsight my dumb-assed fucked-up mouthing-off to Trips hadda been just one big fucking *my BAD*! I hadda *justa fucked my world* to the tune of a mistaken ideal hitched unto a thoughtless act of superb stupidity! Daze laters, I'd awaken-it to done found my dumb-ass laid-it up in a *some-to-nowhere* Central America junglized St. Elsewhere mofo, a make-shift missionary open-air mud-floor po' assed-out Catholica medical clinic yet word be that every dark cloud gots a *Hi-ho Silver* lining and being assed-up as swells assed-out in dat mud hut done proved-it to be no different than any other parts this world because when I hadda awaken-it in that shit-hole of a clinic dat fickled mistress *Fate* hadda been mostest kindly unto my faithless black ass seed the Universe done sweeten-it my blackberry pie *Happy Birthdaze to me* cause inside that piss-ant little hut-room there be a drop the fuck dead gorgeous candy-striper *tank-ya' you dumb black ass wannabe Messykin, mofo Trips tank-ya berry mucho*! Inside the room there be a Heavenly Angelic vision, a young all-natural baptized Azteca *sister-in-waiting* a brown-skinned babygurl Nunya with two of the mostest soul searchingly deep topaz bronze-hazel eyes just a sweet honeydew me cause she be the one to done lookey-looked my dumb-ass up the one side then down the other. BabyNunya the fine Azteca jungle *Playboy bunny* be da' shit on the reals babyNunya be a super model flygurl big-*say it aint so*-butts what a waste of the prime rib womanhood already vowed-it *death do we part* to a Roman-dago mythical yet tain't nuttin liked the sweet nursing from one of God's co-signed on the habitual line lovelies and babygurl Nunya be health checking my vitals on the daily-double! I done awoken-it from day-to-day bleary-eyed in a medically induced coma just to done seed dat jet black long haired Honduran bronze-skinned tits-til-Tuesday *don't fight the feeling* draped in a Nun's habit whose sight to be seen became a lust-filled *dear Penthouse* habit fo' me! Sister Nunya Nurse done hauled a chunk of Christianity certified junque in da' trunk witch no thread bare nun's habit could hide *Whoops* there I be a happy ass all Hell alive peeping all dat sanctified joy, Babycakes! I had been waning into then out of that induced-it coma when outta that coma shit after lustfully peeking-it Sister Nunya, I had been trying real fucking hard to retrace all the *whats* dat done fucked-it all up my short-time dancing topsoil as swell all thems mis-steps that had led me to be done floated-it assed-up, assed-out down a shitty money hungry shit creek! Big-*oh happy day*-butts *Good God* the view, the can this be real heavenly feel of Sister Nunya! Nurse Shorty's hands be fucking spectacular and felt swell worth the ride! Good God-damned Gwad-a-mighty!

Chapter 9

Screaming balls to the wall jet fighters thems F-4s and F-100s, crazed-assed flyboys strapped inside them mechanical *Metallica* birds done sky-jockeyed theys high powered death's a'coming real man-toys bursting-out low-leveled sorties green and red lines of trace-fire followed by live bombing runs dancing to the tune of sporadic 70mm wet-fire, big man-sized bullets Babycakes fuck *Little Daisey* and herns *Sharpshooter* rifles the real shit be *da' sheet* Babycakes there be 70mm, 105mm, M-16, M-14, M-1, Russian AK-47, Chinese SKS, automatic plus thems single loaded rifles and every combination of Biggy-smalls cannons and handguns knowed-it to man all aimed and dedicated to the stopping of thems yella gooner chink fucks! All kinda weaponry done popped-it the fuck-off big ***BOOM! BOOM! BOOM!*** Everywhere there be a where be thems the *All-mighty God be jealous* man-made explosions ***BOOM! BOOM! BOOM!*** Slant-eyed peoples both thems soldiers ***BOOM! BOOM! BOOM!*** and thems slant-eyed civilians ***BOOM! BOOM! BOOM!*** Theys all the both done tried to pull-it out South Viet-Nam ***BOOM! BOOM! BOOM!*** Thems scared to death slant-eyed peeking folks done begged-it in all kinda gibberish speak and broken English to convey theys *gotta-go* message the each to every one of thems mofo be fighting to survive! It be the real truth, Ruth that all of thems wayward assed-out slant-eye desperados hadda been hollering the same damned ting theys all be whistling the slit-eye *dixies* final tune, Hell, yes the fat lady be showing herns sweet fat yella chink-ass as swell to done shit herns fat assed-out granny-panties the *Opera* be over!

We be the firstest of the last batch of American grunts and we'z done understood-it exactamente what the each to everyone of thems slant-eyes be hawking seed them rice-bugs be asking to be tossed-it theys small yella ass-cheeks up and into one of them awaiting jolly greens! The jolly greens be US Navy troop carrier dual-prop *flying green turds* thems drab-green helicopters be hauling *the friendlies* people doing the last of the last forays outta Nam therefore thems rice-bugs be on the holla *Yes, Virginia, there do be a Heaven witch I'll see mucho-much mo' Sooners iffn I can't gets my funky ass-cheeks smashed into one of thems copters* that shit be the on the reals the translated verbiage that all thems friendly South Viet-nam peeps gibberish speak be done communicated! December 74' the start towards final pull-it out Viet-Nam it be the official *freaky-deaky* and all the chaos be centered-it at the US Embassy Saigon where bye-bye all da' shit done been splattered against the fucking yella-assed fan and mo' than mostest us ghost-turds had been needed to save them USN *stick jockeys* and them US Navy Sea Knight CH-47 helicopters from all thems frenzied friendlies peeps attempting to defy death be *In-coming* with a big green loogey lodged in its slanted-eye! Embassy Saigon be a big assed compound that consisted of some 5 tan-yellow bullet riddled two-story buildings formed in a squared-off kinda octagon geometrical shape and there be a big concrete courtyard in the middle of the complex. Inside that courtyard and out-side the Embassy walls all the shit reigned live with pure ass slant-eye chaos everytime thems jolly-greens twirled theys *duck yo' fucking head* blades ready fo' the take-it all off! The embassy had been under siege by allied friendlies all of thems *be friendlies* slant-eyed folks had been praying fo' a miracle in the form of a slant-eye *Oprah* to done hauled herns big ass over fo' the shout-out *you get a seat, you get a seat, you get a seat, everybody gonna get a seat* thems fucked peeps be trying deathly hard-on to get the fuck-outta country and just liked a reel Hollywood war movie a Hell-of-a-lot of extras had been needed for the real live start of final Embassy Saigon pullout that Dec' 74. At that time, I had been assigned to temporary-duty aboard a US Navy aircraft carrier witch be justa big *landing strip atop* a four-clawed bathtub. I had been trained a *shock-jock* to work on them *General Electric* J-79 jet engines witch powered them F-4 Phantom *Screaming Death* be a'coming fo' jo' *China-chink yella slant-eyed funky putrid* ass an air to land assault aircraft. I be an aircraft mechanic by military trade and justa a'nuttier pair of fucking jungle-rot these boots done hit the fucking ground bye-bye USMC standards both be all to the good cause that embassy shit had gotten my ass up then offa that fucking floating scrub tub! I'd been sitting in that flat-head for mostest too more than 10 weeks after my virgin tour boots-to ground Nam started first week August 74' through half the October 74' Big-*Goofy in the Whitehouse*-butts President Gerald R-*real goofball*-Ford done wanted-it to give Ho Chi Minh dat *hoe-she-mean* one bad breath bitch assed-out chink bastard an early Christmas present thus that shit be why Uncle Sugar-n-rice poppy fields done needed me and all thems other ghost-turd extras thems hundreds of other scrub boys that had been just sitting China bay whilst we'z be shiting and chipping-paint offa that tub.

A *jolly-green* had transported my skinny black ass along with a thirty+ full live-crew locked and loaded to the embassy compound there I had been assigned an attack position atop building-five South Embassy. It had been close to a week, all that time the day through the Black knight I been slow dragging-it with *Geraldine,* my babygirl, my sweet soul-sista *Siren of death* my Uncle Sammy done issued-it me M-16 then from my superior position atop building-five south I'd done thumped-it thems full-metal jackets anywhere and everywhere down into or outside that courtyard compound where bye-bye chink mofo on the daily-double da' shit had been getting progressively foul *Yes, Hell to the yeah,* Babycakes, it had been automatic rapid-on wet-fire and it hadda been *Right-on*! A chopper laid propellers first crashed-it down inside that courtyard that Sea Knight had been downed by desperately frantic short-leggetty yella assed-out slant-eyed men who'd done clung hopelessly unto thems whirlybird skids during final take-off and it had been theys friendly folk combined extra body weight witch caused the tuna can to done plummet-it into the ground of that courtyard! Grown-assed boy-like men be killing the womens and kids justa take theys places inside them jolly greens. It wassa horrible sight to have viewed under any circumstances yet fo' the Nam war/police action it all be par the course! Everywhere *Straight-outta Saigon* horror done reigned down inside that courtyard and outside thems embassy walls.

The skinny had been that there should have been only about a tree to four thousand chunk of the friendlies more or less at the embassy big-*gots family*-butts then thems official friendlies done told-it to theys own personal family-friendly ties then those peeps must have pimped their own groups *Emmett Till* damn near the whole country of South Viet-Nam done showed-it theys assed-out asses upon them Embassy doorsteps in hopes of being one of the lucky few to get air-lifted outta harm's way! The Viet-Cong be just outside Saigon City limits and thems fucking gooners whores had been justa jimmy-jamming theys little China-chinks wannabe gooner asses closer and ever so mucho-much closer to a full-scaled Saigon chink commie bitch-bastard take-over! Thems commie gooner bastard motherfuckers had not been justa knocking on thems Saigon city doors big-*gooner*-butts thems yella whores done cut loose the big bad fucking lobo-wolf and dat bitch-bastard be a'huffing and a'puffing and bouts to blow the whole damned city down! It was no fucking rumor just straight-up one-hundred percentile true jungle vine-juice that the VC gooners thems yella-chink asses hadda plan to reeducate all those friendlies whom had justifiably collaborated with the infidel dogs from the land of a *coke and a smile*! Reeducation gonna be real easy-like on them VC professors in that theys skank-hoe smelly slant-eye asses onliest had to simply line their pupils up and in front of thems made-in China chalkboards then proceed to erase them eager beaver students with semi-automatic weapons that been made-in the land of the not-so-friendly *nemba-tree Son* slant-eye chinks. It be thems well-informed students fucking-it up justa everything down below inside and outside the courtyard walls because of that *In-coming* reeducate program! Slant-eyed peeps jungle law be judicated alive and in-living yella slant-eye Hell front-street center-court and it wasn't pretty! My first order of the day be to place a live round into any and every soft-target that hadda tried to scale them embassy court outside walls. The 2nd order of the day had been to place a round into any soft-target dat done managed to negotiate that outside Embassy wall thus death be a jacketed round unto all thems yella no-longer friendly-asses! All fucking week long, I'd been bumping hard to be done sent-it theys yella asses to theys final eternity just for thems lucky whoops *not-so-lucky* yella asses making-it theys last dire mad-dashed attempt to done grabbed-it to done clung-it unto any parts thems *jolly green's* during take-off! The shit be wicked, Babycakes! I done told-it, I done laid-it down a cutting-edge stream of the .223 rounds cause *Geraldine* be my bitch and she be *tits-til-Tuesday* full automatic bursts plus I done followed-it up *Geraldine's* deadly sweet swan song cause I be straight-up clowning thems fools on the full blown home-grown automatic straight-outta the Chocolate City jump'n jive! It had been Geraldine's sweet-ass aria bumping gums *brrrrup, brrrruup, brrrruuup, brrrrup brrruup, brrrruup, brrrruuup...* followed-it up by Zeke's live ass jive *"Here's to you, Babycakes, let me sock-it to ya! I'm just a rabid dog, Nam' just a sweet fucking wet dream gone awry, please don't wake me!"* then justa little sump-tin sump'n a little mo' of the Geraldine solo act thus it be our sweet little duet *brrrruup brrrruup brrrrup, brrrruup, brrrruuup, brrrrup brrrruup, brrrruup, brrrruuup...come to Daddy bitches, gits jo-self an ass load the good shit, baby!* thus together we twos be a *Jo' yella boy, holla a fucking Right-on to mi Grandpapi when ya' flips dis bitch, git-jo yella ass some, Babycakes come git-yo' slant-eye ass sums this bitch!* Yowls, Sir me and Geraldine be singing to the choir! My heart hadda pumped mega-juice and I had done *bumped-it with the big fat-woman* mega-large *"this here be the last song, Rucky Rucy! I'm gonna keep on trucking, you slant-eyed jinxy mother-fuckas! Poppa gotta brand new bag!* Fuck'n A-baby, I'd done had a gigantic choir of Ja'renes and Navy scrubs and theys babygirls full-throttled bursting loose justa rip-roaring the back-up chorus! Every one of us grunts *down-on-the-duce* defending that there embassy hadda done knowed-it fo' a fat fact, Jack that 31st Platoon Company 1F- 2nd Battalion- 24th Marines- 3rd Marine Division would be hauling ass outta Saigon quicker than shit through a Canadian grey goose's water sealed tight ass-cheeks once the last of thems choppers done stopped-it theys twirlings and swirlings and that shit be on the reals, Babycakes!

Chapter 10

THE FINAL DAY OF THAT week be when it had fucking all happened and the shit done happened lightening fuckin *Jack Flash* quick-assed *ZOOM BABY ZOOM* there atop building-five south, a straight-up *WTF* done been burst-it forth to done knocked me unto my sweet black ass cheeks! I'd never to *Medgar Evers* done saw that skinny po'dunk ass nonya the times on the ship nor at the Embassy big-*sneaky*-butts that po'dunk skinny redneck asshole done jumped-it outta the shadows a straight-up *Poof-fucking-Poof* from outta of the fucking blues hisns rail ass done thrown-it one Hell-of-a-haymaker, fuck! TOP be a tall skinny as all Hell sandy-haired blue-eyed white devil *angel-eyes mofo* a fucking po'dunk redneck gyrene dick-head peckerwood, be dat mofo! I hadda on the laters done learnt-it the mofo hadda been one of them college educated rich southern white-boy grunts a *ed-u-ma-cated* redneck po'dunk who done wiped hisns redneck rail ass with accredited shit paper then that mofo hadda just said *fuck the fuck'n cow-tech schooling* to done stupided-it up, Ja'rene! Swells, it had been dat ballsy po'dunk mofo' that *off the fuckin cuff* done justa stepped-it over unseen to done one punched-it, a fucking outta the no-fucking-where donkey-punch to done damned near *momma said to knock you out* cold-cock my skinny black ass! *Surprise Surprize Surprise Sergeant Carter* big-surprized-butts the kicker hadda been in the process of sucker punching me that whisper thin-lipped death *choking on a soda-cracker* mofo' WTF dat not even in'a pinch mofo hadda done snatched-it *Geraldine* right the fuck outta my Black be beautiful hands befo' my ass be done bounced-it offa that shell riddled rooftop! *A'gin-n-juice* WTF! Trust it dat assed-out skinny redneck mofo done indeed delivered-it hisns fuck'n message loud ass let's be clear, dat whitey mofo hadda gottens hisns ugly assed self a pair! The punk-ass fool had some stereophonic balls to done talked-it big shit *"Look hear, Shine, I run the fuck'n show around here,! Now, take yo' pussy, Baby-cakes"* dat *Ragin Cajun* muddafucker done shoved-it hard Geraldine, bad e'nuff dat fool done gots my Babygirl, in hisns po'dunk white-trashy ball-scratchers big-*ballsy*-butts that damned po'dunk mofo done pushed-it *Geraldine* hardtack and frog-pussy tight back into my chest! *"One cunt snap, mofo! Listen the fuck up you gawd damned jungle-bunny! All I wanna hear from yo' fuck'n bitch is one gawd damned cunt snap!"* he'd done growled that foul fucked-up shit on the up-close range up-front into my perplexed hand-some gingerbread brown face with some of the worstest funky-assed breath that I'd ever done smelled-it fo' the life of me that po'dunk fuck's breath done smelt itself a mixture of daze old stale hog-shit littered with da' CC nasties and tree-daze old *Chesterfield* cigarettes big-*ballsy*-butts all the while the mofo' done stayed kneeled on bent knee atop my black ass with hisns fuck'n angel-eyes locked-it up tight onto my chocolate orbs thens dat fool done continued with thems *do as I fucking say* direct orders *"Put yo' bitch on semi! We gots unfinished business when this dog and pony's over. Square yo' ass, jigger-boo! Semper-fi!"* Then that skinny-assed bad-breathed TOP done pushed to me a camo-bag filled-it to the brim with full-metal *Slab city* fillers then the fucking racist mofo stood-it up just as quickly as he'd done stepped-it WTF over onto that rooftop the fucking sneak-thief done walked-it just as quickly the fuck away! I'd done thunk-it dat from the lookey-looks dat skinny mofo' be too damned weak seed hisns boney-assed arms didn't appear to have any kinda *put a mofo on hisns ass* punching power big-*cold cocked*-butts I'd searched my memory blank and the deposit slip didn't lie seed it be straight-up that the po'dunk slim-shady mid-night creeper mofo hadn't worn brass knuckles nor had hisns white-knuckled boney-assed fist been gift-wrapped-it around a bankroll of nickels big-*lucky*-butts *God-to-be-Gawd* damned, second-time around always be butter than da' firstest! In a few mo' hours I wassa gonna be thumping-it live no-jive straight-up wet-fire with hard to the Corps Ja'renes! Holy shits, Babycakes!

Chapter 11

THE LAST OF THEM JOLLY greens cleared the Embassy a group of fiddy-something Ja'renes straight off the bump we done dropped-it down into the streets of Saigon led by TOP skinny-*educated*-butts that ass bite's pasty-white skin be the lucky *winner-winner chicken-shit dinner* ticket that done punched hisns ride atop the White skin-ship train and that be why dat proud assed peacock mofo strutted front-runner the hometown *get ya' big boy pants on* parade! Moving forward dat fool be destined to tweak the very *tip-o-the-titty* the widow's peak: Sergeant Major of the Marine Corps SgtMajMC TOP be accompanied by a tough as all fuck not justa looking-it tough big-*psychotic*-butts the Devil be hisns onliest Godless friend, an on the reals serial psycho gook-killing ass-kicking Mexican-American jarhead G*unny* Gunnery Sergeant GySgt *Sooners* to become a Top himself bumping the call sign *Trips*!

Thems two *hard-to-theys-Corps* mofos ventured us fiddy-something grunts on a one-way trek *Death Valley* VC-gooners yet onliest some 30-something us ghost-turds done managed to come puking our guts out on the other side near bye-bye a landing strip where we decked the last banana boat outta Saigon. The short trek to the entry tunnel TOP done brief-it *"Listen up dumb-fucks the fucking assholes yella commie-bastard gooners have probably cleared most of the boobytraps in these fucking tunnels because the end of the fucking war to keep the good slant-eyed gook-people of South Vietnam from the fucking rice-belly chinks and commie ass-fucks of this here world has near ended. The gooners probably using these fucking tunnels for transit, Cover your ass!"* It had been less than 2-hours offa the tickety-tic-tock mayhaps some 2 *no mas* than tree-odd miles of trekking distance throughout the mostly pitch tar-baby black *whupped dat ass* inside thems last big-*ballsy*-butts my firstest of VC tunnel entries! In dat titi time and distance, my shit chest bumped-it a big fucking freaking love-jones, Babycakes! My shit be lit, adrenaline be whats thems junkies tagged *da' spike* swells my shit done flowed-it over the edge big-*free falling*-butts *Good Lawd* rollin' them tunnels, my shit be liked them Niagara Falls, Babycakes! My shit went up to then flowed with an unheralded-it rage *Right-on, my Brotha* the fuck over the edge of *No Return* double-Dutch the freaky-deaky deep down into the abyss of *Com' on motherfucker, take a free ride*! Bury the dead in dem tunnels meant grab yo' Bro' *may he rest in peace* dog-tags to done snatched-it up all hisns weapons/ammo whilst on the *snatch dat ass* hot foot thems damned deathtrap tunnels a city under sieged and all dat shit be live, baby!

TOP and Trips little war party/tunnel venture had been my unofficial unwelcoming to the real Nam war funk and dat shit hadn't been nuttin like the Hollywood reels warfare I'd done seed-it on the boob-tube reruns nor even my virgin tour boots to ground Nam for what that little bite of the dumb-shit hadda not mattered! The tunnel witch we entered had broken-it off into a series of other little tunnels witch be all the fucking same in that theys all be dark as country mid-night the onliest parts light came from trace-fire or flash-bangers also thems damned tunnels smelt-it a pure Hell, a living shit-filled dirt encrusted chasm banging rotting corpses witch all parts to pieces of thems buck-tooth rat eaten skeletons lay every-*fucking*-where with an added bonus human/animal blood and waste had been smeared onto every fucking thing. A *God awful* stench permeated the stale arid air there be little breathable air inside them *fuck a gooner whore in hisns yella ass then feed the fucking slant-eye dick-head soup* half'a man size tunnels so we grunts had to walk a steady bent the fuck over just to move about the further we done stepped-it through thems bitches! TOP had brought a 12-foot steel pole witch be front-man J-O-B a position witch he done rotated frequently, it onliest be fitting cause *every swinging-dick got to sit hisns ass up-side down inside dat barrel*! The sweeper be pushed ahead to check fo' any lethal bullshit placed along the *follow the slant-eye yella-ass brick* road as a deterrent to fuck up any fool-ass dat done stepped-it balls-deep into theys tunnels thems *fuck you asshole* gooners done laid-out a deadly welcome mat fo' all interlopers *ding-dong Avon bitch* calling with baby-girl in hand to done sweet-talk thems little bitch gooner bastards into taking a hard and deadly pause bye-bye a M-16 *brrrrup brrrrup brrrrup* sale's pitch into becoming dead little bitch-ass gooner fucking slant-eye bastards! There had been spots with a few still flickering battery operated lanterns and it be in thems rare spots I done seed-it up-close all the rotten body parts as well the bloody shit that thems gooner whores had smeared on any and everyting.

TOP had in hisns hip-pockets a plan witch had proven itself in dealing with thems big as small dogs be outta jo' wildest fucking nightmare *fuck me* bucktooth tunnel rats! Thems fucking rats be living offa the dead and theys be sum scary-assed nightmarish shits when we done ran upon a nest of thems fucked-up rats asses gnarling dead gook ass and theys be all intertwined as one big fuck you up knot whens thems knotted-up bitches be scurrying about we couldn't just shoot em' in theys asses we just to done tossed-it a single flash-banger into the nest when dems bastard *my little pony* rats be underfoot the onliest thing you could do would be to stomp thems rat bitches because it be *No fucking shooting* the possibility of an errant *WTF dumb-ass* ricochet Hell, we couldn't even bayonet thems bitch-assed bucktooth gook-rats because of the darkness you might done speared yo' foot or stabbed yo' Bro's foot in the process besides yo' weapon might done just accidently discharged to done *blowed yo' fucking dumb-ass the fuck away* fo' sho'nuff it be bye-bye to yo' mofo feets!

TOP be not yo' common dumb-ass peckerwood that skinny *how much wood can a woodchuck* chuck hadda on the reals to done knowed-it hisns shit. Befo' we done entered-it them tunnels he and Trips made us stop thens theys both done double-checked our uniforms and gear and made for sure with theys own filthy shitty *what you looking et* lying-eyes be assured that our pant legs were tucked inside our boots, long sleeves unrolled and down plus every button buttoned with helmets strapped, snapped and that we'z be fully flack-jacketed no loose-ends and that shit had proven to be worth its weight in pure rotten-ass gooners twenty-fo' carrots fool's gold especially on thems rat encounters iffn one of them rats hadda done runned-it up and inside a mofo pant leg fo' sure as raw ape shit sticks to a furry monkey's sore ass dat unlucky mofo be tagged *Ihop*! When that jolly green had hit the flight-deck thens and rights there TOP done made every one hat-up to the med-clinic for an *instant grits* tetanus shot and rat bite screening.

The real shitty drawls deal inside thems tunnels besides thems damned rats be the lack of breathable air and when we did happen upon a fucking usable non-mud-hole actual still operational *Tank'ya God* for dis *honest Injun* earthen outside air-vent then we'd all stopped-it to done sucked-it all that good vented above ground air down into our starving lungs liked a fat-ass head diving-it into a bag of *Snicker-doodles*! After the first hour we really hadn't encountered too many braved assed *let's party* gooner bastard badass billy-slant-eye whores whom be willing to die in that almost officially over police action/conflict yet liked always where so *Medgar Evers* you happened-it to be this world the all tings being equal theory hadda reigned-it fast and furious because inside thems tunnels there had been dat taste of the proud thems fucking hold-outs gooner fuck fools whom just hadda scratch dat itch and it be thems gooner left-overs thems itty-bitty-shitty rice-bugs dems last of the last theys dumb-asses be mighty good eatings to a war starved man! Thems gooner *Johnnie wee-wee wang-wang* hold-outs hadda done made that little venture quite the enterprise dat hadda been swells worth the wiles *Yes, Lawdy* because in them couple of hours more than justa few times we done ran upon a few *fuck-it we be* idiotic gooner bitch bastards suffering the last-minute *can't help it* need to scratch theys *deaths a'coming* itchy raw-dog ass! Thems be the mofos couldn't just let sleeping dogs lie thems slant-eyes likely done thunk-it that theys held the upper hand in that theys gooner bitch-whores asses done knowed-it the ley of the land where bye-bye all thems *in case of emergency* break dat yella-ass escape routes be thus thems billy-slant-eye bitch-bastards would test-fire a bite thens scramble *yella egg gooner fuck-faces* away! Lord, onliest knows dat shit be good and it be fo'reallies fucking good cause I hadda done caught the fire of that spike and *Hell, yeah* my shit be free-falling like a mofo, Babycakes!

A little sumptin-sumpting hadda happened-it upon my black ass that I couldn't shake it loose there had been a darkness, a some kinda *It* ting done bitch-slapped my ass to done come along fo' the ride. A darken kinda ting done hung its cap on my rack to done cast its eerily shadow about my world liked the from outta-town family fucking visitor who just wouldn't tarry hisns lingering ass back to hisns own damned home seed that darken mofo done settled quarters to done runned-it up a flag pole that *it* be here to stay though *it* be an eerily feeling on the stranger-danger side of all tings this world mayhaps just a bite beyond! I done knowed dat *it* hadda done runned into my small-patch garden to done planted its secret deed yet *it* done kept to its darken self just a two-step outside a WTF *you be looking et*, Mofo!

The last day Embassy Saigon the whole fucking day hadda been the big bang, Babycakes dat firstest *grand ole opry* the Alpha not the Omega the firstest meet-it up day *Yes, Sirrrr* dat day hadda been my *in the begin-*

ning unwanted-it futuristic living-arrangement amongst them two badass *Ja'renes* as well the day that the *let there be light* done just packed-up its *How'dy doody* happy ass shit *Adios mofo* to done returned to the darkness, Babycakes! That be the day of reckoning dem two knuckles TOP and Trips with theys hard-to-the-Corps process seed thems two clowns be hardcore deliverers of life in the guise of slinging-hash in all the differ forms of death on a shingle unto a'many enemy's raw-dog ass! The day of the unforgiving, the onset basic steps that done taught-it to me to jitterbug muddafucka don't git caught slow dragging-it this be the life, baby! The day, I learnt-it to done pimp-walk thems ghetto streets inside the mind's inner-locked and loaded workings witch both the educated and the *pass me dat dubbie* busters of this here world termed consciousness! Life's a dance, Babycakes! I's here to tango!

Chapter 12

Embassy Saigon had been a foul batch of the sloppy-seconds, the second time around that my jet-engine mechanic by military trade big-*tooling*-butts the USMC standard first-tings first command be combat boots to ground thus I done hit Viet-Nam on the dead-run! The first kiss and tell had been a fo'reallies eye opener iffn not a straight da' fuck outta Hell nightmarish epiphany! August 74' things had been getting real busy for the official US pullout, I had been detailed to the cannibals, a Black man be in da jungle, just gotta be a cannibal! There be lots of downed aircraft all over that country thus *Unk' Sugar-n-rice-poppy-Fields* hadda done found-it hisns police action conflict combating ass to be in a real dill-pickle and Unk-*death to all VC chink*-Sammy be an on the reals a full-time junkie in need of a fix! Uncle-*Sorry Charlie*-Sammy had a real need for aircraft mechanics to strip away the vital parts on them downed heavy-metal birds by the time of my enlistment, YES I did say enlistment WTF summertime 72' mo' bouts dat volunteer shit laters big-*full disclosure*-butts fo' the thumbnail:

Uncle Sammisky be done thunk-it that he the smartest po'lack on the war block therefore he'd done figured-it that the war and or the police action/conflict be long on the gone dat shit be fucking bye-bye because thems long-haired hippie-freak American whiteboys done put hisns war loving ass in a full-body check with theys all as one rebellious cry run amuck *Hell No! We won't go!* Not surprisingly, the US military be forced to assume the VC conflict a straight-up royal flush yet to be officially ended thus them military five-star General pin-heads done started-it to train troops to be mechanics in-lieu of ghost-turds in-order to extract mostest to all theys downed aircraft and the aircraft's intelligent parts witch mostest of thems *intelligent* parts had been introduced into this world by the process of reverse-engineering system utilized by the US military on parts that had been stripped away from recovered/downed UFO from a'nuttier world aircraft, yeah I done said-it thems UFOs be on the reals, fuck yo' *Star Trek*, baby! My self-analysis theory be that the US military had felt it to be of the utmost importance to recover their intelligent parts prior to thems commie bastards getting theys wuddle hands onto them intelligent parts then turning thems said parts over to theys big lemon-chicken-head chink brother from a'nuttier slant-eye mother outta China! Thems Chinese chinks would then re-reverse engineer everything the US military had reversed engineered thus Unk *sorry Charlie* Samuel didn't need thems commie yella chinks to be producing stronger more capable pieces of shit fo' thems *rucky-roosey* slant-eye bastards to done throwed *It be War* back at the all-American way of racist life!

Anywho, I had been assigned temporary duty on the same flathead mentioned earlier because I had been a part of the newest military late 60s think-*let's train these ghetto turds to be aircraft mechanics*-tank the USMC done trained me to be a J-79 jet engine mechanic. Thems late 60s ushered in the official era of the Black American combat soldier then comes the early 70s General *McCharlie* po'dunk done got force fed to done learned-it to trust Black soldiers, Airmen and Navy scum to go to war as well to be trained to remove all those intelligent reverse engineered parts from theys high powered highly intelligent war machines. The Nam conflict the Brother done gots hisns Black-Billy-badass on like *Whaddup* motherfucker because the actual US military desegregation done come about through the boot stomping-it to the po'dunk white-asses of thems 5-star Genitals of the Pentagon by the greatest of US Presidents Lyndon Baines Johnson, LBJ done told thems General fools *no mas* the janitor, chauffer, cook, busboy all-in-one olive drab green decked Black ass latrine digger! President LBJ utilized hisns Executive Office to done force fed dems po'dunk Generals to train, accept and treat its Black grunts with the dignity and respect due unto any American citizen dat be a'nuttier reason LBJ be my main Presidential man, Baby! *Tank You dear Lordy* fo' thems cowardly Whiteboys draft-dodging cowardly assholes! Hell No, tank God youse chicken-shit assholes didn't go!

The Navy used thems jolly greens to transport our 40-man team of aircraft maintenance dumb-asses to a point somewhere mainland Nam then from there we done dry humped-it that jungle fo' two days to a deep sway past the boonies outpost camp. I had arrived that outpost camp and the scene for me had been T-totally surreal to my young, dumb and full of cum naïve ass! What I encountered be nuttin that I'd *Medgar Evers* read abouts nor seed-it in nary a Hollywood war movie neither had I heard diddley-squat nonya the skinny about thems outpost camps on the jungle-juice during my short one-year plus a couple months military career big-*WTF*-butts life be bouts to done changed Biggy-smalls my skinny black ass seed arrival that outpost every grunt I done seed be *off the fucking hook* I be talking every damned *hey you* swinging dickhead mofo in dat outpost be stepping-it to a bee-bop beat of hisns very own damn tune and dat shit had been the what that be kool, real fucking laid the fuck back dope smoking, beer drinking Kool-as-all-fuck raspberry *Kool-Aid* kool, Babycakes! Though I didn't indulge neither them doobies nor thems brewskis not because I be some *hey, Molly the mouse-kerr-teer* big-*goodie two shoes*-butts onliest and mainly because my hood had been chockfull thems *living dat life* grown-assed assed-out alkies and junkies sprawled all about thems brownstone buildings just likened Unk' Zeke's pond had been flush full with all dem tall over-grown wild weeds it be a fat fact Jack in my hood there be a wino-junkie every door stoop! Hell, no need fo' numbered addresses in the hoodie jo' house got knowed-it by the wino out-front dat shit be liked *don't' even fuck with dat house that be toothless Rufus pad,* baby! The camp be loaded with big assed Black Panther *party-party get yo' party-on* afros alongside long haired hippie-freak bastards even thems gibberish speak illegal to work big-*jumping beaner*-butts good nuff' to fight Mexicans be sprinkled in the mix and every one of them GI Joe sum-dey-bitches had been or were on the verge to be smoking dat doobbie, huffing hash, spiking dat smack and or knee knocking-back them brewskis, Babycakes! Them war torn GI mofos be at home in da' jungle! There usta be a whiteboy song on the radio bouts *the lion sleeps at night* well dat mofo lion raged-it hisns ass a full fucking snore-on in that camp! Those war hardened *gyrenes* be chilled fucking *Holy shits, Batman* mostest them grunts be pulling a once-over or more tour *Hell to all south-*

ern belles Nam! Mo' than tree-quartas of them G-Company grunts had done cut then re-fitted their uniforms to appease theys own specialized no *plain vanillas* be theys *Tasty-freeze* combat attire thus to my virgin eyes dat *do as I fucking well please* combat style of theys damned dress as *I fucking, po-leese* shit had been combat *Superfly*! My bros be chilled-out liked a motherfucker! Hot-damn, Good Laud, Babycakes!

The mostest thems fools be theys big bucks, po'dunks or illegal Messkins them mofos had come to play with theys babygirls slung-low, the muzzle pointed-downwards slung over their shoulders diagonally across and down their backs! Theys M-16 be assed-out, assed-up and all theys bitches done gots herns head diagonally going-down Marilyn Monroe Holly-*on-my-wood* style! Hell yeah, fo' my youngblood ass dat be *da' Shit* Babycakes! I'd come to find-it out laters, that mode of rifle tote discipline had come by way of them *Jew-boys* working-it thems inter-cities along the Gaza! Jew-boy style of rifle-toting made for instant *kiss my grits* with just a mere flick-o-the-wrist it be combat mode-on the fucking Superfly jo' *Goy-boy* be assault ready like a mofo! A Jew-boy banging-out the rifle in that position when comes the *Surprise Surprize Surprise Sergeant Carter* attack all the funky-cheap-assed *kike* gotta do be to stop pinching hisns pennies long e'nuff to grab the muzzle with hisns off-hand then the rifle's barrel and body gonna move diagonally down hisns back beneath his funky unwashed hairy-assed arm-pit all the whilst he done continued to pull that muzzle forward hisns strong-hand stinky-finger would simultaneously slide along her gams to glide past them two itty-bitty-titty bumps beaded onto the topside of the trigger housing to done all-natural liked to done dropped-it below them yips to easily trip herns clitty from safe to semi-auto or automatic befo' sinking hisns funky-assed stink-finger tight and deep inside herns furry clam and the *bump be on* thus *Kosher-nuts* be poised a ready-on point instant cunt-snap rapid combat-fire to done blasted-it a *rag-head mofo* outta this realm and dat shit be no bullshit cause it be straight-up *da' Shit*, Babycakes!

My virgin combat eyes done locked and loaded upon all dat shit in all its glorified visual not asking nuttin bouts the whys to nor any thems hows it be the reality thus my conclusion had been dat down the back rifle tote shit be outta this fucking world! Thems bad-assed grunts done called theys babygirls by different names according to theys own personal cultural thus it be *Suzie Q* for them po'dunks, thems *Ice-berg Slim* ass-kicking muddafuckas done tagged theys sweet-sixteens *Lucille* then thems gibberish Mexican mofos hollered-it *La chula* sweet-heart!

Chapter 13

FIRSTEST EARLY MORNING THAT CAMP before the day done broke, the First Sergeant/1Sgt had gotten my newbie ass up from a deep sleep and told-it to me that hims and me be going on patrol to scout for sniper gooner fucks dems *zipper-heads*. Fuck there be no breakfast, no nuttin justa *Git-da-fuck-up cunt-scab-n-take yo' morning piss*! The 1Sgt done made it real clear to me during our little recon trek the immediate life dangers to be encountered by hanging *high-n-tight* amongst Golf Company's *Alkies*, *Pot-heads* and the *Cowboys* dems mofos had to buck dat big white bronco's funky white ass just to be alive, he'd said them beer guzzling, buzz-headed and shooting gallery rejects couldn't be trusted to save their own Gawd damned lives and that it would take a real fucked-up *fool-of-a-fool* to done trusted his life to thems fucking ig'nant bastards that done built their castles in the fucking sky and that be the only reason my rookie ass had gotten *Blessed* to be in hisns pristine presence amid all that early morning *In-coming* slant-eye sunshine! The *first-skirt* had a verifiable fucked-up *Welcome to the jungle* baby-boy speech big-*orator*-butts I couldn't do shit big-*hungry*-butts let dat proud as a peacock cracker git hisns preach-on witch in all reality be hisns fucked unabated *listen-up dib-shit* pre-ordained speech seed that numb-skull 1Sgt be self-assured that I'd onliest been in-country less than tree-days thus it be dat country-bred asshole musta thunk-it I had not the fucking time to be a hops-head, hop-head nor a strung-out junkie hopping from foot-to-foot and justa scratching all them imaginary bugs that be hopping all overs dat junkie's all too real strung-out ass! The pasty-faced talkative first-skirt bastard hadda seed my late knight arrival and that I hadn't drank any of thems *Welcome Wagon* brews, not toted-it dems roaches from witch the sweet dreams be made of big-*nerdy*-butts fuck the calm before the storm bullshit, Babycakes! Crude as he had been about that shit the Sarge hadn't had to done *shake-rattle-rolled* nary a hairy nut nonya bouts any self-inflicted suicidal death due to dope/alcohol bullshit! Hell, buzz-heads, Mary-Jane girls and boys, dope fiends, winos and *oil can Harrys* had littered the streets all over the CC dat fucking getting high while awaiting the sho'nuff visit that be a'coming from Brotha Death horse shit be the hoodrat life!

Hell, I could have sat pat the CC to sip death through a paper cup, puffed the magic dragon, bronc da' pony on any daily-double 24/7! The main point of that little trek had been all about God, no the Sarge be no jack-legged country choir-boy decked in an olive-drab monkey suit, Nawl, nuttin liked dat fucked-up shit seed in the Corps a full bird aka Marine Colonel mofo' be God and God be due in-camp that day because it seemed thems Company-G *pot-heads n' cowpokes* been kicking asses while taking gooners slant-eye names in the most fiercest parts of that jungle. The Sarge had told-it to me that God done loved hisns Marines because they had killed so many fucking gooners and that God had a'riding alongside of Hisns Godly nut-sack a pocket-full of little tin stars, silver medals and little red, white and blue ribbons witch God hisns own damned unHoly assed-out self be pleased as plum pudding punch to have the honor to be pinning onto mostest every chest that be 1st Platoon Company G- 2nd Battalion- 4th Marines- 3rd Marine Division come that early morning! The Sarge said that thems gooners probably done knowed-it that God be a'coming to theys party and that our mission be to search and destroy any *zipper heads'* aka enemy gooner slant-eye snipers dat we done encountered along the way. The briefing had culminated bouts 30-minutes into our walk when the slant-eyed sun done risen high e'nuff to done cast-it a shadow then we had reached the top of a ravine with a semi-muddy bed some 12-feet wide about 8 to 10 feet below the place where we toppled-out that little trail witch be the spot where *the skirt* done told me to *get-alone little doggie* he aint no faggot e'nuff of the holding my fucking hand. The Sarge told me to go and check out the northside of the ridge, Hell I hadn't knowed-it north, east, west nor south cept'n my asshole be south cause my empty rumbling stomach be to dropping thems gas bombs every other step dat slant-eye sermon on the mount trek! The Sarge must have seed the perplexed look of WTF this cracker fool be talking about etched all across my gingerbread brown handsome like a mofo solid golden sun baked *tank-ya-tank-ya mucho Aunt Hannah* face cause the Sarge had done stood there arms akimbo then shook hisns big ass coconut in a feign disgust whilst he mumbled some shit about I be too dumb to know that iffn the sun took its morning piss in the east... *blah, blah, blah...* finally he done pointed-it across the ravine with a parting ... *that be the fucking north, dip-shit*!

That little trek with the 1Sgt, I hadda been a'tinkering to myself cause I be only half-assed listening to the ramblings of that cranked old cracker-barrel and I had begun to thunk-it that Nam' be not mo' nor less any different than Unk' Zeke's pond in that all the shit be chockfull the greenery onliest with large bushy stomps seed I justa couldn't move myself to done thunk-it them stumps be any kinda trees thems slant-eye stumps skinny assed-out boles barely topped-out 10-feet at bestest theys looky-looked-it a bunch of no good extra-large purple, orange and yellow spotted bean-shoots. It be on the reals all kinda pretty forest funky green to meself being a person steeped into Ma' Nature plus the dirt had smelled just as fresh as Unk's Zeke's pond even old Aunt Hannah still done smiled-it the brightest of herns brown-suga smiles thus befo' I'd done knowed-it, I done kinda felt-it justa little to home and had started to little by little to be feeling myself mostest *et' ease Soldier* "*UUUUHHHHHmmmmm Campbell beef-n-veggie soup good*!" I had also been kinda tinkering to myself that would my world ever to *Medgar Evers* be done changed?

Chapter 14

There I be bumping a slant-eye jungle and it all be all the same ting just the same old shit and not even a different day! I'd done split from the Sarge dropped-it outta sight down into that semi-muddy creek bed then I crossed over to the other side of the ravine. I'd done made it near that there northside spot witch the crank-pot Sarge had pointed-it out then I started to climb-up the northside of the ravine's weed infested wall stepping upwards towards a small berm that when I hadda done looked up towards it whilst standing inside the semi-muddy bed of the ravine, I done seed that berm hadda looked-it to be justa Biggy-smalls thicket of dead limbs and branches bouts a tree-foot high 8 to 10 foot-long step-over. Top of the berm, I seed that I hadda guessed-it pretty much accurately the thicket be justa piece of Moms pineapple up-side down buttery bunt-cake a super easy liked a Sundae moaning crossover. I'd done thunk-it to justa done shook-it loose a'nuttier one of thems funky-ass empty-belly farts to justa done blown that little bitch patch of worthless thickets plum the fuck away!

I had just taken my firstest step forward on the top-sided that berm when POOF fucking POOF the *magic fucking slant-eye dragon* my lying eyes hadda done seed-it *Holy Shits*, Babycakes! It be a fucking are you for reals, real shit fo' my lying assed baby-browns because the shit theys done pictured-it up be the fucking unbelievable FUCK! FUCK! FUCK! I'd unbelievably done looked-it directly at a very small-like impish wisp of a would be man or butter yet a yella assed gooner manchild justa runt of a man decked in cheap-assed black pajamas and that little man-runt slant-eye cunt bastard be on the fucking rise! Surprize Surprise Surprize Sgt. Carter the done raised-it up mofo be justa steadily coming-it up and from outta the inside of that little thicket of dead branches and dead leaves *Holy the fucking shits, Batman all Hells-a-fire*! The fool ass gooner be just a puny assed-out bastard, he couldn't have been no more than 4-foot-6" dat little runt fuck gonna barely topped-it out nipple level my hairless chest iffn I'd had to done guessed-it the little gook fool be lessor than a 100 pounds soaked in skank rice-water *Sooners* I'd come to learn that be extra-large for a gooner's runt son-of-a-yella-commie bitch! I'd come to done learnt-it on the out-camp party-line that gook-fuck yella-assed fool had probably been regular army Chinese.

The *fuck-me* fool done held within hisns tiny wuddle yella-assed gooner bastard hands a fully done growed-it up grown assed man sized Chinese SKS semi-automatic rifle WTF! *Yes, Sirrrr Bob's me uncle* that little gooner runt-cunt whore done held within hisns tiny yella chink commie black gloved-hands the slant-eye number-fucking-one killing machine there on the fucking quick I'd done thunk-it a differ opinion of the big gun welding slant-eye yella mofo thus dat little bitch bastard's stance instantly done became a Hell-of-a-lot bigger as well a super imposed demonstrative WTF! The fuck-bastard had been wearing black threadbare clothing with faded thin unraveling black electrical tape covering the rips, tears and other would be openings on the mud-caked encrusted tattered black pajamas and he had what looked to be a scuba diver's hood covering hisns impish child-like pointy-head that hoody be embedded with a doubled-row of allegedly poisonous darts. Thems little darts done looked-it like halfa-inch thumb-tacks pushed-it pointy-side out from the inside on the topside of that diver's hoody thems thumb-tacks spikes pointed outward to done trailed that black hoody front to back in a double-row. I'd be damned iffn on the instant grits lookey-looked in all its evil intended totality *fuck-me* no shit thems two rows of tiny little spikes done looky-looked-it exactamently liked a zipper just the fuck liked the Sarge hadda just done told-it to me, OMG!

The Sarge told-it them zippers would head ram a body as a last resort to embed them poisonous thumb-tacks into their enemy's guts in a finalized act of disciplined defiance! The parts dat be seed of that ugly yella-assed zipper's fuck-face had been painted black and he had been wearing dark green flat-round welder's goggles. A spot on that bitch-runt of a slant-eyed gooner whore had glinted a shiny bright metallic quicksilver flash *FUCK-THE-HELL, NO*! that little runt-of-a-cunt gooner bastard had mostest likely to done just hastily sheathed a blade, hot-fucking damn! That little gook mudda-fucker had intended to done knifed me! The little bitch fucking yella gooner mofo hadda done thunk-it to blade-n-grade my skinny dumb-ass, WTF! No fucking way! *Lawd Hava Mercy* on hisns funky little sorry yella-ass worthless soul!

Tank God Almighty there be a problem a big Black skinny-ass problem witch be for the both of us in-that I had been dumb-ass lost inside my thoughts and because I hadda been a fucking numb-nuts day-dreaming dip-shit all caught-it up in comparing the raunchy assed-out slant-eye jungle with the paradise of Unk' Zeke's pond then I had not instant grits stopped-it when my lying-eyes firstest done peeked-it dat yella-slant-eye fuck! Believe me, it t'was not because it hadda been love at firstest slant-eye gooner sight neither had I changed my course of action nor direction because it be my firstest boots to ground Nam big-*dazed*-butts my mind had been else-the-fuck-wheres Good *God Amighty* thus I be big-*dazed*-butts I be not perplexed therefore because of natural reflex I had continued to done stepped-it forward a'gin-n-juice my mind had not been on-point *Tank God* thus I had refused to accept the fucking image my lying-eyes be flashing my way. I had been utterly unaware the immediate dangers of the situation, I had kept to moving forward a'nuttier step therefore when the reality had begun to done concrete itself then the little fuck-less yella chink commie gooner whore be no-less than a foot directly in front of my no-longer day-tripping ass and dat fool ass commie bastard be one quicksilver flashed justa short-armed donkey-*momma said to knock you out*-punch away! I had a thought to sucker-punch hisns fucking *gonna knife my big black ass* itty-bitty yella fucking lights-out yet again and a big plus for the dat little runt-cunt of a whore be that I hadda done on the up-close be so personal firsthand to done seed the real truth, Ruth that the gooner-fuck had the wuddle finger of hisns right-hand on the trigger of that gigantic SKS rifle witch be nestled into hisns little itty-bitty right shoulder-socket thus I had instant grits re-thunk-it dat sucker-punch a slant-eye motherfucker out shit, NOT!

The fucked-up part hadda been that *little gooner fuck* by all logical, physical and scientific rights, seed I hadda stood some 2-feet above hisns on the rise besides hisns runt-cunt shit-fo'-brains commie-whore funky yella ass be less than a foot away, angled diagonally to my left yet directly in-front of me then I should have been looking directly down and into the barrel of the little fuck's SKS! My little brown lying-eyes had for surely done peeped-it both the itty-bitty-shitty yella gooner runt and hisns big-ass *no mo' life fo' you Blackie-boy* killing-machine yet fo' whatever the fucking dumb-assed gooners bitch-bastard's unreasoning the muzzle of the little gooner fuck's high-powered weapon had not been aimed directly at my dumb-*I be fucked*-ass! The rifle's barrel had been cantered high just a bite over my nappy-head as swell for my black ass the muzzle be off to my outside left, over and away from my body! Can the gospel gooney-goo-goo choir holler *Oh happy day Happy Birthdaze to me* in-order to shoot my dumb-ass that little gooner runt-fuck would have had to done swung hisns whole wuddle bitty gooner shoulders some 6 plus inches to hisns left and down justa bite to actually place a round in my dumb unlucky lucky like a mofo day-tripping ass! *Fuck-me* I be one lucky skinny black ass, Mofo!

I'd done looked-it directly at the totality of my *aint's ready fo' the grave* fucked situation because bye-bye then I had done shifted-it thems fucking imagining gears sway the fuck outta Unk' Zeke's pond, fuck-it *Toto, this aint Kansas* to done fully engaged my situation thus I be like WTF be up with this fucking dumb-ass gooner this bitch be teasing a mofo like it be prom night, shit the runt whore gooner bastard be fucking collard-greens *stoopid* dat puny little pygmy fuck hadn't done knowed-it the fuck what he be doing, FUCK dat dumb-assed gooner bastard! It be in that instant grits and I'm talking nano-seconds thems itty-bitty *give me life you can just keep yo' fucking death* seconds be when the gook bastard had done tooken-it upon hisns funky-assed self-assured *gotz this black mofo by the balls* gooner ass to done used thems precious *titi* nano-seconds of *this be my life* flashing *bling-bling-bling* befo' my lying baby-browns to hava done did the fucking ludicrous mostest insane shit evers WTF! The fucking little gooner runt done lifted-it hisns fucking little gooner left-hand off the rifle's barrel then moved that same funky wuddle left-hand downwards under the barrel passed the trigger housing the little runt-cunt gooner continued to done moved-it that fucking yella-ass scratcher down to hisns fucking pie-hole where *bye-bye sweet world of mine* the little fuck done hissed-it a crazy assed-out "*zzzzzzzzzzssth*" at me WTF! All that damned time that SKS muzzle never wavered plus the little skeeze ball be eyeballing me though I couldn't actually see hisns funky skank shitty beady ass orbs a'rolling because the gooner whore be wearing thems dark green welders goggles yet all the whilst this shit be going on my bigger than life lying-eyes done frog-eyed popped-it a WTF, MOTHERFUCKER!

It be liked at that moment hisns little gooner ass be too damned busy and that I needed-it to wait a fucking minute for him to done placed-it a full-metal jacketed chink-round into my dumb fucked ass or maybe dat bitch bastard gooner whore done thought that us two be in a fucking library and dat I be making sway too much noise topping-out that berm so he done tooken-it upon hisns dumb-assed self to done shussssed-it me then again justa mayhap dat yella-bastard gooner whore hadda thunk-it my Black ass be a US WWI, WWII and or a Korean war soldier, justa uniformed camouflaged *Negro only* domestic help, a fucking Black assed butler standing tall a slant-eye jungle about to done served-it hisns skinny yella-runt little gooner ass a bowl of wonton soup!

Tank God, there be a good news witch I swear to God, jo' God, Oh My God, the fucking little gooner's *Tet* God justa anybody's fucking God that this ain't *No God damned* macho bullshit, I had not been a'scared big-*fearless*-butts SURPRISED SURPRIZED SURPRISED SGT CARTER like a motherfucker *HELL THE FUCK, YES*! Big-*on the lookout*-butts no fucking shit, I hadn't shit my pants nor pissed my boots! My drawls be bald-headed white-assed *Mr. Clean* sparkling streak-free and my socks be Arizona desert bone dry! I be damn swell fucking *tits-til-fucking-pay-you-Tuesday for a hamburger today* alive, Popeye! My senses be jacked the fuck-up and all 5 dems sense whores be on full alert *Death Comm 5 immediate threat, Danger-Danger-Danger Jolly Rogers* all 5 of my senses be as keen as a motherfucker and on-point ready, my sense of smell had been super-fucking hyped that bitch gooner done smelt putrid liked a rural southern outhouse fo' redneck kin banging road-kill eating po'dunk trailer trashy backwoods the hills be alive with hillbillies God awful po'dunks *tells ya' no lie* that gooner bastard had smelled-it the pure assed skunk-bitching bush-whacked funky skin-bag of the stale human shit, days old piss, blood and puked the fuck-out guts why the fuck I hadn't smelt that funky yella-commie ass mofo earlier had been the fo'reallies WTF mystery of that day!

My eyesight be mo' butter than my sense of smell thems lying-eyes done locked-it unto every little detail surround-sounded me dat purple-orange slant-eye jungle liked thems fucking slant-eyed tings gonna be the lastest tings that I'd *Medgar Evers* be done seed on the humanly side dis world! I seed-it every little rip in the gooner fuck's cheap-assed tattered black pajamas and on hisns black vinyl hoodie witch hadda firstest glance looked kinda like a scuba diver's hood big-*cheap gooner ass*-butts when actually intently peered at hisns pinhead be covered by one of them little Pan-Am Airline little vinyl tote-bags that theys used to done gived-it away when you decked one of their jets fo' to be yo' doggie bag. Anywho the gooner bastard wore one of them little vinyl bags spray-painted black witch he done wrapped-it around hisns pinhead using the bag's straps what a fucking Jew-boy wannabe *cheap-cheep* gooner bastard!

My mind had never been more lucid, inside my nappy head be a fucking mantra justa solo-act mono-soundtrack stuck on the repeat *after me muddafucker* mode an ode to the fucked of this world done played itself an over to over dedicated shout-out dat my world bouts to gets its *fuck me, on*! Voiced by Gunny Phil Curry that bad-assed *who'dat* had been my bootcamp DI*DrillInstructor* and that dickhead mofo' just kept a non-stop flight *"Keep yo' weapon in yo' fucking hands and yo' finger on the trigger like a Gawd damned 16 year old freckled face red-headed peckerwood keeps his pencil dick! Or you gonna find yo' self in a world of shit!"* Fuck, I truly done found me selfie in a world of shit! *Geraldine* be slung over my shoulder canted diagonally across and down my skinny-assed backside seed my babygirl be clinging to my black ass just the way I'd seed them Company-G *Potheads* toting theys M-16s the outpost last knight and that shit had looked Super-fucking-Bad! I'd done that shit to *Geraldine* the minute the 1Sgt had gotten outta my sight, *fuck you, first-skirt*!

My senses had been jacked, I could feel my heart pounding like a motherfucker from deep inside my chest. My heart had pulsed to the beat of dickhead Gunny Phil Curry's mantra…*keep yo' weapon in yo' hands like a...* my hearing be *Superman* tuned to the max *fuck me* my hearing be on the loud and the crystal fucking *alls clear*, Babycakes! I could hear the giggles of the flea as he hadda on the fly ass-fucked the ant under one of thems funky yellow-orange-green stumps! Fo' the firstest time in that jungle I had begun to done heard its real and all natural sounds seed I'd done heard the chirpings of strange birds, buzzing insects, the crinkling snaps of breaking twigs alongside the bustled cracklings of them dead dry assed leaves as I hadda done kept on stepping forward whilst that funky slant-eye zipper-head done kept to rising-it up from outta that thicket then I done *heard it through the grapevine* it hadda been kinda faint justa *whip-whisk-whip-thud-thud-whisk-whip* to witch I'd done barely begun to done recognized-it big-*Tankz God*-butts it had been them mechanical sounds getting louder-n-louder *WHIP-WHISK-WHIP-THUD-THUD-WHISK-WHIP* thems fabulous sounds be the what that had mostest to likely done saved-it my black ass cheeks. Them swishy-swish-thuddy thud sounds be made by the whirling blades of an *In-coming* bug-eyed old assed Korean war helicopter and it had been then and at that moment that the fucking zipper had taken hisns only real viable chance. The gooner bastard-bitch done let fly with hisns locked and loaded SKS super loud ass *Devil farts* fuck *BLAT-BLAT-BLAT-BLAT* witch had not been aimed at me a'gin-n-juice big-*Tankz God*-butts at thems sounds of God *In-coming* from on high! Good Lord, God done jumped hisns funky unholy po'dunk ass into the mix and dat mofo be riding-it high and tight inside an old assed-out Big Bertha!

God be skying one of them old assed helicopters with the big grasshopper bug-eyed looking bubbled-glass canopy. I hadn't actually seed the copter *Emmett Till* seconds after all the shit had done cleared the slant-eyed fan! Even then I'd only seed the copter's rear-end hauling ass over teacups the fuck outta there! I didn't get a glimpse *Emmett Till* onliest after that funky-assed gooner bastard done bounced-it and God already done flipped-it dat glorified bitch that be when I'd done peeked-it God hauling hisns un-Godly selfish ass outta there to the from whence hisns kingdom done cometh on the quick be furious! Fuck, WTF even fucking God be leaving my Black ass all alone to deal with the slant-eyed *brotha death* be a fucking runt-cunt gooner fuck!

What hadda happened-it be when dat funky assed bitch gooner had fired-it BLAT the firstest fucking earhole shattering shot because of the intense and heighten awareness of my fucking senses being Jacked my lying-eyes done seed the all of it, theys done looked-it the flume, the round's burst of flame flashed live flamboyant *Liberace* fucking alive with bright-assed reds, oranges, yellows followed-it up by a wispy bluish misting smoky white plume! I'd done seed it all exploded outta the barrel of the zipper's SKS since I be standing fucking startled-it *deer in headlights* like a motherfucker so close-up to be a personal assistant to the little itty-bitty-tit fuck! Simultaneously my nose done dived-it ass down head-first into the freshest smells *Medgar Evers* to done filled my world of worlds them boogers inside my nostrils be doing happy-assed back-flips because all my senses be alive and on the full bumped-it up cardiac alert, I done tasted-it the fresh burnt offerings of the raw-dawg cordite witch smelled as swell done tasted a black peppery acidity flavor with a pinch of ammonia. The flume's Heavenly aromatic aroma like instant grits done jimmy-jammed my nostrils with an ecstasy such that it be the nectar that could onliest come from the Gods! Good Gawd damned that gooner bitch dumb-assed fuck be rolling the same thunder that we Ja'renes done packed, right then to the I be fucking there, it be love, *Babycakes*, my love-jones got lit as my nostrils flared and my big lips be slant-eyed fresh kissed with the taste of war! I'm surprized I didn't nut my pants that shit be on the reals big-*later fo' love*-butts I be outta there cause dat shit be not some BB-gun kiddie humping a shitty-diaper infatuation, Babycakes!

Chapter 15

It be liked dat first piece of ass, dat first table dance, dat virgin teenaged kiss be bumping dat thang! It hadda been all dat and a bag of fiddy-dolla casino chips been rolled-it up and into the one then given to the one *who'dat* be there! Power to the people! Black be Beautiful! Make war fuck love, jo' boy be strung-out nose wide the fuck opened Zeke dawg be jonesing like a muddafukka! All the whilst my skinny black ass done on the fucking quick be quickest *Jack flash* to done dropped-it down to be outta the fuck you dumb-ass gooner sight my black ass be bye-bye gooner fuck! I'd done jumped-it backwards to belly-flop onto all fours yet mostest my upper-body *Peace be still* atop the edge of that northside berm. I can only surmise that fucking little gooner runt-whore hadda done on the early seed it in my idiotic baby-browns the exactamente moment that I had recognized thems *whip-whisk-whip-thud-thud-whisk-whip* sounds for what da' fuck thems sound bites be in that theys be sounds of an *In-coming* helicopter therefore it must be God rolling-it in from on high! That fucking gooner must have saw that recognition light-up in my baby-browns and that I done just knowed-it *which way be up* it be then dat little gooner fuck decided our fates and called the impromptu meeting a *let's just part ways as friends* draw! I stated that in all honesty, because come the future *Mz. Experience* gonna taught-it my dumb-ass that in the face to face, hand to hand and specially the experienced verses the rookie combat encounters that kinda up-close be personal eyeballing to eyeballing contact shit be the ultimate *get yo' spike on*, Babycakes! That eyeballing shit sho'nuff lets the experienced combatant to be done knowed-it for sure when, where and just how to strike in the crucial moment because dat gooner held the far more superior position hisns God awful putrid ass had acted with all the confidence and experienced knowledge afforded-it the cat-bird seat to done whatsoever hisns funky little ass wanted done at hisns own fucking leisure the lucky slit-eye fuck!

I can't swear to it because that little runt whore gooner bitch had been wearing them dark welders goggles therefore I couldn't peek hisns itty-bitty-shitty slanty-eyes little-*gooner*-butts my senses be full alert so I hadda done felt-it the moment when that little gooner runt whore had locked and loaded unto my baby-brown orbs with hisns *gots yo' black ass* confident like a motherfucker! Thems lying eyes of mine be screaming on the loud and clear as mud *I be fucked* big-*lying*-butts that be the lie that got relayed to the self-gloating slant-eye chinny-chin-chin gooner fuck to be so super fucking secure in hisns superior position as to done taken hisns sweet assed-out gooner time to firstest done hissed-it hisns gibberish shit dictating to my dumb-ass to cease and desist *stop rights there mofo* whilst he grabbed a moment to take-down God! The fuck doing that unnecessary act of total confidence big-*gots balls*-butts on the ghetto streets that shit be *Word-up* seed the whoremonger gooner done let me to be done knowed-it hisns itty-bitty cock-sucker tiny ass fuck done sho'nuff sported a pair! That little gooner motherfucker done strutted-it hisns gooner shit front-street the *Tri-City slant-eye* farmer's market to done straight-up laced thems big red size 22 inch floppies onto my big assed feets thus the yella-ass whore done officially clowned my Black-ass! That dumb-fuck butt-fucked little gooner whore done thunk-it the thought that hisns little *bite my ass* gonna teach-it the *who'dat* done had the misfortune to have strode directly unto the path of *hey dumb-ass* death' be a gooner semi-auto rifle toting slant-eye BITCH mofo!

At the firstest of that done been flashed-it sight of that colorful flume from the fucking dumb-assed gooner's SKS quick as speckled bird-shit droppings on a freshy waxed bucket, I'd done jumped-it hardtack backwards away from the fuck, the 1st BLAT onliest my legs be over the berm to dangle over the ravine's wall *bye-bye mofo gook* the 2nd BLAT my whole body be down below the berm to be scrambling along the ravine wall to the left-side of the itty-bitty-shitty gooner whore! I be whitegurl flat-assed against dat ravine's north wall befo' the 3rd crack done strung my ears, *youngblood* be long on the *fucking bye-bye* gooner mofo I be gone! I had landed on my hands, elbows and boot tips in that tall bushy green wild weeds covering the wall then onliest because I had been on the same side of the ravine's wall from witch I had done comed-it up from when I'd made my initial approach then as the gook fuck made hisns 2nd set of controlled trigger pulls thems fuck the Devil's ass farts BLAT-BLAT-BLAT-BLAT I'd done side-saddled low-crawled-it to zig below and to the right of the cunt-runt gooner! I had on the Superfly to done crab-crawled it backwards as well downward towards the ravine's muddy bed all the while I be whitegirled hidden as bestest I could beneath thems scraggly over grown wild weeds yet justa bite more than less to the right of that fuck-less zipper fuck in a big-*full retreat*-butts zigging-it the here to done zagged-it there quick as all *Hell to redneck southern belles*! I had crab-walked-it big-*on the run*-butts using onliest me elbows and boot-tips in-order to stay low as I had listened-it hard for thems booming the Devil's ass farts *death be onto jo' black ass* thunderous sounds! Them shots initially be 2-sets of a controlled 4-round bursts each aimed at God because them rounds hadn't been a'coming my way.

I hadn't done knowed-it at the time big-*gun slinging*-butts later the Bros of Company-G had shaken a moment to done schooled me in that the SKS clip only held 5 rounds plus the one locked and loaded inside the chamber thus the zipper had fo'reallies done knowed-it hisns shit seed that putrid skank ass hoe had trigger control 4-rounds to done smartly left-it one round inside the chamber whilst leaving that last round in the clip just in case inside of those precious few nano-seconds I'd done growed-it up a grown man's coconut hairy pair, fuck dat shit! The fucked gooner bitch done knowed-it the fuck what he be a'doing big-*gots skills*-butts dat bitch-hoe chink bastard gonna realize dat hisns chink ass be stranded at the fucking altar of the slant-eye dream to fucking do God big-*jilted*-butts I had on a purpose done a slid-it on my black ass justa bite to give that fool a target near the semi-muddied bottom big-*whoa*

Nellie-butts I had not been so dumb-assed stoopid as to have actually done gotten-it into that semi-muddy ravine bed. The gooner's 3rd set done sounded-it justa little different *BLAT-thud-BLAT-thud-BLAT-thud-BLAT-thud* as them intended for my black ass rounds fell well short and far the fuck away from my black ass not in the clear yet most assuredly backs and away from my previous inferior and endangered position. I watched keenly as thems rounds done plowed into the dirt along the left-side of that ravine wall near the place where I had firstest approached the zipper that dirt done did a buck-wild dance of death be *a'coming yo' black ass* way big-*lucky*-butts youngblood be on the opposite side further a'sway definitely mo' deeper into the brush backwards crawling looking-it to be a'watching that slant-eye dirt do the *boogaloo*! I'd done stayed-it more back aways and to the left of the zipper all the while on the look-out for a safe haven because I done needed-it bad-fucking bad fo' that zipper to have to either stand along the berm's topside edge where hisns funky little gooner ass be a sight on scene silhouetted bye-bye gook mofo the rising slant-eye sun because then hisns gooner ass would be in the fishbowl *Gotcha* or *Po'leease God* fo' the gook bastard to done *due drop-in* hisns funky little gooner ass down into thems wild green bucktooth weeds to done let's us just party-party mofo alongside that northside ravine wall!

I done knowed-it instinctually that I couldn't cross to the other side of the ravine nor to done holed-it up in its semi-muddy bed because that kinda a'scared-assed rabbit dumb-shit on the full *run Blackie boy run* strategy would have made it just sway too easy for that gooner fuck to be done stayed atop the berm then to done put hisns funky chink-rounds into my out in the fishbowl of the ravine bed dumb-ass! I may had been the dumb-fuck big-*day dreamer*-butts I be knot to ever be confused-it as a'scared rabbit toting squirrel nuts stupid dead-fuck oh the Fuck-No, Babycakes! I hadn't been trying to be nobody's damned hero neither therefore I hadn't risked returning fire at the gook slant-eyed *bump dat shit* that kinda foolishness be justa a'nuttier don't you dare bust dat fucking dumb-shit move because any return fire shit would've been an out-right dumb-assed giving away my *Peace be still* inferior position with nuttin big-*flimsy*-butts slant-eye bucktooth wild weeds for covering! To Hell with God, I gots to gets my skinny black ass backs home to done kissed-it mines own chocolate cooties infested hometown brown-suga Babygirl!

God being God he just had to done saved-it hisns own Black ass just liked I hadda with hisns help *tank-ya kindly* mofo done gone and saved-it mines!

The itty-bitty-titty fuck must have stepped-it up-close enough yet not to be seen nor silhouetted to done peered-it over *the slant-eye rainbow* the outer top edge of the berm to done took an afternoon delight quickie lookey-look because when he tossed-it a'nutter 3rd set of rounds my way dat gooner cunt-whore had sent them rounds to the place where that the brush had left a trail after I had on a purpose done flipped-a-bitch to done ass slid-it thems weeds justa mite, good keep it real, slant-eye mofo! Dat gooner bitch whore must have been doing Chinese arithmetic to done fucking wrongfully figured-it that my Black ass be dumbfounded e'nuff to done fucking hooched-it up bottomed-it out inside the ravine's muddy bed, Fuck you gooner slant-eye bastard! Me and the posse had sway too many battles out in Unk' Zeke's pond for my skinny on the run-run black ass to done falled-it in love with my very firstest slant-eye hole! Anywho to all the youngbloods take note, never to *Medgar Evers* to be done falled-it in love with yo' very firstest fur-lined hole! Get the fuck-up, get the fuck-in then get the fuck-out and justa keep-it pumping, Babycakes! During my high-stakes retreat I had taken the time to regroup my illogical fucked-up thought process ergo I'd done put *Geraldine* up-tight against my hairless chest plus babygirl be held tightly inside my right fisted-hand *like a freckled face red-headed peckerwood keeps hisns pencil dick* tank you fucking Gunny Phil Curry! The fucking first-skirt cracker mofo had been absolutely right *fuck dem damned cowboys n' dem pot-heads* theys all be justa chunk of the aint's knowed-it good fo' a'nuttin high as a fucking kite stoopid, Mofos!

Five-clicks ahead I'd done spied a cave along the ravine's lower end there be a hole along the wall big-*safety*-butts not so damned Skippy close to the semi-muddy ravine bed actually it had been justa small hole a wan-nabe nappy dug-out *Yes Lord* I backed-it big black ass-cheeks firstest into that rose by any other name *due drop-inn* ass up belly down once nestled safely it hadda been from there that I'd done started-it to stinky-finger *Geraldine* tree-round controlled bursts just liked that zipper hadda done *I'm alive no fucking jive* learnt-it to me warfare 101 taught by a skank hoe slant-eye chink gooner zipper-head mofo! Book learnings taint gots nuttin on real world teachings, liked *Jethro Bodine* from dat Hollywood TV show the *Beverly Hillbillys* it be *"lookey hear granny, eyes done grad-u-ate-it the sixth grade!"*

I had *Geraldine* toss dem sweet my Soul's afire *death to yo' gooner ass* kisses *burrrup-burrrup-burrrup* Biggy-smalls pause fo' da' cause *burrup-burrup-burrrup*! After my 2nd tree-round blast I'd done heard-it the faded yet familiar sound *burrup-burrup-brurrup-burrup-burrup-brurrup…* full-auto blasting uninterrupted the full-tittied big-pimping *song of the Sirens* that be the sweetest sound in the world to an on the run-run GI holed-it up in a slant-eye jungle, Babycakes! Thems *brrup burrups* be the sounds dat onliest an *Uncle Sho-gun* genuine issued M-16 the widow maker the baby-boy taker could burst forth! Life be great and justa getting mo' butter when ya' all alone playing at war to be done heard-it a'nuttier babygirl cackle that sweet swan song of life, liberty and the pursuit of pussy every GI done knowed-its hallowed warble by heart *burrup-burrup-brurrup* sing yo' song, babygirl! *Sing dat song, sing dat song you bitch* dat be a Rich *da' shit* Pryor shout-out! The 1st Sgt had burst forth with the full-pledged chorus to done let me knowed-it that hisns Sundae early morn preaching cracker-barrel ass be bumping-it *Hi ho, Silver* newbie Black ass mofo, the calvary be *In-coming*! Sweet-tea Jesus, the 1Sgt done covered-it my *sweet sweet-back* black ass! *Jungle bunny* he'd shouted-it that shit loud and on the clear seed earlier during hisns impromptu field *preach-on* briefing the 1Sgt hadda done told-it me that he liked hisns people on theys raw nerve edge *"I don't want any happy-asses at my back, to me you dumb-assed bastards are all rednecks, greasers, wops, niggers, spics, kikes, coons, crackers, peckerwoods, needle dicks, eraser-head-pencil-neck geeks, goobers, fucking Gomer piles sums-dey-bitches!"* He'd done put it so kindly *Fuck you, Cracker* had been my *fired* up return from inside that rose canyon piss-pit of a nappy dug-out!

Chapter 16

THE SHIT COULD NOT HAVE lasted no mo' than 20-seconds from the zipper head's rising, hisns gooner ass controlled 4-round blasts and my sporadic tree-round controlled *bust a'move* returned fire big-*shooting*-butts all the shit done happened incredulously in real time lessen a mere 20-second span, Good Lord, I be alive *aint's life grand* Babycakes! After all the energy done been spent, God rolling away, the gooner fuck done split then the Sarge arrived on scene. The first-skirt took a quick lookey-look over the area then he done asked-it me iffn I'd chased the gooner from outta hisns hooch over to the berm? I hadda just kept it simple fo' the Sarge seed I done told-it dat me and that gooner bitch done had a meet-it up et' the prom and it tain't' polite to kiss and tell! Big-*knuckles*-butts the 1st Sgt done knowed-it how to track so after giving me a *you some kinda smart-ass* grimace he did a full WTF happened survey exactamente accurate on-point like a motherfucker as to the how, when and where every bite of the shit-sandwich had went down! The Sarge *snoop there it is* tracked-it everyting from my approach to the fucking hooched-it out hole whilst I done took the lonely cowpoke's strong big-*quiet*-butts silent stance. The Sarge after hisns survey grabbed ahold my silent dumb-ass then dragged me abouts the area pointing out the differ events exactamently as they hadda done on the real truth, Ruth unfolded-it firsthand as iffn that dickhead mofo hadda been overhead to done watched it all happen from on high in hisns own fucking Big Bertha bug-eye in the sky! The first-skirt showed-it me where the slant-eye zipper had jumped-it up from outta his hooch to done peeped over the berm to search my dumb-ass out! The tracking accurate mofo done laughed-it a bit as he commented-it that I'd been kinda busy *elbows over asshole* low-crawling-it the fuck outta there! "You musta been a'scared ass, look at those boot-tip and elbow-dents" The Sarge paused a moment to give me the silent dead-eye befo' he let me to done knowed-it *fuck the fear* I hadda made the right call in getting-it up onto my stick-horse to be riding the fuck outta harm's way the numb-nuts went so far as to say it had taken a pair just to make-out like a *freckled-face puss-hound* on a first-date. The Sarge done showed me the evidence that my Grand Canyon had mostest likely been the fucking little gooner's hide-out hooch. Hell, the Sarge said that we could have been standing right above the little gooner-bastard just before we had split-it up and iffn that fucking little zipper had not been so dedicated to his mission witch the skirt believed-it to be to takedown God then dat gooner fuck could have taken the both of us out!

The Sarge had done a WTF peculiar ting in the aftermath of hisns on-point tracking he done sniffed-it my dumb-ass and the air all-around me *fuck* I hadn't to done knowed-it then the whys of it all big-*sniffin'*-butts that shit hadda seemed more than just a bite kinda strange ting even fo' dat cracker-barrel mofo to have done. Thems G-Company cowboys and potheads had informed me that the 1st Sgt had just been checking to done seed iffn I'd done shit my pants or pissed my boots be the *4-1-1* skinny! The Sarge had let thems knowed-it that I hadn't done neither then them gyrenes had given me big ups followed-it by mad props. Theys probably would have given me a lot more theys big-*happy getting mo' happier*-butts I had done stopped-it theys *happy let's celebrate* asses to let it be knowed-it to the one and to thems all that I considered my body to be my Temple and that I didn't defile my Temple with nobody's alcohol, smoke nor all to any kinda dope that shit be strictly forbidden because me and my Temple be headed-it to the promised land in the up-coming months when my hard time be up then thems Bros would be paying theys hard earned-it re-enlistment cash-money justa watch me kick my killer jump-shot in the NBA, yeah Brother got game! Them Bros countered that shit by tagging me *Shirley-fucking-Temple* fo' the next plus fiddy-daze and theys done told-it that my Shirley Temple tap-dancing minstrel no-show *Mr. Bojangles* ass would have a better chance of finding a virgin fiddy-year old Momma-san in-country than to *Medgar Evers* come the day that I'm gonna find my skinny black ass taking a single shot in the National Basketball Association that day on and unto the Black knight them company-G grunts had taken theys sips, spikes n' they totes in my honor and to done the Monty Python *Holy Grail* theys done "*farted in my general direction*" Mayhap it had been a contact high or whatsoever big-*confessional*-butts anywho I'd done belched-it up the reality of my full-throttled retreat then thems cowboys and potheads had been even way mo' kool with my doing whats-just had to be done theys be *youngblood you did the right thing, fuck God*! Theys be like *God gotta handle his own* because as theys had put-it to me the number-1 rule in that slant-eye jungle be staying the fuck alive, Babycakes!

It probably ain't no breech of national security big-*secretive*-butts justa little further down that same *happy-assed trails to you* I'd done learnt-it the real truth, Ruth behind the Sarge's *whiff n' sniff* actions and what them potheads and cowboys had failed to tell me hadda been that mostest newbies in theys firstest wet-fires would either puke their guts, shit or piss their pants or burst all tree simultaneously for the main fart and it had a'nuttin to do with dat bitch-hoe bastard *brotha fear* it be just liked what done happen-it upon my dumb-ass during the surprized encounter with that gooner-whore witch hadda been my firstest live up-close on the personal engaged combat scene! In mostest live wet-fires specially the firstest when outta the fucking POOF no-fucking-where thems mofo 5 senses be running senseless caused theys be enhanced by the sound, the taste of burnt cordite, the smells and sights of raw guts, brain matter and all other kinda bloodied body parts that be flying around then landing all over theys body or theys Bro's body not to even mention the horrific sight of thems exploding itty-bitty little gooner fucks thems fucking *KA-BOOM* exploding slant-eye gooner body parts be flying the fuck all to and every fucking where plus all thems exploding body parts shits be coupled-it up with thems fucking constant loud assed *bitch-slapped bitch* screams!

Chapter 17

I REALIZED-IT THAT IT HADDA been more than just Luck being a *Sophisticated Lady* that had saved my rookie-ass from the zipper! The reason that I believed-it that the fucked *zipper* whore had not shot me had been because he had found himself to be in the exactamente same fucked position liken unto my own fucked selfie. The key to all real estate transactions be location, location, location seed fo' hisns ass bye-bye pure fucking buzzard luck of my mindless day-tripping I hadda chosen a path that had put me directly atop hisns putrid gooner-ass! The gooner hunkered-it down inside a thicket of dry leaves and branches could not move lest the risk dat I'd have heard the rustle thus I had gotten up-front personal on dat motherfucker big-*stepp'n*-butts at such a close-up range the back-spray of my body's exploding fluids would have jammed hisns semi-automatic weapon instant grits! An automatic weapon when fired produced and left a small trace of burnt gunpowder in the chamber then iffn that trace of gunpowder got wet by any means then the rack wouldn't slide and the weapon be jammed liked a motherfucker! The most prudent thing to have done be exactamently what the putrid little nip-fuck hadda done did in that he brought the fight to me big-*upper room*-butts from hisns far mo' superior advantage point. I also believe the 1st Sgt on-scene assessment of the little bastard's hold-card in that the fucking zipper be a well-disciplined slant-eye gooner mofo dedicated to his mission and that hisns fucking mission that day had been God. My interloping had just been a minor distraction evidenced by the *laissez-faire* attitude witch the little fuck had used in casually dismissing my ass bye-bye hissing the gook gibberish speak "*zzzzzzzzzssth*"!

Big Bertha showing up when she did had been monumental and

the only irrational luck that I had received therefore I done come to the conclusion that it had been God on high that truly done saved my Black ass! My self-serving logic be most accurate in that given a choice between my pagan ass and God that fucking zipper had chosen God! There you go, I'm shoulda done written epistles to them *Molly Mormon Jello-eater* door-knocking *you want to hear the good news* motherfuckers to send me a medal or sumptin-sump-tin for going to a foreign land then causing a pagan assed-out whore to choose God on high at the crack of dawn in an *In-coming* iron-fisted battle! Some may argue that the little gooner-bastard had given me my life yet even iffn dat shit be true on some cosmic level thesis meta-physical philosophical thang it be a fat fact, Jack that anything received along one's chosen path through life had to have been well-earned or at the minimalist's least a preconceived well planned-it act from the git-go sway afore that slippery-sloped slide outta theys momma's fat preggers ass! The real truth, Ruth for me be dat creation be, had been and always will be a self-made theology witch no one sect can be right whilst all dems others be wronged! I have chosen to remember dat day fo' me to be a time immortal witch I done capsulated into the one all-encompassing *Holy Fuck* cause *I loves me some me-me-me* on the personal that yella bitch-hoe done taught-it war not onliest be Hell, big-*let's get it on*-butts war be mucho-much butter when the kill or be killed action be eyeballing to eyeballing on the up-close dis shit be personal!

Chapter 18

FUCK DAT SHIT, PRIOR TO the encounter I hadda had some 5 plus years of superb OJT on-the-job training in identifying then utilizing the proper mostest accurate form of the how to rid one's self from the onliest real enemy that be this world witch be dat skank-ass hoe *brotha fear*! I'd done been properly schooled in the knowledge and equipped-it with the hands on experienced know how to done kicked dat dirty bitch-hoe bastard *brotha fear* balls deep into hisns raunchy a'scared ass thus that moment be *Not* the firstest time *Medgar Evers* that I done locked-it thems horns eye-ball-to-eyeballs with death's cold assed-out icey touch *In-coming*!

I be 13 when Dad and dem Unks of mine started to teach me how to drive a car on them snowy iced over dirt roads that be all around the country side of the CC iffn you'd ever had the nightmare of driving along a snow or ice covered road then you'd done knowed-it fo' sho'nuff that *brotha fear* the mostest evil of the most evil assed bastards of this *its all in yo' head* world taint fo'reallies real in that *brotha fear* be justa figment of one's *I'm a'scared* ass's quickly unraveling imagination that hitch-a-ride hitch-hiking bitch bastard mofo didn't just to done thumbed-it hisns awful raunchy bugged-out ass a ride inside yo' nappy-head seed brotha fear dat skank-hoe he just of hisns own accord uninvited ass done jumped-it into yo' hoop-tee to done sneakthief hisns way into your mind's inner workings. You knowed-it dat brotha fear done brought hisns skank-ho' ass to the party iffn there be an accident or a bad experience of any kind, the first ting to happened-it be the music done stopped and everything had in an eerily fashion be to done slowed-it way the fuck down to the slowest possible infra-fraction of a second to be playing tricks with yo' ig'nant mind yet in all reality that slo-poke onliest be played-it out inside yo' mind's inner eye and yo' mind's inner ear. That there moment of the slo-mo shit inside yo' mind be the brain-child of dat mofo *brotha fear* seed dat skank-ho' justa be fucking with yo' head. Brotha fear be displaying what be on the reals a fast-moving entirety of a bad situation yet in the a'scared ass mind brotha fears bumps dat shit into its most intimate and slowest forming detail and that right there be the part where brotha fear be a'dancing with yo' a'scared ass! The slo-mo shit just be that imaginary whore's modus operandi to be a'showing you just how he gonna fuck you up big-*scardy*-butts good, Baby!

Dad and dem Unks' had had for themselves an old wrecked bucket, a 58'buick *Oldsmobile Roadmaster* when I be at the wheel of dat O*lds*, Dad done rode shotgun and dem Unks' had filled-it the peanut gallery as my a'scared ass be creeping-it along that slippery iced-over mess at less than 5mph and theys all, Dad and dem Unks' would be justa hollering for me to *speed-it-up young fella don't be a'scared ass* then at any given point along the drive Dad woulda done reached-it over and jerked that steering-wheel in my trembling hands to make dat hooptee start to asshole over tea-cakes spinning fastest as all *Hell, get me the fuck outta there* that hooptee be a twirling ass spin-top rolling fast, mean and furiously outta fucking control! In my young buck no-experienced knucklehead daze when that hooptee done begun to skidding to done spun all over everywhere in my mind's inner eye everything would have done been slowed-it-down to an eerily slowed-it down creepy *I be fucked* slo-mo' yet my lying-eyes on the reals, thems two brown peepers done seed-it all *In-coming* jackrabbit fast and my real ears done heard-it everything going on inside that hooptee with all thems tings justa full speed flying past or a'coming at me, Dad and dems Unks'!

Outta the gate my eyes done seed the *coming of the Glory* as that hooptee careened-it to done slid in long looping circles *Sweet-tea Jesus* a'headed outta control towards thems big trees, bridges and metal railings that jalopy be ass hauling-it towards all that shit to witch I had Not done wanted-it to hit with no-parts that bucket. All the *please, fuck no Lawd, po'lease don't let dat young fool hit them bitch ass trees* dem Unks' be cussing and laughing it up in the gallery and justa talking pure shit about *Zeke be a fucking a'scarred ass dat young bitch punk-ass bastard be a'scared ass who'dat gonna fuck-it all up n' us too* big-*talking*-butts over time I done learnt-it to done tuned-it out dem Unks' jabber mouthings and even turned a blind-eye to all that passer bye-bye *In-coming* shit as I done skidded us out-of-control along thems iced over roads. My Dad, my personal shotgun riding hero done learnt-it to me just how to settle my nerves then to navigate dat hoopty past all thems real obstacles *Emmett Till* I had of my own accord done learnt-it how to completely out-source all the slo-mo as swell dems Unks jive talk to a place *somewhere over the rainbow* and as mo' time done passed-it then experience had crept into the mix and I done replaced thems earlier a'scared ass moments with live on the spot instant grits corrective actions. I had done learnt-it to listen fo' and onliest fo' to done heard my Dad's deep resonating reassuring baritone *steady she goes silky smooth* voice a constant reality check fo' my dumb-ass justa calm steady flow of the swell needed-it and sho'nuff appreciated stream of instructions *"Don't be ah scarred, Son! Grip that wheel tight, left-hand ten o'clock and right-hand two o'clock, turn into dat skid, tap them brakes gentile like, turn the wheel a quarta-turn into dat skid, tap them brakes again all gentile like, now turn them wheels outta the skid, Son! Nuttin butts little itty-bitty quarta-turns Son, all easy liked don't be a'scared justa keep a doing dems quarta-turns justa like dat over to over don't be ah'scarred-it Son, there ya' go dats all ya gonna do keep ah doing justa dat til ya done straighten dis motherfucker the fuck out"* Dad be joined-in on by a chorus of dems backseat driving Unks' *"don't think about it, dats just brotha fear, fear be in the thinkin' napfew! You gots to be in the doing, Son! Its all about the doing, due-da-due, Son! Its all in da' doing! Do it, Son! Kick dat mudda-fucker brotha fear funky ass outta ya head! Napfew youse gots to do the doing, its all in the doing, do da do Son don't be a'scared!"* Dad and dem Unks' hadn't done knowed-it a damned thing about panic nary a thought bout how it be the fucking panic that brings on the anxiety attack that done kept my trembling hands frozen to dat steering wheel and not performing the corrective actions needed to save our asses. Thems menfolk theys hadda justa onliest knowed-it dat one brother of a motherfucker, brotha fear and that you had to kick hisns raunchy ass outta ya' head firstest thing first by doing the due *"don't be ah scarred, its all in the doing, Son justa keep on doing the due! That's it Son, its yo' thang, do the due! Its all in the doing, due-da-due, Son! Handle ya beeswax, Zeke due-da-due!"*

Talk about shit yo' pants to done pissed ya' boots dat hadda been it for me especially in the beginning when I had done rode-it high and tight with dat fucked-up justa gonna fuck yo' black ass up brotha fear it be many a times dat fool ass mofo be done jumped the fuck outta my head to be sitting front-seat rights there betwixt me and Dad! In the beginning it be that raunchy imaginary mofo be done justa shotgun pumped-it all kinda fears, what nots and what iffns my way seed dat mofo be skull fucking my a'scared assed mind yet over dem times, I had gradually done learnt-it to kick brotha fear's freaky-deeky funky-ass outta my head and even butter I done learnt-it to bump hisns bad-breath bad-news imaginary ass right-on outta dat hooptee! Zeke hadda on the Superfly be to done learnt-it to *do the due* I done gots learnt-it from the bestest of menfolk *Son, just due-da-due*!

Five plus years constant practice of thems repeated learnings inside that mint-jalopy had done taught-it to me that fear can and always will be overcome by action, it's just that in the thinking about thems highly most likely *shit happens* possibilities of the imagined consequences conjured-up within the imaginations of the mind because it be all thems bad assed iffns that can make one want to run away or the freeze the fuck-up and just to do nuttin! All of brotha fear's mis-guided worry-whats be designed to cause someone placed within a bad getting worst situation be to do nothing not nary an ass saving *Mighty-mouse here I come to save the day* ting because it be that frozen still non-action that be the what that gives brotha fear hisns powers to be thus by the time that little runt-of-a-cunt rice-belly be on the rise-up and outta dat thicket of dead ass branches then and to the there I hadn't done become a *frozen chosen* nor to done panicked because I'd done been properly and professionally trained in the act of *due-da-due, Son*!

It had been just dat exactamente *due-da-due, Son* training what done stopped-it me when I hadda done thunk-it the thought to done *Sunday* punched dat little gooner's tiny slant-eye lights out yet in the moment of that truth my lucid mind hadda done let it be done knowed-it to me dat that shit onliest hadda been brotha fear and hisns *it all be imaginary* ass done stepped-it up inside my mind's inner-eye to done let me knowed-it for sure that gooner's wuddle finger be slo-mo tap-dancing on the trigger and that I had no time for the thinking I had to *do the due, Son* it be *due-da-due,* time! I have always felt-it in the stone-pit of my cold iced over stone-cold heart that I had a *Hell of a lot* to do with the saving of my own damned life to done belly-flopped and low-crawled-it away seed that retreating action had truly been a death denying act of *due-da-due, Son* a preconditioned automatic response action to being all caught-it up in a bad situation be the *what* that done saved-it my black ass! Tanks mucho-much to my Dad and dems peanut gallery Unks! Their fore-sight to have had trained-it my skinny black ass in theys theory of life *taints no time fo' the thinking* in an emergency *do the due, Son* be the onliest way to done snatched dat ass from the jaws of death. Not to get it twisted big-*do da do*-butts dat gooner's self-discipline and dedication to hisns mission be a major help *Yes, Lordy* dat disciplined shit hadda been mucho much appreciated!

The world will never change and nobody done knowed-it that damn shit any butter than thems Jew-boy Hollywood film makers them *show me the money* producers of all those great war and cowpoking movies that I usta watch on the black-n-white then reenacted-it all the goodie-stuff parts with the posse *as a babe in them woods* just to the out-skirts of the Chocolate City down et Unk' Zeke's pond! Hollywood heroes are and always have been created in the *how can I squeeze da' copper outta this here penny* scheming hands of thems *MGM* grand mongrels thems *Shylock* motherfuckers dat buy-buy simply allowing everyday peoples to believe in their lying-eyes have been, be and always will be both sound judgment and a highly lucrative business seed dat *gots paid* be the onliest reason behind the *Jew-boy* big picture show business dem Hollywood whores be all about Benjamines bumping all dat green folding paper thems money-changing whores be *Fuck the facts, homeboy* lies sell and the biggest lies sell like pop-corn, Babycakes!

In the little time spent in the slant-eye bush some fiddy plus daze, I'd seed more than a few good men go down in *da' shit* though I may not have really knowed-it thems Bros on the daily-double yet them Bros be theys nerds, racist turds, potheads, cowboys, alkies or straight-up hoodrat numbskulls likened unto myself them Bros be Marines and that meant theys all be my Bros' and a lot of Bros' got lost to that war, police-action, conflict the official witchever be the politically correct name of that day! I hadn't done needed-it to send out no damned *tank-ya* notes to that fucking zipper-head bitch bastard wannabe commie-chink neither what I had needed-it then had just been the time justa every bite of all that time back atop the flat-head to all over a'gin-n-juicy *Rucky Roosey* to be done learnt-it just how to hate thems gooner-bitch bastards for all da' Bros' thems straight-up fo' sure sho'nuff ghost-turd fighting side-by-side heroes who didn't get no Hollywood *happy ending* to come back to home and kissy-kiss theys on the reals all the way live Babygirl!

Chapter 19

My first *doo-wah-ditty* boots to ground tour with 1st Platoon Company G had lasted about fiddy-plus days and nuttin much hadda come of it after that firstest recon day *empty-belly hungry liked a mofo* trekking-it with First Sergeant John *Big Johnny* Tidwell fo' sure there hadda been a few mo' wet-fires big-*bring it on*-butts mainly thems fiddy-daze I hadda just cracked my knuckles cranking thems tool-boxed wrenches against downed aircraft while I flexed my military muscles under the watchful command of a young *East Jesus State* jr. college po'dunk whiteboy who had gotten hisnsself expelled-it from *Cow tech little U* and a real live in the dumb-assed flesh pendant motherfucker field Lieutenant a WO2/2nd Warrant Officer hooked on the power such that damned backwoods Georgia-*rotten peach*-pit done thought-it hisns-*redneck*-self to be a gawd damned demi-God! WO2 Arthur M. Shuttelford aka *Pin-alley* hadda micro-managed G-Company platoon to the point he'd done told-it to everybody when to fucking piss! We'd be humping a pack or stripping thems parts offa bird when da' asshole woulda done from the tippy tipped-it top of hisns weak-assed nicotine-tar drenched lungs shouted *"fucking FISH BAKE"* he'd actually done said *piss break* big-*boom boom*-butts shell-shocked ears didn't ring so swell! We be a fo'dee man aircraft-mechanics team witch every fucking body even ourselves amongst ourselves hadda done called *cannibals* in polite company. Thems candy-assed flyboys would have reconned-it a downed aircraft then relayed its location back to HQ whom radio communicated the bird nest to thems G-Company potheads and cowboys that be live-ass no fucking jive-ass veteran ghost-turds whose *number-one Son* job be to done provided a secured perimeter of protection whilst we torque monkeys done turned and hand cranked thems *Snap-On* toolbox wrenches! Once the coordinates be transmitted then all us boots to ground-pound ghost turds and nut-jobbers together done hauled-it ass over thems teacups to find the craft and strip-away its most vital parts to be refurbished then re-used on other planes thus the name *Cannibals*! Law of the jungle rule number-2: Don't get all caught-it up in a fucking name! Law of the jungle rule number-tree: wins and losses to the game hadn't mattered *titi* witch be Nam gibberish speak-easy fo' the smallest bit of any iota seed in the jungle onliest one-fucking shit be done mattered-it and dat shitty ting be just to done learnt-it *fuck the game, love the players and when ya' pass Go collect twenty scrip dollars,* Babycakes! Thems pot-heads/cowboys of the Company-G would form a protective shield, a locked and loaded perimeter around us and aircraft then at the firstest sound of *ping-ping-zings* to done got heard ricocheting offa them downed recon birds thens we woulda done dropped *socks and cocks* to done grabbed-it up them babygirls then everybody gotz in on the fray, it be boo-coo trigger-time, Babycakes! The trigger-time shit hadn't happened all too often mostest to any fighting with VC would normally be away from where we would be removing them parts even though thems times be few big-*let's get it on*–butts them wet-fire encounters be Biggy-smalls because mostest thems VC straggler troops be justa chunk of starving slant-eye *Raggedy-Annes* lost in the fucking jungle gooner-boy bitches and theys fucked asses just liked-it unto ourselves onliest be stepping-it in-transit thus fo' my nappy-happy black ass dems *git the fuck outta my way* meet-it ups betwixt two ships passing through the Black knight, be da' shit, Babycakes! After the dance, it be business as usual recon, hump dat ass then strip dem parts, on the norm, a cannibal operation took no more than 5-days to complete from radio coordinates of the bird nest to the back to happy campers end-it up hump.

Pin-alley had presided over a platoon that be roughly some 90% Black Americans thus we were being led through a fucking slant-eye jungle by a whiteboy wannabe a somebody *VeryIg'nantPussy* VIP! *Tarzan* had been the name that I would have tagged hisns super-egotistical ass excepted dat I hadn't never to have done heard-it nonya G-company to have ever called Pin-alley the *Tarzan*! The quirk on Pin-alley had been that iffn that po'dunk semi-educated punk-ass thought himself important redneck had been given just the slightest titi of opportunities then he had always tried to show-off just how much *smarter than thou* hisns flunky-hunky po'dunk redneck ass be by dishing out the quotes and talking *Joe College* shit witch none of us aircraft techs nor the majority of G-company had a fucking clue! Hell, Pin-alley dat mofo had even done on an impromptu uneducated guess managed-it to done changed hisns own damn unofficial nickname/call-sign seed behind hisns redneck back the platoon both the White and all the Black had from the jump always called him *Bowling pin* witch to the 90% of the platoon had meant a tall, proud stand-it up *whiteboy* pinhead with a red stripe around hisns neck bout to be knocked da' fuck down by rolling Black thunder! Pin-alley had changed hisns nickname just about the exactamente minute he hadda done firstest heared of it. The Brothas told it, *Bowling-pin* hadda gotten the word bouts hisns fucking nickname so he'd called a platoon meeting out in the fucking shit piles of bucktooth wild weeds, check this, the nerdy mofo done explained to thems dumb-ass grunts that Pin-alley would be easier to pronounce that be hisns semi-educated dumb-ass, "*pro-noun-ce*" seed Pin-alley done just lived-it to use them big *tree-dollar* words, dem jawbreakers of the pendant world big-*country pumpKin*-butts Pin-alley had had just one major big assed problem in that most of hisns platoon be mucho-much dumber than theys and we techs had done looked-it liked so nobody had for *Medgar Evers* fo'reallies understood half the shit that be done bounced-it from hisns thin GI-issued toilet ass-wipe tissue paperclip lips to done clogged-it our fucking earholes! The truth be knowed-it from all the rap throughout my fiddy-daze tour G-Company nobody had given a real shitty-turd either way about the nickname.

A'nuttier ting why the Brothas had called hisns po'dunk ass *Bowling-pin* had been because the lame fuck be a Marine Gunner Warrant Officer witch the redneck be so proud of that the goofy dumb fuck be done popped hisns fucking field dress collar to done showed-it to ever damned body in eye-sights dat exploding bomb insignia stitched onto hisns blouse. *Sooners* everybody had took to calling the once tagged *Bowling-pin* by hisns self-created new nickname *Pin-alley* then by the time I had dry-humped-it to that platoon Pin-alley had become hisns unofficial official po'dunk call-sign. The way I seed it, Pin-alley hadn't been a fo'reallies big-time racist po'dunk redneck a'tall during my boot camp in South *Kak-ka-lac-key* and technical schooling in thems redneck swampland counties of the eastern *Ali-bami* panhandle and all thems *nigger don't let the sun set on yo' black ass* gulf ports stretching from the *Yallens'* to the fucked-up Gainesville, Florida, I had experienced mucho-much worst the racial hatred redneck unchecked, unfiltered definitely unwanted early 70s America bullshit! Pin-alley had been more liken to dat *Archie Bunker* typecast from that 70s TV show *All In The Family,* I can't ever to remember Pin-alley having said *nigger* in anger mayhaps a time or two in jest big-*laid back*-butts never ever on the personal one on one, man to man *hate yo' black ass* basis seed hisns country-ass word fo' Blackfolk had always been either *jig, boo, zig* or the many combinations *jigger-boo, zigger-jigger-boo, boo-jigger-zigger* each a straight-up racial trigger big-*redneck*-butts mostest dem times he hadda been answering back to what he hadda just been called-it plus mostest of the times Pin-alley done limited them racist names to just *jig*! The Brothas liked to holla "*yo' hunky* blah, blah, blah...." to the Whites then Pin-alley and all thems other Whites and even the Messykins would holler-back with a furious "*yo' jig* blah, blah, blah ...." Pin-alley hadn't busted-ass when he'd done heard-it *cracker on deck* or Bro' go get dat *peckerwood honky-tonk L-t on the horn* during my little short-timed stint with Company-G that bad-assed platoon had ebbed and flowed without much ado nonya them serious racial tensions.

The problem be dat mofo Pin-alley done wanted-it hisns egotistical ass a straight-up a pure unadulterated GI-jungle respect from everybody dat platoon seed Pin-alley that pendant mofo be liked "You mofos eating my bread therefore you gotta sing my song" then all the Bros be liked "Fuck-you hunky mofo! We only eat ya' fucking bread because life be a shit-sandwich and the mo' bread you got the less shit you gonna eat!" Some nights the platoon done had themselves a Fry-knight fish-fry 'cepting theys didn't have no fish to fry them mofos be frying dat fresh caught ass in that theys done hadda themselves an all outta da' way Mofo, clear the fucking deck no bull all bullshit *out front-street the slant-eye jungle shoot the shit* session witch I must admit had been *da' shit* fo' me cause then da' shit would be full blown and raw-dawg *Righteously, all Right-On, mah Brotha*! *Please to leave ya' piss soaked shitty-drawls at da doe you emotionally sick skank-ass hoe*! Pin-alley and them few Whites-bros from both groups our maintenance *screwball nut-jobbers* crew plus all thems high on something G-Company long-haired *Harry Hippie* freaks woulda been full-stream ahead and done told them lame-ass 60s antiquated racial jokes *"Say jungle-bunny, ya know how we curb a jigga-boo's temper in the great south? We stretch his big fucking nigger lips over a curb-side then kick him in the back of the head"* or something along the lines of *"Why jig bitches always drink bathtub gin-n-juice then masturbate? Cause you fucking zigga-boos aint got a lick-her license"* The Brothas had dem same old tired-assed big-*fucking Right On*-butts older than dirt barbs seed theys done countered-it back with sumptin-sumpting like *"Yo' hunky, ya know why a Brotha can't fuck a fine feathered bird in the lousy fucking south? Cause Polly wanna cracker!"* or the just gotta fucking laugh *"Yo' pencil dick, why can't hillbilly cracker bitches own vibrators? Cause it chips they one and only tooth"*

During them sessions I had been a wide-eyed green as Hell horny-toad frog skin wet-behind the ears mofo justa listening to the shit and it had seemed that there had only been a couple of words dat be off-limits in them bull-sessions and both were just two simple yet mean as fuck cultural fighting words for the Brothas thems two outta limits *don't you fucking dare* words be *"Yo' momma"* and for the Harry Hippies theys two off-limit *not fucking cool* words be "*You faggot*" even dat part of the shit had been *Captain Crunch* dipped in strawberry *Kool-Aid* kool because both sets of *bad git yo' ass kicked* words be communal seed for the Brothas playing *the dozens* talking about someone's momma be a just and righteous cause fo' *a time to educate dat ass* when some fool done shouted "*yo' momma be a skank-ho bitch…*" sho'nuff fighting words that kinda the dozens shit talk be winner-winner chicken dinner *get a great big black boot stomped into yo' fucking meat-hole, Mofo* in any inner-city ghetto! Fo' an ass-whupping on the other side-of-them suburbia tracks dems Whiteboys hollering *"cocksucker…"* or any kinda implications that theys whiteboy ass done personally been bent over a barrel and or to done sucked dick swells Mofo the shit be just cause to do some real country-boy hippie-freak *hee-haw* ass-kicking thus thems foe' motherfucking words be the onliest outlawed-it bullshit in dems bull sessions dat be off-the-fucking *Captain Hook*! Fuck thems *Messykins* theys gotz no dog in dat fight! There had also been a 3rd set of the off-*the fucking*-limits to the out of bounds witch be t-totally off the fucking plantation chatter-whal big-*fucking*-butts dat shit be on the personal and hadda mattered-it onliest with much-ado abouts nuttin big-*sulky*-butts Pin-alley *suck shit thru a waxed straw* big worded pendant White-boy ass more than anything cultural.

The Brothas hadda told-it to me and thens them hippy-freaks along with thems Messykins theys all the tree-sided groups had done barked-it the same shit fo' the fodder in that Pin-alley had been a real fucking green po'dunk horned-toed tinder-footed redneck son-of-a-bitch *I give the fucking orders* fuck-rag douche bag when he'd firstest done gotten-it to the unit justa bout a click more than less a year befo' I'd gotten there and that the shit had done happened-it quick and fast unto hisns furious you best to holla *Yes, Sir* ass! According to all thems ghost-turds it went down kinda liked this: the platoon had been slow dragging-it through a rice-paddy just doing theys daily-double *circle-jerk* jungle trek when theys done runned-it upon a portion of the norm everyday encountered slant-eyed peeps working theys big-*it's a hard knock life*-butts off in a rice field. The group be comprised of justa chunk of old gook men and old ass momma-sans huddled-it up with a handful slant-eye crumbsnatchers when WTF! All of a sudden, an old assed grey-haired pot-bellied momma-san had runned-it the fuck upon then hugged-it frog-pussy tight the fuck outta the platoon front-runner WO2 *fucking I be in command* Bowling-pin then just as quickly dat old grey-bird hadda on the Superfly done let that skinny po'dunk punk-ass redneck bastard loose all the while screaming *bad juju! bad juju! bad juju!* big-*old ass*-butts dat old slant-eye biddy as swell thems grunts hadda used-it the slant-eyed gibberish speak wording for *bad juju* witch I done fo'gots. Anywho old fat gray ass granny momma-san hadda done runned-it a few more back-assed steps away from dat fucking Bowling-pin all the while on the scream *bad juju bad juju bad juju* and dat old slant-eye biddy done pointed herns old ass non-wrinkle free pointer-finger at Bowling-pin all the time! That old ass momma-san granny be looking bug-eyed hardtack at dat po'dunk's white redneck ass when she done flipped-it a full fucking bitch to done jumped-it belly-flopped style into that fucking shallow assed rice-paddy to justa done blown herns old gray-panther slant-eye self the fuck away! Everybody there had gotten freaked big-*crazy old bag*-butts Bowling-pin hadda to be done gots gang jumped-it by them Bros because he'd wanted to cut-loose with hisns *SuzieQ* on all thems other slant-eyes that be working dat rice-paddy big-*yella*-butts liked I done told-it thems other slant-eyes hadda been the usual slant-eye rice-paddy populace of worker-bee folks justa bunch of unwanted rice-bugs, old men and old women with a chunk of the way-too-young baby rice-bellies in tow. The platoon having had lots mo' experience with dat kinda shit than dat fucking tree daze *Lt. Wonderful* thus the platoon done chilled-it the fuck-out on them civilian gooks because theys done figured-it that old momma-san's hand had mostest been forced-fed bye-bye the local VC hiding-out and probably eyeballing the shit in-play. The Bros' done knowed-it a fat fact, Jack that old gray assed-out momma-san had braved-it that VC strong-arm shit and in the process she hadda also done saved-it Bowling-pin's fucking redneck life. That shit hadda been huge because old assed momma-san had freaked-it hard when she done firstest touched-it that flunky-hunky po'white trashy bastard's ass seed all them Bros be theys Black, White or Messykins hadda done learnt-it on the fly straight-up in thems killing fields dat thems Nam slant-eyed peeps be super fucking ceremoniously seriously furious about theys dead and especially about whom theys done died-it with thus for what-so *Medgar Evers* the reason dat old assed momma-san hadn't trucked-it no parts of traveling into the next realm with any parts that be of a redneck gung-ho whore-assed bastard with the call-sign Bowling-pin trucking hisns personal own fucking *kkk* little Missy-sip-pee and Ali-bam-mee karma! Bowling-pin had been made to realize on the real quick-liked that nobody in G-Company be gonna back hisns dumb-ass in any kinda fucking shooting gallery so dat redneck po'dunk cracker had to done sucked-it up hisns harsh fucking raw-dawg nerves and feelings through a fucking drive-in movie wet wax-paper soda-straw on the fucking spur of that blown-away granny slant-eye moment!

It be summertime later that year when it done happened-it that Bowling-pin hadda ceased the I'm Lieutenant Wonderful shit then that damned whiteboy fool hadda done renamed himself Pin-alley thus the asshole that I'd done met during my fiddy-day short-dog first tour boots-to-ground trigger-time Nam witch be Not the enchanted Unk' Zeke's pond big-*fake it till ya' make it*-butts just a conflicting *agent orange* blasted slant-eye jungle! The 3rd thing that had been off the fucking limits any bull-session had been any fucking reference to Pin-alley and that old assed momma-san done met-it up day because then Pin-alley would get thems *sorry fo' my redneck nobody wanna die with me down in the dumps* bluz then dat lousy feeling sorry po'dunk asshole woulda done forced-fed an on the fucking spot dry-hump right then and to the there or very fucking sans the breakfast come the next early morning!

Chapter 20

ANYWHO A'NUTTTIER QUIRK BE THAT right after a wet-fire or just late night for the Hell of it all WO2 Pin-alley would order everybody to pray aloud one *bye-bye* one *"Pray for the souls of those gooner fucks that just died and for those gooner fucks that are about to die"* he had commanded. Back then I could have done counted-it all the pussy even all the glorified poontang gook-pussy that I'd *Medgar Evers* done had on one fist! Truth be told, then I be more into self-love than the love of anybody's fucking God, so during prayer time I be *my Soul satisfied* to done prayed-it loud, Black and proud for some pussy *"Lawd above and Hey You, dickhead below, please to send me befo' I die some pussy any pussy, Black pussy, White pussy, Blonde pussy, Red pussy, Yella slant-eye pussy, Brown pussy, Rainbow pussy, big*-tanks-*butts please God-o-the-Pussy don't send me no damned Grey assed pussy!"* I had done dat shit just to trucked-it with Pin-alley's pinhead cause he was so stoic plus him being a backwoods half-assed Joey-college educated po'dunk redneck that be way too damned serious about bouncing hisns owned damned self-inflicted fucked-up manchild *Son of man* Vatican City demi-god mythological affairs unto the lives of all us folks that be other wise! I hadn't thunk-it to tink dat Pin-alley knowed-it nor cared-it that I hadda done learnt-it bouts hisns old ass momma-san *no love fo' yo' redneck ass* affair maybe he just hadn't wanted-it to make the platoon take a long assed instant grits field hump because of the foolishness of one dumb-assed fucking fiddy-day boy-wonder shock-jock jigger-boo fuck!

What da' fuck could he have done, I be a jet engine mechanic *who'dat* be temporarily assigned to a Navy flathead just a'nuttier shock-jock screwball nut-jobber as thems ghost-turds done told-it the J-79 engine be no more than a big assed battery charged pain in some bitch's ass souped-up vibrator no-more no-less justa one gigantic crotch-buzzer that thems pussy-ass jet jockeys split theys cotton candy soft pink ass-cheeks atop on the daily-double plus my shock-jock ass be just a'nuttier passing through playing the fucking game a *Nobody* to theys fool asses! The only reason that I had even been in dat bush was come August 74' the hard rocking Corps had wanted every nut-sack laced-it up in combat boots to get the *wonder lust* just a small bite a-bit-o-the-taste trigger-time action afore the US Congress hadda put a formal and final ending to that police action in layman terms that shit meant that every cock-with-balls mofo' dat be hard to the Corps had to squat a shit about two to tree months boots to ground inside that slant-eye bush befo' them damned church bells done bumped-it theys finale peal! To put it in a more ex-laxed super loose shitty-ass perspective bye-bye the time I had really got-ten to done knowed-it dat fucking Pin-alley, I be back shitting in them flat-head open-air latrines and justa be banging on them F-4 jet engines or chipping paint with thems fucking insane brainless nut-jobber Navy scrubs.

One thems late the Black knight patrols me and Pin-alley in-accordance with hisns po'dunk ass motif *gotta meet-it up with every swinging dick under* my Supreme command the numb-nuts had assigned my black ass and hisns cow tech ass to a hilltop to done scanned the *valley of death* whilst G-Company done slept-it off. It hadda been that darken knight atop hill number 21358914 where just the two of us done had ourselves a meeting of the minds witch hadda mostest been dat fool ass whiteboy be preaching-it to the atheist big-*amen*-butts told in hisns own its God's world theory in such a way that hisns dumb-ass done thunk-it himself to be the firstest fucking po'dunk polish Pope! *Blessed art thou my child* now bump dat shit, Babycakes!

We had been taking turns using them night-vision goggles and that there be the main reason why we be on the talky-talk seed thems earlier version night-vision goggles be the of latest technical reversed-it engineered captured alien shit. Thems goggles had the capability to done made a moon-lit night looky-look near-beer perfect the same as iffn it be an overcast pre-dusk bring on the evening sky lighting! Peeping through thems night-vision goggles every damned ting hadda dark to lighter greenish tint little-*green men*-butts because there be no real perception of depth while using them goggles theys made fo' a mofo to become sleepy *nappy nap-time little doggies* as all *Hell, to redneck southern belles* and that be why we had been rapping and swapping out on a regular basis them night-visions. That night had stepped-it with a tree-quarter moon witch be a'nuttier negative when using thems new-fangled goggles seed any moon larger than a quarta-moon would reflect a quick flashed-it highly bright yellow-greenish light offa any and the every fucking ting out there in that damned gook jungle so that when looked-it at through thems night-visions the reflective shit be done bright flashed-it *bad juju* to the wearer of thems goggles cause thems bright flashes be blinding! It be sorta liked walking-it sneak-thief in the dark then outta the *no fucking where* some rent-a-cop fucking *Dickey* pant security guard done justa beamed hisns cheap-ass wannabe a po-po flashlight directly into yo' eyeballs, fuck!

We had been swapping them goggles for some time when Pin-alley done axed me what the fuck I be doing with my obviously young gungho ass out there in that jungle because I be way too young to have been drafted. WTF had he done knowed about it, I be 19 yet dat po'dunk inquiring mofo only be bouts tree to foe' years older than my sway too young to have been drafted ass so I'd begun tinkering WTF dis corny-ass peckerwood be ups to big-*redneck*-butts anywho I had given him the thumb-nail sketch about my Marine Corp buddy-buddy, 2-year volunteer enlistment plan then he'd hollered back that he'd hoped that I hadn't gotten the royal flush meaning my hometown recruiter hadda done a *two fo' the money* fed me a straight-up pile of the Queen's rotten-ass shit witch sometime later to be determined gonna gets washed-it down by the King's syphilitic piss! Our rap-session had ended with Pin-alley telling me that I seemed to have an intellect bouts myself in that I could speak the Queen's English dat be dems po'dunks sway of saying *I can see with my evil assed angel-eyes that jo' black ass bees a big*-nigger-*butts you don't sound colored*! Pin-alley be hawking some BS bouts given first chance, I should jump fucking ship then jimmy-jam dat GI bill and further my education. It had all been to the good big-*pendant*-butts kinda strange in that the asshole hadn't even used any hisns usual tree-dollars words nor thems joe college quotes a'tall big-*smarty pants*-butts I just couldn't force-feed meself to done trusted-it a po'dunk peckerwood because that be a'nuttier reason my black ass be in that jungle. I hadda just kinda left-it fo' hisns bullshit to be filtered through them grains of the sands of time to be the teller of tall tales be they lies or be theys the real truth, Ruth cause my mind had done cut-off that cracker somewheres along the way then went around the bend to see a man about a dog!

To wax Pin-alley there hadda been a Black power quote witch I'd done learnt-it my freshman year of high unschooling fo' the Negro only big-*thinker*-butts I hadda done kept in my hip-pocket just fo' a time liken unto dat hillbilly's bringing on the bullshit seed da' Brotha Adam Clayton Powell Jr. had eloquently stated to always *"Beware of Greeks bearing gifts, colored men asking for loans, and whites who understand the Negro…"* thus a Brotha justa couldn't afford to put hisns trust fund nor trust in a po'dunk whitey besides my momma hadn't birthed an idiot and albeit true my pops done raised a living Hell yet my dad had not raised a damned fool, fuck-you Pin-alley! That there pretty much done summoned-it up my firstest boots to ground-pound Nam witch done ended-it with a sermon on the slant-eye mount bye-bye one Mr. Charlie *nemba-10 son* lying-ass po'dunk WO2 Arthur M. Shuttelford aka Bowling pin aka Pin-alley!

chapter 21

After Embassy Saigon, TOP, Trips and that little fucking VC tunnel venture be distant relatives dems unknowed-it 3rd cousins once removed a'gin-n-juice my skinny black ass done found itself dropping SOS bombs *Shit-On-a-Shingle* chipped-beef and gravy atop burnt toast a'nutter 6-months would done passed and I would still be temporarily assigned the *love boat* witch had been out to sea mostest of them there times justa doing the nasty thems lap-dances big wide *round-in-round* turns from Diego Garcia, a little refueling island with big-*nuttin*-butts Navy ball-sack scum-bags shitting on the pebbled-beach sand no parts pussy done inhabited dat lil isle witch be some-to-no-fucking-where the middle of the Australian Ocean big-*lonely*-butts outside yonders to the east be thems Falkland *Oye Matey* Islands where buy-buy we done gots our groove on with the *big teeth* lassies of the British knight *twenty-pound tree shillings* to pound away the Black knight then it be back to the Bay of Guam and iffn lucky them scum-bucket Navy scrums would chuck anchor to dock that tub then R&R with dem Guam Island girls *las chamacas* fine assed café-latte tan brown-skinned islander shorties! Cha-ma-kas be Guam gibberish speak fo' barrio itty-bitty with big titty rental bitches!

I hadn't really minded any of that shit because the dog days be upon my lucky-mofo ass not that summertime July through September heat of all the fucking summertime blaze shit big-*shorty dawg*-butts I'd done enlisted using the buddy-buddy plan witch according to my calculations it be that my ass onliest had to done sat-it upside-down in dat fuck me hard to the Corps steel strapped barrel fo' 2 count'em fucking two years then I be free swell just as free as any Black man living in 70s America could have thunk-it hisns Black ass free! The good news and onliest news had been dat my 2-year stint had justa been about the fuck-up, *Yowls sir*, my fucking ship done sailed, baby its all over big-*dumb ass*-butts the shout-out *Adios motherfucker* mo' bouts dat fucking done volunteered shit in a CC moment! The flat-head being out to sea thus mostest them days there be barely little to no flying thus I had been assigned scrum duty witch dat shit be the worstest of the worstest of ship duty shit seed I done chipped-it paint alongside thems Navy also-ran undrafted scrubs and we done chipped-it paint all over dat damned tub. Thems old hands, Navy and Corps be justa a chunk of the dirty-dawgs salty old dumb-assed 30-something-year-old clueless sea whores be thems fucking scaly-wag crusty motherfuckkas to deys fucking rotten apple-headed Corps because they had been drafted theys done told-it to the everybody with ears that theys dumb-fuck asses had been force-fed the Corps or the Navy big-*lifer*-butts the pukes that done volunteered swells we pukes had signed-it up fo' the shit so thems *LIFER* whores LousyIg'nantFuckExpectingRetirement mofos hadda just poured theys worstest and most shittiest jobs on us dumb-asses liked a maniac 80-year old motherfucker beating-off hisns skank lifeless dead to this world meat and it hadn't mattered one fucking shit whether the volunteered puke hadda been Ja'rene or Navy scum thems old heads justa mixed all volunteered-it undrafted asses into one big fucking shit-pile scrum work-platoon and dat da' way it be on that flat-head 24/7!

My *yes in-deedy I did done volunteered-it* dumb-ass hadda drifted out to sea upon a funky kinda vibe dat rolled-it unto my ass on the *slip-n-slide* mysteriously cause mentally I be living with an eerie *who'dat* darkness and that shadowy mofo *Mr. Darkness* done made-it himself *Welcomed-to-home* in the penthouse of my sub-consciousness and dat darkened Brother be busy building walls, doors and shutters to done kept *Ol' Aunt Hannah* rays of the sunny sunshine, lights out! I hadn't done knowed-it then big-*dumb ass*-butts dat overwhelming darkness dat I hadda done met-it-up with in them damned VC tunnels hadn't shaken its ass back yonder the land of the slant-eye nips! Oddly enough the ting dat be hadda been dat I had been kinda fo'reallies raspberry *Kool-Aid* kool with dat darken presence of mind in that I hadn't challenged the mofo a'tall in fact *Mr. D* had done kicked-it up its fucking heels thens us two be buds fo' life *Oh, cloudy day let it rain* chilled the fuck-out jimmy-jammed in lounge chairs on the veranda in a welcome-home Babycakes dis be yo' Bar-B-Q, *Burn Baby Burn*!

Anywho there be some thems bright-spots to be founded liked it be kinda both funny iffn not so sunny in how one day it be that I couldn't justa wait to leave a fucking place then decked-it out on a flathead *chisel and hammer in hand* fucking chipping away at dried-it up flakey battleship grey paint with Navy scum that got gone *Oh happy day* away from hated-it bastard of a place done bounced-it had all of a sudden become a *Paradise* Lost! The mindset gots its games big-*hide'n seek*-butts its bestest not to done stepped-it up to that plate lessen ya' black ass done come to play! I hadda taken that tub scrum time to daydream smiles upon smiles about them days of yore dems bitches be not lost though theys hadda done gone the way of the not too long ago sway to the bye-bye befo 'my dumb-ass hadda done just realized that dem daze weren't a'gonna *Medgar Evers* to be a'coming back! Thems back in the daze memories had stayed strong tho' even to done built-it themselves a memorabilia alcove thus I done had meself a *Love-me Love-me wall* dedicated to the me because *I loves me some of me-me-me* plus there be a neon sign out-front dedicated to Mr. D the marquee done read: Don't you dare step yo' visitational only uninvited darken ass into nor onto my own the personal Love-me Love-me man-cave! My own little spot witch be my 4-cornered room a *Happy birthday to me* happy place to done rewind my real time back-to-home growed-it up with my Boy's memories. Mostly them daze when me and my Boy's hadda became youngbloods, those looky-look at me, we'z be up and *In-coming* them pre-teenaged hoodrat *in the beginning* years sway too innocent to do the thuggish doings of the hard to theys fucking core inner-city ghetto career criminals yet way-way too young to chase them fine assed coco-puffed *Say it loud, I'm Black and I'm proud* foxes with the bushy bush in the front of theys young wagging tails!

Chapter 22

I BE ABOUT THAT COMING of age thang! Yea, Babycakes and it be on, *Right-on, mah Brotha*! Before I starts-it up that trip down the backside of memory lane, I gotta clarify a little sump'n-sumptin cause I don't want it to get learnt all to the wrong seed I hadn't to be *hate'n* on them thugs cause it be them thugs that set and done kept Blackfolk free in America! Crack yo' mind, Nat Turner the Brother who done led the greatest of a'many American slave rebellions it be quoted by thems po'dunk slave-owners in his-*lying ass*-story that Brother Nat Turner once a *fuck this shit* slave turned Black freedom fighter done said-it *"I didn't choose the thug life, it chose me"* Hell, even fucked-up slaveowner sway-back Mr. Charlie had to dub the Brotha *Natty-T* hisns proper props! Iffn whitey po'dunk done gone and given my Black *Brotha Natty-T* a place in hisns-*all white lies*-story dat had onliest to done meant that Brotha Nat Turner had to have done afar mo' than hisns fair share of fucking-up thems cracker barrel slave-owner's and all theys shit! Nat Turner done knowed-it be the real truth, Ruth in hisns *"Baby, I'm a thug"* Soul, a shout-out to my Brotha Trick Daddy! No, I hadn't been serving-up da' *Haterade* bouts dem thugs and the thuggish things theys do, Baby! Them thugs be lit, them thugs be the onliest ting that done stood the test of time between po'dunk whitey taking over da' hoodie to be kicking our po' broke Black asses to da' curb! Po'dunk whitey pissed hisns unshined boots just the thought of that ass whupping them thugs had awaiting iffns hisns white ass be done broke up-town, baby *Oh Hell nawl*! Thems thugs be the keep that done kept! Mr. Charlie redneck peckerwood po'dunk motherfucker done thought-it long then hard against taking da' *A-train*, Baby!

In just thems almostest 2 fucking *it's a hard life* years, I had done learnt-it dat military philosophy witch *KeepItSimpleStupid* be the KISS factor thus to sum up the *living dat life* hoodrat I justa gotta bump Pin-alley to quote the authentic author of the *King James* that there mostest famous wordsmith William *Billy-bad-ass* Shakespeare cause that mofo done said-it bestest tho' I gotta break off the little floozy *Misery* cause in the da' hood we'z be po' big-*empty pockets*-butts we be not downhearted weeping willows thus my personal touch in da' hoodie: It be not *misery* big-*replacement*-butts Poverty "...*acquaints a man with strange bedfellows*" and in da' hood Mz. Poverty be a big butt double-Dutch bitch big-*sumptin sumpting*-butts she gots hernself a sweet lil booty bumped *Cuz* called Miss Necessity everybody done knowed-it Necessity *be the Mother of all inventions* dat be why in da' hood summertimes it be a *good thang* to be tagged motherfucker that be why we Brothas always bumpin *hey-hey motherfucker* cause dat pimply faced whore Mz. Poverty gots hernself a couple of bad-assed chambermaid hoes Mz. Desperation err *oh fuck* Mz. Hopelessness and iffn a hoodrat ever done had the ball-busting pure assed-out misery to done made either one of those two dead-beat dead-end big-butt bitches deys onliest fuck-buddy then dat homeboy be a'headed-it assed-out for the slippery slope big-*lucky*-butts iffn a hoodie done gone to done *snuggled bunny* up with Miss Necessity then dat righteous big Black mofo gonna be da' Motherfucker! Those thugs had-are-have been-still be and always will be the *keepers of the gate* staving off *the Man* to be giving a hoodrat's scurrying ass just e'nuff time to untangle hisnsself from the entrapments of the butch bull-diesel dyke trio of thems bad-ass bitches Poverty, Desperation and dat weird-it assed-out hoe Hopelessness! Iffn ya' ever happened to be fo' whatso *Medgar Evers* the reason it fucking be to done founded-it yo'self to be on the light-tripping-it to be toe-tipping-it thru da' hood, dap-up a thug, show'em some luv, thug love, Babycakes!

Nuff' bouts dem damned thugs! Let' em fucking be! Yo' my main boo-coos, does ya' members? Friday nights be *jazzed* big-*party*-butts *Sat-nites* just pure assed swang! Thems streets in the hood be alive! *"Ba-baba-ba boom boom-boom ba baba boom boom-boom doo-wah doo-wop,* Baby!" Youngbloods dems processed *slick-back* heads as swell thems the nappy-heads with the clinched black-fisted pick sticking atop theys big happy-nappy afros all thems teenaged foolish ones on the rise be stompin' the good foot a'coming up or thems dats be slippery sloping on the down-low cause fo' the one to thems all a'nuttin mattered 'cepting dat theys done gots theys *Doo-Wop Doo-Wopped* on! Thems ghetto street corners *Dr. Jukebox*, *Mr. Radio* and *Nurse Store-bought hi-fi stereo-phonic* come Sat-nite justa keep yo' electrified/battery operated dumb-asses ta home! *Thugs, hoodlums and bums dey bees* My Moms alla time hated on them smooth crooners as theys done did their mellow melody justa sugary sweet harmony thang on each and every block. Mostest them brothas fo'reallies weren't thugs seed the most had played or be playing college football, B-ball, baseball, running track and field justa all thems major be minor college sports American style et all thems education be for the Whiteboy only universities because to thems higher educational white schools the athletic brothers be *fieldhands* across America! Even more of them same suave crooners done toured-it or be headed liked me-own-damned *Sooners* to be self enroute to a happy-assed tour de fucking boots ground-pound Viet Nam, baby! Big-*give it up*-butts summertime come the Chocolate City then its all fo' one and the one bees all justa everybody dats to be somebody be to home *get yo' big black ass a seat* we'z done comes it backs to home away from thems white colleges that let ya' play on theys sporting fields and B-ball courts big-*racist*-butts to done never let a *Brotha* sit them university classes and just liked Nam all-American Whiteboy colleges be the fucking *gooks got to be damned*!

Big-*rock'n roll*-butts them fiddies, sixties and seventies come Sat-nite in da' hoodie a'nuttin big-*bitchin*-butts the *Hawk* and hisns cold-assed *brrrr* winds be the onliest ting to *Medgar Evers* put bumpers to a Sat-nite's high-stepping-it Black be Beautiful ass! Fo'gots ya' troubles 'cause troubles be! Come the hood, Sat-nite everybody be grooving on the one to a'nuttiers vibes be theys good or even butter be theys bad-assed *Super-Bad cold-sweat motherfucker* vibrations! A Babyboy justa had ta done have'd hisns Babygurl! Sat-nite the hood bumped-it live, Babycakes! Us be say'n it loud tanks a ga-zillion million ta ma' Brotha James *B-say it loud, I'm Black and I'm Proud*-Brown da' Godfather of Soul! *Yea, baby* we'z be poorer than church mice rolling bones at the foot of the altar door big-*taint nuttin*-butts a thang comes Sat-nite nobody chumped-it theys cheddar! We be alive, together and driven by the soulful songs of the ghetto! Thems on the block crooners dem *doo-wop* boys be giving big-Ups to: Marvin-*Jealous Kinda Fella*-Gaye, Smokey-*Tears of a Clown*-Robinson, the Four-*Give yo' baby a standing ovation*-Tops, the tempting-*My girl*-Temptations, the Dells-*Oh What a Night* dat shit be live and on the impromptu, baby! Would that a foxy young brown-sugah' done swung-it low herns sweet tight-ass chariot passed dem hoodlums and dem bums then a *Medgar Evers* so slow down on the bass low serious rendition of the Dells-*Stay In My Corner* trilled the air da' Brothas with their bass, falsetto, tenor and musical purity laid low some down-to-home harmony and believe you me theys acapella reigned *Supremes* holla at jo' boy because thems thugs rhythm done jacked to done bitch-slapped dems bad news blues! Not an instrument to be sighted mostest thems brothers couldn't read sheet music nor play any kinda instrument 'cepting mayhaps a gospel goo-goo-gooney's tambourine big-*Hallelujah*-butts dat shit be fo' church mice not fo' the sho'nuff Sat-nite hoodie bumpin' da' hood! Nonya dems on the reals fo'reallies Brothas *cuttin dat tune* could afford musical instruments anytohow yet theys done finger-popped, foot-stomped, toe-tapped and crooned the snap, crackle, pop of a serious *Stagger Lee* soulful strut! Guys with their gals creeping-it from one juke joint to the next theys be Superfly bump'n hats with the wide-brims, jump-suited double-knits, *Stacy Adams*, red mini-skirted micro-dresses, tear-dropped hoops and put *on yo' red* high-heeled sneakers strolling, dancing and rapping a line of 100% pure ghetto bullshit every-be-where!

Juke joints be nuttin more than home cooked rib-shacks with a red we be Open neon sign flashing the sto' front window and a coin-operated 45 rpm record player bumping-it in the back corner that done belted out some *good and a'plenty* company to any and all *who'dats* that had dared to enter the joint with coin open palmed-it *all hands on deck*! Moms and Dads with theys whole families, Ants and Unks, the tree-gees: Grandkids, Grandmammies and Granddaddies all out Sat-nite and we'z done sat-it on thems slumlord brownstones, parked cars, leaned-it against the most dangerous dilapidated crumbling buildings and walls, hung-out of flats-tops and broken windows to done leaned-it over roof-tops or justa stood wherever an opened space happened to avail itself. Foreign visitors would have most likely done thunk-it the thought that we'z be fucking crazed black assed loons awaiting *Mr. Charlie's* its *Macy's Turkey-day P-rade* in the middle of a'nuttier hot-assed African summertime Black knights and in a way we'z be because *sho' time* be just a'round the corner big-*loony toons*-butts mo' bout dat *sho' time* in a CC moment!

Chapter 23

Meself, Gettis and Mr. Bobby would to be hanging tight jumping from rooftop to rooftop in 69' we tree be the *trio*, the one fo' the one and the tree fo' all, Babycakes! We tree hoodrats be thems damned mannish youngbloods justa 14 rounding 20-sumptin and liked all big-*bad assed*-butts we be full of the pomp and looking for them circumstances! Gettis be black-ass mid-Knight *can't afford a candle* to be seen in the dark and at a great distance the peoples done called him *Crow* cause hisns shiny blue-black skin and thems two big black stare yo' ass down befo' the beat-down lying-eyes. Gettis played baseball and run track, my Brotha be built for speed big-*brawny*-butts he's healthy, thick arms with even thicker muscular legs. Gettis could plow you over and never be done knowed-it dat he had hoed your row! Mr. Bobby, yeah, Biggy-smalls it be years hence and still I gotta call my skinny-ass rat-tailed Brotha *Mister Bobby* he light skinned and *light in da' pants* skinny-*po*-butts heavy on attitude. I done seed it with my own and I be damned iffn theys be lying-eyes the time Mr. Bobby's skinny ass done on the *Superfly* he whipped-it a grown man's *don't cha fuck with Mr. Bobby* ass big-*stupid*-butts when it hadda done happened-it Mr. Bobby be at the tender age of 12 seed that drunken *Irish Rose* wino skunk drunk grown-assed man hadda tried to take Mr. Bobby's baseball-glove right offa Mr. Bobby's strong hand the left-hand dat *light in da' pants* fool be a south-paw then when that drunken sop hadda failed the attempt dat done growed-it-up fool had the nerve to done called Mr. Bobby *light in da' pants*!

Hell Mr. Bobby had a tee-total hatred fo' baseball skinny-*po'*-butts that damned worn tattered baseball glove be the onliest ting dat hisns sto' front jack-legged *gotta git the fuck outta here* preacherman daddy done left-it to hisns skinny black ass befo' breaking wind a new sho'nuff trophy woman/wife number-tree plus mo' than anything else this world Mr. Bobby hated fo' peoples to refer to hisns lithe, wiry, slim body as *light in da' pants* my Brotha could eat halfa plow-horse, chuck down a bucket of oatmeal laced with chocolate ice-cream yet never ever did dat skinny-*po*-butt never done managed to gain a solid pound of the saturated fats! He'd never to ever gots close to tipping them scales mo' than a buck-fiddy and that's with him a'hiding steel plates in both thems other-wise empty assed hip-pockets of hisns *light in da' pants* high-yella ass yet he done whupped-it a sho'nuff grown-ass man's drunken dumb black ass on the enraged fly. That shit dat Superfly kinda super-human strength shit be the what must have aided Mr. Bobby's skinny-assed *light in da' pants* body dat fated to make hisns skinny black ass *Ghetto famous* day! It all went down in broad assed day-light at a crowded public park when he done whipped-it that grown-assed man's ass big-*dumb*-butts good then as an added measure, after Mr. Bobby done burst-it that drunk's nose and that done growed-it up ass be bleeding like a stuck-pig motherfucker justa stinking up the place lying all bewildered-it a'wondering to himself how the fuck did hisns drunken ass be sprawled-it out floundering on the park's grassy lawn it be then that skinny-*po*'-butt done told-it *"from now on motherfucker, you will call me Mr. Bobby"* All through-out the CC dat *light in da' pants* mofo hadda done earned-it hisns skinny-*assed*-self the name *Mister Bobby* though at a further than a far step peoples be knowed-it on the low-whisper to have uttered *light in da' pants* hisns grown-assed man ass-kicking way!

Mr. Bobby had moved-it to da' hood befo' me the skinny-*po'*-butts right after hisns store-front preacherman daddy had skied-it up with dat newest of trophy wives seed Mr. Bobby be bouts 9-years old then and dat boy could box, I mean to tell ya' dat skinny-assed *light in da' pants* mofo could box hisns skinny-rail ass off, might to be why he so damned skinny all hisns life! All hisns older brothers could box theys asses off too and theys done fo' the mostest of damned near 9 *straight outta the ghetto* years, thems boxing fools, thems older brothers of hisns had taken the State of the redneck hillbilly *I-n-mybabysis-Diana* high school boxing championships year after year, belt after belt weight class after weight class hence 1961. Thems older box-yo'-ass-off brothers had done built-it themselves a make-shift small roped-it off canvass covered the otherwise concrete floor boxing ring in the basement of their not so runned-it down brownstone two-story house that theys done runned-it away *jack-legged preacherman* daddy had done bought-it for thems and theys *she still be drop-dead gorgeous* momma ex-trophy woman\wife number-2 just befo' the push! Theys boxing ring had been homemade just straight-up ghetto as all Hell!

There be tree 4 by 8 foot ply-wood boards placed together dyke *tongue in groove* mode thems boards be laid atop the basement's concrete floor with 5 piled-it up layers of gunny-sacks tucked and tacked onto the tops of all tree boards with a stretch of canvas pulled-it balls tight over thems done been tacked-it on gunnysacks. There be 4 steel fence posts and each one of them posts be welded atop a size-14 steel tire rim then the 4 fence posts be threaded with 4 thick ropes and that there be the most ghetto-est ghetto boxing ring *Medgar Evers,* Baby*!* Someone heavy-assed, a fat-body always had to stand atop each one of thems tire-rims and hold hard onto them poles just to keep them ring ropes high-n-tight. It be said that one had to bite some of the bad in-order to get to the delicious *the goodie-stuff* and it hadda always been the goodie-stuff to get into that make-shift ghetto ass boxing ring and fight them other kids from around the way big-a'*scared*-butts that bite of the bad had been pure Hell!

Thems older brothers trained Mr. Bobby yet theys in all ghetto reality be eight of the done growed-it up assholes that just beat the living Hell out of me, Gettis and any and all thems other neighborhood and passer bye-bye kids that theys grown-up sadistic asses be done *snatched dat ass* walking along them nearby mean assed ghetto streets and alleyways! That be the bite big-*dumb bully*-butts when thems older fucked-up brothers done snatched-it a wayward kid *walking home alone* ass offa them Chocolate City streets then me and Gettis got to give that other kid an ass whopping too *Yes Lawd* to done jumped-it into that ring to done *whupped dat ass* be the sho'nuff goodie-stuff! Seed them older brothers of Mr. Bobby be grown-assed menfolk each and everyone them sadistic done growed-it up whores be daze past the 18th year+ and thems whores-assed grown-assed men be kicking all kinda little kids in theys little kiddie asses on the daily-double under the guise of teaching the po' misfortune snatched-it offa them streets chillens a boxing lesson.

What hadda went down be dat them older brothers would snatch a kid's ass offa the streets then drag that kid's ass kicking, screaming and crying down theys brownstone basement steps to theys make-shift boxing ring witch be ghetto legend then one or two of thems fool-headed cold heartless mofo older brothers would take that captured kid's crying black ass over to a neutral corner of the basement and start showing that kid how to throw and block punches. Lesson time, thems sadistic fools would toss super slow-mo super cotton-candy soft upper-cut punches at the kid's face and body all the whilst thems fools be *skinning and grinning* and justa kept to telling the kid to *bob, weave and move yo' head* thems sessions be *fucked-up* gentle liked punches and giving much praise *yeah young fella you doing good, Good job, kiddo* theys bumped-up the a'scard ass kid's courage with lots of encouragement *Emmett Till* one of thems *growed-up little kid ass kicking* bastards couldn't starve off theys hunger fo' new innocent blood then thems vampirish *gotta make him bleed* whores would haul that unsuspecting kid's innocent young naive ass front and centered tossed-it up and over into that make-shift CC ghetto legend boxing ring!

Once the kid be inside the ring then on the quick to be done seriously thems sadistic fools done sped things up thus them slow training punches would start to come faster than mostest fastest until theys done come so fastest as to done knocked that captured kid's ass cold the fuck-out! Fo'reallies for thems done *growed-up little kid ass kickers* it be *Momma said to knock you out*! I had done lived that to done did exactamente that and I hadda done gotten knocked-it the fuck-out just liked that bye-bye one thems sadistic boxing bully whores in that exact same *m.o.* Dat be why I hadda done knowed-it all too damned swell theys Not so private details the hows, the ways and the whys all about thems grown-assed fools and theys kid scam boxing lessons to be t-totally bullshit!

Chapter 24

DAD HAD JUST THAT DAY done moved us from outta the *Small Farms* out to Unk' Zeke's pond in the country-side to center-court the hood and I had only been there about halfa day walking about and justa looking things over when *WHAM BLAM No thank-you ma'am* one of them older fucking done been growed-it up *little kid ass kicking* older brother of *light in da' pants* had done grabbed ahold my 10 years awaiting-it ass then tossed-it my screaming and crying a'scard black ass down theys fricking brownstone steps to done flung my WTF startled ass into that basement. On cue, one of them bully mofo big older brothers be in a back corner of the basement to done given me that useless game of the pity fricking patty-pat befo' he done toss-it my ass into that ring! My firstest be *light in da' pants* then Gettis then befo' I done knowed-it *witch way be up* one of thems older fucks hadda jumped-it them ropes into that make-shift ghetto ass ring and that *little kid ass kicking bully mofo* be the son-of-a-bitch bastard who done knocked-me straight the fuck-out!

Later, that same nite, it done been the firstest time *Medgar Evers* I'd done fo'reallies heard-it my Moms give Dad a good sho'nuff *cuss dat mofo out* and let me tell ya' my Moms could fo'reallies cuss! My Moms be madder than all-get-out at Dad fo' firstest to done made-it us tenants and the 2nd to done caused-it herns most precious babyboy child to suffer all over hisns handsome liked a mofo gingerbread brown babyboy face! I hadda done always sided with my Moms on any to whatsoever family matters that be why Calvin usta always done called-it me a *Momma's boy* even so much mo' dat nite because of the ass whuppings that I had done taken big-*lookey look*-butts also because my Moms hadn't never wanted-it be no damned tenant in the firstest of places. I hadn't done knowed-it exactly what a tenant be big-*dummy*-butts iffn my Moms didn't wannabe one then I didn't wannabe living in a raggedy old Injun's musky assed-out tent neither! I remembered-it Dad hadda argued-it back with my Moms *"Beautiful, that the boy aints no baby, he gots to get growed-it up and he gots to done learnt-it to fight for hisns own self someday. I know its tuff but dats the only way for a man to get along in this world"* Dad always hadda done called my Moms *Beautiful* come the day or the Black knight be he mad or he happy fo' Dad my Moms hadda always been *Beautiful*! Dad would prove fo' me in the short-run outta the long stride to be absolutely *Right-on my brotha* righteous because thems kicking little kid ass older brothers of Mr. Bobby and that make-shift boxing ring would become my *Hell, yeah, mofo* ghetto-pass throughout my tenancy as a resident tenant center-court the hoodie justa right-up and *Emmet Till* Uncle Sugar hisns old white-ass finger pointing selfish self be done snatched-it my dumb-ass offa thems mean-assed streets of the CC to done gave me the bootcamp pity patty-pat combat lessons befo' hisns old white-*I Want You*-ass done toss-it my dumb-ass center ring boots to ground-pound Viet-Nam, baby!

Nobody and I mean no-fucking-body done messed with me, Mr. Bobby nor Gettis seed we tree wet-behind the ears young blades hadda become the bad words to be a'coming outta anybody's mouth on them ghetto streets where we done jive talked-it from the one to all mofos with 6 of the quickest fists *Medgar Evers* to done whupped-it upside theys big ole' watermelon cotton-pick'n heads and when thems fewest times be necessary we done brought-it out thems crazed kid ass-whopping older brothers of Mr. Bobby to handle the heavy-lifting. In dat ghetto nonya to nobody ever wanted-it us trio of the young gun Billy-bad-asses nor them sadistic older grown-assed done growed-it up brothers of Mr. Bobby *In-coming* theys po' black hoodrat ass!

Thems older brothers always done trained Mr. Bobby because he theys baby-brotha, theys each had done licked theys funky-breath chops as theys done awaited the day he'd done stepped-it to home to done stepped-it down thems brownstone basement steps with hisns very own chalky white Slate of the redneck racist hillbilly *I-n-mybabysis-diana* boxing championship ring, belt and trophy big-*bully*-butts that day never done did nor shall never ever come to past because come year 1970 the great mis-State of *I-n-diana* done passed-it a new writ to outlaw high school boxing *they* done said it be not a sport just pure brutality thus it be time to be rid of unnecessary aggression in *they* high schools. Mostest folks hadda put it down *"Dem fools at state capital don't ever be wanting to give another Simms brother hisns title and ring ever again"* theys done said more big-*rumor mill*-butts it don't do any good to repeat such stuffings in polite company. A'nuttier thing bouts them older kicking little kids in theys hoodrat crumbsnatching asses older bully brothers be just after Mr. Bobby hadda done whupped-it up on that fool grown-ass man's flunky drunken ass to done told-it that grown-assed man he bestest to be calling hisns *light in da' pants* scrawny little ass *Mr. Bobby* from thens on swells thems fooled assed older brothers would done thump-it up on me and Gettis even mo' *Emmett Till* us two dumb-asses liked all thems other street-smarts black asses of the inner city hoodie hadda done learnt-it by way of theys fisticuffs the Word-up be that all us hoodie residents done started-it to call Bobby that there newly earned-it hisns own self-anointed nickname *Mr. Bobby*! Self-anointed called-signs taint restricted to just the cow-tech little U whiteboy pendant, *Fuck you*, Pin-alley!

I played baseball with Gettis and my Boy's, boxed with Mr. Bobby and hisns older nut-job big-*bully*-butts done growed-it up *little kid ass kicking* older brothers yet my onliest true love hadda always been/was *Peace be* still B-ball, damn it! I hadda just lived-it to done chunked dat rock and I be built fo' the game, I be tall, agile and walked on the balls of my feet and I had a jump shot that be pure *Land-O-Lakes* butter, baby! In them mean assed streets of the hood, I hadda had my own set of personals seed nobody done be perfect this world therefore the peeps done knowed-it justa how to *puff wind in my cheeks* them peoples woulda done called-it out to me on the backside whispered-it *rooster claw* thens theys best to done runned-it liked a motherfucker cause it be on, baby! Justa to done remember-it dat shit done riled my ire, Hell I can't even hold sway ta tell the *whys* and the *hows* of it all right now I'd justa get too damned mad big-*irate*-butts I do promise to relay mo' about the nature of that hoodrat *fuck with me iffn you wanna* nomenclature in a CC moment big-*brothahood*-butts me, Gettis and Mr. Bobby gonna be friends for life, a trio of Billy-bad-asses fo' *Medgar Evers*! We tree be the *trio* and the bestest of mean-assed friends walking thems ghetto streets taking names, dishing out lolly-pops and ass-whuppings on the daily-double to all thems hoodrats cause theys be justa chunk of the all day *suckas*! We be all the time fooling around one with the other two, in sickness or health we be tight as *Kelsey's* nuts, mess with the one and you gots yourself a mighty heaping of the other two, oh yeah, we hung as tight as old crooked *Jewish* fingers to a shiny new copper penny! Nobody else hadda ever really penetrated into our trio though some tried *Sooners* it would only be justa us tree taking them hoodrats names then kicking them ghetto fabulous asses! Looking back, I hadda done figured it be 'cause we hadn't had a fo'reallies given leader of the pack seed for us it be whoever came up with a plan of adventure fo' that day then that day-planner would ramrod the event yet fo' mostest gangbangers theys done needed an established leader to answer to big-*follower*-butts we tree done fought it out amongst one a'nuttier all our young lives yet nonya be done *Medgar Evers* emerged any mo' dominate than either the other two!

Moving to da' hood had really changed my lifestyle seed no longer be there thems famous daily BB-gun rifle-up wars out to the fabulous Unk' Zeke's pond and not only had I made new friends big-*smarty pants*-butts I had also learnt-it new skills even butter I'd done learnt-it newer words the tree words that became my mostest used, enjoyed and fav' of all the words I be to *Medgar Evers* done learnt-it in dat hood be *fresh prune juice*, baby! Thems tree words be a solid gold tribute to Old Ms. Jackson, a straight-up *who'dat* usta leaned-it outta herns brownstone 3rd floor window to done shouted-it out to the many mini-skirted hot fine-assed young hip-swinging caramel delights that done strutted theys fine assed goodie-stuff on the buy-n-buy along the sidewalk beneath "*Hoe, quit try'n ta show off dat dried up prune everybody knows it aints got no juice! Git ta home and cover yo' skank ass!*" I be either still 10 no more than 11 when my *Cuz*, the infamous Bug done let me to done knowed-it the hows, the whys and the do's about *fresh prune juice* in that it be all abouts getting the stinky-finger though neither of us had ever had a stinky-finger big-*wishful*-butts dat same summertime later Bug's Momma, Auntie *Katie-Lou* hadda musta have done somehow be to done overheard-it me and her babyboy child, talk about getting and a'wanting some *fresh prune juice* thens the next ting I done knowed-it the tree of us be sitting theys cat-claw kitchen table with a quart-can of *Del Monte* Un-sweeten Prune Juice and only two glasses *whoa Nellie* I be done plopped-it them purple plums for daze!

Chapter 25

Sat-nites any Sat-nite in da' hood be just as good as any a'nuttier Sat-nite big-*gots big love*-butts one particular Sat-nite done always stood-it out in my mesmerized memories of the bestest of the best of times *the goodie-stuff* especially when I be chipping away et all that damned battle grey paint on dat fucking floating flathead. I remembered-it dat Sat-nite summertime 67' it had started-it with me, Gettis and Mr. Bobby jumping from one brownstone roof to a'nutter, Mr. Bobby had decided that we would drop a couple of water-balloons down unto the heads of two wig-wearing street loving Ladies of da Black knight, Ms. JoAnne Alison and Ms. Christina Jones then those two cinnamon crunch nutmeg brown street-strollers hadda commenced to string together a line of *"Mother-fuckers, sums-dey-bitches and rug-rat crumbsnatch'n asshole bastards bestest to be mind'n yo' own damned business beef fo' I ..."* dat naked real truth, Ruth! The kinda truth dat be the official ghetto resident's compliments stripped-it bare to the neckbones, everyone within ear-shot hadda peanut-butter jelly smelly-belly rolled with it and it be laughter abound cause *back in da'* daze, evens in da' hoodie, ladies didn't cuss not the Mothers, Aunties, older sistahs nor even them sweet *walla-walla holla-holla* loving little ladies of da' pleasurable Black knight life nonya the womenfolk cussed-it unless somebody truly be in need of a cultural lesson in *Southern* po'folk hospitality! *Yes, Sir* dat Sat-nite, school be in session, Professor JoAnne and Maestra Christina sat the podium then theys done dat *EF Hutton* thang wherebuy-n-buy theys done cussed-it our dumb asses Biggy-smalls and justa everybody done stopped and listened! *"Give them lil dumb-ass bastards Hell, Girlfriendz!"* Those two fine-assed ladies didn't miss a beat with their blessed little *rent me buy the halfa-hour* hearts thems two done stood center stage, drenched in water, wigs cocked, hands on hips akimbo then theys done taken care of their business because their world had been rocked, laughed at and punked-out by a trio of fist-pumping pre-teen-aged crumbsnatchers thus theys would not nor could not be ousted front street by a trio of big-*dummy*-butts justa mere daze fo' being outta theys shitty-diapers! Hell, justa one peek at us tree *diaper-dandies* then folks done knowed-it a fo' a fat fact, Jack that we'z tree be a trio of the sway too *wet-behind the ears* skoolyard hoodrat knuckleheads thus *gurlfriends* done gots down to the dirty on our young *Punky Brewster* black asses!

That Sat-nite had its minor personal distractions turned the public spectacle of mass entertainment. A few fights, fine-ass young mommas done caught theys just gots paid-it poppas strolling-it with someone else's daughters, some *jackass* got da' *4-1-1* that a'nuttier mule been kicking-it in hisns stall thems minor doings small-*poo*-butts sideshows of distraction that hadda kept them streets alive to be jumping *Emmett Till* the main event justa one-man band witch all of us hoodrats had awaited hanging jive, live and tight fo' the gala of dat one Man's gallant entrance! In the hood, the Reverend BD *Kenny* Bemus*bee-muss* be *da' Man* and *the Rev* rarely failed to disappoint hisns fav jive-ass peoples lessen hisns Sat-nite drink-on, dance-on and whore-house chase-on done gotz the butter of hisns man-*amongst men*-self big-*tanks*-butts dat Sat-nite, round the mid-nite the Rev be on schedule some *who'dat* squatting the watchtower done gave Word *"Here come da' Judge*!*"* The Rev had come on the strong-side of tings to done stumbled to done bumbled hisns nappy-head held high, spirits high and just plain assed high from hisns testy taste-tasting thems fermented grapes to make sho'nuff hisns own self that dat da' wine still held wisdom big-*preaching*-butts onward and forward had strutted-it the Rev BD Bemuse to center-court. The Rev BD Bemuse done loved-it nuttin butta than to done gotz hisns own personal *take it to da streets young-bloods hear me a'coming* Sat-nite come da' mid-night preach-on! Dad had told it that it had been just such a Sat-nite, years back that had begotten the Rev hisns lovable user-friendly nickname BD. According to Dad it had happened liked this backs in the daze, the Rev's wife then a foxy young brown-skin by anybody's rights stood on the curb-side in-front the *Shakey Puddin* witch just happened to be about a block and a half southeast of center stage as swell the Chocolate City's most infamous house of the ill-reputed where the widow Mrs. Fanny-Mae Mitchell done runned-it all by herns-*gets dar paper up-front*-self the affluent gentleman's fancy-schmancy *come da' one cum all* whorehouse! The Mrs. Rev done managed to have gotten-it a'hold of herns nephew's bullhorn seed at that time the Mrs. Rev's nephew be the announcer at thems Froebel High school football games and cause he old and be of the old-skool flavor just liked Old man river aints no *changes gonna come* hisns old-assed ways seed he still done used hisns bullhorn instead of dat newfangled-it *Inspector Gadget* electrified gizmo a microphoned sparkling for the Negro only new 10-year old used public announcement system to call the play-by-plays fo' all thems gridiron frozen tundra games. Swells Sir, dat super-fine in herns owns rights the young Mrs. Rev copped a'hold of dat there bullhorn then with horn in hand out-fronts the *Shakey Puddin* she done the shout-it out for all da' hood, the goodtimes to be had ladies working it inside the *Shakey* and especially the Rev Bemuse *who'dat* at the time just happened to be amongst the clientele inside shaking all dat Puddin! The Mrs. Rev shouted-it into that bullhorn for all to done heard-it *"Big Dick Bemuse get yo' scrawny black ass up and offa dat wrench and bring it on home!"* Dad told-it the Rev hadn't preached-it that Black knight big-*a'scardy cat*-butts the Rev done taken a'liken to hisns newest *a good wife giveth* moniker plus he'd just done hopped-it hisns rabbit-ass up to be outta the *Shakey* to done runned-it to home on the hot-foot likened he'd been ordered-it to do *bye-bye* dat pretty little wifey of hisns whom had dat Black knight sho'nuff summoned-it up all *Hell to southern belles* in them streets as swell she managed to done made a Heavenly name for herns-*most lovable*-selfie by publicly standing tall and proud for hernself. The mostest them peeps hadn't knowed-it fo'reallies sure iffn that pretty little wifey hadda done wanted-it dat the Rev to done brung hisns scrawny black ass or dat big black dick home either way the were of it all be legend in da' hood! I can recall from a tenderfoot that peoples always done axed-it the Rev BD Bemuse, in polite company *"How it be dat pretty little wifey of yourns'?"* For ordinary folk, being caught at the *Shakey Puddin* and getting your Sat-nite drink-on, be just goodtimey big-*gossipy*-butts fo' the Rev BD *Kenny* Bemuse, who be the pastor of the biggest baptist church in the Chocolate City and whom done acquired a consorted passel of the naturally envious and ruthless enemies outta both the Black and the White thus hisns frequent Sat-nite visits to the *Shakey* may have not necessarily been the most politically correct asset for a good man of the cloth to have done staked-it hisns infamous claim with hims being a righteous man! That shit be a *no brainer* no matter cause in da' hood the beloved Rev BD *Kenny* Bemuse be good *damned Skippy, Right-on mah brotha* good peeps!

City Blockhead Baptist be damned near a city-block long and at both ends it be tree-tiers high with standing room only every Sunday afternooner when the Reverend Bemuse stood the podium. Mostest of all us dissident inner-city residents that done hung-it out da' hood thems Sat-nites didn't even go to church, 'cept'n maybe an Easter Sunday or an early Christmas morning and then onliest justa show the whats what and the *who*'dat's gots it! My Moms, Dad, dem Unks' and Gee-Pees theys all epitomized the typical Sat-nite hood resident awaiting the Rev BD *Kenny* Bemuse to come and get hisns Sat-nite preach-on yet just liked mostest to all us *in theys right mind* peoples my Moms, Dad, dem Unks' and Gee-Pees didn't cotton to nonya a nobody's church nor never be to my knowledge *Medgar Evers* have even to be done peeped-it the insides of a nobody's *church mouse* in the house of lying-asses hawking-it dat theys lying-assed selves be the true teachers of the living word! Nobody center-court the CC done stepped-it nowhere near a fucking church not even City Blockhead Baptist lessen it be done happened that one of theys owned be done gots the Saintly or Satanic touch-up *bye-bye* the icy-cold *tasty freeze* finger of Big Brother Death come to visit then the ex-resident be boxed-it up, ready and in dire need of an address label fo' hisns ungodly ass's final shipment!

My Moms, Dad, dem Unks' and Gee-Pees hadda always claimed-it "*We the ones dat done raised Kenny, so, it's Ok to hear him lay-low the law*" plus theys always had a *roll-out the carpet* red-hot on the ready handmade excuse fo' to be caught center-court comes the mid-nite Sat-nite preach-on "*That boy couldn't talk*" Dad told-it *"he strutted around like a Rhode Island rooster calling peoples he didn't even know skinny, excepting he couldn't talk too good, so he'd call everybody 'Kenny' and now us peoples just naturally done returned hisns flavor*" Gee-Ma had bragged *"I made cussing church folk a religion way before thems Molly Mormon morons and thems damned Jehovah Witness fools done gots deys firstest backsides tapped by a fast-closing doorknob. I just loves to hear me some Kenny gettin' hisns Sat-nite mid-nite preach-on*!" My Moms claim to fame hadda been dat she done needed to visit with herns gurlfriends "*I don't set the hour nor the day but its us gurl-time all the same*!" Dem Unks' be liked *"Hell, dat boy my main man, I just gots to hear me some Kenny kick'n dat shit! Kenny be fucking all thems whores up*!" Needless to say the Rev BD Kenny Bemuse be liked family and be well loved in da' hood! Hell, he born *Right-on my brotha* center-court the CC witch be the intersection of 15th Ave. and Jefferson St. hisns daddy had been a cement finisher and mason and hisns momma had been the onliest Colored schoolteacher back in da' daze. The Rev's moms done taught-it to everybody and anybody theys first through fourth grades of schooling for the Negro only and usually that would have been the entirety of theys schoolings cause *po' chillums* being raised by po' peoples gots to work! The Reverend Bemuse graduated Harvard law school he had gotten a'hold to some kinda special interest scholarship big-*lucky*-butts after the graduation he couldn't get a worthy enough job in the Chocolate City area to put shoes on hisns big-assed feets nor food in hisns growling empty belly. He had moved his practice from city to titty then he'd sold the old school house took the cash and somehows done ended-it up in Paris, France a'fucking with alla thems frenchy *frog-leg eating* Mofos! Ironically that old schoolhouse got purchased by Mrs. Fanny-Mae Mitchell, then dat schoolhouse done become the *Shakey Puddin* so in a way the Rev be not really partaking such the wonderings of a whorehouse chase-on so much thems Sat-nites as he simply be gitting-it back to hisns roots in an around-the way hiatus it be hisns back to home fo' a Sat-nite *we be family* re-union could the Rev help-it that all the rental furnishings be alive so dark lovely and beautifully re-arranged!

The Rev talked that *Frenchy* too plus on the daily-double he done read dem European rags then done related-it everything going on in the US from a Europeanish *thems peoples* aints such the racist snobbish assholes of this world point of view. *Word-up*! You wanted the real deal, needed-it that real truth, Ruth then you besta bump ya' gums and comb ya' naps alongside the Rev BD Bemuse! The Rev's lawyer stuff done kept-it many a genuine sneak-thief outta the big house! The Rev done told-it in the original America the Blackman made-it, given it to the Redman then the Whiteman comes along to done stole-it thus the Negro aints stealing he just be borrowing what he done slaved hisns whole life for therefore its onliest natural the Blackman *git-back* be exactamente what originally be hisns thus it ain't stealing iffn the river of time done runned full-circle its course back to its original and rightful owner! Legal papers, gubmint troubles no problem seed the Reverend set yo' ass straight befo' he done gots yo' black *caught in the act* ass freed! He hadn't charged po'folks a penny even iffn theys could affords to pay it. *They* thems gov'mint ass-haulers thems authoritative po'dunks hadn't liked him firstest and fo'reallies mostest onliest cause he Black secondarily because the Rev be hisns own man thus it hadn't mattered a *damned Skippy* that it be thems harden times for any a Colored man living in America thems fiddies, sixties *Emmett Till* thems seventies brung *the awakening* to the racist land of the free! The Rev be the pastor of the biggest church and following in the CC dumb-*racist*-butts mainly *they* hadda hated the Rev because he done be the one *who'dat* done kept hisns peoples tight! *Do right by the Rev BD Bemuse and he gonna Do right by you* that be law one of the CC and folks done seed to it dats youse done learned-it law-one the Steel City before you cut your first diaper-less fart! The Rev BD Bemuse loved hisns hood backwards to be forwards no two-ways around it or be abouts it thus to my young-ass it be a mutual thang with all the peeps in da' hood it be *We loves our Rev*!

Chapter 26

The Rev done arrived-it center stage dat Sat-nite, the first thing he'd said *"Them redbones' so light damn near and wish to be white skinned knee-grows got the nerve to be snubbing good folk for coming to the Easter Sunday church. To Hell with them, Bastards! I'll preach it in the streets!"* We done loved-it mostest when the Rev talked down hisns own haughty-taughty high-brow congregation witch be mostly thems uppity Coloreds and Negroes of the day with theys justa smattering of the po'dunk uneducation of the Negro only and a little coin in theys hip-pocket! Now iffn ya' thought regular whitefolk po'dunks nots to be confused with thems low-life redneck po'dunks be a problem fo' the Negro then you musta never done had a meet-it up with an uppity Negro seed them uppities done wrote-it the book *how to cop an attitude on a po' black ass*! Hell look-it up the word *attitude* in the Webster and iffn there taint a pic of thems uppity Negroes then just throw that damned dictionary in the trash, it taint no damned good a'tall! They say *shit rolls downhill* swells them uppities be dat there last most leastest unexpected-it bump that dat rolling-shit be done hit just before rolling dead smack onto our po' Black asses chilling in the basement seed thems Negro/Coloured uppities done made-it theys *God as my witness* J-O-B for damned sure that we po' assed-out Blackfolks living down et the buttamilk bottoms done gots-it ourselves the mostest stank outta thems full-of-shit rolling downhill shit-smackens! Thems uppities had a future that didn't entertain nonya parts hoodie thus we had responded to the Rev liked always with a caterwaul of clappings, stompings, hooterings and a'hollerings "*Amen, Rev BD, Kenny, fuck dems uppity whores, Preacher man*" you had a'many blessed-it to done cussed-it choice of endings at the Rev's Sat-nite mid-nite preach-on! That be the way the Rev be done did it on the *Superfly* preached-it in them streets, he'd lay out a few bits of wisdom then step-back a bite to await our response befo' moving on thus it hadda been more liked a personal conversation than a served-it up full-fledged sermon from the mount yet instead of it being man to man it hadda went down the most enlighten on the part of a slightly tipsy leader to a happy sometimes too damned too happy-nappy assed drunken mob of the rowdy *all Hell done broke loose* crowd! The Rev BD Bemuse used God, good wine and a hell-of-a-lot of colorful language to drive home hisns own *special K*(Kenny) brand of thems there handful the Gospels.

The love affair between the Rev and hisns peeps be on the reals and a'nobody and I mean to have done told-it dat *Nobody* gots too damn close to be near the Rev when he done began hisns done preached-it in dem mean-assed CC streets because iffn the Rev could then he'd done grabbed-it ahold of yo' black ass to done made you lead confession, say a prayer from the heart or sing an old timey spiritual right there center-court in front of God *be there be a* God and the whole of our world! That particular Sat-nite center-court the Rev done stopped a police cruiser, a *po-po* wagon justa passing-it bye-bye then the Rev done made the white Officer Rubezynski get the fuck-out, stand and lead the *Lord's Prayer*, it hadn't mattered one *swit the Devils spit* to the Rev that *Cleotist* and *Ray-Ray* be handcuffed-it in the backseat of that po-po bucket! Next he done grabbed ahold to Ms. Ida Mae Carlson a *who'dat* mostest assurdidly hadda been on a tear, a worried hurried woman on herns way back to work seed she hadda done stepped-it out to done stepped-it home and checked-it on herns passel of the bad-assed chillums the original *Bae-bae's* chillens and more than likely she'd been in sway too much of a hurry to get backs to herns job and that blues band on stage such that she'd completely done forgotten-it be Sat-nite and the mid-nite preach be on! Ms. Ida Mae sang them downhome dirty blues around the corner aways over at the Apollo, not yo' Up'town Harlem venue big-*happy*-butts our CC brand witch be number-one on the chitlin circuit, a look-alike rendition of that famous New York City jumping-jive juke-joint. The Rev had gotten hisns-self a good hold onto her lithe *well-stacked fine liked a mofo* body why the Rev hadda caught Ms. Ida Mae by both herns shoulders to done spun her a full tree-hundred sixty degree turn-around for all the crowd to done seed the special prize he'd done plucked outta his hat to sho'nuff let it be known dat he done found-it the goodie-stuff! *Hell, Yes* when Ms. Ida Mae done finished singing *Precious Lord* grown-assed half-drunken men done wiped away crocodile tears from theys blood-shot eyes!

CC Rider, named after the train big-*pimp'n*-butts I can't relate that story swells not in polite company, a zoot-suited *pimp-daddy* ass, the buzzard's luck would have done had it when CC Rider had turned the corner hims a probably all caught-it up and inside hisns big pimp'n thoughts whilst he be looking fo' hisns top-flight gurls thems two professor doctorates JoAnne and Christina swell dat fool ass done tripped-it up to done fell on hisns skank pimp-daddy black ass outright sprawled a'front the Rev! Back in the daze, CC Rider be the hood's onliest resident to be done dressed-it on a par with the Rev seed thems sweet never to home flat-back ladies of the Black knight always done kept hisns skinny pimp-daddy ass stitched in the finest of silken cloth and dat Sat-nite hisns ass be tucked inside one of them light-grayish Italian silky suits with matching kerchief and blue ostrich feathered stomps! The Rev had been very polite and on the careful side to done kid-gloved-it with a series of personalized questions fo' dat *pimp-daddy* ass to answer to seed thems questions in all reality hadda been character credible prompts by the Rev befo' he done snatched-it dat whore-mongers ass and tossed that scum of the ghetto into the roaring Hell's afire! The damned skinny-assed pimp-daddy done cried hisns personal evil-assed confession for mostest damned near 10-full minutes afterwards *Oh my God, its a miracle* dat scum-bucket pimp-daddy low-life on the reals hadda proceeded to done emptied hisns ill begotten whorish gleamed monies from them clean eye-tile-yen silky-silk pants pockets to done tossed-it out all hisns ready cash be free-falling down onto that dirty ass ghetto street! It be a mad dash fo' da' cash dat *Indy 500* came a bite on the early side of the street dat year and everybody that hadda just so happened-it to have been close 'nuff done runned-it to done stuffed-it theys thread-bare worn-out brimming over with air-borne dust mites empty assed hip-pockets as the balling hisns fucking evil eyes out scum-bucket done confessed *I been touched*! The Rev had been quick to shout-it out to all us peeps to *"come and get this booty"* then the Rev hadda let it be knowed-it to all mankind that *"booty begots booty*! *That be a biblical fact"* I done knowed-it right then that it be a good ting that I be up on dat brownstone rooftop beside Gettis and *light in the pants* cause come the 'morrow CC Rider gonna be drinking *VO* whiskey and kicking-it to all the po'black asses of all thems idiotic money grabbing fool *who'dats* done taken advantage of hisns *I's be justa honest-man doing the Devil's work* faith! The Rev. BD Bemuse would lay bare your soul big-*preaching*-butts as Dad at times put it "dat Rhode Island rooster done laid bare more hens than souls" Even back then at dat young and tender age I'd done knowed-it there be a chunk of *rooster claws* in the CC and dat there be dat anger dat I hadda on the earlier front done bottled-up cause I be sway too mad to conversate abouts seems there had been a time when my Moms and Dad had done stepped-it theys separate ways fo' a minute and da' talk always walked da' walk in da' hood big-*gossipy*-butts what you don't know you won't know dat be *Word-up*, Mofo!

Generally speaking always after a good confession likened dat dope-ass fly pimp-daddy CC Rider done laid-it down to sleep then to done followed-it up with all hisns ill-begotten whoremongering monies break-dancing thems curbside gutters that be when the Rev be done jump-it outta the bag of tricks to done kicked-it with a certain flare of the uncertainty bringing-on the shit that be *da' shit* baby! After all the mad-money be passed from the bitch-slapping hand to done replenished all thems empty fucking hoodrat hip-pockets it be then the Reverend stood up-right to done jammed some *Baby I'm fo' real* preaching!! The Rev done brunged-it down all thems colorful peeps in the Heavens and raised-it up all thems fools dat be redneck sinners outta Hell! Fo' years I hadda done thunk-it that God had damned Adam, only to discover that dat be just the Rev's way of blaming Adam and all the menfolk in general for all the evil inhabited in this world and especially fo' the loss of Eden. I don't to never member' having heard the Rev blame Eve no parts fo' the eviction notice "*She be innocent and naïve*" hadda been hisns choice words bouts the gardens one be onliest fine-assed Babygirl seed the Rev had liked unto always claimed *"her real name be Na'Eve, the na being she be all natural, she wore a natural and natural be a word which comes from nature and nature be naturally innocent then Eve, well Eve that be her po'dunk Catholica Roman dago given name yet folks done needed-it to learned her real name be Na'Eve. See it had happened thissa away. Poor Na'Eve got hood-winked by the Devil hisnsself, he bees all dressed up in a two-thousand dollar-bill snakeskin suit. But dat Gawd damned Adam took one gander at Na'Eve's heavenly endowed breastestes and here we all be outside the Eden hob-nobbling in a God damned ghetto!"* The womens blessed heaps of heart felt praise upon the Rev followed-it up with a sassy wink of an easy baked smile seed thems womenfolks done praised him a' *good-n-plenty*!

Now, the Rev would be quick to compromise cause he loved all hisns peeps equally, the womenfolk a whole lots more and most definitely physically than the menfolk yet he hadn't wanted to done t-totally alienated the menfolks *"Can't blame a man for sinning, Gawd damned Adam be the first man on earth, he's done walked and talked the talk with God and he done sinned, Gawd damned Adam, he lived in Paradise and he bees the first to have sinned but it be a factual that mostest womenfolk be built big breasted like Na'Eve therefore Gawd damned Adam may have been the first yet he won't be the last of the menfolk to be done sinned!"* The Rev always spoke volumes about hisns seemed-it to me favorite patriarch of alls thems bible thumping folk, *Brotha Noah* and that Sat-nite be not any differ *"Brotha Noah be a man dat Blessed be he by the great God Almighty His Ownself! Brotha Noah be Blessed to populate this here world after man done caused its destruction through willful and out-right sinning, enslaving God's Chosen and all the while running high and tight with that evil one, old brotha Satan! Now, Brotha Noah Blessed be he of God, be a wine drinking man of biblical proportions, Brotha Noah be chosen by God Himself to go out and come to populate this new world. Therefore it be a real sin against God All-Mighty Him's Ownself iffn a man don't drink good vintage grape and do his damnest to come and populate this here New World!"* At that all the men along with all the women had reason to done *Whoop there it is* and the holla be loud and strong with theys laughter after witch every-damned-body crowded before the sermon in the streets done lavished great praise upon the good Rev *"Oh he be talking good now, Go tell it on the mountain! Kenny gettin hisns preach-on! Holla mah Brotha! Say Amen! Ahhh shucky-shuck! What he say! Preach it Kenny! Dems churchy-fied folks be sinning sho'nuff!"*

The Rev BD Bemuse knowed-it hisns audience all so well, dat Sat-nite, he put the spin on Sampson and Delilah *"Now Delilah, dat high-yella up-town gal did only what a grown woman should have done, taint natural for a man to be running around with locks. I can't stomach a processed-head. Grown-ass men visiting beauty salons trying to take the naps and kinks from theys God given natural napped hair. Brotha Noah had an afro, Brotha Ham had an afro even Gawd damned Adam had an afro, you Gawd damn right they did! Sampson strongest man on earth running round beating up on whole armies with the jaw-bone of an ass cause he the mightiest man on earth be a God damned Goldie-locks processed-head of an ass, damn them Goldie-locks! A processed-head fool tain't got God's good sense to buy a cup-o-coffee! All he got in his hip-pockets be hair fare! Hell Goldilocks be a woman! What the Hell a strong man like Sampson doing running around with a processed head? Good Lawd! I hates me a processed-head fool!"* All the processed-heads, theys the men whom done visited-it a beauty-salon having the sole purpose to done had lye conditioned into theys hair where buy-buy the lye had unkinked theys natural hair to done made theys nappy-naps relaxed and straight then it be dems processed-head menfolks done mounted protest *"AAahhhh he just jealous! The nappy-head, dat fool don't be a knowing a'nuttin bout nuttin! His ass ain't golden they oughta lock-up hisns nappy-ass head! Wished his nappy-head had hair liked mines!"* Everybody took to laughing and clapping the shout-outs "*Amen! Hallelujah! We like yo' fro' Kenny! Preach to thems fools, Kenny! Let dem nappy-ass naps be!*"

Whenever the Rev had need be of a pick-me up of the fermented juice he always done firstest tipped us by starting anew to preaching-it about the grape *"Jesus loved himself some good wine, my Brothas and my Sistahs! Yes indeedy, he did, knowed it for a fact! He went to a block party and they had no grape for the Holy One. Jesus told dem teetotalers it weren't natural to be celebrating without the vine juice. Then the Lord, God Himself, took two jugs of water and turned the contents of thems two water jugs into Heavenly wine. Wine-a'plenty, He called it. Ya'll already knows my good Brotha Noah loved his wine and what you say? Good Lawd! Yes, he blessed of all men for it...*that night *Bucket* a city-councilman stepped-it up to done tipped the good Reverend's sacramental cup. The Rev hadda stopped-it in the midst of hisns sermon to done personally blessed *Bucket* for his good works amongst the peoples as swell the replenishment of his vintage grape! The Rev preached some biblical women, the woman at the well that be the married lady *who'dat* done gots caught-it creeping and the Rev BD Bemuse worked her with a good-foot *"The Devil his self always dressing up in authoritative clothing and attacking some poor innocent woman cause her husband done run off and she can't get no job but she still be needing to feed her chillens. This time he dressed as the temple elders and thems fools done paid a married woman to fool around with a good man of the cloth"* He had looked directly at our crowd and gave us the *wink-wink* followed by the nudge-nudge *"Then they bring her up before the Master Himself, hollering the lie she done got caught when the truth be known she got entrapped"* the crowd spurred him on-ward *Amen! Kenny! Preach it Brother Reverend! Word-it-up, Rev!* The ladies seemed to fo'reallies have loved that twist *"But the Lord Who Be God sayeth unto them devilish fools and all their followers 'Ye without sin cast the first stone!"* Again the peeps interjected *Sho-nuff Rev! Did dat there* *lady duck? Ahh shucky-shucky*! *Give word Kenny*! *Dat rooster can crow*! Word on dem streets be that the good Rev had just recently got caught by the associate ministers of City Blockhead Baptist with a married female of the congregation then the jungle vine swore that dat Mrs. be doing more than justa kneeling confession at the Rev seated on a pew back of the church! The Rev had started to move hisns hands high into the air as he had stepped-it to an imaginary beat *"Them fool devils say but Good Lord, this woman, she committed sodomy…er adultery"* The Rev twirled, danced backwards a few more steps then jumped-it into the air and he done ended-it with a full split ala *James Brown*! I can't prove it, big-*dancing*-butts I truly believed-it in my heart of hearts that when I hadda firstest done watched it that movie *Flash dance* and viewed the scene with the young brothas *break-dancing* in them streets that wasn't new a'tall fo' me caused I done fo' many a years believed inside the pit-stone of what be left of my *heart of hearts* dat the Reverend BD Bemuse had invented break-dancing swayback center-court *"But my sweet Jesus wassa just ah cutting bait with them fools, cause you wanna know what he the Lawd done said? He sayeth unto them impish false prophets"* there the Rev had paused for the full effect, locked-it eyeballs to eyeballs onto as many of us peeps as he possibly could before he laid bare the law *"Adultery be not a physical act! Ya'll know Brotha Noah populated the new world and what? Damn right! Brotha Noah be blessed of all men for it!"* that gave the crowd a chance to pipe in *Don't be forgetting he wore an afro Rev*! *That sure be the fo' reals real truth, Ruth*! *Preach word, Kenny*! Then the Rev had done preached-it the lady Mary Magdalene into a mini-skirt "*Mary was no refrigerator*" He'd said *"That woman couldn't keep nothing, she be the first to preach the resurrection in the streets. And I'll tell it like it be, a'many of you women out there tonight would do the same, just commence to run into the streets and scream and shout Hal-le-loo-yah unto the high Heaves iffn Yo' man done rose again!"* That done did it, everybody justa stepped-it buck-wild! *Say it Kenny*! *Swing dat stick, Rev*! *Preacher man, on the holla*! *BD Bemuse laying da' word, Baby*! *The Rev be off the hook*! The Rev BD Bemuse be at hisns bestest when taking hisns double-Dutch chocolate fudge Sundae-noon sermons offa the pulpit into them mean-assed streets of the CC where he done cleaned-out the gutters, waxed mother's wit and conversed on a personal level with hisns beloved peeps *We the Peoples*!

chapter 27

WE ALL DONE KNOWED-IT FO' a fat fact, Jack that when the Rev began to preach them harlots it be time to take the young'ums and the innocents to home because the Rev be winding down hisns Sat-nite sermon and them harlots arrival be the onliest warnings you gots that the sermon of the Sat-nite mid-night preach-on be near to done ended and a parent just hadda to done ushered-it thems *git-alone little doggies* to home at to near bouts that time because at the very end of hisns Sat-nite sermons the Reverend BD Bemuse did not ask nonya nor nobody to bow their heads, not to join hisns uppity *knee-grows* onliest church, not to join hands within hisns wine soaked hands nor to join theys alcohol or MaryJane girl enriched hands together for the utterly hapless foolishness of prayer. The Reverend BD Bemuse got raw-dog on that ass and he cussed-it and *Word* be dat he done cussed-it good too and he cussed-it a'plenty the Rev cussed-it everybody and anybody doing wrong, did wrong or just be done got plain ass wronged! The Rev always started-it with hisns own personally writ law numero-uno *"I don't pick the cotton neither do I pick the ass to cuss, I lets po'folk without it and God All-Mighty Be to do thems pickens then I do the cussings and fuck the gawd-damned cotton-picking fool that gets fucking motherfucking mad!"* he'd continued *"That Gawd damn Jack-shit John fuckin-fritz-gurl Kennedy done run his monkey do-do ass to Berlin, leaving good men to be died in them fucked-up sugarcane and tobaccky fields of Cuba! Dat be why his own rednecked whiteys sent his po'skinny skunk ass down Dallas, Texas way then lead-plugged dat funky-hunky's peckerwood ass!"* That had riled up the peoples ire *Don't be getting it Ugly, Rev! Damn, Rev you above all done knowed-it we loves our Jack! We'z gotz hisns picture on the wall! Take dat damned ritz down! Tell it, Rev!* The Rev continued the Presidential tirade *"Fuck Lyndon Banged-up-the-ass Johnson, he sending all our young Black men off to fight in Viet-Nam just so Mr. Du-you get the fucking-Pont can get mo' richer selling his fucking paints and chemicals all of it be evil ass hoe monies made from the use of Oriental child slave labor, fuck that fucking ass licking cock-sucker the french-fried frog"* Since mostest of us had no damned idea who the Hell dat DuPont the frenchy ass-fuck frog be thens all the peeps had a chance to chime and chirp! *You be dropping word Brotha! Show ya' rights, Rev! Dats a fat assed fact, Jack!* The Rev done rolled *"Fuck the mule-headed mayor cause that motherfucker should have just sat hisns fat* *po'lack jackass down when the peoples done spoke"* at that them peeps a-gin-n-juicy Lucy went buck wild with theys laughter and banter *You still be chewing dat bone! Cough it up Kenny! Fuck dem Whores! Dem sums-dey-bitches I hates 'em too! Tell it like it be, Kenny!*

A year and some daze backwards November 65' *We the Peoples* of the CC hadda done gone and elected-it the Rev BD Bemuse as theys newest and onliest firstest to be *Medgar Evers* black City Mayor by write-in vote because *thems* gov'mint ass-haulers wouldn't place the Rev's name on the ballot big-*racists*-butts the Rev done won dat mofo city election by a landslide yet the Superior Court of the Grated Slate of the hillbilly pumpKin *I-n-mybabysis-diana* done claimed-it that the Rev BD Bemuse did not exist. The peeps hadn't knowed-it hisns real name be James Robert Bemuse such dat mostest thems peeps the ones that done knowed-it to write done writ Rev BD Bemuse, Kenny Bemuse, Kenny, BD and or Rev on theys ballot! The incumbent po'lack mayor and city gubmint hadda petitioned the Courts to have thems write-in votes throwed-it out the open door. January 66' one cold ass-freezing day thems gubmint courts done ruled-it to done tossed the write-in vote along with one James Robert Bemuse right the fuck offa thems City courthouse steps! *Good Lawd,* my *sweet-tea Jesus* the Rev hadda done stood liked a grown man possessed cause he done cussed the Courts, the State gov'mint, the re-appointed po'dunk ex-mayor, the city hall, the governor, and all thems po'dunk racist of the shitty-ass kkk mis-State of I-n-diana right then to be there big-cussing-butts justa bite *to the left-to the left* of them deputized white po'dunk *po-po* with billy-clubs in theys evil redneck assed white hands bumping a wide-legged stance atop them City courthouse steps!

It seemed the Rev loved to cuss the ministers of all thems other CC churches mostest of all thus it be just fo' dems motherfuckers dat the Rev commenced-it to done swishy walked-it and effeminate lisp talked-it *"Fuck them processed-headed faggots, I hates all them sons-of-bitches! Da' Whores! Nasty assed boot-licking cocksuckers is all that every one of them sons-of-bitches be!"* That kinda not-so-friendly fired-up *brothers of the cloth* hatred be on the personal and dat shit always played itself out as a major part of the Rev's Sat-nite thems big-*idiots*-butts it gots doubly intensified around bouts the spring 65' when Dr. Martin Luther King Jr. had held a rally protesting unfair housing in the Windy. Thems local ministers had formed a bloc, signed petitions and went to the whitefolk media requesting the head pastor of City Block Baptist Reverend Bemuse not be invited to speak at the rally because he's an embarrassment to the city. The local media had pounced on dat shit with the majority of *they* stories be the real truth, Ruth about the Rev's lewd and drunken mid-nite parades along center-court. Thems clergy fools and thems gubmint ass-haulers done taped-it the Rev and hisns Sat-nite mid-nite sermons thens the media used *they* radio *Hell to the yeah* we'z done listened tho' the goodie-stuff be flipping bleep-bleep-bleeped over! *They* had also photographed-it the Rev entry to done exited-it a visibly much happier man from the *Shakey-Pud-din* looky-looked *theys* black and white photographs it could be easily seed the Rev be bumping a drunken strut and *they* printed pictures of the Rev urinating in public with pics of hisns drunken attempt to write his name in the wintery piles of snow witch made fo' a'nuttier reason to *don't eat yellow snow*!

Thems tree-summertimes mostest every Sat-nite, da' hood had been privy to some of the bestest damned cussing-outs *Medgar Evers* to done buzzed a hoodrat's ear *"Every dog has his day*!*"* the good Rev had continued to modulate *"What comes around will swing around*! *I'm a rabid dog and them dick eating faggots gots on milk-bone underwear*! *I'll chew that ass, I'll chew me some of theys uncle fucking-the Tom asses cause all good things cometh to those that wait*! *And I tells it outright to all you motherfuckers gathered here what be the real truth, Lawd knows that I be one patient muddafucker*! We hadn't done marched-it with Dr. King in 65' big-*missed out*-butts dat Sat-nite we'z done stepped-it strong stride fo' stride alongside the Rev every stomp of the way *Tell it Brotha Kenny*! *Get Ugly with it Rev*! *Play the dozens on them Muddas*! *Bring Rudy-ray Mo' on them fucks*! *Kick theys uppity-ass, Kenny*! *Big Dick Bemuse long-stroking it deep to them faggot muddafuckas*! The peeps had hung tight dat Sat-nite *Fill Yo' cup, Brotha*! *Come on Kenny*! *Work dat ass*! *Give 'em Hell, Rev*! *Give-em Gawd damned Hell, Big-dick Bemuse*! *Preach-it in the streets mah Brother*!

That Sat-nite the crowd had lingered-it and the Rev had time to call out all the local hustlers, petty criminals dat be thems straight-up sho'nuff thieves of the den amongst us the Rev cussed-it thems country fools then he even cussed-it out *Mr. CC Rider*. The Rev done told-it *CC Rider* be a *low life whorish ass pimp-daddy scum of da' hood, taker of the lost and innocent Soul-Sistas and that he'd pay the fiddy-dollars to done seed to it fo' justa anyone to long dick that whoremonger in hisns getting rich offa the innocence of innocents pimp-daddy ass*! The end, at the berry very end of hisns Sat-nite preach-on the good Rev BD Bemuse did done doned-it as he'd always done did done-it after a good *Yessum's Lawd my Soul be satisfied* Sat-nite mid-nite sermon in thems mean assed-out streets of the CC, the Rev done turned hisns back unto da' hood, lifted the coat-tail of hisns hand stitched peaches and cream Italian silky-silk suit dropped-it them expensive trousers and purple silk boxers! Then the Reverend BD Bemuse gave our gathering hisns final blessing! *"all you black-assed motherfuckers can kiss my sweet Black ass Good Night! Gawd Bless! Now tarry yo' po' black asses home muddafuckers! Let the choir say, Amen!"*

Chapter 28

IT BE A VERY SAD occasion in America when the good Reverend BD Bemuse did done got hisns *git-back* to them bloc-headed ministers and city ass-haulers comes April 4, 1968 a great American, Dr. Martin Luther King Jr. be gunned down, heinously assassinated under the watchful eye of thems *Whites only* federal piggly-wigglies Fat Bald Idiots FBI then nationwide all Hell done broken-it loose from the established po'dunk limits! All around and inside Black America there had been big time riots everywhere from the smallest of po'dunk burgs to the biggest inner-city ghettoes and the Chocolate City had been no different for about 2-weeks chaos and bedlam reigned mornings, nooners and all throughout them *fiery Burn Baby Burn* blazing Black knights! The city ass-haulers hadda shutdown the buses, schools and mostest all city and State governed functions. In da' hood there be no Sat-nites, no bums, no hoodlums, no Rev BD Bemuse it had been just some bad and saddened dem times be from the mostest of all to everybody 'ceptin dem damned klu-less klutzers and theys redneck klan thems po'dunk skinny whore-ass whiteboy *nazi jump-boot* bitches be ripping it up inside theys newly deputized *Jethro, I said to raise yo' right-hand* po-po suits under the guise of restoring law and order to the city!

After Dr. King's funeral, the local ministers had reformed their bloc and them bloc-heads along with thems po'dunk po'lack city ass-haulers had planned a march through downtown the CC ending with a silent vigil honoring Dr. Martin Luther King Jr. that was to be held on the steps of City Hall where a statue of a sitting Abe Lincoln done decorated the lawn. It had been theys dual plan to honor Dr. King with the greatest form of flattery by imitating his rally fo' civil rights commemorating the march on DC at the Lincoln Memorial witch had given the world one of the greatest speeches *Medgar Evers* orated by Dr. King. Thems bloc-heads and gubmint ass-haulers wanted the vigil to coincide with the city's annual Juneteenth celebration and this time, *they* had done invited the Reverend James Robert Bemuse pastor of City Block Baptist to join them then thems assholes done made-it a public spectacle outta the colorful non-printable and not for the public audible *you cocksuckers can kiss my Black ass* decline that the good Reverend had giveth unto all them whores.

I have to stop fo' a fat fact, Jack of an authentic *they* wouldn't print-it so Blackfolk had to tell-it a Black oral tradition and not a his-*fucking lying white ass*-story. I done knowed-it there be few peeps outside the CC to done knowed-it what I done touched upon earlier seed mostest Black-folk be liked *What be Junteenth, baby*? All the po'dunks be liked *What the Hell is Junteenth*? I shall now relate what little I done knowed-it about the mostest celebrated Black America holiday celebrated with the *Midas touch* by Blackfolk in the done knowed-it living-it up in an *I can't breathe* racist America!

Junteenth be abouts our celebrating the unofficial big-*party party*-butts a celebration by any other name still gonna be a *party-party get yo' Black ass party-on* seed *Junteenth* be the weekend celebration of the official end of Black lives legally bonded into slavery in the United States! Oh Hell yeah we'z be free! *Junteenth* be a very special day in the CC fo' us hoodrats plus all thems uppities kicking-it in the Negro only suburbia parts of the inner-city. Mostest to all us's Negro families had migrated *Tank God* ups from thens outta *da' delta cotton pick'n bluz* witch be redneck central lil *Missy-sip-pee, Lou-easy-Anna, Alley-bam-mee* and *South Taxdatass* thus we be accustomed to the celebrating of *Junteenth* as the official day that all slaves be freed in America. *Junteenth* be an official nationally knowed-it unpaid holiday celebrated by all Blackfolks and po'dunk city *ass-haulers* in the knowed-it and dat shit bumped live! It be a fat fact, Jack dat *Junteenth* in the CC be liked *ho-hoe-ho Mary* it be da' fucking Christmas, *tricks-fo'-treats Bitches* fuck jo' *Hallo-weenies* and yo' black ass on the personal *hey-hey, world I's be here* birthdaze party seed theys all be rolled-it up and into the one *Hell of a par-tee* big-*happy nappy*-butts justa dancing in thems streets party-party, baby! In the CC always come the Christmas time it be ass-bite freezing, snow, ice, sleet, -15 degrees below zero and all that *Billy-bad-ass* weather bees on both the outside and inside of a hoodrat's crib because thems po'lack slumlords done turned-it off the heat plus many a'times a body didn't to never to *Medgar Evers* be done got no damned Christmas presents cause bills had to be paid and that *bills gots to be paid* theory done held its cheap-assed sway for a'many birthdaze to boot big-*no gift*-butts *Junteenth* be the cure-all because *Junteenth* be celebrated in the summertime bees the rights time *to get jo' groove on* when it be African hot like a motherfucker and the celebrating be even hotter! Juneteenth be set *to get yo' swerve-on* the weekend of June 19th and dat party be not justa house-party not evens justa block-party big-*bring it on*-butts the whole damned city done blocked dat party! Family be family and it all be about *yo' skin dark then yo' black ass be a free ass swells yo' black ass be family* and the family done came from all thems parts USA to celebrate *da' Freedom*! It be dems goody times being multiplied by mo' giva-me mo' dems goodtimes fo' jo' Black ass!

The menfolk *bar-b-qued* and smoked thems meats and fish and just the freshest catfish been caught outta Unk' Zeke's pond and ya' bestest to done knowed-it dat yard-bird thems step-lights gots slow-pressure cooked-it then slattered-up with the good sauce cause in the hood *Bar-B-Q* slow-grilled-it be the chicken and babyback ribs done ruled-it *Supremes*! The womenfolk done cooked-it theys mostest famous recipe soulfood, theys done baked all them goodies at home to home and a'nuttin be sto-bought *Yo' crazy Bitch get yo' ass up n' outta the A &P Fuck dems ready-mades youse gots to scratch that itch* it be all to the good because nobody broughts bad-stuffings to the party, people done talked-it a whole nuttier year bouts the last *Juneteenth* thus it be dat nonya thems womenfolks didn't wannabe bad mouthed-it fo' over a whole year to come! Juneteenth be *bitch, you best to crock* that *Betty Crocker* shit and bury dat *Pillsbury* po'dunk mix *Hell to the nawl* nonya that *ain't cha momma on the cover of a pancake* box whitefolk sto-bought bullshit, real butter and real cow milk there be no oil nor water nonya that gov'mint issued powder shit, it be *Junteenth* baby! Thems da' times for the goodie-stuff to be and nuttin big-*baking*-butts the goodie-stuff such that all them goodies be the bestest of the homemade from scratch specially dems cakes, pies, cookies even homemade ice creams and candies all kinda flavors a mouth *Medgar Evers* done tasted-it be done passed through the biggest fattest of lips that hadda burst-out the *we'z be Free* celebrate!

Hell, fo' *Junteenth* you didn't even have to be Black nor family seed all thems bums, thugs, uppities, hoodlums, rich, poor, bloc-headed ministers, city ass-haulers, po'dunks, Ricans, Mexicans, Eye-tile-hens, Po'lacks,

Injuns, Chinks, educated or just anytobody plain assed illiterate even thems all *Hells southern belles* justa all the motherfuckers be well welcomed to its our *freedom party*! Iffn a body done showed-it up to done celebrated *Junteenth* then dat body partied, celebrated and done et the broken bread with all us Black and any other bodies present, it be the *Junteenth* motherfucker and dat shit be lit, Babycakes!

The city provided the fireworks and live music and the shit be on the reals big time fireworks alongside the real deal musicians not that damned musaz shit blasted outta extra-large bullhorns assed-out strapped-it to the rooftops of station wagons big-*party be on*-butts thems all too real live fabulous famous musicians dat be to performing live free concerts party-party come *Junteenth* weekend! *Good Lawd* the stars done mic'd it up alongside dem downhome blues bands and theys all done performed-it and it be all free onliest thang to be paid be to done find-it a space fo' yo' empty-pockets to done sat upon! Thems city ass-hauling sons-dey-bitches done got-it-together fo' *Junteenth* thems straight-up *Mr. Charlie be pollack jew-boy white assed* whoremongers put-it on the *Ritz*, baby thems fucking po'dunk fools done rolled-it out the *Baby, I'm for reals* red bad-assed carpet-beggars fo' the *Junteenth* celebration!

In them parks there would be all kinda cook-outs big-*we gots eats*-butts I remembered the best thing be that all the peoples be happy, I'm talking on the reals happy-nappy asses and fo'reallies enjoying themselves in celebrating *Our Freedom* it be a great time to be alive, Baby! I don't done knowed-it what thems lying assed *his-story* whitey lying-assed uneducation for the Negro only books done said iffn theys po'dunk lying asses done mentioned-it anything et tall in print about *Junteenth*! On the personal, I aints done never read anyting abouts *Junteenth* in *NO* his-*white lying ass didn't*-story during my 2nd class citizenry and unskooling for the Negro only just as well because thems no-count pages of those po'dunk *his-story* books be filled with straight-up inaccurate falsified opinions big-*fucking white lying*-butts cause it be *his*-Mr. Charlie-*story* when it concerned any parts Blackfolk then WTF ever be printed on thems pages swells it be gonna justa gotta be chucked-up the ya-hoo hillbilly pumpKin redneck ass with umpteen white racist lies!

My lovely Great-great-grandmother from my momma's side hadda done told-it to us the real truth, Ruth because my Great-great-GrannieG had been born a slave on a plantation somewheres to near Hazlehurst, Mississippi thus she be there when it all had went down! The ting be dat my GrannieG didn't read no *his-story* po'dunk whitey bullshit lying assed-out books for the one she hadn't knowed-it how to read et tall and fo' the number-two Great-great-GrannieG had done lived-it them times thus my GrannieG done told-it dat which she done seed, heard and *Oh, Hell yes* done lived! Great-GrannieG done told it in that when she be a young'em no more than 5 or 6 dems Union soldiers had come to done told-it to herns ma and all thems other slaves on that plantation that theys be freed big-*great news*-butts the Great War to free all mankind be still going on and that theys should still work the land big-*freed*-butts onliest from now *Emmett Till* the end of the great *John Brown* gonna free the slaves war theys would get food and scrip from the Union fo' theys work then when she be round 7or 8 thems Union soldiers done come back and told them ex-slaves that theys all be freed big-*ain't gonna work no mo'*-butts nonya thems had to work that damned plantation anymore and thems angel-eyes blue-coats done told-it to my peeps that the Great War for Freedom had just done ended and *Tank God* theys be no longer slaves! She said that herns family and a few other families done got it together and theys had done walked-it for mo' than a week to the town of Hazlehurst, Mississippi to done settled-it down on the land scattered abouts the woods nearby! My Great-great-grandma GrannieG done said-it that during the Great War for Freedom dat some of them wealthier low-life pole-cat crackers dems with the real money thems ones that didn't buy into any that worthless confederate scrip *phony-money* dems there plantation owners had moved theyselves and theys slaves to *Taxass* because Taxass be supposed to be free land not affected by the Great War. GrannieG done figured-it dat she and family must have been in dat po'dunk burg a'nutter 5 to maybe 6 years after the Great War for Freedom had done ended afore she done seed any of those slaves dat hadda got marched-it to Taxass big-*freed*-butts theys done returned to the area with the good news and even greater the printed word! Those Taxass relatives hadda done told-it to everybody with ears attached that theys hadn't done knowed-it that theys po' black asses be freed until June of that year and it hadda been thems *who'dats* tho' theys be the last ones to be freed big-*freedom*-butts Great-GrannieG done guessed-it to be a biblical ...*the last shall be the firstest* because them finally freed Tax-ass ex-slaves done been given paper bulletins bye-bye the Union soldiers that had June 19 printed on them showing it to be the official Freedom Day.

We the Peoples done chose to celebrate *Junteenth* as our never to be forgotten official unforgettable day because June 19th be the day when fo' the mostest all of us dat be of the *Who'dat* Nation be done knowed-it that We Be Free, baby! That hadda been especially true for mostest all Colored/Negro families that done lived-it the harsh hard slave life in the little Missy-sip-pee delta, southeast *Taxdatass, Lou-easy-Anna*, and *Alley-bam-mee* racist mis-States of the Union then the mostest Negro families done hand packed-it theys *Junteenth* celebrations as a carry-on whence we'z done migrated-it to all parts north, east and to the westward-ho just to be away and a'sway any parts thems redneck swamp lands of the lousy south. That be my great GrannieG facts of life not to be confused with his-*Mr. Charlie lying po'dunk ass*-story embedded with all hisns mythical racist opinions as facts witch in reality be just a mixed bag of thems big fucking white lies and dirty-assed tricks concerning any and all things Blackfolks!

My GrannieG's rememberings of *Junteenth* hadda always been good 'nuff for me big-*dummy*-butts e'nuff of the skooling put down dem pencils and crayons! The good Rev's *git back* on thems bloc-headed ministers and dems city-ass haulers done begun early June 68' the Sat-nite mid-nite one week prior to *theys* heavily advertised vigil Saturday of the *Junteenth* weekend an *Oh my God* somber as swell sober Reverend BD Bemuse done walked-it center-court the CC and laid out a simple plan to be performed by a simple peoples "*Fuck them church mouse faggots and city ass-hauling bastards!*" He'd said, "*We gonna meet at City Block Baptist Church next Saturday morning at 10am and march peacefully to Gilroy stadium in honor of Dr. Martin Luther King Jr. A peaceful march to honor a peaceful man because God don't like ugly and We Be a Beautiful Peoples*" He had done even kept hisns silken trousers belted-it up whilst he done a solid on the reals hand held high tripled-cross Blessed-it our tipsy dare I say stunned-it crowd then the Rev Bemuse just turned and walked away! Needless to say, we hadda all been collectively shocked bye-bye hisns stoic mind-blowing discipline! Most be shocked that it be Sat-nite and the good Rev BD Bemuse be plum to be damned sober! Hell, word be dat Sat-nite the good Rev hadn't even paid homage to the *Shakey Puddin*! The good Rev done repeated-it the same game plan that Sunday morning and afternoon from hisns pulpit at City Block-head Baptist. Word be Deacon McManus had coughed-it up blood-clots and the associate ministers of the City Block-head Baptist done tried to protest yet nonya that foolishness had mattered *titi* to the Rev. I was told that the Reverend Bemuse gave word of his plan then turned his back on hisns uppity *Negro only* congregation to done lifted-it hisns robe when he had walked-it right the Hell out of City Block-head Baptist the same as he had done it fo' us earlier round the mid-night center-court thus the beloved Rev hadda left both hisns fav congregations collectively stunned and sermon-less.

Vigil Saturday as the bloc-head ministers and city-ass haulers had named it comes 10am seemed the whole Blackfolk world, the whole city plus busloads of Blackfolks from Chicago, East Chicago, Hammond and Michigan City, I-n-diana just a great Biggy-smalls chunk of *We the Peoples* done stood patiently out front the City Block-head Baptist *Emmett Till* the good Reverend Bemuse and Deacon Daniel Davis done led the throng of *We Shall Overcome* singers tree-miles of marching and singing through downtown the Chocolate City passed the vanilla suburbs surrounding Gilroy park then onto the Gilroy stadium grounds. The city ass-hauling officials had tried to refuse our admission yet we hadda done bum-rushed thems and the stadium gates! Some of the older young men from the march had scaled them stadium chain-link fences then *they* hadda done conceded-it and the city ass-haulers unlocked all the entrances into the facility and hooked-up the audio. The bloc-head ministers along with thems city ass-hauling officials had attempted to get onto the stage *"Git back to Hell, the same way ya'll crawled out!"* be what the beloved by hisns peoples Reverend BD *Kenny* Bemuse had done shouted-it at thems low life pole-cats! The peeps hadda gave the Rev a serious round of applause *Tell'em Reverend! Pay the cost to be the Boss, Kenny! Ride them Toms-n-pole-cats outta there, Rev!*

The Reverend Bemuse read Dr. King's *I Have a Dream* speech followed it with Dr. King's Selma, Alabama sanitation worker's speech then gave a great American a great eulogy. The rest of the day be filled-it with mo' speakers along with some recorded Dr. King speeches and sermons plus the Rev done let other ministers and many a choir to done got-it up onto that stage to done preached-it and or sang theys hearts out taints nuttin butter in this evil assed two-faced world than some down-to-home *I gots my Soul saved* gospel choirs on the reals stirring up the Spirit! Thems gospel gooney-goo-goos done sho'nuff gang-banged some Souls dat day, baby! I a'gonna done told-it thems church-chimps swung-it from tree-to-tree as theys done sang theys unholy Roman-dago mythical lied to *Peace be still* enchanted hearts out, *Right-on, mah brotha-man!*

The Rev did a very strange thing after all those speeches and the goodtimey gospel singings seed the Rev got back unto dat stage and began to whisper hints of *strange fruits* amongst We hisns chosen Peoples, the Rev began to praise the great efforts of one President LBJ *"That great American President Lyndon Baines Johnson has given us Black people a chance to be somebody, for the first time Black men are being trained to be real soldiers.... LBJ has enacted a series of social reform programs ..."* that shit had been a real life shocker to all us center-court peeps on the holla back *Yo' Rev dat be the same banged-up the ass Prez Johnson you preaches about? What you talking about Rev, how comes he so great, now?* There be mo' much-o much mo' to come! The Rev Bemuse had complemented everybody about their beautiful and neat afros and colorful dashikis big-*set em' up*-butts forewarned that we might just need to be sending them colorful rags *Right-on* back to Africa and replacing thems all with Mohawks and buck skins, Huh? The Rev told us that the truth had been set free and that the great seal of white lies done been broken and that the few white lies as well theys Roman-dago enhanced-it myths that be left unto this world won't stand the test of time, he said to go forth unto and into the universities and colleges to train and learn to use our minds in an intellectual and educated way yet we should be prepared to dump ninety-percent of all the fossilized white lies and worthless classes that we will be taught in thems same universities! The Rev said it was gonna be the best time *Medgar Evers* for Black men and Black women in America in that we were going to be free for the fourth time that be a'nuttier ting that I done loved-it mostest about the Rev in that he's a very intelligent man with an innate talent for eloquently breaking off large chunks of intellectual truths into digestible sound bites and edible pieces then dishing-up them bits that be pieces into the language that be spoken, consumed and understood by hisns beloved peoples! That day the Rev had set his table well as he done broke bread to the leastest that be the crumbsnatcher level come some fiddy-odd years hence the Rev's vaulted wisdom hisns gifted knowledge done managed to resonate, permeate to done danced along the under currents and vibrations of my inner most thoughts thus the Rev be educating my dumb-ass throughout the long-haul and thems on the reals truths be cresting atop the da' waves of a whole new computer generated enlightened world! A world whereby most thems antiquated thousands of years old white-assed po'dunk lies formed of the white man fo' the po'dunk through his-*lying ass*-story be proven on the daily-double to be out-right racist opinions witch that po'dunk done knowed-it from the jump hisns *his*-lying-*story* be a collective of the falsified opinionated bull-shit rhetoric yet hisns po'dunk lying ass fo' eons be presenting that bull-shit as factuals!

After a great gospel day of singing spirituals, preaching, speeching, eating and enjoyment of the general good mood that done ebbed then overflowed what could bestest be described as *Junteenth* fellowshipping then for the encore, the Reverend Bemuse stepped-it back up and onto that Gilroy stadium stage, he didn't say a word he just done stood-it there looking upon hisns peoples all proud then slowly and Good Gawd Amighty *Medgar Evers* so slowly the righteous Rev had begun to raised a clinched black gloved right-fist high into the air as the stadium loud speakers played James Brown *"Say It Loud I'm Black and I'm Proud"* the crowd went buck-wild with the madness, Black fists pumped-it into the air without a care *We the Peoples* shouted the words loud and proud over and over again all thems Black fathers and mothers and their generations, grandparents and their generations, children and their children's children generations stood in unison shouting *"Say It Loud I'm Black and I'm Proud"* with a raised-it on high Black fist pumping the air! The mostest of us *We the Peoples* especially the uppity Negro elders be uttering those iconic soulful up-lifting words of self-praise and self-esteem in ourselves for ourselves a great communal Blessing unto ourselves as a peoples for the firstest time in theys *it's good to be me* beautiful Black lives! *We the Peoples* raised as one a solidarity clinched and proud Black *"Say It Loud I'm Black and I'm Proud"* fist!

We the Peoples as a People must have been collectively dreaming the good Dr. King's dream because that day that moment the good Reverend James Robert Bemuse done killed off for *Medgar Evers* the Colored, the Coloured and the Negro for generations past *Tankz God* and generations to come fo' hisns beloved *We be the Peoples* of a darker hue! That *git-back* day the good Rev had simultaneously resurrected from within us the Black Power as swell the intellectual Black Man from the inner to the outer thus our world be awoke loud and definitely Black Power proud!

Chapter 29

Them days at sea be just dazed at sea for my black ass not much fly-ing with lots of down-time, chill time, chip all that fucking paint time witch be *cue the lights* it be selfish times justa harken back and gaze upon my very own *love-me love-me* wall! What the *f'n* else be there to do on a flat-head idly floating whilst chipping paint with them jerk-off seamen scrubs dat shit had been totally mind numbing as all *Hell to all southern belles* won't somebody *Po-leeza* to get me the fuck outta there! WTF the fated day cometh *fuck me*, I got called to the Captains Deck wherebye-bye a po'dunk whitey *Mr. Charlie* USN Rear Admiral Lower-Half complete asshole had presented me a personal set of the *You Be Fucked* papers, Official USMC Orders to report to Paris Island, SC fo' USMC RECON training and I be liked WTF be this fucking training RECON bullshit my black ass be outta this shit-can in a CC minute, I onliest gotz two count em' two fucking months left to be banging on the Man's fucking war drums, MOTHERFUCKER!

I had gotten into a real shouting match with that fucking Navy Admiral about them Orders to report, that Rear jackass mofo hadda been a real jag-off of an asshole plus hisns flunky-hunky ass be Navy so hisns *I give the fucking orders* ass hadda gloated liked a motherfucker justa super elated to done kicked-it to the ass-cheeks of a sea faring bell-hop! The asshole fuck done knowed-it full and well that thems Orders to report be a real fucking *Surprize Surprise Surprize Sgt. Carter* fo' my dumb-ass thus it be official that cowtech shit-head Pin-alley jabber-mouth pendant muddafucker hadda been two-stepping-it to the correct fucking beat hisns little sermon on the mount, fuck! The King's syphilitic piss be reigning hardtack on my dumb ass I be fucking royally *FUCKED*! WTF stunned *deer in the head-lights* standing tall the Captain's Deck my shit gotz twisted, bye-bye my calculations I even done took off both my boots and re-calculated then I had less than tree-months befo' my dumb-ass be outta there dat barrel a'headed-it fo' the *good Lawd* 4-years living the reserved non-committed life of the ex-ja'rene a full-circle thems *welcome wagons* backs to a full-time sitting fat-n-happy on my ass civilian! Previously, I had done gived-it the thumb-nailed onliest as to my volunteer-enlistment sealed with a big-*stoopid*-butts KISS*KeepItSimpleStupid* What had happened be, I had done signed-it up for the *buddy-buddy* plan because during the Nam draft there had been a military enlistment option called the *buddy-buddy* plan that only the Marines offered and that had been the onliest reason that I done chipped-it the paint, thumped live full-metal jacket rounds and cranked me some wrenches comes the firstest *Gawd damned* place! It hadn't mattered *Bo Diddly* squat dat I hadda kinda sorta peanut-butter-n-jelly jammed the babygirl action during both my little pound-ground squat dat black ass in an agent orange covered bush, stomping slant-eye bucktooth rat asses big-*jam on it*-butts *Good Lawd* burnt cordite dat shit be banging, baby! The CC hometown lying-ass Whiteboy Marine recruiter done told-it iffn I and a buddy enlisted together, we onliest had to do 2 years each active-duty then the each of us done did 4-years non-active reserves at home the CC with no strings-attached, no meetings to attend nor nuttin to do active nor reserved USMC *Medgar Evers* again unless during those 4 in-active reserve years Uncle Sugary-Pops gots hisns Billy-bad-ass self into a'nuttier war big-*war drums banging*-butts only a *Baby, I'm for reallies* real US Congress deemed-it fucking war, *damned Skippy*! My dumb-ass, hadda done taken tight a full grab of that 2-years *no mas* shit to done runned-it to done gots my Boy' by the nut-sack Willie Shields, *may he rest in Peace* so that us two-homies be done to out-smarted the *big bang war be a'coming* system! In the late 60s and thems early 70s the Viet-Nam conflict had been escalating full-auto and sweet Uncle Sugary-Pops be going about hisns business of drafting strong from all walks of American life. Once dat old wrinkled-it up wizen-assed shitty-finger pointing *I Want You* Uncle Sammy done drafted an ass specially iffn dat ass be inner-city Black then just fo' dat drafted Black ass it gonna be Army infantry, 4-years active duty followed by a'nuttier two years in-active Army reserves *bump dat shit,* baby! Army bootcamp be 5-months with a'nutter 2-months rifle training, 30-daze leave then *Boo-coo jigga-boo Howdy duty Vietnam*! Hello, over tree-fucking years boots to pound-ground Nam, *Hell to the nawl*! I had done did the math big-*calculating*-butts the Marine Corps and onliest the Corps offered-it the buddy-buddy plan and that lying-assed whore po'dunk recruiter done told-it to get accepted into that buddy-buddy plan an un-drafted ass and friend both had to voluntarily enlist into the Corps big-*lying*-butts the plan onliest be available and applicable before thems two friendly asses done been drafted then *Luck be a real lady* fo' dems two because then it be bootcamp 8-months the last two of those 8-months be rifle training, thirty-day leave justa click past 1-year Nam' next stop for the young intelligent brotha be home sweet home thus dat fouled-assed CC recruiter done sold-it to me and my Boy' Willie Shields, *may he rest in Peace* a sack full! That ass fuck low-life po'dunk done concluded hisns all bullshit sales-pitch bye-bye jiffy-popping-it out 2 USMC enlistment contracts along with two *Bic* black ink pens one each for us two fine outstanding young men. Dat there chicken-shit be the how comes us two black-assed intellectuals of the *Negro only* uneducated fools, done stepped-it up to done hung our hats onto hisns fucking lying-assed bullshit one hot summertimed day August 72, FUCK!

Late October 72, after me and my Boy' Willie *may he rest in Peace* hadda been forced fed the hand to play on our high school football team seed nobody in dey rights fucking mind never to *Medgar Evers* done thunk-it to play fucking football in northwestern Indiana because come the end of September the ground be on fulltime winter frost-bite frozen solid alert it be liked playing on illegal Messykins poured-it concrete especially those last come the late October games. The only way the school could field a football team be to done forced-fed all the track, b-ball, and baseball players to done lined-it up and take an index-card numbered 1 through 4 seed this card game bullshit happened-it right after the firstest baseball game every springtime done sprung! The hand played itself out when the fucking yella-tooth skinning be grinning fat-assed po'lack football coach called out the *I'm fucked* number that done placed yo' unlucky ass on the team iffn you didn't done showed-it up to choose a numbered card then automatically it be *winner-winner chicken dinner* because it be a sho'nuff given that the no-show black ass gonna be a first-string every gameday starter fo' that up-coming season. That spring 72' me and my Boy' Willie *may he rest in Peace* had each done grabbed-it ourselves a tree and I'd be buzzard-luck damned iffn all us big black bucks standing there a'holding onto a damned unlucky-assed tree-card had done gone and won that dumb-fuck po'lack's football lotto, FUCK! October 72' the basketball coach Xiomar Franklin hadda done stepped-it onto the football practice field to done pulled my Boy' Willie *may he rest in Peace* along with two other football players aside to done told-it on the personal the bad-assed mis-State of the redneck hillbilly *I-n-babysis-diana* latest fuck a brotha up bad news because theys had the asthma then the mis-State would no longer allow them to play b-ball fuck big-*cough it up*-butts theys could playout the rest of the football season then dems fools be *Fuck you, Adios Motherfucker*! Dat no b-ball shit had done kicked-it in the ass fo' my Boy' Willie *may he rest in Peace*, my Boy' hit thems bricks to the bootcamp then to the there, Kool mofo *I aints mad at ya'* sour grapes *Kool-Aid* fucking kool!

January 73' *they* done stopped the fucking draft and there I and my Boy' Willie *may he rest in Peace* be freaking stuck with them two-fucking volunteer years, active-duty Marine Corps *Motherfucker* FUCK! FUCK! Dat be a'nuttier super-imposed upon the brain reason why I don'ts never

ever a'gin-n-juicy Lucy put my trust a lying-ass bastard fuck po'dunk nor any kinda whiteboy bumping gums hisns fucking aint's *sorry, I gots to fuck you Negro* informative white ass! Willie *may he rest in Peace* comes June 73' be back to home to done seed us fools to be done graduated it the skooling cause it be hisns thirty-day back-to-home befo' Nam tour, FUCK, FUCK! July 73' my Boy' Willie *may he rest in Peace* never made mainland Nam. He had taken the tub over there yet there had been what the Uncle Sammy mofo letter to hisns momma done called-it complications, official records stated that an unavoidable accident had been encountered with the tub to land transport vehicle after breaking the underbelly of the ship. The skinny be my Boy' Willie *may he rest in Peace* and all them Bros had been packed inside the *chicken of the sea* tin-can transport big-*unlucky*-butts that Gawd damned fucking amphibious tuna-can done flipped-a-bitch then all thems Bros inside the can done drowned in the drink FUCK! FUCK! FUCK! July 73, come one fucking week befo' my official deck day, I sat my Boy' Willie's *may he rest in Peace* funeral FUCK! FUCK! FUCK!

The bastard of a Rear Admiral Lower-Half asshole done laughed-it most hardly when he done told-it to me that my contract for thems two-years buddy-buddy plan had been null-and-voided out the gate because one, I had been onliest seventeen and didn't have my parents signature on the document as fo' the second it be that I hadn't become a rifleman and the last number-tree ting be because the fucking Corps done invested their time and money to done trained my numb-nuts to be a jet engine mechanic therefore I would not be discharged come July 26, 1975 as per my null and voided buddy-buddy plan contract signed-it one hot summertime intellectual day August 72' FUCK, FUCK,FUCK! Furthermore he'd continued that I be in for the full-ride, the *death till we part* 6-fucking years witch be a full-stretch because I be just one dumb-ass jar-head Mofo who don't know shit from *Shinola* how to read a fucking contract! The Rear asshole told-it that I had to pull them firstest 4-years active-duty because of the shock-jock training and because I hadda done volunteered during a military conflict era then thems other two-years gonna be tacked-it on as active duty also and last yet not the most leastest be that my dumb grunt-ass would do WTF he or *they* done told-it for me to do *Emmet Till* July 1979 FUCK! FUCK! FUCK! FUCK! FUCK! FUCK!

To done topped-it all that bullshit off dat USN Rear Admiral Lower-Half asshole justa fo'reallies be laughing hisns funky-fat old white ass off that bastard old assed whiteboy whore had stood there across from me behind hisns gun-metal grey desk and dat ass-fuck done laughed-it liked a cockamamie homicidal motherfucker! I gots me a'nuttier full-stretch, 2-weeks in the brig for having jumped-it across that full-metal fucking desk to done snatched dat laughing white *you just been informed* ass, FUCK! FUCK! FUCK! The onliest smear on my military record be the incident on the Captain's deck seed yo' boy hadn't attempted to kill the messenger justa done ruffled hisns fucking white chicken-shit feathers a bite big-*man gotta do what a man gots to do*-butts because I had been more than capable in the performance of my engine, chip fucking paint and boots to ground duties according to the USMC *Tops* and *Gunnies* co-signed by thems scaly-wag sea scrum Navy Officers no further charges be brought up against my dumb-ass that be how that Rear asshole done put it to me befo' he slammed the hatch-door closed STF*ShutTheFuckup* tight on my big-*madda than a mofo*-butts truth be I done fo'reallies need-ed-it thems two-weeks of *chill dat ass* in the fucking isolated cooler to done chilled-it the fuck down, FUCK! FUCK! FUCK!

Thems old-heads rolling the brig done told me the *Baby, I'm fo' real* deal, theys schooled-it to me on the *wink-n-sly* seed thems talking-heads done told-it justa mite bit mo' differently than what dat Rear lowdown old ass-fuck dirty shitty asshole hadda done told-it. Thems fools done bumped-it that I had an *Angel* somewhere in the Corps because that Rear asshole had really wanted to rip-out my then still be to dis day virgin ass-hole to done tore me a new one just so nonya dems other Ja'rene bell-hop pukes be tempted-it to do the shit that I had justa thumped-it upon hisns po'white trashy ass big-*stupid*-butts with a hardline KISS! Theys done told that the Marine Corps upper echelon done straight-up told-it to that Rear Asshole to shove hisns candied-ass fucking feelings up hisns damned fat-ty white ass-cheeks then to go get-it fucked! Them talking-heads told-it dat the Corps officially ordered-it dat po'dunk bastard Rear Admiral iffn he wanted-it to hisns been punched the fuck-out hurt feelings ass could dry-docked my Black ass no mo' than two-fucking weeks then get me to Guam and or any fucking else where he could tote that fucking tub to done put my black ass on a transport bird homeland fo' a thirty-day because my black ass-cheeks will be decked Paris Island come due-date thems fucking Official Marine Corps Orders! FUCK-YOU justa fuck you Rear Admiral Lower-Half full circle-jerk asshole *deez-nuts*, Motherfucker!

chapter 30

AUGUST 75' MY ASS CHEEKS be smacked, cracked and squeezed as you damned well po'leased deep inside the rear-seats of a Trailways bus liked I be one dems friendly slant-eye asses aboard a Jolly-green excepting I be not one happy-nappy ass camper. My still pissed da' fuck-off big-*recruited*-butts not pissed on black ass be passing through them racists po'dunk mofo lousy fucked mis-States of the South thems lousy fucking still wannabees the *confederate south* thems major loser mis-States of the little *Missy-sip-pee, Ally-yo'sistago-bam-her* and call all yourns nuttier po'dunk male kinfolk to *Gee-orgy-her*! My pissed-off ass be enroute to done returned-it to the exactamente fucking jump-off where all my Ja'rene bullshit done firstest squared its rotten to the Corps ass seed I be justa bouncing black ass babyboy rolling back into the po'dunk land of the redneck klan aka Paris Island, South Kakka-lac-key! In all the karmatic dat be poetic justice there taint no butter place on earth fo' a pissed-it the fuck-off Black man in America to be! Blackfolks oral tradition be the real truth, Ruth of the actual not *his*-lying-ass-*story* concerning all dems southern islets, ports and points justa every fucking one all thems places Paris Island, Hilton Head Point and mostest to all them islets along the *Carol-lyin* redneck *Gee-orgy-her* coastal shorelines. Ole Honest Abe and the Congress done right after the Civil war mainly because *they* po'dunk whites all be justa chunk of the redneck sons-dey-bitchin assholes who wanted-it to keep us's the newly freed *We the Peoples* of a darker hue hurdled-it all together in one worthless place that be easy access to whens *theys* redneck asses done petitioned-it theys po'dunk *White males only* Congress to done reversed-it all thems toothless paltry anti-slavery laws witch the Union closed a winked-eye to its anti-slavery laws witch then done gotz overrun amok by thems mis-States populace of redneck losers *johnnie rebs*! Modern daze inner-city ghettos be of the same purpose as to all thems worthless isle-junkets just to be an uninhabitable place to keep Blackfolks nearby big-*outta sights*-butts not so far away dat Black ass be long on the gone! Thems loser *johnnie-hoe cake* mofos wanted-it spots within easy access to whens thems anti-slavery laws done gots reverse-engineered thus it be no furloughed conclusion both sides of the fucking racist coin hadda done felt-it that them islets along the Carolinas and Georgia Atlantic shoreline to be sway too isolated to be ports because a ship couldn't breech to any nor be thems bits of lands capable of producing any kinda crops yet thems islets be ever so close to thems plantations so *they* both purported to just give all them useless worthless islets over to the newly freed Negroes only. *Tank-God* for Biggy-smalls flavors caused *We the Peoples* done on the spot loved it to be glad just to have had thems wonderfully sunshiny islets with no po'dunks, no cotton to pick, no tobaccky to plant, no cane, no caning, no whips nor lynchings *tank God* nonya the heir-apparent real time reality of living Black amongst thems no-good evil-assed johnnie-reb po'dunk rednecks thus it be dat *We the Peoples* done gave a hale and hardy heart-felt *Tank-ya berry mucho* to both old Honest Abe and hisns pasty-white po'dunk body of Congress to have done given us Blackfolk in-accordance to *johnnie reb's* assessment that land that be worthless junkets and islets!

We the Peoples whom hadda been lucky enough to done inhabited those islands had from the git-go been superbly happy-nappy black asses to be outta sight and to be rid of thems *kill a muddafukka's naked black ass* cotton, sugar-cane and tobaccky fields. *We the Peoples* the new-owners of thems little islets be comprised mostest of a peoples whom hadda all been ex-slave fieldhands thus mostest to alls thems beautiful Black peeps hadn't been taught-it nor allowed-it to even speak English. That be why *We the Peoples* isolated of theys own accord done created for themselves a personal language a user friendly language a viable communication system a necessity for the any hurdled mass of any peoples. *We the Peoples* with the helpings of once *a'gin-n-juice* the Mother of inventions *Mz Necessity* seed motherfukkas go sway back into the Black man's daze upon this land big-*talkie*-butts *Mz. Necessity* stepped-it up to *We the Peoples* isolated freed Black asses *living the life* upon theys *Stevie* wonderful islets a world of wonders, a tranquilled peace for the Black be beautiful Black man, woman or child alone to theys Black selves away from the mainland theys done coupled-it up all friendlies-liked with *Missy Necessity* to done devised-it theys own and onliest theys own language. The language be formed-it outta a slop-jar mixture just a swell blend of sound bites dat be pieces of remembered African tongue and a shit-load of the gibberish speak Spanish, French, Creole and glued it all together with the spacklings of rural po'dunk English. Isolated-it away from the mainland of redneck po'dunks, theys done the right thing firstest in that theys educated their Black selves to love their Black selves firstest things first! Thems peeps being isolated done took the time to learnt-it to teach each to the other to love the one and all the others unconditionally then the time comes when *We the Peoples* mainland could no longer communicate with *We the Peoples* living on theys islets because thems damned *Ghee-chees* had theys own *Ghee-chee* islands and theys done learnt-it onliest deys own *talk Ghee-chee to me* damned language!

We the Peoples not sent-it to those worthless islets big-*ignorant*-butts living mainland became the problem seed we'z done been unschooled in the systemic southern redneck bigotry *they* 2ndhand readings, writings and speakings with all of it taught by the assed-out uneducated racist po'dunk. *We the Peoples* began to emulate the bullshit we'd done learnt-it from that redneck illiterate especially hisns firstest thing first witch be the White man's most prized worldly possession as well that shit be an unwanted pox unto this world witch be hisns po'dunk ass racist ignorance then before we done knowed-it WTF hadda done happened upon us *We the Peoples* mainland done become big-*uppity Negro*-butts the evil shit didn't stop there because shamelessly we'z hadda done turned-it all the po'dunk whiteboy racist shit inwardly to done served-it thems same shamelessly shitty-ass white turkey racist stuffings onto our chillens and our chillens children witch became a communal atrocity. *We the Peoples* on the mainland hadda unknowingly learnt-it the po'dunk out-right bullshit lies his-story as theory witch included mis-information abouts *We the Peoples* living isolated on theys islets and speaking onliest theys isolated language through the white man's po'dunk systemic unschooling for the *Negro only* to done learnt-it to done firstest thing first to done imitated dat redneck and hisns racist bullshit then it simply be *monkey see-monkey do* and we began to done called-it dat major chunk of *We the Peoples* living the good life on them islets thems damned know-nuttin gots shit fo' brains, lazy-ass, black ass *Ghee-chees* living foolishly on theys worthless shitty-ass *Ghee-chee* Islands!

The fucked-up ting be the hatred be real just as real as all the other racial hatred that has permeated and thrived unchecked alive and always *moving-on up* in a racially divided America since *1492 when dat greasy ass dago-WOP mofo Columbus done sailed the ocean blue* all that inter-cultural self-hatred be an all to the raw dog shared-it collective of the racial hatred bullshit witch be the onliest ting that fo'reallies of this world be all-American! Anyone living and educated within the American way of life has by systemic default an inherited all-encompassing pre-programmed racial hatred of all peoples this world evens iffn thems hated peoples be theys own damned Black asses and that chicken assed bullshit just be fowl like a muddafucka! In my youthful ig'nant daze iffn a'nuttier Black fool be to call an even nuttier Black fool a *nigger* then the shit be liked *K-kool mofo show yo' rights* big-*dumb*-butts iffn that same Black fool hadda done called-it that samed a'nuttier Black fool a *Ghee-chee* then da' shit be on and the switch-blades be clicked opened then put-it to no-good use because dat *Ghee-chee* calling muddafukka done needed-it hisns Black ass self an on the personal razor keen touch of the uppity-Negro hospitality thus dat *Ghee-chee* calling black ass just gotta be cut! The *Ghoula* Language be a beautiful language with sounds that be on the Superfly fo'reallies musical tones iffn youse to *Medgar Evers* gets-it to hear the spoken words of times ageless *sho' ya rights* its gonna be a sho'nuff treat for yo' big ass ears!

Chapter 31

TOP DONE GRABBED-IT MONKEY-FIST TIGHT ahold my black ass inside the bus-station, I'd done recognized-it that po'dunk skinny-ass soda-cracker the minute I'd stepped-it halfa-fucking black crusty uncut toenail inside that terminal, an *Angel* my ass, *Fuck me*! It hadda been *Beelzebub* hisns own damned evil assed self that done shooken-it my black ass offa that tub and outta dat brig! Rights there I done knowed-it dat RECON shit be justa gotta be gonna be all fucked the fuck-up! TOP be *toss me yo' shit, jigger-boo* to done snatched-it up my grip witch he flung the duffle into a Willie's jeep befo' he proceeded to done runned-it my *I knows I'm bouts to be fucked* ass in semi-dress khakis and low-quarters dems black leather dress shoes in'a fucking CC moment I be a'running hard a'pounding ground on paved roads bumping dress low-quarters, FUCK! The po'dunk cracker hayseed mofo had brought along Trips fo' the enjoyment and thems two insane idiots be on the living-it up in the land of po' assed-out country-pumpKin redneck *Hillbilly-bad-asses*! TOP and Trips theys had me sucking raw eggs as theys low-LIFER asses done runned-it me about 7-miles to theys backwoods RECON camp. TOP stood the back of that jeep, Trips drove da' mofo' and all the fucking way TOP done chained-smoked hisns funky assed unfiltered *Camel* cigarettes and everytime I'd done a fucking hang-dog, the mofo done flicked a lit butt offa my not so happy-nappy head *"Jitter-bug-eyed motherfucker, I gots you, I gots both of my good fucking eyes on you"* TOP be justa shouting a hardline stream *howdy pay ya' dues, Mofo! Welcome home scumbag did ja' sleep wells* hisns insane po'dunk shit be *In-coming* non-stop the each the every fucking stepped-it live *"Why youse little fucking jungle-bunny reject, I own you, I gots yo' black ass, jigger-boo! You tried to run yo' black ass to a fucking scrub-boy tub-house brig and miss out on me,* FUCK YOU, MOFO! *I own yo' black ass! You will perform by the numbers, you will square yo' black ass because as long as there is a red-tailed Devil reigning over Hell yo' jigger-boo ass will Semper Fi!"*

We done rolled-it through a straight-up red to da' neckbone hillbilly town seed I'd runned-it passed a full grown *Knights of the Columbus* billboard that read *Nigger, don't let the sun set on yo' black ass* a straight-up shit-burg be dat town and thems fake bewildered bemused looks on thems town fucks agaped *wide the fuck dick sucking open for business* ragga-mouths because theys all be just a chunk of the hillbilly fools withs theys one-n-onliest snaggly yella-toothed filthy pasty redneck *cabin shack in the hills* big-*pumpKin*-butt ugly faces justa all thems assed-out backwoods southern redneck peckerwoods had been t-totally bitchin *tits till Tuesday* looky-look that *Run-Nigger-Run* shit! Them soda-crackers had a look of the a'far taken back on the outsides theys ugly one be toothless fuck-faces that scene of a nigger-skinned uniformed Messkin driving a *Willies* jeep while the tall proud mofo standing in the back of sad assed jeep be a USMC full-dress blues redneck peckerwood dat done talked-it *theys* kinda *johnnie-reb* glory daze racist *aints gonna happen* bullshit to an on the hot-foot black mofo theys *a'suuueeehoooooowhoo-eeee baby Sue looky the niggra run* shit be the exactamente what fo' theys po'dunk redneck fucking hayseeds asses because to thems townsfolk fools it be *the south gonna rise* Heaven! Truth be told that welcome-to-home *homie* mat hadn't been nuttin special to a nonya dumb-ass *Welcome aboard* Mofo to the unit because that had been just exactly how TOP and Trips done re-acquainted themselves with each and every one of their special forces of voluntarily forced-fed recruits seed dat damned jeep be dems two raw dawgs *Welcome wagon to Hell*, Mofos! The fucking *Trailways* and *Greyhound* be the only public transportations into then out of that po'white trashy-trailer park of a hillbilly backwoods shit-burg *one stop-light be one too many* town when you arrived the meet-it up with TOP and Trips then theys done runned-it dat ass however the fuck that ass be dressed-it them 7-fucking miles to southern home fucked cookings!

TOP and Trips had been in the process of assembling theys personally own RECON team and thems two mean as fuck mofos be not clowning around! Theys hadda remembered me from theys last minute impromptu VC tunnels escapade, in fact mostest to all thems pound-ground through a shit-burg *racist aint the word it's the law* town on the hot-foot be the survivors of that *yo' wait a fucking sec* here be a last minute tunnel drop, Mofos! The main core of their RECON team consisted of a reserve unit of some twenty-five shit-fo'-brains *Messykins* and justa put it mildly them Mexican-American ex-reserve boys done gotten it the worstest seed us OTMs*OtherThanMessykin* mofos had all been active-duty big-*fucked*-butts thems Messkin reservists had been once a month week-end warriors, Hell them boys be almost full-fledged civilians and all of thems be from a reserve bare base fuels unit outta the southside of Tucson, Ari-*fucking*-zona thems beaner-boys been eating sto'bought tacos and farting refried greasy-ass pinto-beans, belching cervesas to be licking theys fucking lolly-pops all day everyday be dems wet-back suckas! TOP done booted em' square in theys gibberish speak asses or *culos* witch be just whats dems ex-reservists *taco-malo* bad-boys done hollered-it *tenemos bastante el culo-* We gots assed!

I done said-it them boys be mostly Mexican-Americans pain in the ass big-*wetback*-butts good *Gawd, all Hell to da Mighty Gawd damned-it* iffn thems beans-n-red chili shitting culos *it's only a dry heat* cacti humping Messykin bastards to done served-it up a real fucking purpose thems culos done gave-it a damned good fucking pause fo' da' cause and for the firstest time in many a'moons it came to be that I'd done gotten a good jelly fucking belly done rolled-it laugh seed *Emmett Till* dat training it be a fat fact, Jack dat I hadda never ever done heard-it that fucking derogatory term *wet-back* big-*I liked it*-butts that funky low-down turd hadda done dropped-it thissa way, TOP done shouted-it that racist assed name to *Elvis "tank-ya, tank-ya berry berry much"* Duramegas seed that *viva loco bato* crazy-ass bastard be alla-time *Thanking* people with a mocking of Elvis in Messykin voice. Firstest time, I had da' pleasure to have heard Elvis say dat shit be when dat mofo firstest done gotten hisns greasy asshole to the RECON barracks seed the mofo hadda gotten gum stuck to the bottom of hisns *zapatos* while running-it through thems redneck streets on hisns trek from the *Trailways* thens for fucking-it up the barrack's floor we'd been on all fours justa have had the honor to done hand polished-it hisns wooden floors then TOP done made Duramegas drop and give him a fiddie afterwards TOP hadda asked-it dat Messkin how'd liked-it that shit then fucking Elvis done answered back with a shake of the head, a twitch of the hips and in dat mocking *Elvis* voice *"tank-ya, tank-ya berry berry mooch-o"*

TOP hadn't never to ever done expected dat *you be clowned* shit from a Messykin cause then the po'dunk TOP had justa fucking done lost hisns redneck mind *"Who the fuck are you, are you fucking telling me that yo' greasy-dirty shit for brains ass is Elvis fucking Presley?"* TOP done made everybody in the barracks drop whatever the fuck dat *swinging balls under a stick* mofo hadda been fuck'n doing then-n-there every-*fucking*-body done had to duck-walk-it over to thems two then TOP made all us recon recruits give up a *fo' bye-bye fo' fiddie*, that's four-sets of fiddy each set and every one thems mofo's had to be a complete to the Commandant of the Marine Corps a straight-up no-bullshit, no-fucking slacked-it off, hard to da Corps push-up!

Elvis's real name be Alberto Duramegas, at that time he fat and out of shape because justa only a week and tree days befo' he'd been a civilian living the good life! Anywho the fo'reallies goodie-stuff done happened justa few days later, we had been on a field trip when un-be-done knowed-it to me, Elvis had gotten stuck crawling through the muck *"What the fucking fuck, a wet-back that can't swim"* TOP had shouted-it that shit from the other side of that muddy stagnant brackish sea water steeped muddy fucking creek bed witch we all be on the low-crawled-it thru and I be just ahead of Elvis then in hind-sight, I done guessed-it dat TOP musta done seed-it the lookey-look dat crossed my copper-toned handsome liked a mofo *children of a darker hue* face done registered a WTF did dat skinny-assed po'dunk whiteboy just call me?

"Not you jigger-boo that fat-ass numb-nuts dip-shit behind you! He's the fuck'n wet-back! You're a fucking black ass nigger ex-jungle-bunny! Know yo' station in life!" TOP shouted-it *"class time"* and done ordered-it everybody who done made it across that muck to get back in dat creek bed face down push-up position arms straight extended and locked then the whole unit be alongside me and Elvis in the fucking mucky-muck. TOP explained-it skinny-*po'dunk*-butts firstest ting he *"Now that dumb-assed numb-nuts jigger-boo-boy jungle bunny be a dumb-fuck* pointed-it hisns skank ass-scratcher et me *he don't know what the fuck is the wet-back* then he done pointed-it et Elvis, *Listen the fuck up! The wet-back, oh, he is someone quite special, he ain't yo' everyday slime scum sucking bastard mofo, not like the fucking greasy haired gee-hee*

speaking WOP! A fuck'n olive-oily ass bastard WOP that cunt-scab is here WithOutPapers that's ah east-coast illegal greaser spic-o-span, a spic he come up outta Porttoe Rico or he spanned the fuck'n ocean with his pig-shit for grease greasy-assed hair all slicked the fuck back, damned Italian dago bastard mofo come cross on a civilian tub all the way from Italy without the paper to wipe his fucking poor penniless cocksucking sister's fucking sore ass with! Not the crooked nosed kike, hymie ass fuck damn Jew-boy with girly braids on his fucking pinhead a gawd-damned fucking cheap-assed mofo who'd steal the fucking coppers off a dead man's eyes and fo' damn fucking sure not you jigger-boos who ain't gots God's good sense nor no fucking any elsewhere to be in God's great white world, woolly haired boo-bastards, I guess we just gonna have to learn to live with then tolerate y'all spooks! No, this here's a fucking greasy-assed dirty wet-back, that there Elvis, and he is something real fucking special like, the wet-back come up outta May-he-co jump his poor dumb no English speaking beaner shit for brains ass in the Rio Grande, splash across to El Paso, Texas then break every damn law known to civilized man. Talk like a spic, hair like a day-go, skin like a kike and smell like a coon! Hell, he is his own damned bag of the mixed fucking tricks!"

When I had done crossed-it that creek TOP made me drop right the fuck there and do a straight-up fiddie fo' laughing so damn hard at dat shit big-*po'dunk*-butts that racial hatred shit hadda been straight-up *Hater-ade*! Later dat nite Elvis done hit me with the down-low the real *fo'-one-one* about Mexican-Americans big-*beaner*-butts I can't lie da' lie, I hadda always done cherished-it to done remembered-it TOP's clowning of another race idiotic version of all the whys to be *how sweet it is* dat a po'ass assed-out Mexican done gots hisns Messykin ass to be a Mexican-American.

Chapter 32

Now to be fair-assed about the shit TOP hadn't stopped-it just with the nigger, spic, dago, jew-boy and wet-back shit that mofo hadda even done broken-it down the real truth, Ruth as to thems damned *collard-greens!* I knows it fo' a fat fact, Jack that mostest folks may or may not done *Medgar Evers* heard-it bouts thems fo'reallies country *pumpKin* folks thems collard-greens though a many done heard-it *collard greens* twells to the well informed redneck po'dunk dat shit don't be about some worthless ragweed growing-it up outta a garden-patch dat the niggras go buckwild fo'! Nawl, Sir seed c*ollard-greens* be dumb-assed inbred cloudy whiteboy slaves whose po'assed-out hillbilly redneck masters mostest times also be theys owns gawd damned fo'reallies by redneck blood daddies! Thems collard greens done been inbred-it firstest by some assed-out redneck having hisns very owned-it po'dunk white wifey to done fucked hisns redneck ass own son(s) to produce hard working dumb-as-a-rock fieldhands or it be the same way with theys own baby-daughters either po'dunk redneck daddy or po'dunk redneck junior would fuck baby-sis to produce fo' theys family a *Bob's me uncle* authentic *aint going no-where big strong* fieldhand(s) just to plow and till theys land! *Collard greens* be justa chunk of the cloudy-white human mules and dat be whys thems white-boys done been knowed-it all across America to done called-it the one to the other *jackasses* cause theys be family, kinfolk on the reals be theys stubborn mule asses!

Yeah Baby, it be *how low can you go* them assed-out po'assed po'dunks be straight-up whoremongers fo' dat paper! Mostest peoples done seed thems latter-day collard greens thems be those skinny-assed hillbilly rednecks snatched outta the country-sides bumped-it the military way then assed-out theys be the ones that done homeless-it up the city streets shuffling-about with theys crayon-written little *work fo' food* cardboard signs hand held all across America! TOP even done recruited a few of thems *collard-greens* fo' the unit bragging that *a man ain't a man, less he's gots himself forty-niggers and a mule*! The collard greens gots theys name same as all fucked-up racial hating names come about this world just liked everything else dat be made in America thems collard-greens theys dub done bumped-it from the way-back in the aftermath of thems slavery *good riddance bye-bye* days where the original authentic collard-greens done be inbred. It be dems times just out-side the Civil war then a po'assed-out po'dunk redneck woulda done married a po'assed-out po'dunk cracker woman big-*poor*-butts both theys po' redneck asses done knowed-it that the marriage be a farce seed the little white wifey onliest gonna be justa a'nuttier slave-mammy, nanny and cloudy-white slave producer to dat po'dunk husband/master of herns thens theys gonna sell herns chillens to thems *let's do business as usual* big-*done lost the war*-butts still plantation owners *johnnie-rebs* whom desperately needed-it *fuck the Union* thems slaves to work theys fields. It worked itself out thissa way seed firstest tings first little white wifey wassa gonna fuck and produce babies from the biggest of the nearby plantation's big Black bucks and that there be where the *collard* part comes from it be thems po'dunk redneck's off-shoot of the word colored. The redneck po'dunk would work the fuck outta the off-shoot(s)of hisns wifey until the younger buck(s) be of an age to breed with hisns own white momma over to over and a'gin-n-juicy Lucy because the most inter-breeding of the white wife to herns sons and grandsons be what done produced the lighter-to-whiter skinned-it collard-greens and as theys all *creme de café-latte* cloudy-white asses hadda done jumped-it outta the little wifey's *Easy Bake* oven liked *kittens offa mittens* thens the redneck po'dunk done sold theys cloudy-white asses to thems plantation owners and that be how redneck po'dunk assed-out whitey done made hisns po'dunk ass dat after the Civil war paper!

Thems once rich plantation owners done lost all theys *Thank God iffn there be a God* monies funding an inept evil assed revolt against the gubmint big-*penniless*-butts theys full of confederate scrip phony-monies asses couldn't afford to pay anybody nuttin thus thems once rich assholes needed-it theys evil asses a'nutter chunk of the slaveries. Thems money-hungry po'dunk hillbilly rednecks began to done made themselves a race of the cloudy-white asses to be bought, sold, bartered and traded-it on the excuse the pun the *black market* big-*evil*-butts business be business as usual under the tables just the same because thems collards be cloudy-white not Black slaves therefore thems gubmint revenuers couldn't tell the difference between a po'dunk redneck and hisns collard-green child slave so thems revenuers done winked-it a blind-eye to done let the redneck-daddy seller as well the collard-green slave owning buyer beware!

Them collards growed-it up into gigantic man-sized motherfuckers with big arms, big thighs and especially big wrists so theys can do the heavy-lifting and toil dat cloudy-white ass from befo' sunrise till a'sway past sun's down! All thems cloudy-whites whether theys be women or men be strong as *all Hell get the fuck outta there* be thems bitches theys be *Sampson* like strong big-*inbred*-butts with all that there inter-family inter-breedings theys be just as proportionally stupid as theys be biblically strong! Theys pure simple stupidity be one of theys major *tell-the-tale* signs of theys royalty and blood-line plus theys outstanding and easily recognizable physical traits be out-right call-signs of theys *a pure inbred* collard-green hereditary be that mostest thems fools be one-green eye and the other one brown theys be mixed-eyed and or cross-eyed motherfuckers as well the possessors of extra fingers, extra toes and all kinda little extra body parts liked nipples even genitalia thems simpleton fools be knowed-it hav'em both, a pussy and a dick thus it bestest be to never tell thems ig'nant cock-strong mofos to go fuck yo'self! Thems collard-greens be dumb asses so stupid dat even the fucking Army draft done rejected-it theys big strong cloudy-white asses bye-bye the shit loads for being too damned *stoopids*! Thems pre-draft set-it ups at rural train stations be dems on the fly recruit depots where po'dunk recruiters simply done tossed-it theys dumb-asses a pair of boots to see iffn theys could lace-em' up, it'd be plum foolishness *Surprize Surprise Surprize Sgt Carter* the WTF results! That there exactamente be the 2nd part of theys name because po'dunks theys gonna always be a'calling the unlearnt-it and the mentally underdeveloped some sorta green shit liked green-horns, green beyond the gills and green onions shit thus mostest thems fools be too fucking green to cinch-down a pair of combat boots!

TOP told-it to us and even pointed-it out to us thems collard-greens within the unit plus he hadda talked-it pure-assed rednecked country dumb-assed shit bouts how theys all be justa chunk of the fucking dumb-assed *motherfucking sister babygirl banging bring the nigger in from the cabbage patch to knock her up family fucking family* pumpKin mofo shits for brains assed-out tricks! TOP done always tried to done paired-it us up with a collard for any survival training seed thems dumb-ass sum-de-bitches done knowed-it full well instinctively what could and what could not be eaten thems collards done knowed-it this shit all-natural liked seed thems fools sniffed-it, examined-it then let ya' to done knowed-it iffn a green leaf or black bug or yella critter egg could be eaten or not and without fails thems cloudy-white bastards be justa instinctually *Right-on my brotha* bouts the eatable and or the non-edible shits of this world! Besides all dat survival shit thems damned collard-greens be the back-bone all-naturelle pack mules of the unit fo' obvious reasons!

Chapter 33

ANYWHO, TOP DONE NEEDED-IT HIMSELF a comm-guy dat be a real live communications albeit language specialist and there dat be how he done liaisoned-it my black ass. I be born in thems mid-fiddies, an April fool, an Aries to the zodiac nuts and horoscope fiends, *what yo' sign be, baby?* The real truth, Ruth be thems fiddies and dems early sixties hadda been the what dat done shaped my black ass for all dat it be to done become seed in all reality that short span of the times be my early years thems momma's tit be da' shit years! Justa pimple on a flea's nut-sack them late fiddies years be big-*shitty diaper*-butts me being a Negro boychild living in kluless klutzed klan-land *Whites only* mis-State of I-n-diana those be my ride or die years. Dad worked-it construction before construction be a living-wage for a Black man any parts racist America, so early on Dad hadda done made-it that paper and owned a shack with a piece of land on the outer-city limits of the CC. The peeps called-it them cabbage patches the *small farms* yet most of them sharecropper lots had been inhabited by po'ass assed-out foreign whitefolk thems *Po'lacks* of whom dems Unks' done told it, *dey bees po' and deys mainly lacks brains* big-*stupid*-butts thems *Po'lacks* be justa country po'assed-out illegal whitefolk not to be confused with po' white-trashy folk dat also be the *Word-up* from dem Unks'! Those types of peeps *In-coming* being newly arrived thus theys hadn't been born to nor had theys inherited dat all too deeply all-American ingrained *WASP*WhiteAngloSaxtonProtestant bullshit sliced outta the all Christian American dogma racial segregated redneck religious shit pie!

The city gubmint started to build this big-ass school in the heart of the hoodie finally fo' us black folks, the school be a huge main building with two wings attached-it and all tree thems buildings be two-stories high plus there be a gigantic gymnasium attached to the complex. The main building and the one wing be pretty much your standard flare American inner-city 19-fiddy/60 school, double red-brick, pane glass windows and rectangular center with flag pole dab smack the middle of it all. The anti-city gubmint peeps fought with them pro-city *Toms* thems dumb-assed Negroes who a tinkering theys be *Mr. Charlie's* favorite uncle about how dat school wassa gonna be a whitefolk college versed what dems *Toms* had purported-it all to be big-*lying*-butts mostest peeps done thought-it that shit be *Whites only* lies told-it by thems po'dunks so the peeps wouldn't steal shit nor vandalize the damned thing being it be situated deep inside the hood. There had been a big reconciliatory gentleman's agreement amongst *We the Peoples* when dat second-wing done got built cause it had no real windows just 12-inch by 10-foot long glassed slits be portioned-it through-out the outside walls thens everybody thunk-it theys *lying-assed po'dunks* a'gin-n-juice specially after that second-wing done gots all thems big air-conditioning units placed-it atop its roof. In the end, everybody done proved-it to be just as wrong as theys be right them firstest 2-years 61'and 62' them *Toms* be the *Right-on*! It be an elementary school for the *Colored only*, I did first-grade then second-grade in the school, *No pro-blame-mo*! The onliest thing be that during all that time, we kiddy-stuffs onliest gots use of the main building plus wintertime we got to play inside the gym. Come spring 63' one warm and colorful for the *Coloreds only* springy day the school hadda opened-it up that one regular-styled wing then it be *Surprize Surprise Surprize-o Sgt Carter* cause we done gots flooded-it up the yahoo with a chunk of wild-assed baby *parakeets* whom be dems damned Puerto Rican kids, dems faster than fast gibberish speaking islander kiddy-stuffs at the lunchtime theys punk-asses done come on the hotfoot thru those finally opened-it wing doors a'hollering all kinds of the gibberish crap *"Jo amigo negro, como se llama? No hablas*! *Besame culo,* puto! Hello, my Black friend, what's your name? You don't speak gibberish! Kiss my ass, bitch! After that day we tree the Colored/Negro and thems Parakeets done learnt-it all our schoolings in both the English and theys gibberish speak Spanish. Every morning all the lessons be taught to us Colored/Negro in Spanish in that first wing then after lunch we'd switch with thems Keets and go back to the main building where it be the same lesson big-*gibberish speak*-butts taught in English. *Tio Suga-risimo* had provided that I be taught to read, write and speak fluent Puerto Rican gibberish speak and I'd kept to the gibberish *Emmett Till* I done graduated high school big-*e'nuffs e'nuff*-butts for mostest peeps when them Spanish classes became an elective after the start of 7th grade, it be *adios Mofo*!

On a personal level that Spanglish-shit had proven to be more than just *All to the Good* because as life went onward and upward thens thems little Puerto Rican girls that hadda bounced-it through thems newly opened-it first wing doors dat 63' lunchtime swells thems small-*pooh*-butts *con* cooties justa few years later thems *chiquitas* done burst-it forth big-tittied muneca's babydolls *Jello, J-Lo' dems creme café-late-booty-bumps n' lady lumps* be da' shit, baby! The fights to get to them caramel-delights big-*bouncing*-butts we done fought-it hard against herns older *parakeet* males *Gawd damned* switchblade toting razor thin skinny-assed gibberish speak ex-island whores thems fucking daddies, uncles, cousins and brothers be a living Hell seed thems skinny assed-out black beans-n-rice shitting putos all thems *cabeza* de *plancha* iron-head *hijos de putos* SOB mofos done talked-it with theys hands then thems ugly assed-out sons-of-bitches done jabbed-it and upper-cut it with *fuck the gibberish* theys switch-blades done spoke loud be clear the perfect fucking English!

Fighting through herns gibberish speak protectors of the *PP&J* be da' Brotha's worst nightmare, I'd be justa lucky nuff' to get a few *frenchy* styled kisses with maybe a super *lucky strike* be to done gots justa dip the tip of my stinky-finger on or ever so slightly near herns Heaven's portal cotton-candy panties covered virgin entryway into the 100% pure *parakeet prune juice can ya dig it*! *Sock-it to me, Mamacita*! Check da' shit out, a ghetto school brand stand spanking f'n new for the ghetto fabulous only, biggest gym in the city, a sniffers chance of getting some pure *PP&J* dat shit be not so bad fo' a Brotha borne of thems *out in the fucking open racist* 19-fiddies America! Oh, oh lest I forgots, after that firstest springy day neither we nor thems the damned kiddie-o *Keets* could bring a sack-lunch to the school thems *Whites only* guv'mint ass-hauling whores done ruled it be no mo' *brown bagging-it* from dat day forward all lunches became free to anybody and everybody somes say *there be no such thing as a free lunch"* Swell, Sir them *somes* bitches be exactamently right!

Chapter 34

THE FIRST DAY OF SCHOOLING past the Christmas break 63' all Hell to beat all fucking Hell done *tasty-freezed* it the fricking over seed come January 64' *they* done opened-it thems last remaining doors to the 2nd wing, the one with no real windows and when thems sums-dey-bitches hadda throwed-it wide the fuck open dem damned doors to dat window-less 2nd wing right at the free-lunch time just after we the Negro/Colored/Keets be all lined-it up for thems free-lunches a'gin-n-juice *Surprize Surprise Surprize Sgt Carter* it hadda been one *Good Gawd Dammed, all-gotz damned Good Gwad Amighty* excuse my *Frenchies* all the soupy shit done splattered across the proverbial fan because all *shucky-shucky* to the *WTF* now was never there to be, we the Negro/Colored/Keets done got the bums-rush by chunk after demented retarded chunks of the po' white trashy dirty-blonde raspberry-pimpled ugly-faced teen-aged boo-bastards! When thems fucking 2nd wing doors be done opened-it thems shitty-shits hadda just bursted-it the whole cafeteria loose with the po'dunk retard *Whites only* teenaged asses thems pinky-faced po'dunk fucks done spread-it out into and unto our free-lunch cafeteria whereby the each and every one of them demented tow-headed cockroaches, thems crippled-it up SOB chowder-head returds gots in-accordance to the racist day of thems openly racist times theys po'dunk white-ass crippled-it up asses done got placed-it upfront ahead of us the Colored/Negro/Keets so theys crippled-it up asses be at the head of that free-lunch program line, kid you the frick not! Thems cafeteria old blue-haired white granny-crones done just walked-it all thems crippled-it up teenaged fool fucks right fricking smack to the front of the free-lunch line and nobody done said a'nuttin! That there granny gangster-shit be thems on the reals racist 60s not thems flower-child hippie-freaks pictured in thems lying-assed *his*-white ass-*story* books hawking a *make love not war Peace* loving 1960s America!

Thems po' white returd trashy bitch-bastards be not your normal everyday type po'white trashy teenaged bitch bastard big-*crippled*-butts thems fools be your *Gwad damned theys be cursed by God justa any damned body's God* Whites only crippled-it ups and thems fools be lame dumb-asses theys be the fricking real Mc-*handicapped*-Coy thems down-right paraplegic fucks be what thems trashy-whitey teenaged whores be! Thems fricking cripple-it up fools be yo' deformed retarded po'white trashy demented sum-de-bitches white po'dunk illiterate fucks! Thems *Whites only* crippled-it ups sums-dey-bitches be the idiotic from the one to thems all plus all theys retard asses be wheelchair bound, steel-hooks fo' hands and mostest thems fools theys feets, hands and arms be born deformed-it in that theys limbs be scrawny, short, partials, prosthetics and or theys outer-limbs be attached to theys crippled-it up body backwards or at some kinda a'nuttier weird deformed angle! Good Gwad damned, added to all that fucked-it up shit be that theys pasty raspberry big-ass pimpled butt-ugly acne white fuck-faces be justa slobbering and drooling *"uggh-ugghh-uggh"* and mo' than a lots thems fools be wearing a white fricking football helmet thems racist returded bastards be the bitches of all dems dat be racist white crippled-it up teenage bitch bastards! First off, theys be teenagers/young adults 15+ we'z be just jo' plain dark chocolate covered almonds with a few gibberish-speak vanilla sprinkles elementary school flare 5 to 9 year-old school non-deformed non-retarded kids. We had to share the lunch room ergo that *free-lunch* program, the gym and we'z done *Sooners* learned-it the best damned free movie theater in the inner-city! The personal don'ts gets no mo' personal than being gathered-it up then force fed to mix-it up with the butt-ugly chunk after chunks of the retarded white crippled-it up teenaged racist whores for schoolmates and every last one be of the *sad-sap* variety fools theys be the mean-spirited worstest fricking crippled-it ups po'dunk fucks to ever done invaded an elementary school for the Negro/Colored/Keets only!

Thems damned Keets had done gotten it just right in theys impish *parakeeting* minds that it be bestest fo' deys asses to done paired-it up with us Negroes/Coloreds against thems white po'dunk returds and help us to fight thems retarded crippled-it up po'white trashy teenaged bastards tooth to theys fricking crippled-it up steel-pincher pointed curved hooks fo' hands! In the blink of an evil pink-eye thems retarded white bitch whores hadda done started-it to pinch, jab, poke and scratch our arms, thighs and any other black and gibberish speak body parts they could snare with theys fricking full-metal pincher/hooks fo' hands thems acne-faced big-*fatty*-butts mostest 'cepting thems of the worstest sadistic genre thems super Whites only racist purposefully cruel bitch whores seed in general the most done left our nappy/straight-haired heads alone yet there be those few crippled-it up evil hillbilly-bad-ass cripple-it ups to done called-it out *nigger boy/island nigger* to done went on the attack wildly swinging theys steel pincher/hooks fo' hands! Thems handicapped sadistic returds always to be done rolled-it theys crip-rides, theys wheelchair atop a Negro/Colored/Keets foot then lock the wheels in place seed it had been war, a teenagers against little tykes war, healthy verses teen crippled-it ups war, Black/Parakeet intellect verses White retard war and alls fair in a gots *no love fo' yo crippled-it up ass* war withs teenaged butt-fucking uglies besides the Hollywood reels done told-it firstest *war be Hell*, Babycakes!

We woulda tooken thems wooden rulers wrapped rubberbands around a handful then we'd done jimmy-jammed them 12-inch power sticks between the spokes of theys rolling *crip-ride* so when dems rulers hit a solid part of the wheelchair both rear-wheels lock-stopped-it on the quick to done send-it theys crippled-it up asses flying through the air aka *Super-Stoopid* crippled-it up boy to done bounced that returd ass down that cripple-it up ramp on the SuperFly, baby! Fo' thems crippled-it up mofos with theys backward assed feets we tossed-it a handful of the BBs onto them handicap ramps then *Bobs me uncle* thems wannabe *Bojangles* shuffling reversed-footed po'dunk bastards be flailing, falling and sliding ass first down thems ramps. Fo' thems steel-hooks that be pinchers fo' hands po'dunk mofos we had started-it to done rolled-it bits of all that green/grey molding clay around pea-gravel rocks then we'd ping thems sum-dey-crippled-it up bitches with homemade slingshots. Thems clay covered pea rocks onliest done stung-it the evil-assed bastards big-*crazy*-butts then the clay woulda done made the little pea-rock stick to theys pasty acne white skin then thems punk-assed peckerwood crippled-it up bastards be shit outta luck and royally fucked! Theys retarded asses attempting to remove a pea-rock pebble offa theys *Whites only* skin with stainless steel pinchers/hooks for hands or even butter yet to have a'nuttier crippled-it up buddy to be using hisns steel pinchers/hooks to assist in the removal, fuck it be thems fucking crippled-it ups returds who done invented the buddy-buddy plan!

The worst part be the cafeteria because we'z done sat-it directly across from thems butt-ugly acne covered white pasty faces witch always be justa drooling and justa straight-up slobbering-it *UGGH-Ugggh—Ugh* it be hard to stomach any kinda meal when you be forced-fed to lookey-looked at that chunk of the slobbering teenaged returded crippled-it ups on the constant with theys endless *ugh-ugh-uggha-googa* shit Good Lawd! We had truly earned-it them fricking free-lunches ergo taint no such ting as a fricking free-lunch in this world! War with them retarded crippled-it up po'white trashy teenaged bastards had been the highlights of my elementary school daze just to be about kicking-it in theys crippled-it up teenaged white returded asses, *Yes, Sir* dat be returded war, and it be lit, Babycakes!

I and everybody be a winner, all the old timey peeps be exactamente right in their own way thems *Toms* with theys Negro only school theory as swell dems anti-city gubmint peeps in that the school be built with other intentions in-mind! *Yes Lawd,* thems po'dunk gubmint whores had intended to make an elementary Negro only be little elementary Negro human guinea pigs that had to done learnt-it to read, write and speak it the parakeet gibberish whilst simultaneously fighting-off a bad chunk of handicapped returded teenaged slobbering *ugh-ughugga-uggha* racist crippled-it ups! I be the *winner-winner self-esteem dinner* because I done formally learnt-it the gibberish speak at an early age, that shit be scientifically proven statistically that early life foreign language training greatly enhanced the development of a preschooler's cognizant thinking then bumping thems uglies with the damned to be cursed returd cripple-it ups in'a it be war, baby! I done learnt-it firsthand to reject all racist white supremacy bullshit be it heard, said and or to done read-it through systemic uneducation for the Negro only schooling that onliest be about promoting all *they* racist Whiteboy firstest bullshit! I done lived-it on the daily-double experienced reality 5-days a week, the real deal of being an all-American teenaged whitey onliest made you a handicapped, retarded, crippled-it up in dire need of an old grey-haired white granny fo' to be yo' butt-ugly pasty face po'dunk crippled-it up redneck ass protection thus my experienced reality refuted the racist Whites only braying jackass that done tried-it to blow any form of the racial inferiority bullshit all-American propaganda smoke up my young Black be beautiful ass! I had on the daily-double *All hands on deck* been force learnt-it to believe the reality of what my beautiful baby-brown eyes done seed and my big wide-opened black ears done heard and that witch my enhanced mind done read of all the prevailing unthinkable *hate the Negro* White folk racist rabble propaganda outta them fiddies, sixties and seventies *bye-bye mofos good* riddance! I be 7 going on the 8-year, thems *tender-roni* most impressionable of years and the very first thing that I had been taught-it be the bestest thing that I would *Medgar Evers* be done learnt-it in this life: Do not for a *CC moment* believe them white lies about white racial superiority because it all be pure 100% unadulterated *Whites only* bullshit lies big-*propaganda*-butts dat bullshit be a well-orchestrated government sanctioned institutionalized systemic Whites only bullshit!

At the up-start to my journey of a Black man's life bumping a redneck America, I done learned-it straight-up the real truth, Ruth the end that justify the means to walk this gigantic ball of dirt like a man as a man then it hadn't to have mattered-it *one swit the White devils shit* whether the done learnt-it classroom be et Unk Zeke's pond or *Mr. Charlie'* by default gibberish speak classroom for the *Negro only* unschooling! I had been given the formal training and day to day experience to done walked through the all-American segregated valley of death been straight-up taught-it to be a man that done learnt-it to fear no evil tho' I'd done seed-it to done heard-it a'plenty abouts its evil vile po'dunk redneck ass! Much love to all my Spanglish teachers a heart-felt shout-out *Grassy-ass, Mofos*! To the po'white trashy crippled-it ups as swell dems *para-Keet-toes "Kiss my ass, you returded crippled-it up motherfuckas and Besame culo, putos*!" To those fine-assed buxom booty-bump done growed-it up Lady-keets, *holla@ya' Boy, Chula*!" I believed-it that my Spanglish schooling hadda been exactly the what that be the how that dat mofo' TOP hadda finagled hisns po'dunk rednecked ass a'sway to *snatch dat ass* because hisns po'dunk cracker-ass had a dope-fiend's addictive need to done controlled-it a'nuttier man's dumbass life! I be fluent in tree languages English, gibberish and *OH, Hell to the yeah* CC jive thus in a world of jumbo jets and gigantic aircraft carrier flat-tops that little itty-bitty bump on a wood tick's nut-sack, my formal gibberish speak schooling hadda technically done made my dumb-ass out to be a tactical forces communications language specialist as swell just a'nuttier *who'dat* done learnt-it to *Semper Fi* Mofo!

Chapter 35

TOP's TRAINING HAD BEEN T-TOTALLY brutal, a straight-up living hell, pound sand then pound sand to done pounded-it mo' sand all the day then all the Black knight be long! TOP be exactamently liked 1SGT *Big Johnny* Tidwell *no happy-asses* at hisns hillbilly backside! Time woulda done proven-it fo' me dat all that *no fucking happy-asses* shit be a fo'reallies ting to be done wanted-it and needed-it by any warrior when the shit be blowing offa dat fan! My dumb black ass just liked-it both 1SGT Big Johnny and TOP done on the jackrabbit quick be to done learnt-it not to want *no happy-asses* at my backside neither because when ya stopped-it to done tooken-it just a peek maybe justa lookey-looked peek-a-boo over at yo' Bro, I hadn't ta never ever done wanted-it to done seed a smiling happy-ass lessen dat Bro be one of thems *collard-greens* whom didn't have a clue as to WTF be up about controlling all theys fucking wild-ass offa the cuff WTF be this shit emotions! Them collard greens always be doing in-appropriated shit at in-appropriated times every fucking minute of the day thus it bestest be fo' yo ass to done accepted-it dat theys minds be lost and all caught-it up into something dat be stupid because thems fools be mentally challenged and totally unstable sway past the point of all that be wild-ass stupidity! TOP and Trips done taught-it and we'd all done learnt-it reals fucking early on to just done accepted-it anything thems dumb-assed fools done surfed-it up then to done justa let theys dumb-shit be!

In the heat of the moment, the zeal of the battle seed the shit that done spooked-it my dumb-ass hopefully hadn't *Lawd hava Mercy* done had the same effect on my Bros locked-n-loaded battling like a motherfucker thus my Bros being unfretted by the calamity of the chaos be holding it *Sweet-tea Jesus* strong a poker-face justa calm steely-eyed locked-jaw thrust-it forward bumping a serene harden-edge straight-out handling hisns business thumping-it hisns babygirl's high and tight ass liked a motherfuck'n killing machine gone awry! Everything be all kool *agent orange Kool-Aid* fucking kool thens I could done settled-it the fuck down to done did what hadda had to be done! Big-*smiling*-butts iffn ya' Bro be wearing a skinning and grinning a'scared shitless WTF mask doing that lookey-looked moment then that shit be justa fucked the fuck-up! Fo' the fun of it when we be justa fucking-it off riding low in thems Herks along the Amazon we usta shoot-it at thems runt monkeys atop thems tall trees then we be justa strumming-it them babygirls popping theys shitty-browns swing-monkey-swing asses outta them tree-tops along the river's edges there always be a shit-load of them small brown yella-ish mange assed-out runt-monkeys big-*swing time*-butts when the one monkey done seed a'nuttier monkey's ass done been shot the fuck-up then dat monkey woulda done skinned-it back hisns lips in a funky kinda grin cause he/theys all be a'scared shit-less, frozen to the spot thus when that one monkey bastard be a'scared liked a motherfucker frozen to the spot then all thems other bitch-asses be frozen too thus theys all be easy fucking low-hanging fruit. That be how TOP and Trips done learnt-it us that the a'scared-it ass Mofo be a monkey dead ass, Mofo! When yo' shit done hit the bottom of yo' tank and you be frying yo' last wits to figure witch way be up then you had never wanted-it to done peeked-it a *skinning-grinning* happy-assed Mofo's ugly-assed mug lessen the mofo be one of them emotionally unstable collards! That be the way of TOP barking the racist stupid shit that woulda gotten hisns skinny white-ass all fucked-up on any inner-city street corner to done clowned mofos every step of the way hisns po'dunk ass be making fo' damned sho'nuff sure dat all us dumb-asses done learnt-it to hold that water and fuck dat *happy-to-be here, Boss* happy ass, shit!

"You red-eyed syphilitic scum-bags, you wanna sleep?" dem times TOP be done awaken us outta a just getting to the goodie-stuff sleep *"Well, you'll fuck'n sleep in yo' Gawd damned coffins, shake that ass, scum buckets!"* My bunk bride be a'nuttier one of them ex-reservist outta Tucson *dry fucking heat my black ass* Arid-zona Pfc. Humberto Castaneda, the mofo be supposed to have been a barber liked hisns illegal assed wetback daddy be big-*run away*-butts he had shucked-it thems *chili-bowl on a beaner's big emptied-ass lettuce head* snip-n-clip to done stupided-up *Ja'rene*! *Who-B-C* be one thems illegal Mexican that done growed-it up in Compton, Ca. he talked-it more jive than any Brotha and *Who-BC* backed dat jive-talk shit with a sweet-ass right-crossed coming at ya' upper-cut that bato had a mean flash followed-it just

as lightening quick with a *Mommacita said to knock you out* left fucking hook! Who-BC be the onliest man ever dat I done to meet in this life dat be a non-vegan mofo who didn't chow-down a step-light! I'd be liked *Who-BC, how'd fuck, you done growed-it up in Compton amongst all them Blackfolk and don't jack-jaw a yard-bird*! He done explained-it dat shit to me in the *Blaxican* fashion to done holla dat he'd be done growed-it up in dems early fiddies there be no paved streets nor sewers so all the poor assed-out peeps just tossed-it theys piss and shit outta window using bedpans and piss-pots *you ain't got a pot to piss in* meant you be one po' assed-out motherfucker who hadda hang hisns pecker offa windowsill to let fly with a morning piss! Who-BC told-it hisns neighbor be an old skool *Bro* raised-it them step-lights and dat brotha-man sold dem yard-birds to dem *loco* butchers along the way! Who-BC growed-it up assed-out po' hisns outta *Met-he-co* family done backstroked-it that Rio Grande thens theys all be living-it po'assed out *nigger-vile* Compton, *Cali-fuck-ya* seed the thing that trucked-it with Who-BC and thems yard-birds be that whenever folks threw theys fucking shit and or garbage outta theys window then all Bro-man's skeleton assed step-lights done hauled-it ass over to dat spot and ate that shit up liked wild fire! Who-BC be liked fucks thems damned chicken-shit yardbirds cause you don't know what the fuck be inside that shit eating, piss drinking, yard scratching fowl-assed bitch! You be what you done et!

Our first break time, TOP done brought in a damned step-light then he had everybody imitate that damn yard-bird's strut to done moved-it on the balls of our feets, summertime later we done had to step across these fucking tree to fo'-foot round 24-foot long assed logs that be about 6-feet above the ground hoisted over mud-pits with hanging ropes. We had to lift one knee high into the air then stretch that lifted-up leg and maintain balance on the ball of the other foot before placing the lifted foot down onto that log on the dead run just to make it the fuck across seed a mofo had to done stepped-light the length of that hoisted *swinging like a motherfucker* redwood thus balance be the name of that game and dat shit hadda been foul! TOP always had some kinda fucking whiteboy fucked-it up reasoning *"Yo' fucking silken-drawls get wind whipped then you find yo' dumb-ass drifted to be a hundred-fifty feet above ground whisked onto a ledge or rock shelf, you best to be stepping light, or you'll gonna be one dead chicken-shit mofo!"* TOP crowed *"You chicken-shit jarhead gyrene bastards, better'n learn to fucking step-light!"*

Anuttier Spring break, TOP done brought in two cages, a big one with two male monkeys inside it and the other a smaller cage witch housed-it the one female monkey. TOP had let them two male chimps sniff round the bitch-in-heat then thems two horny-assed bastards done fought-it to the death do theys part for herns monkey hairy ass affections! Thems male *blue-balls aching* chimps hadda bumped-it up ugly tooth until the bigger horny assed monkey done died! The larger monkey had started out with a smallish patch of white hairs on the bottom of hisns big funky-monkey ass big-*funky*-butts by the end of the fight mostest those funky little white hairs be missing. TOP made us, those amongst us dat done knowed-it how to count, to done counted-it the each unto the every what hadda been left of them remaining white hairs on that dead monkey's filthy ass *Good Lawd* the funk! *"God do the choosing, when God place an ass before you it don't matter how big or how fucking strong that ass be! You gotta snatch dat ass*!*"* TOP swung through the jungle like *Dolomite* bumping gums survival of the fittest instructions *"kick, punch, knees, elbows and ass-holes, bite that ass, do whatever the fuck it take to snatch an ass, monkey fight, never fucking ever forget the white hairs on that dead monkey's ass Gawd damn-it! You ghost-turd mofos want to survive this world you best to learn to snatch that ass*!*"* Boy did we fight besides our inner-group fighting there be regular boxing, kung-fu, jujitsu, street-wrestling and bar-room brawling and all the running, jumping, face-slamming push-ups plus the regular physical training *side straddle hop* fucking Marine Corps *get jo' ass some mo'* PT! We trained rifles, ten-inch blades and hand-guns in those eleven months my trigger-finger had gotten so raw-dawg that I thought I would never again be able to scratch a *shakey-puddin* big-*lucky*-butts whilst on 30-day leave after the camp *tell-it-all Thelma* done shouted-it down from herns mountain perch dat my trigger-finger be justa fine *Kool-Aid* cherry punch fine!

Chapter 36

Under the unwatchful eyes of Prez *slip and fall* Gerald *I'm-a-fucking-goof-ball* Ford our specialized platoon hadda pretty much went and did what the fuck-ever when the fuck-ever and where the fuck-ever TOP hadda had a hankering to venture just to done stepped-it both balls knee deep into a somebody's foreign non-virgin asshole onliest to done fucked-it up theys gibberish speak day big-*fighting*-butts all good tings gonna end thus Prez *dry-roasted peenutz* Jimmy-*I gots soggy peas fo' nuts*-Carter musta done drank-it sway too many of them *Billy beers* then that bastard country-hick Presidential mofo' done thought-it that he the Commander and Chief and dat hisns dumb-ass be running the fucking show because that britches-hitching hayseed mofo' done officially ordered-it us to crack our nuts *soggy-bottom* style confined to them wet-bushes of the South East Asia and to firmly grasp and understand hisns words *No fucking place else*! Shit, I hadda done thunk-it that goober-bumping bastard be a *God-fearing* country bumpkin pew-boy! Anarchy, revolts and up-risings and all kinda shit be happening world-wide big-*pewboy*-butts *JimmyC* hadn't wanted-it fo' a handful of empty-headed ja'renes rolling upon some 3rd world country to be fucking-it up for thems diplomats yet all *Hell to redneck southern belles* them diplomatic dip-shits be doing too good a job of fucking the shit all the fuck-up all buy-buy theys damned selves!

South East Asia, I done popped-it my RECON cherry somewhere Cambodia 76, dat virgin tour lasted-it about tree-months, *poncho* city, no tents nor mummies/sleeping bags just one rain shitty-ass slicker fueled by the field bacon dems voles, rats, snakes or starve! The mission be a search-out to destroy a group of gooner-chinks running an anti-aircraft communications jamming system deep inside that slant-eye jungle. We be a 16-man training unit and everyone had hisns very own and separate section of dat jungle to search and secure. TOP and Trips done mapped-it all, assigned it all then thems two had set up HQ within range such dat every tree-days you buzzed the mike to let my dumb-ass to done knowed-it dat you be still alive. Every day-tree iffn I hadn't gotten them 15 clicks by noon and clickety-clicked it HQ then the search fo' dat missed-it unclicked, da' mofo be on! Good thing be I done always got my clicks, the bad ting hadda been thems fucking daze on end of the tireless boredom seed I be all the fuck alone to that fucking wet assed constant rain drizzled jungle justa lonely assed-out mofo on an island and I hadda no clue as to how to control my mind. My dumb-ass had no idea how to tender thems thoughts and still be alert to scratch, sniff then fucking destroy! On the daily-double it just be me, *Geraldine* and a few of herns bestest girlfriends: the M-1 carbine throw-down rifle a manual single-round load emergency back-up the fuck up rifle, a *Smith-Wesson* .357 wheel gun witch a'gin-n-juice be hand-loaded using dems speed loaders, *Colt*.45 auto, grenades, C4 and a small cache of other personal combat weaponry at the ready all the whilst I done scanned-it for thems fucked-up slant-eye soft-*commie yella* ass-targets. At first, the loneliness done deeply penetrated to done messed with my not so happy still nappy like a mofo head! It be the firstest time Medgar Evers fo' me not having a'nuttier person to fuck with swells that be the fucking shit that trucked-it *dis shit be over* my dumb-assed head just all the emptiness! The bullshit questionable living arrangement all alone and nearer to the edges of an untapped intellect be liked *Zeke, what the hell you be doing here, Bro? Why you be up in this wet-assed tree? Ain't nuttin out there butts cheetahs and leopards, take yo' monkey ass to home*! In time, though I done got ahold the ley of the land to done learnt-it the key to that RECON profession be learning to live life within yourself!

A man had to on the daily-double be to done mentally challenged-it hisns mind in the setting of limits, goals and boundaries fo' hisns thoughts then to done kept thems corralled-it thoughts hurdled together in one easy to get to place liked the po'dunk done kept us *who'dats* on thems worthless *Ghee-chee* islets and all theys inner-city ghettoes *Emmett Till they* can chain us backs to slaving thems fucking plantations, news flash *aints gonna happen*! That mental shit be more important than the setting of physical goals liked how much ground to cover and most importantly when the fuck and what the fuck to eat yet that being my firstest mission then my dumb-ass be nowhere near privy to that kinda self-containment of the intellectual and logistical knowledge big-dummy-butts my inner survival of the fittest be on the looky-look out fo' some that self-acknowledged wisdom shit! The good thing be that I hadn't had to done learnt-it dat shit on the fly, I hadn't had to dodge that curve-ball all by my lonesome self it just so happened-it and totally unknowingly I'd been toting inside my rumpsack a friend fo' the ages. TOP in hisns infinite wisdom and *Hell to the yeah* I cussed-it that skinny po'dunk backwoods redneck mofo' for a solid week big-*looking out*-butts TOP hadda strapped-it the blinders to my big nappy head to done kept me focused along the narrow path seed that skinny po'dunk bastard done *Saran* wrapped-it two books and placed them two fucking books where my food rations were supposed to be secured inside my rumpsack. When I had discovered that shit, I be hungry as all to *Hell with redneck southern belles* then I done just gots it even mo' madder than a motherfucker *who'dat* just done strolled-it upon a'nuttier mule kicking-it in hisns stall!

Every time we hadda jumped-it into a training-zone that fucking mofo' TOP done always taken a combat boot to the asses of two maybe tree of us pups cause we be justa bunch of the fucking retread retards

TOP would take a'nutter dumb-ass fo' a little walk-n-talk outside the hangar where we'd be awaiting a *fairy Herk* then the fucking psycho Trips or a'nuttier assigned trainee done replaced-it that talked-it to one's reserve chute with some of TOP's educational material thus we'd all learnt-it quite quickly very fucking quickly earliest on in jump-school training that there gonna be dems times witch you only had the fucking one-shot at them rip-cords, *Don't Fuck-it Up*! I'd been prepared fo' dat shit big-*ass-hole*-butts that shit hadda been training big-*dummy*-butts me being in that Cambo' jungle and it be a live real world fucking on-fire mission thus the question be, why the fucking bullshit? Answer, because there will always be the BULLSHIT!

I hadn't been a total dumb-fuck dumb-ass, I'd hidden beef jerky any-to-everywhere in my packs, on my uniform, taped to my body and I had been rationing that jerky *Emmett Till* I had gotten to the point of a fo'reallies fucking starved-ass Ethiopian *skin-n-bones* fucking hungry, mofo! Hell, I hadn't even checked-it my food supply because I hadn't wanted to be tempted thus when I hadda done opened-it that rumpsack then firstest done peeped-it thems fucking two books wrapped in plastic that be when I done knowed-it a fat fact, Jack dat po'dunk asshole TOP done removed my foodies then I'd gotten madder than a country-hick mofo unlacing hisns fucking boots to do Chinese arithmetic! I had damned near chunked-it them two fucking non-edibles big-*fucky fucky long time*-butts it hadda been something quiet a whispered-it on the inside kinda queasy feeling that had urged me dumb-ass to just calm the fuck down my illiterate mind somewhat then that same silent-voice witch be running thems background checks hadda persuaded my dumb-ass someting powerful *Peace be still* to done kept me from ripping apart them two fucking paperbacks yet outta selfish-pity and pent-it up anger I'd done tooken-it meselfie a'nuttier week befo' I cracked-it open the first book. I gots me a copy of it to this day, the book be titled *As A Man Thinketh* by James Allen seed it be a fat fact, Jack that Mr. Allen done wrote that little book way the fuck back in them early 1600s yet them sweet kisses from hisns muse *Wisdom* be a valued commodity as swell a learning tool dat be timeless because herns honey sweet cutie-pie kisses of sustainable knowledge be eternally priceless! I believed-it that book helped to save both my sanity and my *Gawd damned I'm a starved* dumb-fuck life and it hadn't mattered one wit that little paperback copy had only 22 leaves from tit to nipple big-*book learning*-butts fo' the mostest parts of some 60-odd days I had suckled-it them itty-bitty titties of truths of life and its concepts then the magic done happened.

The proven knowledge opened-it up a totally new experience iffn not a whole new and exciting world of thought based reality to be fo' *Medgar Evers* unleashed upon my dumb-ass fo' it be then to be there the daze I'd totally rejected all the *no mo' bullshit* unschooling for the Negro only! Mr. Allen reeducated my ass to the point that I just voluntarily done up-chunked all thems worthless dago-roman falsified myths systemically force-fed my black ass *Tankz God* fo' you Mr. Allen, fuck-you po'dunk mofo TOP! After reading *As A Man Thinketh* thems firstest tree to four times, I had begun to write down a lot of my thoughts to done placed thems thought bitches of mine in the fishbowl to done scrutinized and cross-examined thems thoughts of mine to see iffn in deed any thems bitches done held water after theys had been somewhat tenderized and filtered through the wise teachings of the sage, Mr. Allen. I wrote those post-comptemplated thoughts into the other book witch had been completely blank just page after page of nothingness 'cept the on very last page that po'dunk TOP done written *You fucking welcomed*! That be why I had cussed-it dat po'dunk mofo hardtack fo' a'nuttier week befo' I'd begun to fill them empty pages with my own self-made newly *slight on the salt justa mild tint peppery* times be a'changing my newest Mr. Allen enhanced re-thoughts! I'd done learnt-it not so quickly big-*slow*-butts to never dwell on memories thems *Memorexed* times didn't do a body any damned good all alone, out in an open wet-assed alive with fucking *kill a black ass on sight* slant-eye gooners and wild assed pumas and nuttier *eat a man's grown black ass alive* critters roaming free! Memories them ego tripping bitches only occupied alert time besides that lifesaving lesson had been taught-it to me twice the fuck over, firstest by the posse et Unk Zeke's pond then the 2nd be by a yella-smelly substitute teacher in the Napalm Valley thus the corrected answer be when alone in any jungle it be not the fucking place nor the fucking time to be caught day-dreaming in some idyllic-stupor of the stoopids.

The most important thing that I done derived from Mr. Allen musings be *I love me some of me* the sage done taught-it to me that your inner most thoughts create yo' outside world therefore the key to be done changed yo' outside world be it jo' circumstances and or reality firstest ting to be done be to done changed it on the daily-double yo' inner most intimate thoughts running amok inside yo' dumb-assed mind! I hadda reread to done reread a'gin-n-juice all my self-made homegrown thems be me alone to this world done thought-it notes handwritten-it in dat book of the blank pages then I done started-it to tinker bouts just how Kool it be cherry red *Kool-Aid kool* some dem thoughts of mine, baby! I had written abouts my daily grind in that jungle big-*wordy*-butts mostly I wrote-it about the whats and the whys I be doing a particular thing at a particular moment, the whats: I be tracking some small critter field bacon its gonna be dinner tonight then fo' the whys: because I be one hungry as all Hell get me the fuck outta here, Mofo! As time done pressed, I adapted to the quiet then I done wrote even mo' shit including plans for my future sometimes real, go to college, work IBM computers and other times jive *Jo' President Zeke how many hoes you be bumping-it up in the big Oval today*? I never did fo'reallies done managed to control my inner-thoughts because of other thought provoking stuff gleamed-it offa shithouse walls *its not the self-made man you worry bout* big-*banging*-butts *you must question the inventor*! I started-it to done retrained-it my way of tinkering thems thought bitches of my inner-mind then big-pimping those newer and younger re-thunk-it hoes unto the streets and sidewalks of my *aints life grand* consciousness. I started to memorize and write parts of *As A Man Thinketh* unto the pages of that blank book just to give my mind something to dwell upon through-out the day. I broke ground with the little tings instead of tinkering my usual thought *I gotta find and kill me some dems fucking yella-belly slant-eyed gooner-fucks,* I began to readdressed that whorish thought to be a little sumptin-sumptin *my mission be to stop them slant-eyed gooners from doing theys evil actions thus I be saving the lives of all them innocent flyboys flying high in the sky in-order to save the world from a commie bastard's yella-chink fucking take-over* seed that be thems rearranged-it to done re-thunk it thoughts of mine, thems younger intellectual thought bitches thus dems newer inner thoughts theys *raw dog asses* be the young hoes strolling with flashlight in hand witch I done pimped-it unto the dark and empty *ghetto fo' life* intricate workings of my previously fo' the Negro only uneducated mind!

The younger thoughts hoe done strutted herns sexy ass bumping stiletto steps to the newest disco beat not thems late 50s and 60s jitterbug oldies systematic rhetoric unschooling for the Negro only gonna be hoodrat fo' life. Mr. Allen enabled my dumb-ass to holla *Hey-hey Mr. DJ drop dat new track* thus saving thems *jet-jockey candied* asses became my inner *my mission* therefore from the inner to the outer theory on the surface I became the newer selfie-made man. My revised thoughts be liked near-beer in that theys be similar beg-*to differ*-butts rearranged in such away to be justa mite less threatening yet defiantly mo' positively as swell potently mo' dangerous fo' that yella-chink-commie gooner fuck bastard hiding out in that wet-assed jungle, Babycakes! It be liked the thing that occurs with a new woman, be she a good woman or a bad woman cause the very firstest time dat new woman walks-it into a man's cave that woman be like *well this is nice* big-*lying*-butts come that second-time around dat be iffn the man done put it down on dat fine ass to be lucky enough to get dat second-entry then that same woman she justa gotta move something inside the man-cave sumptin-sumtin small-liked some slighted itty-bitty ting a foot-stool, lamp or the plastic crate set aside fo' yo' homeboy to prop hisns ass-cheeks upon whilst the two of youse watched thems *Sooners* whump dat ass on the black-n-white TV. That be what the wisdom of Mr. Allen done taught-it to me, to be as vigilant and tactful with my thoughts liked the new woman be on her newest man's dumb-ass man cave *God forbid* to tink like a woman! Babydoll hadn't kicked-it the man-cave's shit to da' curb big-*slight of hands*-butts she done definitely yet subtly reset the small and the simple by slightly rearranging the crate thus I tried to do the same ting inside my once big empty nappy head with all my dumb-assed thoughts running amok just to be done tweaked-it them whorish thoughts to done made them thoughts mo' positive and justa bite mo' simple big-*intellectual*-butts dat task hadn't been so easy as you'd done thunk-it to be fo' a simpleton to actually simplify hisns most wildest free-flowing unlearnt-it thought bitches bumping hisns shit-fo'-brains! I started-it on the reals to done trusted-it Mr. Allen and hisns gifted wisdom big-*still a dummy*-butts there be times a Brotha be a' tinkering the *what iffns* shit liked *what iffns* I does do all them rights kinda tings to done learnt-it mucho much wisdom thens gets all the way ups to Heaven having a rap session, a one-on-one center-court with *Who'Dat* the originator of all tings that be then I'd bees unto God, *yo' Brotha Man*, yeah mofo the whole world over done knowed-it fo' a fat fact, Jack that God be Beautiful thus it be a given dat God be Black! What iffns I takes the time to done axed God All-Mighty, *Yo Bro, what truly be the meaning of life*? God be liked *pass me dat blunt youngblood* then after God done taken-it Hisns Wholly-Holy Godly Self a good e'nuff' good God All-Mighty mega-hit offa dat doobie then the Holy-One doth sayeth "*dat be a solid question my young uninformed Brotha, let me go ax the wife*!" I must stop the bullshit to done gived-it that po'dunk TOP, hisns fucking propers cause the Mofo did on the reals done did the *knick-knack paddy-whack* to done rolled this Devil Dawg a bone!

Day 81 of the mission, Cpl Daniel Lopez, *EL* for short, hisns Messy-kin half-a-brick ass hadda stack Army issued shit-paper in hisns boots to tap-out the 5-foot 6-inch height requirement of the Corps! *EL* done liked-it to always be hollering them *hillbilly* jokes on the raw-dawg the dumb hillbilly hating ass had gotten us into a *Hell-of-a-fight* couple of months back with some *rump rangers* Army Airborne mofos seed we be at Fort Bragg, North Kakka-lac-key it's a big ass Army sad-sack jump school. Whilst hanging-it out in a huge open-air hangar awaiting the dark of knight and thems *Herk fairies* C-130 *Hercules* cargo planes thems can-died-assed po'dunk USAF flyboys be the sum-de-bitches always done took us somewhere anywhere everywhere World to do all the fucking fighting! That particular night we be to do some low-ceiling black knight jumps over the Atlantic shoreline befo' the jump a restless feeling him-self elfin *EL* done walked-it up to some kinda *Special Forces* unit and asked a big 6-foot-8" 200-fiddy-pound red-to-the-neck hayseed big wrist mofo whom sho'nuff just hadda be a collard-green *"when y'all divorce here in north kakka-lac-key is she still yo' sista?"* *EL* done found-it our targets then everybody done assembled-it all together by day 85. TOP formu-lated a plan of execution seed there be some 12 gooners holed-it up in a hillside cave equipped with all theys gooner shit and combat arsenal then come the day or night at least 4 them gooners done sat-it to done ran-it theys gooner-chinks *jam on it* shit while the other fuck-gooners done slept or sat watch the surrounding area. Them outside the cave dwellers gots theys little itty-bitty-shitty funky gooner-asses a personally assigned pup to send the each off on a one-way bon voyage *bye-bye mofo* a'nutter realm unbeknown-it to mostest men living this universe. I had gotten-it on the lucky *sunny-side of the street* my watch guy be on scout duty big-*WTF*-butt hisns chink snoring like a motherfucker yella commie bastard ass never done heard-it me, hadn't seed-it me nor felt-it the smooth-edged ten-inch blade wrapped tightly in a *Blue Angels* silky! Hell the nip-bastard hadn't even gurgled-it a fucking blurt on hisns way outta this world justa a small mummer bubbled-it up along the outer edge of my flat-steel that musta been some kinda wake the fuck up *Mofo you be on the other side of all tings not this World*! After everybody done sprung-it loose on theys personal escort gooner fuck look-out/operator then Trips took Priest, he'd only do Catholic girls *may he rest in Peace* to done blown-it up the cave and all the gooner equipment shit asunder! We done a tree-day dry-hump along thems tree-lines to the deck thems *In-coming* rescue *Hueys* then it be tree-weeks R&R *Yello, Momma-san, I nemba-one GI*!

Chapter 37

Not all assignments sailed as easily out then back to port, as my firstest, a short wiles laters on a'nuttier tunnel-mission in the Philippines there be a jungle group of the mofos *Pot-poi*, *Pot-pie, Pot-heads, pot-something* big-*flip'n*-butts theys dumb flip-asses done had the big misfortune in that theys giddy-yup boots done clashed-it hardtack alongside Mrs. Marcos elegant evening heels! Those fucking *we gonna take-over this island* bitches done hooched-it theys fuck asses inside *copy-cat mutherfuckers* elaborate VC style death to all interlopers tunnels complete with shrapnel, grenades, steel-wire, bam-boo pits, thems same fucking big as small dogs slant-eye bucktooth rats eating offa months/years gone way the bye-bye dead bodies and a'plenty of human/animal waste and blood on everything and everywhere. The 3rd week, 3rd tunnel of the 3rd wet-fire that mission be for my dumb-ass a fucking the 3rd turd nightmare dat fucking unlucky tree it be then that I done fucking runned-it upon one dems *Billy-yella-slant-eye* mofos inside a tar-baby pitched black bastard mid-night flip tunnel where it almost became my fucking *bye-bye sweet world of mine* tunnel! I done a sho'nuff meet-it up with a *Bruce Lee* Rucky-Rucy mofo and dat *rucky-roosey* fuck-flip bastard done had the balls to done stabbed me with a worthless flip-open pen-knife it be true like a motherfucker that life be cyclical seed most GI peeps done called dat little two-inch pen-knife that the flip-fuck done used-it to attack my big head a *zipper*! The rucky-roosey mofo slashed jabbed my shit just above the right-eye only mere seconds befo' he'd cut a throaty buck-toothless smile across my *fuck the kung-fu, bitch* dis be a ten-inch blade counterpunch! The flip doc at the Manila hospital put-it to me in pretty good big-*gibberish*-butts broken English that had the flip rebel's aim been justa eighth of an inch either way up, down, or all around then I'd have been the one-eyed motherfucker we done chanted about whilst out a *Jodie* run!

I truly believed that I been freaking jinxed that mission cause while I did the rehab at a Manila St. Elsewhere Mr. Bad-ass *buzzard luck* done gave my horny-toad ass a'nuttier mostest personal on the close *howdy do, Mofo* visit in the fabulous form of an *all get the fuck out* flip-Babygurl dat be stacked liked a motherfucker yet she be not a *Sadie Thompson* hawking thems bedpans big-*floosy*-butts Good Lawd, she be one all-time super *how you doing* babyflip-gurl a foxy brown fine-assed *show me the money* lbfm LittleBrownFuckingMachine! The LBFM good Gwad fine ass be not pimping thems flip hospital hallways fo' the monies that bad-ass bitch wanted the ass, she be squawking a fo'reallies piece of the big black ass cake, baby! The temptress knowed-it herns shit all to the swells cause I be liked *Jack be nimble* to done made the big mis-stake an almost gravely err seed she done helped-it me to done bounced dat hospital bed and tubes then I done hooched-it up with herns fine-assed flip RN sexy-self as the world done twirled-it big-*lucky*-butts the heavenly flip-nurse RN babygurl done turned out be nurse fucking psycho *flip dat bitch*! The LBFM had some major mental issues witch she be gonna strap-down double-fisted fucking tight atop my horny unawares dat trouble be on the hotfoot *I'm coming* black-ass!

What had happened be, the young lady's ex be a *flyboy* one thems Air Force candied-ass mofos seemed flyboy also be a chocolate thunder jet-tech big-*lucky mofo*-butts not quite near so ruggedly dark, tall and handsome as me it's a fat fact, Jack that the one thing thems flip-flopping Flips done prided themselves on be that theys nosey-Rosy asses be in the done knowed-it all abouts the every damn thing that slithered-it in or to done slithered-it out a grunt's water-tight asshole yet *Bro' man* managed to pull dems stakes, popped them caulks to done hauled-it outta the land of a ga-zillion million banana-faced flippity-flops without so much as to done giveth her a *"kiss my sweet-Black ass good-bye*!*"* At the met-it up, I hadn't done knowed-it then that little snippet of vital life savings information abouts me lbfm crazy-ass Nurse flip *Shortie* befo' the horny toads done settled-it in liked wet-back poured *O'la puto* concrete upon my big-*git dat booty*-butts I done *Sooners* to be done *all Hell southern redneck belles* got learnt-it the hardtack the no happy-nappy ending way! Mr. Buzzard-luck done writ upon the bamboo walls that my little brown-skinned rump-shaker and herns family *got faced* when flyboy *Homie* done *flipped dat bitch* Homie be ass-cheeks over soki teacups *Elvis done left the building* on thems flippity-flop mofos thus psycho Nurse Shortie and flip-family deys all be a shit-sack of the sad bitches done *gots faced* asses! Baby-flip RN *Shorty* needed-it sumtin powerfully bad to done extracted-it fo' hernself and family a pound of the flesh now, the pound hadn't much mattered-it to her nor herns we'z done been punked family, it could have been any old pound big-*dumb ass*-butts the flesh that flesh it just had to be jet-tech Black that be where *bye-bye* flip bitches my dumb-ass had entered-it front to center staged left justa mite off to the left because nuttin be right bout dat done flipped-it shit! Not that I wasn't so dumb nor had I not been forewarned by TOP whom done told-it to the one to the all of us that *iffn a woman be more beautiful than any other woman you've ever been with and she's not asking for your money then that woman be wanting a piece of your ass to take to market, like a fucking kidney or something other, be aware Mofos! Don't wake the fuck up naked inside an iced downed tub*!

Yo' boy be in love and my love be an on the sly tight-booty flippity-flop psycho bitch big-*Romeo*-butts baby-*pineapple*-gurl be finer than a mudda, she wasn't even one of my nurses on the regular yet she'd done visited-it my bedside mostest days justa check-it in on me with thems *I kinda missed-ya* big round semi-slanted baby-brown eyes then she be bursting forth the light banner chit-to-chat witch she'd queried my dumb-ass mo' times than not seed Babyflip done mentioned-it in a kinda passing sorta way bouts my long on the gone daze when I usta be a shock-jock seed then and there I hadda more than sensed-it dat sumptin just didn't smell fishy bouts *the fish in this barrel* I even to have done knowed-it that Babygurl flip done peeped my bedside med chart cause the Corps had not changed my MOS*MilitaryOccupationalSkill* the one ting my horny-toad ass did done knowed-it be that Babygurl-flip be finer than a motherfucker! The LBFM be equipped with a set of them humongously all natural flip God given tits dat be topped-it all off with two perfectly chocolate-drops thumb-sized-nipples to match Babygurl flip done *put the right-foot in, went into the hospital and took the dumb-ass out, we did the hokey-pokey then she let out a shout* Yo' homeboy be in love, Babycakes! Baby-*pineapple*-gurl hadn't used much to cajole my horny-toad ass to done broke like a motherfucker that damned hospital gown made the mad dash to herns home just to done kicked-it inside that little rice board apartment hooch somewhere the Manila Bay airport whereby I be putting it down with a Black be beautiful righteous slant! It be luv Babycakes! All be fair grounds in the love that be war specially when onliest the one fined-assed whooping and hollering brown-skinned LBFM be the side of the love-fest that be the onliest side to done knowed-it that fo' this black ass Injun the wagons be circled-it up because RN flippity flip be on a war party, baby!

It all went down comes the late night early morning t'was bouts oh-two-hundred-thirty hours 2:30 am-ish that 3rd night a'gin-n-juicy rucky-roosey them buzzard luck trees, 3rd night of the 3rd day almostest the 3rd hour be the bewitching hour when I hadda from outta the deep happy-nappy *done gots my swerve-on* sleep the shit be that I done gots awoken-it by a blood curling banshee scream, my lbfm Baby-*pineapple*-gurl freak hadda sung that song of the evil alternative let's just fuck *Tarzan* then bury the hatchet in hisns *sleeping like a newborn* black ass dat shit be straight-up slant-eye jungle love! The fine-ass flip dat bitch done *yelled-it from the chest* pierced-it a death tune upon my eardrums *Emmett Till* my lying eyes done popped opened-it WTF to done seed it a living screaming banshee Sista Death be *In-coming* and she be a Flip'n banana face *Hell's belle*! The LBFM herns fine-assed self be free-falling forward all the whilst clamped two-fisted tight unto a two-foot machete witch dat bitch done double-fisted between thems so succulent big ass *lovely brown big'ums done come to town* all-natural born non-*Silicone Valley* top-shelf be thems big-assed golden sun tanned all natural tits! Nurse psycho bitch be a standing tall between my legs justa screaming banshee and free-falling forward when I had on the just awoken-it *Tank God* I done reacted mostly outta the fear of what the fuck be going on here little sweet-thang, *Hell to the fucking No* I hadn't to done bitch-screamed-it, I gots balls, yo' boy done growed-it up hisns selfie a pair of thems big coconut balls, Babycakes! My lady-killer instincts hadda done kicked-it auto-pilot such that I had thrust both my hands closed-fisted justa straight-out and straight-up, hitting Baby-*pineapple*-gurl hardtack herns just fo' me in dems last tree-daze herns little boney brown savory scrumptious shoulders tips yet with herns tiny weight aided by the gravity of the situation my fine-assed lbfm RN flip fucking nurse psycho bitch done *Peace be* still managed-it to place a nasty-assed quarter-inch deep, two-tree inch gash across my chest near the upper part of my sternum, Fuck! Check this funky-ass shit, herns fucking flipping *flip dat shit* neighbors hadda done wigged-out whence theys done heard-it herns pre-warned to be warned louder than a Mofo banshee fucking free-falling scream followed-it up by my loud assed *WTFs WhatTheFuck, Bitch*!

The next ting I'd done knowed-it thems brown-skin slant-eyed whore hound neighbors of herns done crashed-it theys skank mo' brown than yella-asses into then through thems rice-board paper thin ass walls or the door as a group to be at and onto my ass in a slant-eye minute because thems stupid little flip-asses musta been exactly just liked my fucking big black ass been startled the fuck awaken bye-bye that lbfm's flipping bitch's loud assed *iffn there's a Heaven yo' black ass be headed to Hell* scream then amidst the chaos all fucking flip Hell done broke-it loose big-*snooping*-butts it onliest done broke that way because of thems fucking interloping flip-flopping flips be not minding theys own Gwad damned business! Thems flipping pineapple neighbor bitches hadda done foot chased-it my black ass decked in field pants and canvas flip-flop hospital shoes through thems narrow assed streets *Emmett* Till we'z done ran-it upon a local beat-feet, as iffn I hadda been the one fucking-it all up! Gotta stop and done give that little *Flip* po-po hisns props though cause he hadda seed-it me a'coming hardtack hisns funky ass way chased-it bye-bye that mob of crazed banana-faced pygmies big-*madder than a mofo*-butts first-est ting dat little flip beat-feet cop be done did after he'd owl-eyed-it to fish-mouthed-it seed dat flipping mofo be small-*boney*-butts that po-po had also been an older yet butt-wiser flip, he hadda gotten shooken-it small-*baton carrying*-butts not shaken therefore he hadn't drawn hisns puny-ass night-stick! He'd probably done knowed-it wouldn't have done any good seed Filipino beat-feet *po-po* didn't carry guns probably some back dated left-it over shit from theys British blimey bastard gook-blokes got ruled daze witch thems fucking the Queen's *ass-wipes* be the Brits number one colonial rule in that all locals in occupied lands couldn't carry weapons no matter WTF theys loco asses be doing! The flip-cop hadda just casually put up hisns empty ass hands to stop all forward movement by me and the mad bum-rush mob witch had gotten even bigger once we be outside and on them flip streets. Hell it be tree in the fucking morning where the fuck did all thems fucking flips come from? The little punk-assed old fart po-po had started-it in with that gibberish talk for all thems *mad assed didn't have a fucking clue as to what hadda fo'reallies went down* neighbor flips to done stopped-it all thems fucked flip asses in deys fucking tracks to be a'listening to that po-po gibberish speak shit! To me the whole of it be liked that Hollywood toon-town movie 'cepting the star the big fella *Gulliver* be played-it out by a handsome as all Hell *get the fuck outta here* Black man and hisns beautiful black ass be chased-it by a chunk of banana-faced yella-brown assed *Lilliputians* and thems little silly Lilly-*slant-eyed*-Pootin fucks be screaming gibberish shit all the whilst Hell bent on tying my big Black ass up, WTF!

When TOP and Trips got to the airport police station there I sat with busted *Frankenstein* stitches above my right-eye and a two to tree-inch big assed grayish red-veined membrane bubble sticking 'bout an inch or two up and outta the center of my hairless chest. What had happened be when I'd first arrived dat stank po-po station this one flip cop had tried to help me then he'd poured-it some kinda alcohol backed sanitary something solution on my chest where be that damned bleeding liked a motherfucker gash from the machete of the crazy-ass nurse psycho flip dat bitch! That flip solution hadda done burnt liked Hell's *fucking set my black ass* afire and that be when that fucking stab-wound done bubbled-it the fuck-up into the big assed tree-inch grey membrane red vein-lined bubble-luscious! FUCK, I done then screamed-it my own damn *fuck me* bloody-shits banshee shrill befo' falling to my knees that medicated fucking shit done burnt-it clean assed clear through my black ass *Burn Baby Burn* muddafukka, Good Lord! I hadn't knowed-it thens nor now iffn it hadda been dat hellacious howl of pain heard all over that little ass flip po-po station or the mad-assed scowl etched all over my handsome baby-gingerbread brown face because I be pissed as all *Hell get me the fuck outta here* mad or mayhaps it hadda been them bursted stitches over my right-eye coupled-it up with that grey/reddish membrane bubble stuck outsides my chest either fucking way, I be thankful to whatever the fuck it hadda been because thems smallish-*boney*-butts flip cell-mates had done given to me a wide berth in that overly crowded skank funky-assed flip jail! To this day both scars are visible the cut in my brow looks kinda natural liked when the barber puts a part in yo' high and tight though the gash in my chest done lost its depth and length yet Peace be still visible liked it be a black divot mole kinda ting and to some womenfolk especially the drunken ones a'plenty done axed-it me iffn I had meself an extra inverted man-nipple like I be one thems fucked dumb-ass never been so fucking stoopid collard-greens!

Chapter 38

76'A HANDFUL OF US GOT a change of scenario, in the latter part of October 75' some rag-headed turds done shot-down a French airliner then we jumped into the ass hot arid desert of Lebanon where there be thems ungodly fucking *hoo-boos* just miles and miles of blowing sand *In-coming* Hell bent that fucking hoo-boo shit be no *Mr. Sandman send me a dream* dat nitty-gritty shit onliest gonna leave jo' sand-papered ass buried balls deep on an endless beach without water! Lebanon be a camel of a fucking different color and since our dumb-asses hadn't been invited to too many deserts TOP had said we were gonna roll coffin city, WTF! The coffin: Dig a hole tree plus feet down some 74 inches in length by some 38ish inches in width then shore the inside of that cavern with whatever happened to avail itself that could help secure yo' ass in all that shape-shifting sand big-*shifty*-butts whilst packing our gear some-to-body on the sly done seed-it when dat black ass psycho wannabe a Messykin, Trips hadda done stored some cardboard in hisns jump-gear and the smartest ones amongst us had done copycats dat shit! A breathing tube had to be affixed topside the coffin thens come the black knight thems fucked *Devil Dawgs* would track yo' *fucking caught in a boo-boo* ass down justa drop all kinda shit, be it bugs, snakes, piss and only Allah knowed-it whatever else that could slide and or slitter down your air-supply tube so ya' had to keep changing jo' shut-eye locations on the daily-double!

The knock be that the master mind behind the airliner attack had been located mad-*bombing*-butts things be sensitive liked on the political front so dat be mostest likely why we be spending all that time shitting in the shift-changing sand yet old *Emir* mastermind rag-headed sand-nigger done had hisns self some kinda medical problem-o that required hisns funky goat-banging *done blowed-it all thems innocent Frenchies outta the sky* ass to cross a particular stretch of the desert to get to hisns rag-headed doc every now come the thens. The day the assignment dat funky camel dick sucking ass done got hisns shitty-ass cheeks in the *Dear Penthouse* up-close and on the personal *he could not believe hisns luck* center-fold them cross-hairs then we'z done tooken-it our sweet-assed turns trigger-tapping to mapping thems camel-jockey sand-whores tills thems left-hand pointer-finger ass-wipes done gotten-it within 800+ meters then the kill zone be set. There had been 4 guards and the target bouncing along in a green/white *Land Rover,* BillyT and me had to take-out thems goat-banging guards then Priest, he'd only do Catholic girls *may he rest in Peace* be assigned to done blowed the transport vehicle below then beyond Hell's afire.

That mofo be one sad-eye puppy when I'd firstest done the meet-it up with hisns *only the lonely* dago ass where we both be stationed on the same tub sitting China Bay. Hisns JOB be a munitions *Mickey mouse* system technician fo' thems Phantom jets then he'd been with me in both my firstest boots to ground Nam and them VC tunnels whatsoever the fucking reason seemed-it like I justa couldn't shake dat sad-eye WOP bitch-hoe mofo fo' nuttin! Hisns sad-eye be always a'crying like a little bitch the word done got-it out that *lil Suzy* dat be the name fo' any whiteboy grunt's hometown sweetheart seed hisns little Suzy hadda done ceremoniously dumped-it hisns Catholica sad-eye WOP assed-out ass for hisns bestest bud via a dear fuck-you *Johnnie WOP-boy* letter witch he hadda carried-it fold in hisns left chest pocket and Priest, he'd only do Catholic girls *may he rest in Peace* dat mofo done taken-it that *adios dago wop-ass motherfucker gotta go* shit hard to the Corps thus him always be a weeping willow justa balling hisns sad red shitty brown-eyes a *good n' aplenty* and him always be a'listening to a portable 8-track player witch the wop bitch bastard had toted-it every fucking where big-*bummer*-butts the sad-eye mofo he'd only play this one and onliest fucking one fucked-up the greasy WOP ass album sung by a *Beatles* wannabe cover band called *Bread* the fucking album be titled *The Best of Bread* hisns fav song offa dat *WOP ass DJ don't cha never drop dat track* fucking album hadda been *Baby I'm a want cha* belched outta the bowels of Hell! Its been mo' than fiddy fucking years hence I done to last *Tank God, for small favors* to have done *Medgar Evers* be done heard-it dat bitch punk-assed ditty strummed-it across my eardrums big-*bummer*-butts I bet cha ten soggy *SOS* turds to a *Dunkin* donut that I could sing dem po'dunk punk-assed lyrics word fo' word any day anywhere at any-fucking-time! Hell, it wasn't the Brothas who'd invented the ghetto-blaster it hadda been dat damned sad-eye WOP mofo' Priest, he'd only do Catholic girls *may he rest in Peace,* him always justa hauling hisns sad-eye WOP ass and dat fucking beat-up 8-track player from the tub through the shit all awhile justa playing that one bullshit *ofay* shitty-assed ditty and justa balling hisns brown shitty orbs the fuck out! My Boy' be so damned fucking sad that everybody hadda done showed-it him mucho love, Babycakes!

The Brothas done dapped-it hisns sad-eye ass up tight seed we done taught the sad-eye all thems newest bad-assed *Right-on my Brotha* hit-me up daps, thems Company-G potheads done chilled theys smoke so as he wouldn't get the contact high cause they hadn't wanted-it to be the ones to done fucked hisns wop ass up any mo' than he all to the fucked be already and on the flathead whilst chipping fucking paint I'd done heard-it with my own damned ears many a mofo singing along to thems *Best of Bread* shit for songs that in all reality be justa a bad restless white noise hum across yo' fucking eardrums! Everybody on that flathead and Nam ground hadda done just let dat wop dago sad-eye bastard mofo play that shit fo' yo' ears *white bread* album every fucking chance he got and dat dago sad-eye mofo gots them chances by the shit loads! Good Lawd, the real truth, Ruth be dat sad-eye mofo be good even butter than good with explosives especially C-4 and that be why hisns sad-eye ass be in the desert with us. After all the smoke done drifted TOP backed-it dat po'dunk redneck skinny white ass of hisns about a thousand plus meters aways from the no mo' guardians, no mo' *Range Rover* mastermind raghead sprawled-it centerfold the fishbowl then po'dunk TOP done grazed-it a single fiddy-mil round into the assignment's upper right-hip socket area some kinda biblical ting, WTF that fucking TOP done thunk-it himself to be the fucking po'dunk Pope! TOP hadn't wanted-it to done ousted the fucked sheep banger bastard it be killing him softly fo' all thems good innocent *frenchy folks* seed dat goat's nuts sucking camel-jock ass done deserved-it and did receive mo' time upon this earth because TOP had wanted-it to play-out a little sumptin-sumptin for what the shitty-finger goat fucking bastard had done to them *Frenchies may theys rest in Peace*! The next tree-days we done rolled-it to *Mr. Lucky* food and water both witch hisns camel-jock be a raghead ass had refused big-*starving*-butts day five, survival of the fitness musta kicked-it him in hisns funky *lookey-look the camel done fucked him in hisns shitty* ass because *Mr. Lucky* dat bastard camel humping asshole with hisns filthy left-pointer finger scratching hisns shitty bloodied ass right hip-socket done used-it all thems shit and blood stained fingers to eat then to done drank-it all that hadda done been rolled-it hisns funky assed way! The skank-hoe cocksucker done et then he done continued-it with thems on the 24/7 *it's me oh Lord, standing in the need* of prayers! From day one that *shot-it in the ass* Mr. Lucky done prayed-it those long-winded monosyllable prayers *oooooOOH----heyyyyaaa-aaahhhhhh—ooommm--ooooooh-aaahhhhhh—ooommm ooooooh-aaahhhhhh—ooommm* either prostrate or a rocking-it to the beat on hisns one good hip! TOP hadda done made one of us to be done prayed-it up-front, aloud and alongside each be every time Mr. Lucky be done fresh started-it up *"Jesus fuck'n Christ! You never fuck'n know who has the better Gawd damned God"* TOP confessed-it *"Never get yo' ass cheeks cracked between a man and his gawd damned God*!"

I hadda 'membered-it thems daze back Nam and that pendant po'dunk redneck mofo Pin-alley so I a'gin-n-juicy Lucy on the loud and proud prayed-it for sum dat pussy! *"Lawd above and Hey you dick-head below, please to send me befo' I die some pussy, Black pussy, White pussy, Blonde pussy, Red pussy, Yellow pussy, Brown pussy, even Rainbow pussy, but please God-o-the-Pussy don't be sending me no damned Grey pussy"* I for the life in me hadn't to never ever knowed-it to done understood-it the *what's sup* with thems skinny assed wafer thin lips po'dunk WASP soda-jerk cracker-barrel red-neck whiteboys commanding a mofo to done gushed-it upon the fucking spot some fucking churchyfied prayers! The only differ betwixt the two numbnutz be that with TOP the rag-fuck goat's ass eating sheep fucking camel-dick sucking mofo about to be done died be laid-it out-front the fishbowl *ah rocking on hisns fucking good hip* center-court our eyeballs.

TOP had let it be knowed-it to the one and all with ears that I justa happened to be one black ass heathenish fool hitching a ride on a one-way crotch rocket bound for Hell! That hadda been why TOP done been mo' than especially happy, no more liked super fucking praised the Lawd be God *gospel-gooney-goo-goo giddy-yup* yappy-ass fucking happy when that man-pussy, the ass fuck Ritz had arrived our camp South America! TOP done preached-it *Word* on the holla in that God in His Own Infinite and Supreme Wisdom answered all prayers and since my heathenish Black ass had prayed for it, TOP hadda done stopped and pointed at the pink-cotton candied-ass DEA mofo Ritz befo' he'd done Blessed-it me with the *there yo' pussy be, you jigger-boo pussy-praying black ass Mofo*!

Chapter 39

83' MY FINAL YEAR OF Marine Corps active and active reserve duty it hadda been my *fare thee well* tour G-fucking goodbye-bye po'dunk TOP and *Adios you aints my amigo* psycho mofo Trips with justa weeks left to my enlistment contract I be et home with my on the reals *Tank God* in the black she be beautiful flesh Babygirl and I be short-dawging it liked a mofo in the *Love Shack* justa me and my Babygirl when them fool-assed fancy fucking *my daddy gots the money fuck you AMA I'm gonna be a baby doctor any-fucking-way* rich white academia college kids justa a fucking chunk of the dumb-assed whiteboy/whitegirl wannabe a doctor fools seed thems educated dumb *Red Stripe* beer guzzling rich skank hoes hadda done gots theys cotton-soft white asses in a raggamuffin asscrack down yonder '*Yeah Mon, You lezzy bones, won't be bringing dem dar babies inta dis world, Mon* fucking with dem jiffy-pops! Prez Nancy, eh' President Ronald *shot in the ass* Reagan had done ordered-it TOP, Trips and the boys away from all those café latte fine *bump dat ass* South Americana S*enoritas* to make a low-ceiling night drop into the Atlantic ocean just miles off the shores of Haiti. TOP the whore-dog mofo knowed-it for a fat fact, Jack that I be sitting on my *Sooners* to be a civilian ass in OKC justa licking my shorty-dog chops seed this big dog be groomed and ready to get the fuck outta the Corps fuck the bullshit, baby then the mofo done sent-it me a personal invite to the party-party mofo the shit be on! That po'dunk redneck mofo done ordered hisns evil ass a *Waffle House* specialty my buttered black ass biscuits on the sunny-side up! WTF why my short-dog ass be on the hidden menu at the ready-point to be served-it up a last minute gonna *fuck dat shorty-dawg ass up* mission! WTF dat po'dunk happy-assed mofo done hollered-it from half-way across the fucking world *serfs-up jigger-boo, Mofo*! Any fucking Vet can tell ya' this truth that the military especially the Corps done held hard-*fucking*-tack bouts letting go a fo' sho'nuff experienced tactical *instant grits* mofo with the killer instinct! Uncle *don't leave me* Sammy be hardtack to done let fly the honed-in dumb-ass roaming-it free onto the highways and all thems *bye-bye mofo I be a civilian* ways without a genuine Hatfield's verses McCoy hillybilly *lets us just git this shit on* family feud seed to thems fucks it be liked iffn yo' ass aints a'married to the Corps thens yo' fucking hillbilly, nigger, hippy, wetback, kiki, po'lack, dago, chink, in'jun ass be fucked, *Semper-Fi*, Mofo! Thems sadistic egotistical bitches be likened unto thems inner-city po'lack dago mofo wife-beating beer-belly white-bread drunken motherfuckers in theys thin strapped white-tees kicking theys po'assed-out woman in herns dumb *why the fuck won't she leave him* ass because little Mrs. SuzieQ done knowed-it for a fat fact, Jack dat stupid pencil dick mofo be no bullshit bouts hisns fucking on the daily-double vow *I'll kill ya' fo' I let ya' go*!

That Grenada jump, I'd been justa little bit more than a spook being spooked *sitting by the door* of that Herk because I'd had all that time to done sat next to that long lost yet never to be forgotten skank-hoe *brotha fear* and us two Mofos done reacquainted ourselves to done conversated *how you dewing* whilst awaiting thems fucking Reg-*daddy*-Bush administration fucks to chime them jingle-jangle its-a-go bells! The unit be strapped-it in at the *all-Righty almighty* locked and loaded ready-point positioned-it inside a gunship Herk with thems props a'twirling justa sweating-it on the runway Andrews AFB, DC. We be on the fucking locked-it fucking loaded-it for over 2-hours, *fuck dat shit* Hell there had been mo' than five fucking hot-refuels whilst we done sat shitting bullets and all that fucking time my dumb black ass be white-knuckled-it talking shit with the skank-hoe *brotha fear*! During all that damned free time I just couldn't shake *brotha fear's* nasty funky-ass and hisns nasty funky thoughts outta my dumb-ass head! I'd been off the fucking leash justa fucking on the short-dogging it back OKC home to the University of Oklahoma *Sooners* and I hadda straight-up been fucking milking dat *shorty-dawg* bone to its gnarly end big-*bony*-butts I hadda on the reals to done knowed-it that both thems two hard to the Corps *clowns* po'dunk TOP and psycho ass Trips loved-it nuttin *peanut-butter jelly* than to done fucked with the inner-mind workings of a *short-dog* mofo, *Semper-Fi*! The short-dog by nomenclature and by all practicality of all that be the reality as to the conception of time not being relative thems big-*everyday*-butts loud-assed tick-tickety da' tock tockety-tocks of the clock on the wall done struck one, it be a real truth, Ruth dat the *short-dog* only gots mere seconds left befo' thems final grains of the sands to hisns *bye-bye mofo* enlistment be done dropped-it completely through the Corps hourglass then *short-dog* be fucking running-it on the *haul dat ass* clear and free away to be totally outta the Corps yipping-it, running-it and a barking-it buck-wild naked-ass be the short-dog *Hey-hey Mofos, I be free*!

Big-*hurry*-butts whilst the shortdogg be eyeballing dems *let freedom ring* doors justa swinging in the gently blowing *welcome backs* to the civilian world breeze it be in thems last of the last mere seconds of the time left on hisns contract the *shit happens* big-*buzzard luck*-butts it always be in thems itty-bitty titi lastest of tickey-tocks be where and when thems two twisted motherfuckers TOP and Trips done dropped-it the Chubby Checker *Let's twist again* track to done called *shortdogg* ass backs to the battlefield thems two heartless gungho Mofos be always a'banging on the shortie-dawg's ass-cake! I'd done seed-it done to a'plenty of thems shortdoggs dat be clocking theys last few hours in the Corps then theys buzzard-luck asses done catched-it ahold of the bad-ending strolling hardtack *fuck* it be *bye-bye Mofo* terminated short-dog ass be over the fucking rainbow, No mas Mofo! Fo' dat shorty-dawg's ass it be *I done seed da light at the end of the tunnel* and that *In-coming* light be the fucking the 5:15 freight train to Hell! Justa ah' coming forth to snatch hisns be the shorty Devil-Dawg ass fo' the final homecoming! I'd done knowed-it fo' a fat fact, Jack that both thems cold heartless hard ass to theys Corps fools both TOP and Trips hadda loved-it bestest of the best whens dat shorty-dawg's ass done got one of theys twisted endings! Thems two snake-bitten fo'ever war Devil Dawgs woulda done digged-it deep into theys harden stonepit hearts to find that last ditched mostest utterly idiocy totally worthless titi insignificantly useless *WTF* assed-out it be small-*pooh*-butts a'nuttier useless mission to done runned-it upon a shortdogg's ass justa chomping at the bit. I done knowed-it firsthand straight-up thems two *shortydawg ain't leaving* shit shitty-assed theory be theys most proudest fucking *trick's in the* bag cause I done seed it all with my own fucking lying eyes done seed the both TOP and Trips justa licking theys putrid chops whilst the shortdawg be all out-front street *Run the point, Mofo* fo' that last worthless bullshit mission!

I justa couldn't slacken them thoughts of *how the fuck* thems two happy-asses done gots thems fucking Jiffypops to upstart shit with thems med school kids that shit be my main worry-what WTF! *We did it! We got shortdogg Zeke by the short hairs! That shortdogg jigger-boo mofo be in love now his in-love black ass be in the trick-bag!* It hadda been thems kinda worry-whats that be exactly liked the fairy Herk's turbo-props turning theys *ugly-trick the trick's* asses over never be over inside my big nappy-head because I could onliest just sit back strapped, loaded and on-point ready awaiting fo' dat gunship to fly my shortdogg ass the fuck out fo' my fucking final titi mission with thems two hardtack to theys fucking Corps clowns! My mind couldn't turn dat fucking bone loose in that my black ass be buzzard bait cause this last mission gonna be Zeke's fucking titi, the set-up mission dat be my very last fucking RECON a bullshit titi mission! Thems fucking *worry-whats* justa rolling thunder lightening quick inside my big empty head sitting-it there next to *brotha fear* thems blades full-tilt a'twirling on the runway, on the wait justa on the fucking stand bye-bye, Mofo! There be nuttin worst for a shortdogg a'holding hisns drawls tight fo' the fight and hisns mind being on the fright because he's gots no parts control bouts the flight or the "*why can't we all just get along*"... Rodney *whump dat ass* King quoted after the Los Angeles po-po done theys evil assed shit unto hisns po' Black ass one fucked-up Knight in the City of Angel-eyes! Why can't this nation just do the ting that be the *Right-on* thing fo' my shortdawg ass witch be to done fucking shutdown thems engines just to fucking cut-bait, Mofos! Strapped-it inside dat Herk, I be liked a starved suckling black babe all up and in hisns mammy's *rock-me please rock-me* arms bouts to make the first installment on the Karma of all the evil I done did this world because I's be a starving-ass newborn and mammy be one fine-assed big tittied bitch with no nipples!

The ting dat I hadn't to never ever done figured-it the fuck-out be how in all *Hell to jangling redneck southern belles* had them two ignoramuses' thems sorry-asses done gots Biggy-smalls gots so lucky the both po'dunk TOP and psychotic questionable Mexican *tar-baby black ass* Trips WTF just how the Hell thems two ig'nant mofos done put-it the fucking trick-bag onto all thems fucking jerk-chicken Rastafarians Jiffypop raggamuffin shit-bags to done put down theys ganja long enough to done taken-up fucking with thems white assed-out baby doc wannabe richy-rich ass college kids, Fuck! Yet there I be, less than a week before I be done walked-it *free the fucking clear* the fuck outta dem wide opened-it *freedom doors* justa swinging-it in the *fuck da' fucking Corps* wind, my enlistment be over, bitches! One mo' week justa one mo' fucking week then I gonna be a good gots damned-it civilian once and a'gin-n-juice *Jo' Ladies yo' Babyboy be Black and back in town*! Less than two days ago, I hadda seed thems *free yo' mind and yo' ass will follow* signs pointing the way to thems I be free doors big-*buzzard luck*-butts WTF there I be *shitting gold-bricks* on a fucking flyboy runway inside a gunnery Herk *all hands on deck* turbo-props bumping!

Chapter 40

TOP's PLAN CALLED-IT THAT AFTER the low-ceiling ocean jump then my shortdogg ass gonna be fucking point-on-point lead dog for the bush-whacking of the airport security team a bush-league Army of the shitty blue jump-suited *Jah mon* jiffypops! Even Mr. Allen could not *helps me Lord* to kick them nasty ass fearful thoughts cause thems fuck-me *worry-whats* be running a gangbang she-bang on my over-thinking it mind abouts all thems factors to the facts of life! It gonna be a low-ceiling over water night jump outta a gunship Herk, there be no light, no line, no ramp and besides topping-it off all dat bad-assed shit the fat fact, Jack be that it be a gunship not the normal C-130 cargo bird and that there fucking fact be for me the major freaky-deaky a'scardy assed point of all the shit in and all of its owned damned accord fo' me that shit be a'nuttier big assed mind-twister because we done never gots the gun-shipped fairy lessen the *In-coming* shit be expected to be just bananas fucking wild to be wicked liked a Mofo! The gunship unliked the cargo bird carried a 105mm or a 70mm cannon either one done sat it beneath justa *free blowing gust of wind* one click south and a tad to the rear of the inside deck door. We would be bouncing-it out port side just behind the number-two in-board engine ergo to the front-side of the deck there be them two turbo-jet engines, their props and theys exhaust iffn a buzzard luck wind gust bounced-it up and offa thems oceanic waves it gonna be *Danger Danger Jolly Rogers Danger* liked a motherfucker! Fuck, to the rear of the door iffn you hadda done a *Howdy-due* meet-it up with that damn cannon stick sho'nuff' fucking fo' sure, ass-kissing that solid carbon-steel *death be a'coming yo' way* 70/105mm dick wouldda just have fucked-it up yo' whole damned Knight, *Jah Mon*!

Even without them fucking *worries-whats* on a shortdogg's mind there be the real tings involved in all them low-ceiling over water jumps witch be *not one spit to the Devil's wicked shit* whether theys done in the day or night the ting was/is/be that there was/be/is just sway too mucho much of the shit to compensate fo' iffn shit done turned sour during the jump then there be sway too little time to re-sweeten dat sour assed-shit back the fuck-up! That peculiar fucking night it hadda been pitch black albeit Trips tar-baby fucking black assed Messykin black with justa few fluffy floating white clouds in the nighttime sky besides I decked-it 3rdman-out behind BillyT, real name Williams Tomas dat fool be the Yaqui Indian Love God outta Gila Bend, Arizona. BillyT gots those two last names for a fucking firstest name because of thems *what a bad fucking idea* dumb-ass Injuns way of naming theys just born git fo' whatever be the fucking firstest Gwad damned ting theys drunken Injun asses done seed-it outside the buckskin tent bye-bye peeping through the front-doe' flap. Once *Ma Squaw* done shit-out baby redskin and dat *Sooners* to be drunken papoose been slapped-it on hisns just born red ass thems dumb-assed Injuns takes themselves a looky-look outside the tee-pee flap to see *what's sup* thus fo' BillyT hisns fucking two last names be outta the ordinary fo' thems apple-heads *red on the outside white inside* motherfuckers yets so mucho-much butter than theys usual flare two-dogs fucking or blind goat falling!

The unit done given dat drunken Injun ass a proper all world-wide the fucking koolest call-sign *Medgar Evers*! BillyT the Injun red-assed mofo not onliest had thems two last names dat mofo owned two world class big assed fucking earlobes witch on sight seen done sent all kinda womenfolks into some sorta freaky-deaky frenzy *no shit fucking A-buddy* on the reals world-wide dems womenfolk be liked theys justa gotta grab to squeeze to suckle hisns big assed lobes right there spot scene! BillyT's lobes be thick-assed like a mofo, theys big as a cup-in-a-saucer then flatten-it the fuck straight-out liked thems two fucking lobes of hisns hadda been pinched-it between the thumb and the top of a curled and fisted pointer-finger then squeezed just tight to be pulled-it forwards! BillyT's lobe-shit be that all *fuck you* natural, the God given born with shit. Women folks be theys Black, White, Red, Brown or Oriental be theys rich or poor, fined be they asses or dems be the plain-Jane ladies evens unto thems assed-out third-world po'assed-out womenfolks seed it hadn't to mattered one unHoly fuck abouts thems womenfolk what be theys lot in life nor theys status single, married, widow or divorced cause it be a woman's thang seed thems womenfolks would all by the shit-loads done got hooked sight-seen on hisns fucking big assed lobes and just nuttin be a common denominator for them womenfolks because thems ladies of the World woulda done lined-it up then the each to every one dat done lookey-looked to done peeked-it hisns big assed lobes hadda justa done rolled straight the fuck-up on BillyT then theys all justa commenced to done pulled-it, bit-it and or all the above to done straight-up suckled on them damned big assed earlobes of hisns the lucky Mofo! Thems gotta grab thems lobes womenfolk be liken-it had been their God-given inalienable rights to done suckled free style onto hisns big assed lobes, the lucky bastard!

BillyT butter knowed-it as *Lobes* seed that big assed lobes Yaqui Love God hadda earned hisns call-sign at a civilian airport in Malaysia when this *drop da' fuck fucking dead* gorgeous slender tea-rose skinned big tittied honey a superb *LBFM* chink variety justa strolled-it herns silky beautiful commie-chink fine-ass straight-up on da' Bro to done suckled-it hard and long on firstest the one thens hisns other big assed lobe right-out front us and fo' everybody in the terminal who had theys lying eyes opened to done seed-it thens rights after she done did dat bad-assed banging shit the *Hindu Goddess* voiced-it just so righteously seed it came about that she done gave-it a hushed yet heated whisper to BillyT big-*lucky*-butts justa sound-bite on the loud enough fo' the rest of us unenlightened dumb-asses to done heard-it *"You be a God in my country"* and dat be the real truth, Ruth!

Bush-Reg done finally given them execution *Orders* then the Herk took to flight to done shit us out portside! I don't knowed-it iffn it hadda been the Love God's big assed Yaqui earlobes or the propwash froms thems two big-*turbos*-butts when I decked-it out on cue, behind Lobes, I done hit a patch of the bad-*luck buzzard*-luck to done bitch-flipped-it my ass thus I couldn't fo' the life in me be done knowed-it *witch way be up* to done T-squared my shit! It be Trips tar-baby mid-night black over that Atlantic ocean plus I couldn't tell iffn I be falling, floating parallel to the waters or be all caught-it up in an up-draft thus it be dat Shortdogg Zeke truly be fucked! On a night with no moon, no stars nor man-made lightings available for the ready-on point referencing then the ocean hadda looked-it exactly liked the nighttime sky with them whitecaps lapping over one inta the other just liked theys wavy asses be thems fluffy white clouds in da' star-less sky *as above as below*... that be the biblical shit, baby dat be *OT* shit on the reals, Old Testament big-*Amen*-butts the ting be I couldn't get a true bearing as to my air-borne status! The Herk be running silent and in the black although I could hear them engines getting theys buzz-on any thems night sounds be surround-sounds so I just couldn't be fo' sure where the fuck dat buzz be fo'reallies coming from fuck I done broke the buzzard fucking luck! I couldn't afford to just pull my chute cause iffn I be up-side down then *instant grits* thems opened silky-silk drawls would envelope me like a sack-o-shit then I'd blue ribbon, you knowed-it I'd be the first one to hit the ocean dat there splat thang be done *bye-bye cruel world* waved-it my beautiful Black ass adios motherfucker!

I be kiting that much I hadda done knowed-it for sure in that my short-dog black ass be caught-it up in and or on an air-stream justa floating with no control though I kicked-it, screamed-it and to the yeah, Hell yes, I done prayed-it *"Lawd above and Hey you dick-head below, please to send me befo' I die some pussy, Black pussy, White pussy, Blonde pussy, Red pussy, Yellow pussy, Brown pussy, even Rainbow pussy, but please God-o-the-Pussy don't be sending me no damned Grey pussy"* I hadda fell bout fiddy-feet a second, I took off both jump-boots to done did the math, I had had to calm my mind, re-tender my thoughts to order thems *Tiffany cuff-links* to square my ass! Word-up this patch of dirt 75% watered down bitch hoe of a planet fo'reallies do be flat, I done seed it from the air a'plenty and done humped-it from the ground a good and a'plenty! Strange but true justa afore dat asshole to beat all assholes *brotha fear* hadda done kicked-it to me square the fuck in my getting tighter and mo' tighter be tight nut-sack,

I had per chanced-it just to done remembered-it the time back on the tub running thems lazy-daze lap-dances between Guam and New Zealand this tight-assed crazed Mofo po'dunk Navy scrub F-4 jet-jockey be screaming from the top of hisns soons to be cancerous fucking *Marlboro* smoky tarred lung-bags some straight-up bullshit bouts how he never flew formation *fuck you, mofo you'll fly dat bitch today* without a belly tank. The bastard had wanted-it us wrench-monkeys be to done put an unnecessary center-line fuel tank on hisns bird big-*fuck you*-butts that bitch bastard scaly-wag jet-jock Mofo just be on a keep'em honest stern to port fly bye-bye thus that white whiny wuss-fuck onliest gonna be airborne poontang-time some tree to five-minutes. The belly tank with testing be a tree-hour nut job and it hadda been a hundred and thirty plus degrees on that flight deck! Fuck dat funky fuming at the mouth bitch-hoe scumbag! Big-*stupid*-butts it had been that dumb-fucked bastard's fuck *I be a whiteboy* selfish entitlement *I'm a fucking Officer* assed-out little weenie-whining dat done saved-it my black ass seed hisns *I'm a white pilot do as I say* reasoning behind hisns whiny assed useless plea for a belly tank had serendipitously banged-it upon my mind's inner ear-drum "*if I hit somebody's jet wash and kited, all I have to do is jettison that center-line tank, the jolt will square my ass outta the fall*" what a spoiled-assed po'dunk bitch I'd done thunk-it at the time when that jet-jock trashy-whitey spoiled-assed po'dunk hadda been full-throttled belly-aching that bullshit big-*whiney*-butts just in case that whiny mofo shit done on the reals held water, I reached and pulled-it a ten-inch blade from my inner left-thigh then I curled my ass into a semi-ball, knees up and angled towards chest befo' I ripped-it open my reserve chute when those dumb-ass books hadda begun bouncing-it offa my big nappy watermelon thems jettisoning books be on the holla *hey-hey Shortdawg Zeke Whoops up-side the head* be upside-down, Babycakes! Quick be the shit I'd done bicycled to done rolled-it over and righted-it to done squared dat ass to let them silky drawls catch theys selves a breath of the freshest mid-night oceanic air even most quicker I'd done loosened them cords all the way max to done slowed-it the descent. Luckily, I'd only missed the dock-it up dingy by about two-clicks. I be alive and since I done growed-it up Unk' Zeke's pond thus the short titi swim to the rubber boat hadda been an appreciated option.

As any Blues man can tell ya' Brotha, *Sir Bad-Luck'* he came in big bad assed batches dat be buckets of the bullshit buzzard-luck fo' yo' big black ass! Later though in all *pass the ganja* reality, it had been just earlier dat same morning be when the buzzard luck done bit my Short-dog ass a'gin-n-juice seed one of thems raggamuffins an unlucky fuck done gotten off a lucky round during the airport intervening and Short-dog Zeke out-front on-point hadda tooken-it a Jiffypop 9-mil lead-ball to hisns left arm just above the elbow break big-*lucky*-butts the good news be the onliest news in that the shot had made a clean entry with an even cleaner exit lucky be my black ass that ball hadn't hit anyting vital big-*lucky*-butts the loss of blood had been quick since I be Short-dog on-the-point then I hadn't taken nonya any mo' thems fucking death be *In-coming* chances, I found a safe haven, clicked the counter, sleeved the arm then injected myself before passing the fuck-out that part be pure *in an emergency break glass* training!

Chapter 41

When I hadda came to the firstest ting first that I had done checked-it because in our unit be it had to be the firstest ting first to be done officially checked-it whether or not my left boot and my left foot be both left in-tact and still attached to my Tank God *not left fo' dead* body! Next, I had noted that our resident medic had refitted-it and properly dressed my broken-wing seed Bad-*to the*-Bone fucking B-double-t-B aka Staff Sergeant SSgt Jared Maxwell dat half-breed mofo be one bad assed knife welding motherfucker that skinny assed tall and lanky witch's brew be a real live cowboy bumping-it up in the rottening flesh outta that Tucson bunch of dems we usta-be reserves seed Bad-to the-Bone's dad be a veterinarian on a cacti burred over grown wild weeds *puss n' boots* ranch some 80 plus miles outside then south of Tucson thus it hadda been all natural that Bad-*to the*-Bone had been our unit's medic being dat he hadda growed-it up stitching cow asses together with cactus quill and bubblegum. *BttB* looked just liked a wannabe *Britt* in the original *The Magnificent Seven* 1960 Hollywood movie 'cepting BttB be the real *mayo'* greasy white bread spread shit! Not onliest had he looked-it liked Britt big-*lanky*-butts just liked dat Britt character in the movie what dat fool ass cowpoke BttB couldn't do with a blade justa couldn't be done this world! The fat fact, Jack in the beginning *Britt* had been BttB's call-sign *Emmett Till* we hadda done learnt-it all abouts hisns Mexican momma situation then hisns fucking call-sign had officially become Bad-to the-Bone. On the reals, beside the Mexican momma thing BttB be mango *Kool-Aid* kool with my black ass besides hisns evil ass hadda been justa liked me in the bestest of hisns evil assed ways in that dat long tall lean and meaner than snake-shit mofo didn't drink nor smoke dope and he didn't do any thems all kinda nuttier drugs neither big-*keeping it real*-butts ever-so-often he'd puff the magic dragon, to done *Cotton-eyed Joe* it up with dat *MariJane girl*, the po'dunk cow-poke said he'd gotten sideways crossed from hisns momma and that her bad vibes be in hisns blood. BttB dat mofo be the firstest sad-sack mofo dat I'd ever had the misfortune to done meet-it up with that had hard-*fucking I hates you*-tack fo' hisns own momma and hisns onliest insane fucking reason be because hisns momma be a real live in the flesh authentic born in Mexico stayed in Mexico *Senorita.* I done seed with my owns beautiful baby browns hisns outright beautiful Mexican moms at hisns fucking big ranch wedding *Good laud* she be a mature *Beyonce* look-alike an older finer than *J-Lo*, yo' BttB don't be sweating-it to be getting-it all swollen cause tis onliest payback and big due RESPECT cause Bro yo' moms be a top-tier world class beauty!

TOP done taken us to Arizona to a big assed Army training center Fort Huachuca, we done trained-it thems Gatlings, big mobile guns and small cannons afterwards we had all hitched-it our dressed thread britches on over to BttB's done growed-it up in hacienda and hisns wedding. I hadn't taken it too damned kindly to BttB's po'dunk redneck Messkin hating daddy a po'dunk whiteboy mule doc serving all thems Arizona and Mexico border ranches thus daddy racist mofo be the po'dunk redneck that done trained and taught hisns onliest git to hate all fucking Messkins even the wannabe a whiteboy's own *Superfly* fine Mexican momma, damned iffn that don't be some kinda racist reversed Oedipus complexible bullshit! Big-*get yo' hate on*-butts BttB had dat Injun *bad blood* in hisns bigoted half-a-Messykin whiteboy wannabe ass and because of that Injun blood he'd done always reminded-it to me abouts my Great-great-GrannieG! *Nawl, oh Hell to the nawl* that half-breed po'dunk a'tinkering hisns *I hates all Messkins even my own damned Messkin momma* wannabe whiteboy po'dunk bye-bye any other fucking name Fuck No *Hells to all dems southern belles* nawl that jackass cowpoke didn't celebrate *Junteenth* nor have any love fo' *We the Peoples* big-*Black Be Beautiful*-butts them twos BttB and my Great-great-GrannieG had done shared-it a common linkage in that theys both shared a mutual profession as swell theys both cantered to a sacred ritual that had been incorporated within each the one as a major happening to theys own personal medical practice.

I hadn't knowed-it anyting personal bouts my Great-great-GrannieG cause she'd been on the upstart into her 2nd century before I done firstest done dropped-it a diaper-less turd upon this big green earth! My Moms hadda done told-it to me mostest all that be my onliest versions of the storied past concerning my Great-great-GrannieG in that she be a natural healer and all thems older peeps done said it be that way because she had Injun in herns blood. When the times be, that everybody hadda done shoveled all theys on the personal shit into a gunny-sack then moved-it up North *bye-bye* little Missy-sip-pee thens theys had theys firstest meets-it-up with Mr. Hawkins and hisns icy *brrrr* cold freeze an ass to death blowing snow winds with hims alla time justa shitting ice and sleet all abouts the Windy and over to the CC! *Old man Hawkins* justa be a pissing-it out hisns evil death threats from both hisns raunchy-assed piss-nuts in that the one be full of influenza and the evil-assed other nut done toted pneumonia then thems peeps hadda come a'running-it to my Great-great-GrannieG fo' the healings big-*thankful*-butts there be dems times when herns regular roots and remedies be not working then the peeps woulda gone out to done brung-it back fo' GrannieG a pipe of that whacky-tobaccky, rabbit lettuce that MariJane girl then GrannieG would smoke a bowl of da' whacky and after a bit of time spent to dancing with thems mellowed-it out hankerings then my Great-great-GrannieG would step-down into the root cellar and come back-up with the mixture to done healed a body all the way butter. Bad-*to the*-Bone hadda done exactamente kinda the same ting for our unit in that every now to a then he'd get a hankering to done rolled-it up a fatty not justa dubbie big-*rollin'*-butts a fat-ass Jiffypop ganja special to done chest bumped-it with the magic dragon and dat be how and onliest dat be how dat halfa-cracker half-breed skank-hoe mofo Messkin momma hating *the whore* of a cowpoke wannabe whiteboy ig'nant po'dunk backwaters fuck hadda in any kinda way fashioned-it be to done in anyways kinda reminded-it me abouts my Great-great-GrannieG!

A time in thems, Philippines on the eve befo' a'nutter mission BttB had done lit-it up a fatty then took a little stroll through the jungle next early morn the unit be walking-it along through a thick be darkened part of that rickety-whacked wicked pineapple jungle where everything be as thorny as I be a horny mofo big-*tank ya*-butts it done happened so fast it be liked a living flash of the Hollywood reel cause what went down be the unit be following single-file along a morning fresh animal trail justa chilling befo' we gets our attack-on then fucking lightning quick BttB runned-it to the front bye-bye passed-it the Shortydawg on-point WTF *bang* BttB done throwed-it tree ten-inch blades into one of thems trees and down the fuck felled-it a lone rebel flip-sniper sum-dey-bitch be all locked-it and loaded with a banana clipped Russian AK-47! Hell, lessen 20 mo' clicks and we'd all have been dead men walking!

There be the time justa routine ranchito raid a'gin-n-juice after one of hisns wacky-tobaccky *out of the blue* hankerings Bad-*to the*-Bone hadda runned-it up from behinds the on-point psycho tar-baby black claiming dat hisns black ass be a fucking Messykin, Trips it be thens BttB justa hauled-it off and done one-punched-it to done knocked Trips on hisns crazy ass *fuck* BttB done sho'nuff donkey-punched that fake Messykin black ass psycho mofo *Word* be that BttB done damned near cold-cocked Trips the fuck-out on a purpose and dat part justa mighta been a wee little itty-bitty the real truth, Ruth because Trips allatime liked-it to done roll called-it *Hey you hop-headed half-assed Messkin wetback with shit fo' brains here's yo' fucking mail* besides punching the fuck outta Trips that *I don't wannabe a fucking Messykin* BttB quick be shit done turned-it all backwards to done shoveled Priest, he'd only do Catholic girls *may he rest in Peace* away befo' he done C-4 blowed-it the fuck away that assed-out ranchito entry door alla while shouting at the top of hisns snake-bitten lungs *"gun moll, gun moll, gun moll"* witch fo' us hadda been the safe *get the fuck up and outta here* word of the day! That particular bitchin ranchito raid had been a fucking death-trap sto-bought readymade set'em the fuck-up in that thems midget fuck-face Aztec coke-manufacturing *we run this jungle* pharmaceutical whores hadda done hauled-it theys *boobytrap'em* asses outta there via an underground tunnel big-*scam*-butts befo' theys done the mad exodus them bitch-assed betos had done placed-it the dynamite, gasoline and all sorts of combustible gibberish *blow a motherfukka-up* shit on the other side of that entryway. Finally, when Priest, he'd only do Catholic girls *may he rest in Peace* hadda done time-release triggered-it the C-4 that whole damn assed-out ranchito shack done big sky danced-it thens done two-stepped-it *bits-be-to-pieces* afore all that shit done ashed the ground! Bad-*to the*-Bone's creepy ass *Spiderman* instincts be of the legendary goodie-stuff within and without the unit to the point that iffn BttB done felt it justa little bit of the sump-tin sump-ting then we as a unit plus any-to-all hitch-hikers justa every-fucking-body hadda just said fuck-it to all and to what all that hadda been previously planned-it then we'd all done did that shit in the whatever however exactamente way as Bad-*to the*-Bone done re-laid it out! Nobody not even TOP nor Trips hadda wanted-it to bump-it up uglies with BttB's funky premonitions big-*Spirit in the Sky*-butts hisns eerily right on, my Brotha to the fucking point hunches done proved-it to be damned deadly accurate like a motherfucker be hisns WTF *Spiderman* instincts!

Anywho Bad-*to the*-Bone half-breed ass done dry-patched my center-punched wing big-*medic*-butts the problem be that *Lobes* done taken-it my 9-mil H&K and two of my tree 10-inch blades plus that damned psycho tinkering he's a fucking asshole Messykin done snagged all my ammo *"Hey, mofo' don't be playing possum"* the Yaqui Love God 'pologized when he'd tossed me my H&K! *"Clip on a pair, mofo"* Trips done challenged *"and grab yo' pussy praying monkey ass some of da' good shit!"* No, no tank-ya Trips there be plenty of fucking ammo somewhere world and *Sooners* that ammo gonna be mines big-*no way I be dancing with yo' psycho ass*-butts *Tanks tank-ya' berry kindly*! I be alive and *Good Lordy* my ass bouts to be *free at last* unleashed unto this world! Fuck with Trips, all hail to the nawl! I'd done been there and hadda done e'nuff that shit on the fuck-me up-close be sooo personal to done *got shot in the ass* learnt-it my lesson all to swell dat death aints a fucking lesson to be done learn-it any parts abouts whilst truck'n with a super deranged Blacker than mid-night Black assed-out *why the fuck you* wannabe a Messykin muddafucker!

Chapter 42

TRIPS BE ONE CERTIFIED PSYCHO mofo whom myself alongside justa bouts everybody and I believed-it evens TOP done held-it a righteous and healthy dose of *brotha fear* when it came to *bumping uglies* up against an engaged with a definite purpose psycho-ass Trips! Iffn not for the Nam war/conflict then Trips be voted the most likeliest mofo to have been a crazed-assed serial killer off the ropes running loose headed fo' all ports bordering unto Bonkersville! I done mentioned-it that checking my left foot be the firstest ting that I did when I done arrived-it my awoke state because that be law numero uno fo' the each and every one of us iffn Trips be any-to-fucking where near bye-bye yo' ass getting wounded. Trips that psycho bastard woulda done taken-it upon hisnsself to done shot-it off a mofo's left-foot in-order to collect a fallen Bro's identifying dog-tag witch everybody wore inside their left boot. Reasoning be dat iffn sum fucked-it up bad-assed buzzard luck shit done happened-it upon a mofo and the icy-cold finger of hisns God be rolling along the crack of hisns crusty ass-cheeks such dat Bro done high-stepped-it the way of the *bye-n-bye* then hisns left boot mostest be likely to done stayed secured to hisns left-foot and mostest times iffn a body got blown to fucking pieces fo' whatever reason the left-foot, the left-boot and the dog-tag seemed to always have remained-it a *tree-piece* combo to be left-it intact. Trips hadn't wanted-it to deal with taking-it the titi time necessary to unlace/cut the boot open seed dat mid-night black mofo' monkey-do-do assed-out psycho bastard would without fail just take-it out hisns Colt .45 at close range, at a fucking close e'nuff to get blood stain splatters on yo' ass range dat crazed assed-out mofo be done blowed-it the left-foot completely offa a body. Iffn the foot still be footed inside the boot dat psycho whore done fired-it yet a'nuttier round to blow the boot wide the fuck opened to done blasted-it that foot completely outta the boot alla while shouting "*Dance mofo*! *Dance yo' last dance with me*" and all dem there times Trips the crazy ass Mofo be justa' skinning and grinning whilst he done danced to the psycho looney-tunes orchestra non-stop bumping out thems crazies surround-sound hisns funky Messykin wannabe psychotic mind! The psycho Trips be justa dancing buckaroo style happy-assed liked a mofo on the holla "*Dance with me, mofo dance ya' last dance with me*!"

The real truth, Ruth be that motherfucker psycho assed-out dancing like a motherfucker be straight-up on the serious biz with that shit! The ting though had been how-*so fucking*-ever dat fucking dancing happy-ass wannabe a messykin Trips and I do give dat psycho crazed-ass mofo hisns credit that be due caused dat crazy-ass Devil-Dawg had some funky yet legit logic for doing dat damned *insane on the membrane* graveyard do-wah-ditty! Trips told-it, when a body gots born tree tings always happened: the body got yanked from it's momma's bloodied ass then slapped on it's bloodied ass and iffn it screamed then them little bloodied assed footsies be printed on its bloodied ass birth certificate thus accordingly by actually seeing the bloody left-foot that shit done come full-circle dems wagons dat crazed mofo said it done made sho'nuff the once born now a dead man's ass most rightful identification! Nobody and I mean nobody

Medgar Evers bothered to inform that psycho wannabe Messykin maniac that he wasn't gonna be shipping the bloody stomp just the dog-tag back to HQ. Iffn there always be a logic for the illogical justification of doing an unreasonable particular thing then it's a given that there will always be a logical reason when caught doing a peculiar thang at the wrong time besides the given reasonable and logical explanation broadcast by the wrongful doer of such tings there always be without exception the fo're-allies reason that a ting done, did gots done in the firstest damned place and in the case of psycho assed-out Trips, I on the reals truly believed-it that the onliest on the real fucking reason fo' hisns psychotic monkey-ass shooting the left-foot off a lifeless body be that fool-ass be just one sadistic Motherfucker serial killer wannabe! First ting our unit firstest made fo' damned sure dat yo' almost dead-ass hadn't been the one to done danced-it yo' last dance with the likes of dat fucking tar-baby black Mexican *jumping-beaner* psychotic Devil-dawg Trips!

Chapter 43

I'D DONE A'PLENTY MORE STINTS big-*crazy*-butts there be a few short-termed memorable other scenarios liked 78' we be balls-deep within the Congo helping them Belgian *ya-ya* waffles and *Pepe Le'Phew* French toasted forces whom be done caught-it raw dog with the rotten egg on theys pasty white-faces because theys done failed-it in *theys* estimation of the local rebel forces ambitious we gots the numbers *lets just take the fuck over* endeavors thus thems Belgians waffles and thems French-fried toasties done needed-it sumtin sumpting powerfully bad a pause to done gotta gets hauled-it theys chunky hunky white-monkey asses outta there and a'sways from the *People's Republic* successful rebellions. Them early 80s, done also ushered my ass over to thems wetland jungles of El Salvador and Nicaragua where bye-bye them little pigmy Aztec gibberish speaking midgets be justa running-it bare-assed naked and fucking with the all kinda peeps down yonders even fucking with the likes of thems midget fucks over the Honduras wey! Thens came thems fucking DEA agents, the pinky-pink pig whores of the dope-dealing world be the most sorry-assed of rich white bitch birthed bastards to ever done toted-it a shiny-tin bronze badge on theys po'dunk deputized-it chest thems DEA whores had no honor, no pride, thems SOBs be justa chunk of money hungry *sons of the skank-hoe white rich* bitches! Ritz be my the sloppy-seconds go-round of an unfaithful lousy-assed *no nuts to scratch* po-po husband outta the bunch because the firstest bastard fuck done up and runned-it hisns po'dunk ass back to the States after just two fucking days of nuptial bliss screaming fo' an annulment! Ritz, what a fucking pussy! *"You prayed for it, good Lawd! Now, you got it"* TOP be the proud strutting El Poppa when he hadda done gloated-it to be done tossed-it dat lazy-assed whore my way *"Serves yo' heathenish ass, right"*

Ritz tanned rich cracker, a fucking Princeton grad, 6-foot, 195 soaking wet pounds of the pink cotton-candied manicured fingernails chicken-shit asshole! The firstest R&R, I tried to done did a good thang, I took dat pink assed punk bastard to meet my favorite Bogota lady of the late knight, *Maricela* tricked-it outta little yellow-green two-bedroom sugar-board shack in barrio *Villa del Gatos Negros* black pussy town located deep inside the city's poorest yet most colorful slum. I done left Ritz the pussy-assed mofo in the other bedroom with *Camilla* dat bitch be a sho'nuff nene straight-up café-latte skinned hoodlum-girlfriend lover roommate yet she be *da' shit* somehow, liken unto a birth mother dat done heard-it the squalor of herns onliest baby child over all the noise on a busy playground, I be damned iffn I hadn't done heard-it dat pink assed man-pussy's gurgle! Buck-ass naked, I done runned-it back to done kicked-it in Camilla's bedroom's waffle thin placard hand-painted aqua-blue with gold-fish trimmings bedroom door witch thems two whores done bragged bouts the paint-job dat shit be *feng-shui* witch be Chinese gook gibberish shit to garner good wind/good water some kinda commie-chinks lucky-assed wealth thing. *Whoops there it is'* Ritz be to all fours, knife at hisns fucking throat, Camilla and herns sorry-ass 90-pound boy-pimp atop hisns pink pulled-taffy rich whiteboy ass WTF! Thems tree horrified bastards justa done frozen-it in-place when theys done peeked my Black be beautiful naked ass burst the fuck-in on thems big-*whupped it*-butts then that shit hadda just gotten too damned ugly for words!

That little ranchito raid dat unfaithful day when my dumb-ass done decided dat it be bouts high noon and high time to fucking dance with the Devil the too damned Black to be a Messykin himself! It be an early morning raid witch had all been about the planning and that shit had been well planned-it to its mostest minute be intimate detail witch 99 point 9 outta 100 times be justa a'nuttier sweet-ass free-money, dog and pony show, nothing the more be bringing-it on nonya the less! The ranchito, an abandoned deteriorating once white stone and rock shack with weatherworn broken pieced-it together red terra-cotta roof a tree-room, one tier dilapidated shit-shack deep inside the that fucking jungle it be just an on the simple *easy money* soft-target. We hadda done surveillance of the place on at least 8 different occasions and dat last time we'd done stayed about and clocked-it thems there *rent*-a-*betos* local guard whores for over tree-weeks justa a'watching theys assed-out non-military asses move abouts the place. 12 *cabrones* goat-bangers secured the ranch and the dope witch theys lame asses done stored-it in a lean-to wooden makeshift open air stacked bales weatherworn make-shift barn. We had done accurately timed each of them *putos* from their earliest morning piss zero-five-hundred-hours *Emmett Till* theys late night ass-scratching zero-a-buck-twenty-hundred hours circle-jerk thens the two late-night guards would mostest often than not cop a tree to sometimes 4-hour snooze and of the two just one of thems lazy asses be riding shotgun in the front room of the ranchito then the other fuck be asleep outside the ass-end of the barn. It be kinda funny how death seems to done always slipped-it up on the lazy-ass fuck napping on watch-duty. Seven *betos* witch be local fucks be stationed outside guarding the house and a'nutter five done guarded the barn onliest during day-light hours, simple enough, a chunk of *tres leche* tree-milks cake! Thems usta be Aztec gibberish speak Injuns short pegged-leg little asshole jungle-bunnies coke-smuggling mofos theys all be assed fucked backwards in everything theys do the small-*midget*-butts theys ass-backwards shit be a cultural thing in that theys modus operandi *little macho-shits* didn't as a norm seed thems pygmies didn't attack each other or no-somebody during the late night. Thems gibberish speak ass-whores done felt themselves *Memo-bad-asses* Memo be gibberish fo' Billy seed theys always stepped-it up face to fucking face in the broad span of the rising Sun thems day-light horas be theys macho shit *mano a mano* man to man, fight by the light of day be a man, Puto! It done tooken-it a real gringo *chingas tu Madre pinche puto* an unhonest Injun fuck-you motherfucker whore to done way-laid-it somebody during the black night! WTF thems midget fools be ass-backward collar-greens justa chunk of the stoopid midget gibberish speak mofos! That shit be in theys primordial dust seed dat shit be theys inherent Aztec midget Injun kinda thing from when theys alien teacher outta a'nuttier world *Quetzalcoatl* done rolled-it hisns mothership upon theys dumb pygmy asses to done built theys damned pyramids backs in thems day-light midget ass saving times!

We were going to strike those particular assed-out guard whores about zero-four-hundred-fiddy-five hours onliest because TOP held boo-coo RESPECT for the gibberish speak native customs, fuck dat shit! The real deal, thems *bato* simpletons would be deep into *la suena dulce'* the sweet-dream that last and bestest part of the early *Momma-mita po'lease I don't wanna get offa this dirt floor to go to a fucking the ass-backward schooling fo' the Pygmy only* morning, Lord hava mercy dream! Priest, Blessed-it be hisns poor little Catholic heart would only do Catholic girls, *may he rest in Peace* seed I can't count the number of lbfms and all thems Latina whores thems skank fine-assed nenes all of whom we hadda done doused-it in some damned tap unHoly water blessed by the *Big Papa* hisns own-*unholy nasty assed Black it be mid-nite*-self Staff Sergeant SSgt Larry B. Pope, the B stood for Bernard, who be the lousy fuck to done named theys onliest fucking male git a fucking Bernard and that fool he be no saint! Anywho after the Pope's blessing bye-bye dousing that fucking unholy piss water onto the rent-a-choochie skank ass then he'd done triple crossed-it thems newly commissioned newly Communioned Catholic ladies of the blessed Knight just so dat sad-eye mofo could get hisns *sad-eye* laid big-*blessed*-butts Priest, *may he rest in Peace* be more than just damned fucking good with C-4, he gonna blow the cheap-ass grated-iron front door to that ranchito offa its damned even cheaper assed-out hinges.

Chapter 44

TOP FIRST-MAN ENTRY THAT RAID, first-man entry that be always the bestest of the best and the most envied position on any entry raid in that you got to see firsthand up-close the stunned look *Good Lawd* the bugged-eyed fish-mouthed *Oooh, I just shit my pants* lookey-look just the awe of it all, followed-it up quickly with a WTGSF*WhatTheGibberishSpeak-Fuck* etched all over theys pinche *nearer my God to Thee* OMG fuck-face(s) cause theys pygmy ass bouts to be departed this world *Adios el mundo* goodbye-bye world theys Azteca cunt face(s) gonna be the latest lost Soul(s) just to done left this realm for other parts unknown-it Universal! *Generalissimo*, first-man entry could squeeze off some 7 to 10 rounds into the soft-target(s) then dat pygmy mofo(s) be a dead mofo(s) befo' first-man done runned-it through to be cleared the entry room. Second-man entry be the most dangerous position of any entry raid because the entry room guard(s) *fuck's* natural reflexes would have begun to have kicked-it in upon second-man's entrance usually the fuck(s) would have begun to return fire big-*dying*-butts not at first-man who *bye-bye* then first-man entry be sway long on the *I be* gone second-man entry be *In-coming* if-fns the big-*bouts to be dead*-butts barely alive fuck(s) had some disciplined well-trained combative instincts then the fuck's lying-eyes outta natural reflex shit be more than likely to done looked-it in the direction of the entry-point from whence the flash of all that blowed-it the fuck up *tank-ya Mr. C-4* along with thems sounds of the entry-way's big-banged explosion followed-it most quick assedly *bye-bye pygmy mofo* the red-yellow-blue flume offa thems .45 or .9 mil high velocity rounds blasted outta first-man entry's weapon witch be the fuck(s) final sounds and last this world vision *I be fucked* delivered-it bye-bye first-man entry's brutal and almost always surprising deadly lethal *In-coming*!

The guard fuck(s) even iffn gravely wounded-it many a times would have fired at least a return round or two at that entrance-way and that be the ting that had made second-man entry so perilous yet not the most least wanted-it position on any entrance raid. That had been a'nuttier big assed difference between the real world not being Hollywood reel world because being shot in the real world didn't instant grits kill off a body there be some time left in the fuck(s) to do major damage even to done taken-it other asses along fo' the death ride iffn the fuck(s) done chose to rattled them bones and held any parts raw-dog in hisns just *got fucked* ass! Second-man entry had to come in high and tight behind first-man in a low all to most kneeling yet runned-it kinda position and second-man entry had to be running-it hard and fast also second-man had to be centered of the entryway because for whatever scientific reason witch my being a by-product of the unschooling for the Negro only dumb-ass be too dumb-assed to know, hadn't done knowed-it then and to this day still don't done knowed-it now the why of it all big-*uneducated*-butts that shit just be the way it be seed in the real world of an attack zone thems bullets tended to ricochet offa wall, floor or ceiling then travel in a straight-line about 6 to 8-inches parallel along the nearest adjacent perpendicular wall, floor and or ceiling. Second-man's mission had been not to take-out nor worry the fuck about any fucked one(s) in the entry-room, second-man be hauling-it ass-over-porcelain teacups mayhaps justa quick repartee with the dying fuck(s) *I see ya' Mofo*! *You be one dead-assed mofo* cause second-man entry be focused as swell hisns ass be low-stepping-it on the quick to hisns assigned location. All the flash banging/C-4 explosions done woke every-fucking-body in the place wide the fuck to be a'scard-ass awake thus speed be the name of second-man entry's game. After the dangerous ass entry second-man had the easiest and safest job of all because usually second-man would be assigned to a secondary room where it be usually secondary rooms housed-it sleeping fucks and sleeping fucks soons to be dead fucks of whom everybody done knowed-it dat shit abouts dead men in that theys monkey-asses see no evil, hear no evil and theys dead asses don't tell no his-*lying ass*-stories!

Third-man entry be the shit because third-man would have seed-it the gun-powder that had exploded from the fuck(s) weapon(s) when the fuck(s) done returned-it fire at the entryway thus mostest of all thems entry raid times it be third-man upon arrival to done on a calculated purpose tooken-it a nano of a second pause for the cause to done looky-looked hisns lucky assed self a legit target(s) to cut-loose at and generally speaking third-man entry be done racked the majority of confirmed kills mostest them raids. Third-man entry hadn't been a bad position to be in iffn yo' blood-thirsty ass done wanted-it all thems accolades thems funky-flunky little tin-medals tied to them little red-white-buffoon ribbons.

Fourth-man entry be an unlucky most trusting bastard on earth, fourth-man entry done rolled-it in hard and tight on the heels of third-man entry with hisns eyes and hands wide the fuck opened because hisns weapon be holstered. Fourth-man entry be to *bag-n-tag* witch meant that fourth-man entry had to cuff/hog-tie any fuck(s) alive or just departed *Adios al mundo* this world big-*goner*-butts theys body be physically inside the entry-room. Fourth-man had to physically secure and disarmed any weapon(s) and that be why forth-man entry be the most hated and unwanted-it position on the entry team. The *Clean-up man* had no time to question whether or not thems firstest tree be faithful to theys duties *Mr. Janitor-man* gotta fo'reallies done trust-it thems early entry mofos with hisns life!

Fifth-man entry be just *a'rootin and a'tootin* blasting lead on the dead-run as well listen for a call to aid either of the firstest tree, fifth-man entry's main job be to keep any fuck(s) distracted-it from the holstered fourth-man doing his thang the bag-n-drag two-step ditty-bop. *Filthy-man* J-O-B be to done blasted-it live rounds into any fuck(s) moving within the entry-room except forth-man! Fifth-man entry be fourth-man entry's protector and an emergency back-up to everybody else on the entry team. It took practice, trust, dedication and timing to be pulled-off successfully yet 9-point-9 times out of 10 thems little dog-n-pony show ranchito raids always done spanked-it easy like a firstest slap to a newborn's gun-powdered ass!

Chapter 45

THE THING MOSTEST DIFFERENT AND difficult to maneuver around in thems jungles of the South Americas versus the South East Asian jungle missions besides thems fine *Tank-ya Big Guy in the Sky* big-tittied nenes and all the bulk cocaine manufacturing/trafficking though some of them gooner-gook fucks done trafficked-it the heroin Biggy-*smalls*-butts in thems slant-eye jungles the biggest differ bye-bye far be them damn *buzzard breaths* of the Central Americas the hired fucking gun that fo're-allies westward hoe! There be no hired gunslingers in South East Asia thus we had done never trained-it fo' thems big-*bastard*-butts in them snow-capped jungles of the South Americas theys be chocked to the *Dunkin* ass cream-filled *Doughnuts* with thems hardline buzzard breaths. All thems little midget injuns done hired theyselves a highly trained-it para-military security force to cover theys ranchitos and theys chili-peppered asses! Every now to aplenty of thens, the unit hadda had the opportunity of done runned-it upon them well-trained ex-military hired guns witch be getting the big payday thems done gots paid mercenaries be thems *un-magnificent seven*! Sometimes theys came in the form of *ex-Nam/ex-rump-rangers* straight-up combat US veterans justa still hooked on that kill or be killed adrenalin spike and them boys just had to get paid and Good Lord *theys* done gots paid-it swell thems ex-Vets done gots papered the fuck up, Baby! Thems drug lord midget whore mofos had deep-love and even deeper pockets fo' thems buzzard-breaths and thems little itty-bitty *can't reach the nips of herns big titties* drug-lord whores hadda done paid-it top-dollar for ex-Nam vets or fo' the mostest any man that done knowed-it the way of the iron-fist! Thems buzzard-breath gots paid though theys be not Barbie's Ken doll big-*stud*-butts fo' sure as all *Hell's a'jangling with slutty southern belles* thems tippy-top pin-heads don't pass da' bottom my big black balls midget Napolitano complexed-it druglord fuck fools done fucking straight-up paper-dolled-it the fuck outta all thems buzzard-breath gun-slinging whores! It didn't matter one wit to a fucked ass shit from witch nation that ex-military Vet done hailed out of yet the mostest big-*gots paid*-butts be American, French, British and thems damned to all *Hell, alongside dems southern belles* fucking bad-asses dat done killed-it the Mr. Jesus fucking Christ dems fucking Jew-boys!

We all in our own little Devil Dawg be damned iced over cold stone-pit hearts not a war justa fucking police action/conflict battle hardened Ja'renes hadda secretly knowed-it for a fat fact, Jack that anybody of us coulda would've been any everyone of thems *Bro gots to gets paid* lucky iron-fisted Mofos hired by thems pygmy druglords fo' a fo'reallies caramelized nougat big fucking extra-large sized *Payday* seed dem big extra-large paydays aints just fo' the nuts! Amongst thems buzzard-breaths it be more than justa few of us, to done runned-it upon ex-bunk Bros therefore an unofficial treaty amongst us and abided-it bye-bye thems it be *so righteous my Brotha to be getting it* paid top dollar Bros be *Word-up*! Normally, in any fucking raid be it a little ranchito or a *grande hacienda* the big family house, TOP done incorporated-it a ready-made *show my Bro da' luv* viable escape route plus there always be the little left-over bite of the wiggle-room for an impromptu on the Superfly give thems ex-Vets theys break-out chance. We'd all seed Nam, some more than others big-*postal*-butts everyone done figured-it that thems ex-rangers weren't gonna try to mucky-muck the shit up because of some silly little discharged without annulment papers nor would them buzzard-breaths try to become a *body-bag* hero out in thems jungles though theys be there for the pay yet on the reals liked us dat spiked *gimme the goodie-stuff* adrenaline rush be done put an itching in dat ass that can't be scratched any a'nuttier way! Secondly most of us be swinging through thems jungles fo' all that fine-assed *Sir Mixed-it-mucho* nenes thems Indian, African, Azteca and Spanish mixed bags of the *fuck me po-lease come fuck me* tricks that be a God given gift to any a happy-assed man! Wars be and all ways will be political big-*grunt*-butts soldiers be soldiers and mostest all soldiers be on the upstart po'assed-out men forced fed into some rich man's too rich to go out and fight hisns own damned *protect my monies* battles. We'd done cut-it loose the *Song of the Siren* the mighty roar of our babygirls popping off full-auto be to done let them vets to knowed-it just who the fuck theys be fucking with and iffn theys wanted-it this could be a friendly *dap-it up, Right-on my brotha, Groovy, Get the fuck outta here, Keep-on-trucking, Baby* kinda thang bye-bye and don't get trucked into a *howdy-doody* mofo wet-fire engagement kinda ting! The sound of automatic fire be *Word-up,* Baby its time to wake the fuck-up and gets fucking long on the gone fishing big-*ups Bro*-butts iffn that alarm be thems controlled tree-round bursts then it be too fucking late to done burst dat easy-exit move cause the shit be on the reals and da' shit be on, *Right-On my Brother*! We be liked *hear me roar* yalls just gots paid asses bouts to learns second-hand *What be going on*! After the raid, iffn they'd done asked-it or needed-it we'd get them Bros an un-official *Herk* back State-side *mums-da-word* transport it be all about the *R-E-S-P-E-C-T* Babycakes!

Them *ex*-French Guillotine mofos be the special forces seed thems Billy/Guillermo-bad-ass bastards froggy-motherfuckers be the firstest to ever clear VC tunnel with theys up-turned pink ass noses *"Gawd damn a fuck'n mofo' got his fuck'n pink-white assed nose in the fuck'n air always sniffing then looking down upon the brown-assed cocksucking pygmy midget that's been feeding him"* TOP swung a double-edged sword *"any mofo' can't respect his betters needs his fuck'n throat bladed and graded! Fuck'em in the ass then feed'em dick-head soup!"* Thems Frogs-asses be afforded-it the same opportunity of life, happiness and the pursuit of *le' pusse* offered-it to them American Vets, war be war, Babycakes!

When thems damned Israelis, fuck thems *ex-Moshads* rode fence then we fucking waylaid-it *no-fucking shit* we just jumped-it the fuck-up onto dems stick-horses then rode the fuck outta there usually to Cali where we done gots it up-close and personally waylaid by them pretty little lightly slightly tan-skinned big tittied keeping-it real street whores until the *Holy days* be bumping thems kosher nuts Jew-boy cut-dick cheap-ass gots paid motherfuckers! Hell, thems bitches theys be the ones that done trained our dumb-asses in the gorilla and urban warfare fight *"Fuck all you Gawd damned Martin Luther-fucked-up the world we loved-King Jr assholes and ball scratchers, you can just fuck'n dream on"* TOP preach it in the nene fur-lined streets *"every teen-aged bastard stroking his dead meat has the dream yet very Gawd damned few have the cajones, the big fucking balls to kick their daddy in the nuts then lived long enough to fart about it! Fuck them Mofo's"* TOP continued *"just wait till that hooked nosed fuck, penny-pinching cheap assed bastard bearded faced Jesus killing braidy bunch kiki motherfucker got his fucking ass cheeks ah' rocking and ah' knocking at that Gawd damned prayer wall"* TOP roared-it *"then we'll kick kosher nuts in his cheap ass 'til he's shitting manna on a one-way street to Jew-boy Hell! Fuck them Whores!"* We afforded the ex-Jew-boy the same thrills as all thems other war Vets big-*cheep*-butts TOP done hated-it thems *ex-Mooseheads* mostest of any to all thems buzzard-breaths. The firstest time, we fought-it a group of them whores, it come to a stand-the-fuck still big-*cut dick*-butts for a time justa wee bit of the time early on we had those shifty-eyed shitty dick-head bastards bottled-it up big fucking time in the big ranch house. We had them rock with me Moses, Jesus killing sums-dey-bitches dead to theys fucking braided hair sissy-girl *fucking-A* big-*kosher*-butts then somehow a second group of kvetched kike Shylock whores dems clipped-dick assholes come up behind us from outta the no-*fucking*-where then we done had ourselves a fucking *Surprise Surprize Surprise Sergeant Carter* moment! Fuck, we'd got dealt-it thems fucking two's and trees from the bottom of the deck because our perplexed caught-it up in a death trap asses be center-court a real live Mexican albeit Colombian jungle stand-the-fuck-off!

Not to knock-knee, TOP seed justa anyone would have done the same ting in the exactamently same way given the natural circumstances of the day. TOP had negotiated a jungle truce with thems sneak-thief sneaky ass done slid-it head first outta kosher cunt ass-whores big-*sneaky*-butts we done gotten-it for ourselves a big royally deep ass-fucking from a 12-inch circumcised dick! Thems give the moose head mofos wanted-it that we move atop a nearby hill where we could oversee theys *just give us time to get our cheap-asses be gone* operation the Jew-boy exit to be self-assured that thems itty-bitty-titty cap cunt-bitches be out in the fishbowl and that the negotiations hadda all been straight-up and over the countertop. The truce called-it for them kosher nut-sack sucking whores to have no more than tree rising Suns to move all the shit theys could carry-out thens whats left at the hacienda and inside the coke storage barn be ours to destroy. The coke had all been baled, bundled and stacked in a galvanized steel barn witch be bouts two-thousand square foot and some15-feet high *basta el culo*/up to the ass in cocaine! The shit be out in the middle of a no-where jungle with no roads into nor to be out from and them ex-Moosehead motherfuckers and theys mofo midget cocksucking bosses had totaled-it no more than 30 peoples big-*lying*-butts only 18 be menfolk and theys only had the five working pick-ups and two sedans to do all the transporting. It be *Hell to the yeah, mofo* because at that time there had been a group of armed-men to the front and a'nuttier group of armed moose head giving kosher-kuntz to the rear besides neither thems nor us done wanted-it to be fucking heroes, fuck dem little tin-medals it done took a real fucking genius to become gopher foodie fo' the likes of an CIA funded Azteca midget Injun dope money, Babycakes! Lessen an hour after the agreement them sons-of-kvetching Jew-boy sum-de-bitches cheap-ass sneak-thiefs thats done killed-it Jesus whores hadda flown in French choppers, *Bell* copters witch dems Jew-boys used to haul pallets of all theys shit outta harms way! Thems kosher kiki sons-de-vetches done drove-it to the hacienda seven half-tracks witch be army troop carrier trucks in that theys all truck in the front big-*fuck me*-butts in the rear be optional use tank tracks and the cargo bed on them half-tracks be open-air capable thus thems bitches can haul all kinda humongous shit! Thems fucking *Jew-boys* done grabbed-it theys chicken-noodle soup shitty-assed-selves every po'assed-out Injun that swung-it through that jungle and paid or theys done forced fed-it them peons to help pack to done moved-it the Azteca pygmy druglord family and all the coke dat shit be a sight to be done scene justa logistical masterpiece!

Some of the platoon wanted to bump-it up ugly like to done *burst a move* down to dat fucking hacienda and kick kike deep in hisns raunchy lying cheap-ass big-*kosher*-butts we'd made a gentleman's agreement thus TOP done told-it *"We rode a dead horse to place but the day gonna come when we'll win this fucking derby"* WTF we gonna do with a little round bolo hat? Thems bitch-bastard ex-Moshads *a raisin bagel aint no damned donut* muddafuckers hadda done moved-it all whilst we done sat, watched-it and protected theys kosher-nuts lying kiki asses from above on our negotiated hilltop perch and thems bitches done moved-it all theys shit in less than a day and a half. They had as a gesture of their goodwill and kindness fo' our stupidity in keeping our gentile word, thems whack-assed kosher-nuts ass-whores done left us the booty on the entry-room floor witch be a shit-load of gold watches and leather belts encrusted with precious jewels that be the valued goodie-stuff of choice then TOP done made us to give it all thems precious gems to thems po'assed-out bastard kids of thems lovely barrio whores breaking bad thems slums of Bogotá, Cali, Hell yes! We hadda done got assed-out fucked-it big-*stupid*-butts the silken purse be dat we done gots our nene *got back* on we done some real time raw-dawg fucking fo' some 30-daze Cali-cunts style because dems ill-begotten kosher cunt jewels done bought mucho pleasure as swell the loving touch fo' our own *tank-ya Jew-boy tank-ya berry kindly* family jewels! A'gin-n-juicy Lucy the good Rev. BD Bemuse had gotten it all to the *Right-on, my brotha* righteousness in that *"booty begots booty"* be a biblical fat fact, Jack! After that *Whoa Nellie* as a norm we avoided-it any *Baby, I'm for real* troubles with them para-military units riding fence because of the Jew-boy's ball-busting *Welcome to the jungle* negotiation tactics the one thing fo' sho'nuff be dat we done gotten-it assured exactamently the *how it be* unimaginable instant grits fire power of midget druglord money on the open black-market of dems South Americas snow-capped jungles!

Chapter 46

We done runned-it on the down-low and for the mostest of parts we just maintained-it our stamina with a slow yet steady diet of that *'plain vanilla low-fat yogurt* popping-it off them betos' while training them cracker-boys of the DEA until dat po'dunk TOP done gotz an *itching in hisns balls* then TOP would send them po-po fucks on a retreat in-order to cut the unit loose on some real live paramilitary trained-it wannabees seed thems South American jungles be chocked-it full up to theys itty-bitty midget assholes with all kinda revolutionary boys trying to oust some fucked *Generalizimo*! The mostest times, it would not be a fair fight big-*kick'n ass*-butts war be war and alls fair dat be fare comes the time to get yo' war wagon on! Hell, yeah it takes more than justa name to play the game because them revolutionary boys big-*pooh*-butts to holla back da' great *Muddy Waters* thems loco revolutionary fools onliest be gibberish speak *Mannish-boys*! We'd be done thumped-it a ride on thems iron-fisted birds the C-130 gun-ships, strapped *Hueys* and *Blackhawks* firstest ting first thems iron-clad birds done swooped-it in on the rebel fucks with a *laid-it down to sleep* stream of live-fire followed bye-bye a done burst-it loose witch be us a'running outta thems tree-lines justa stomping-it hard to the Corps, boots pounding ground the jubilant smell of burnt cordite rolling black thunder on thems revolutionary pygmy jungle-bunnies the shit be *all hands on deck* thumping them Babygirls! Hell justa 30-something of us under the cover of them *dirty birds* done over run hundreds thems *gots the knocking of the knees, run pygmy bastard mofo run,* it seemed liked onliest yesterdaze dat Injun pygmy ass done dreamed-it hisns filthy po'assed-out ass be a soldier big-*dream on*-butts hearing the song of the Sirens *In-coming* then hisns midget ass done woke to the fat fact, Jack he bouts to become just *a'nuttier died in the woods* gibberish speak soldier-boy! TOP called-it getting back to fucking basics the re-training of our *kill-kill-Kill* killer instincts so we don't be done loosed-it that hard done earned-it hard fought fo' competitive combat edge.

We be nobody's heroes nor anybody's fucking Arch-Angels though some thems whiteboys be fucking cut outta the Devil's ass sho'nuff *Angel-eyes*! We be justa chunk of trained adrenaline junkies and liked-it or not we be one to the same as thems gots paid buzzard-breaths minus the *moola*! Heroes gots the girl next door with a heart of gold big-*saved the world*-butts we gots the pay to play *Sugar-babies* with a running meter beneath herns all natural *rent-me combat-ready-daddy gumdrop nippled succulent* titties! Damned Skippy, we and dems buzzard-breaths the anyone of us could deliver a newborn baby then blade-n-grade an uncooperative parent's fucking throat dat done questioned the very act of our delivery! Now, don't go jumping on that high horse and riding outta there, *Shane*! There's a ting about "*befo' you judge a man, walk a mile in his shoes*" Nawl, I ain't taking off my boots, you might be Army, no need to walk a mile in dem bitches anyway instead dwell upon that day of reckoning to be sated that it won't be your crusty *God as my savior* ass-cheeks that's gonna be cashing my gravesite check!

Reg-*daddy*-Bush administration be always sending *in the clowns* every other coupled months some-to-body DC VIP and flunky come to inspect the unit thems pussy-boys needed-it a little adventure dat be why we always done scouted-it out some little outta the way ranchito that be patrolled by an inexperienced *rent-a-bato* crew to be avail whenever that *VeryIg'nantPussy* done popped-it down for theys done lookey-looks then we'd run deys peek-a-boo VIP asses up a real live flagpole! The Sunshiny, yo' Mr. *psycho* Devil Dawg *let's just me anda youse to be done have ourselves dat fucking dance* day seed that little ranchito raid, should have been a piece of possum *pumpKin* pie! There be four outta DC pukes surveilling the raid and theys VIP asses be just inside the tree-line yet well away from the *its really fucking happening* shit theys lying-eyes be bouts to see besides theys had thems collards as theys very own personal VIP bodyguards.

Ritz and I had both been assigned the house entry-team. Priest, he'd only do Catholic girls *may he rest in Peace* exploded that iron-grated door all to Hell! TOP first-man entry blasted-it the entry-room fuck Blam! Trips, second-man entry JOB be thems sleeping betos inside the bedroom just off to the left of the kitchenette area. I be the glory-seeker and keeper *the best little whorehouse in Cali* entry-position tree, blast anybody and everybody that moved-it in the entry-room then take down the kitchen fucks! Ritz the dumb-assed money-grabbing wish to be a fucking outstanding hero bastard wannabe motherfucker entered fourth with hisns onliest cotton-candy ass job be idiotically simple seed all that pink-assed *just follow the fucking orders* nut-sack breath whore had to do be to bag and drag the one fucked fuck in the entry-room. After blowing the iron door Priest, he'd only do Catholic girls *may he rest in Peace* be Filthy-man.

BOOM-BOOM fucking BOOM! The iron-grated entry door be blown the fuck away from its cheap-ass hinges. TOP on the dead-man's run done placed-it a 9-mil almost centered the head of the just awakened outta fast asleep *bye-bye* sleeping on duty guard fuck! Trips, done hauled-it ass and I'd done heard him a'placing thems 9-mil mints into all thems bed pillows in the secondary room fo' dems fucks nappy-time be over! I done seed it with my owns lying-eyes that the force of TOP's rounds had knocked the *goat-fucker* against the opposite wall from the entry door some 12-feet away and the fuck be propped-it up in the corner diagonally to the right furthest away from the entry door, the fuck looked-it liked a used tampon, red blood gushed from hisns head and flowed-it down hisns asleep on watch-duty ass. TOP also done placed-it a couple 9-mils in the fuck's chest area and the shotgun be near bye-bye fuck, you be a goner! I tossed him a couple of 9-mil *goodnight sweet-heart* body kisses befo' I be in the kitchenette to done rinsed-it away thems two left-over dishrags! Ritz the dumb-bastard returd fuck-up bitch bastard musta have gotten-it all caught-it up in the excitement of that being hisns firstest entry raid because the po'dunk piggly-wiggly DEA fuck had not followed hisns official orders just to bag and drag instead the whoremonger man-ginna ass-fuck had followed me into the kitchen. Filthy-man, Priest, he'd only do Catholic girls *may he rest in Peace* tooken-it two-rounds of number four-buck full-blast short-range fired *bye-bye* that soons to be dead this world fuck from the not secured shotgun held in the dying fuck's uncuffed hands! The fuck's two last shots had been a direct fucking hit that struck mid-center *Lord, knowed-it that mofo done toted a lonesome broken-heart* hisns sad-eye chest. Bro' Priest, he'd only do Catholic girls *may he rest in Peace* the die be cast because the unlucky last breath fuck had fetched-it to done fired-it twice the *870 Remington* shotgun that Ritz had failed to bag thems double-ott buck pellets done severely impacted big-*lethal*-butts not penetrated through the re-enforced steel armor plate on the front of Priest, he'd only do Catholic girls *may the sad-eye now rest in Peace* bullet-proof vest BLAM-BLAM!

BLAM, at the sound of that cabron's firstest shotgun blast, I quick turned-it so fast to done knocked Ritz the fuck down even to done runned-it over hisns DumbEagerAss as I commenced a *Chuck Berry* duckwalk outta the kitchen back into the entry-room just in time to done seed a dying Priest *may he rest in Peace, Lord done fo' sho'nuff knowed-it that sad-eye mofo* who'd only do Catholic girls hisns lonely broken heart done be in need of a good rest yet that WOP mofo done held on high a ten-inch knife in hisns raised right-hand that he done commenced to *swing-low sweet chariot* to done bladed and graded that lucky-fuck cabron a toothless full throaty-grin justa mere seconds befo' our sad-eye Bro' Priest, he'd only do Catholic girls done made peace with all things sad-eye this world!

After the shit had cleared TOP, the dope, thems VIP hunky-flunkies all be loaded-it up into transport Hueys headed to Cali, it be then that psycho ass mofo Trips because hisns ass be the HNIC*HeadNiggerInCharge* dat psycho mofo done tooken-it that exactamente opportunity to go real hard to the Corps at that fuck-up pussy-fuck Ritz with everyone's silent blessing big-*let's dance*-butts not mine! I had quick-liked done grabbed-it me dumb-ass selfie a pair of thems hairy-assed coconut fit-to-order mid-knight special clip-on balls then I done gotten-it betwixt dat rabid Devil-Dawg and hisns cotton-candied punk-ass bone, a BIG FUCKING mistake because old Devil-Dawgs never die, theys just shoot-it a too dumb to know-it mofo that the onliest hero this world be a fucking deli-meats *submarine* sandwich *at the Subway* as swell that the HNIC Devil-Dawg gonna shoot ya' in jo' dumb black-ass then bay *Word-up* da' next full moon!

Chapter 47

Dat be the honest Injun the real truth, Ruth shit as to why I be laid-it up, in a tree-room mud-hut that done served as a missionary hospital a fucking mofo make-shift medical clinic somewhere deep in the Colombian jungle with its brand *spank dat ass* newest patient justa praying hisns heathenish black ass a brand to be newest fucking prayer "*Lord God, above and yo' St. Dickhead below can yall helps a Brotha out? Po'lease Lawd don't let this young Honduran nun humming them gibberish speak hymns and sweet nursing me* *with thems silky-soft sponge bathe-me babygirl, po'lease bathe me softest hands to ever roll along this harden to the Corps gonnabe body. Lawdy, po'lease helps me, let Baby-Nunya-gurl be not too fucking addicted to an unholy pre-ordained matrimony"* to da' world's mostest sexiest *bump-dat* Nun, I done said-it loud and clearly in my bestest of the gibberish speak *"Ola, mi Chaparita! Que tal?"* Whadd-up, Shorty! How you do-in?

Sommertime laters, still at that St. Elsewhere dump, dat mofo TOP dropped-it in on my down-in-the-dumps feeling sorry fo' my sore black been shot-it up ass partly because Baby-*Nunya*-gurl be all too fucking faithful to herns fake fucking vows to an imaginary God whom mostest likely just be the *Oz* veiled smoke behind a guiled silken-screen big-*busted*-butts TOP and me rapped-it on the reals fo' *Medgar Evers* real *Emmett Till* we'z done held-it ourselves a let's straighten it out pow-wow then to the *Hey-hey* there we two heathenistic war dawgs done had-it fo' ourselves a straight-up this be the farting of the ways! TOP had been pissed at me for having bounced-it hardtack Trips way, he'd said-it that I had pulled Trips fucking Ace in the hole card, WTF else be new and that I had forced fed Trips to play a dead man's hand with my numb-nuts playing the starring-role of the dead man! TOP backed dat shit-up in that Trips had only nicked the surface of my black-ass cause we both done knowed-it dat psycho ass Trips straight-the-fuck-up be dead-eye accurate at any range and the shot that he'd done plugged me with had at best been no more than 6-fucking feet away! Yeah, yes in-deedy dat shit walked the talk that done clearly made me the fucking dead-man big-*dancing*-butts the shoot the handsome man in hisns Black ass shit hadn't been nuttin personal fo' psycho ass Trips dat shit be justa *move bitch, get the fuck outta the way* kinda ting! TOP diplomatically backed-it dat shit up a bite justa half-step when he added that I'd probably done what had been bestest for the unit because an enraged Trips whom every damned body done knowed-it be a fat fact, Jack that when the psycho fool be riled-it up he done toted-it just a pair of eights inside dat damned sway too darkened wannabe Messykin skull of hisns and that thems two eights inside dat dumb fuck's skull be sho'nuff *Crazy-Eights*! Trips for sure woulda done shot and killed-it that damned rich-whiteboy pussy mofo' and killing that dumb-assed fool Ritz would have justa done brought-it out the bestest interlopers from the gang atop Capital Hill! Thems Reg-daddy-Bush administration gangbangers and thems pentagon pent-fucks giving the fucking orders at home from the rear guzzling stale assed *Billy Beer* just fo' the entertainment the whole unit would have had to stood-it *hat in hand* before the nation's most brightest 5-stuttered Genitals at the Pentagon!

It hadda been during that little *ain't life a bitch* chit-to-chat that I had dropped-it the hardlined turd TOP's way. I hadda told-it to TOP that I had been a'tinkering long and hard and that this ghost-turd needed a change of the kitty-liter seemed to me that he, Trips and I needed-it sumpting sumptin powerful a parting of the waves big-*taint nuttin personal*-butts the Surprise Surprize Surprise Sergeant Carter had been fo' me because TOP wasn't to no-ways near to be mads bouts my pulling stakes then punching spurs to dead horse's ass! TOP done told-it that he understood my predicament in that there be only so much shit one's mind could shovel! I'd been on my second enlistment the Corps with justa about a year and a half out then I be done. I'd told-it to TOP that I was gonna step outta the shit and into the kitchen to done scrubbed-it them pots and pans in an IBM computer civilian suit *bye-bye, Mofo* the time, I'd left the Ft. Sam Houston hospital re-hab TOP had done worked-it outs fo' my dumb-asse to extend the remainder of my contract for a'nutter year-plus of active-duty to cover my electronics retraining. TOP had set-it up for me to jump ship from ghost-turd to computer technician for free bye-bye utilizing an Uncle *tech savvy* Sammy's flyboy technical school then go USMC active-reserves for justa stint and become a front-center ultimate warrior where you got yo' cake seed the Brotha gonna be paid and ice-cream knocking da' boots civilian with a *gyrene* one-weekend every-month and just two weeks per year straight-up reserve just liked thems Tucson Mexican-American boys usta be befo' theys big-*basta el culo*-butts gots commandeered-it into the unit. I done knowed-it full swell just how TOP done worked-it hisns official *in the trick-bag* shit fo' thems unlucky beaners *good Lawd* thems reservist got fucked-it hairy-balls deep big-*culo*-butts I don't be a psycho wannabe tripping-it Messykin! I got shipped-it to a communications school for electronic maintenance training at an Air Force base near Wichita Falls aka *Whiskey Faults*, Taxdatass a'nuttin special happened during that year of the flyboy schooling.

Chapter 48

THE LUSTFUL DAZE OF YOUTH thems crazed *teenaged pussy* No! Wet dreams a'plenty Hell Yes! Thems fist-pumping years all them dreams I done chased-it after the one and the onliest chocolate-drop *Hersey's* kissed *who'dat* sweet sexy ticket in hand fo' the trip the light fantastic! I'd never seed the face nor caught-up to the damsel in a micro-mini it be circa dem 70s' *Afro Sheen, Old Spice, Binaca*, halfa-wallet $.35 a'hour cheap-ass ends, the Temptations *Just My Imagination* eight-track rolling-it the boat, in bedroom and always in my head, a racist hillbilly mis-State of *I-n-babysisdiana* learner's permit, sultry smile, twinkled eyes, snapped went the fingers dat crackled to done popped-it justa lean mean virgin skinny Black be beautiful sex machine with the power sign turned on! I always burst it loose down to *Guitar Zan's Blues-n-Ribs Shack* to done double-clutch parked my wish to God she be my S*horty*! Rosie Leigh Robinson, babygurl be a butter-scotched sweet hip-swinging soul-sista #1 and dat beauty be totally clueless to herns superior position within my wet to be so wild late-night dreams, *Rosie-tripleG* be the starlet and I be the startled though it mattered little that Rosie-*GGG* be not then nor would she *Medgar Evers* be privy to that real truth, Ruth because back in the daze I be aways too far girl shy to do anything to done realized her seed I justa hugged-it tighter than a mofo my booth riding-low my *homies*, Mr. Bobby and Gettis fo'sure yet I'd done kept to taking them ever so on the sly glances herns way, Rosie-*tripleG* be my ultimate fantasy! When we be 12, Rosie-*tripleG*'s nipples slipped-it through her training bra liked two loose *Sugar Babies* big-*good Laud*-butts come the 16th year Rosie-*tripleG* had the eyes that hypnotized, hips that mesmerized and thems tits gave me wet-dreaming fits! She'd be at *Guitar Zan's* with herns own two super lovely *Supremes* Thelma Mae Williams and Geraldine Louise Whitestone thems two babygirls sho'nuff be easy on the eyes big-*Superfly*-butts Rosie-GGG lit up that joint! Every Friday-nite' that juke joint be thumping-it hard and the genie be outta the bottle bumping gums Rosie-tripleG *GurlGotsGams'* Rosie-tripleG gots herns self a perfectly matching set thems big brown chunky peanut-butter thighs smooth be theys creamy and not so damned easy to spread dat gal be lit ol' Aunt Hannah hadda cop a pair of the gold-rimmed *Ray Bans* justa shine-it bright upon herns genuine red-bone selfie *who'dat* be my personal 8th Wonder of the World! Rosie-GGG dat girl usta set my world afire! Nylon stocking-cap, *Dippity-doo*, white boxers, Am-transistor radio, my Mom's gots dog ears, fluffy pillows, ironed sheets, Vaseline, and the torn-out pages of the lingerie section from a *Sear'* catalog cause Rosie-*GGG'* be done flashed-it me the broad side of a honey brown tenderloin and the nighttime bees the right time to make it about my all too reals yet always too imaginary *Shorty*!

Big-*virgin*-butts shit happens and we should be wary of what we done dreamed-it for, asked-it for or done prayed-it for dat lil' bite of straight-up this be the real world real reality done hung its Christmas stocking my chimney grate earlier with me, my Auntie Katie Lou, my cousin Bug' and dat quart of Mr. *Del Monte* Un-sweeten Prune Juice! Years laters, my fucking pussy prayers done brought me that fucked-it up DEA candy-ass Ritz-cracker *aint he the motherfucker* into my dumb-assed fo' life! All thems Pacific rim jobs plus all thems *Generalizimo* South America countries the law be that any to all kinda monies could be pressed to the flesh thus I no-longer needed-it to pressed the flesh big-*wanking*-butts to done managed-it to plant my cherry tree a'many times over big-*pimping*-butts that shit hadn't counted fo' diddley squat because it all be *poon-tang* justa store bought pussy and poon-tang taints to ever be confused-it up with the homemade home grown fo' reals live to the touch pleasingly plump spread-eagled *hey-hey babygurl done dropped-it likes its hot* on the reals! Tain't nuttin like live-pluckings offa dems limbs spread wide *pussy willow* tree witch sho'nuff be the tree of life! Fo'reallies in lessen time than it hadda tooken-it me to palm grind-it with *Rucky Rucy* and herns fo' *ugly assed step*-sisters creeping Thumb street, Fist City I done plucked-it the fo'reallies alive in the startling sepia flesh the chocolate-drop starlet that I done fo' *Medgar Evers* chased through-out all my lustful cream filled extremely wet nightly visions through-out all the *hey-hey daze* of youth can the choir say *Amen* and to sing a *Yappy Nappy-Pappy Birthdaze* to Zeke!

Oh God, please, please All Mighty God please be to You, God, purdy please, God, please to justa let me fart! Just one, God! Let it be a big one, Lordy, please Big Daddy in the sky be done let me have justa one big assed gigantic earth shaking nut-rattling she usta be my girl kinda fart!" aside I done prayed-it that *Brotha Man* atop thems Heavenly stairs done gotten-it justa bit usta to my personal concoction of the oddball pleas because I done needed-it meselfie a real God and an on the reals vaporizing thems sins forgiving God at that! I be curled-it up into the fetal position on that floor for so long that dust bunnies began to form themselves under my black ass cheeks! It be outta desperation that I began to calling on all callers of the Cosmos! Inside that apartment, Heaven's own lil' *Love Grotto* witch up to that shit happened *all Hell done broke ranks* seed my Love Grotto be justa liked *Disneyland* the most happily happy ass place on earth, rock-steady my brotha! The Love Grotto be the place I done shared-it with my fo'reallies one she be my onliest Babygirl, my Shorty, jo' *Temptations* holla@ya'Boy "*My girl, my girl, talking about my girl...!*" my Babygirl, she be mines and mines all to my no-longer lonesome Black be beautiful self *"You are going to die, damn you, Zeke! You are dead meat, Mister! Everyone warned me about you! Oh, Momma please forgive me because I didn't listen, Noooooooo!"*

Babygirl, my Babygirl done bumped that slip of the tongue evil commissioned wayward the boneyard crap all up and into my handsome like a mofo gingerbread grille plus my Babygirl done spewed evens mucho-much more such foolishness whilst my black ass-cheeks done hugged-it *Pillsbury dough-boy* biscuits tight onto the napped carpet floor. I be enthralled with the worstest *Medgar Evers* da' shit be gut wrenched pain an unbelievable f'n pain and agony yet it be she the beautiful one who be mad! *"Oh how, I hate you, Zeke!"* Normally, my Babygirl be nuttin big-*beautiful*-butts a spoonfull the sweet-tea Jesus big-*don't hate me*-butts my Babygurl be not yo' gospel goony goo-goo love child fo'reallies she be a lotta lot mo' Biggy-smalls sweeter and a whole lotta most kinder big-*pissed off*-butts *Lord helps her* my Babygirl's blessed little green-eyed jealousy filled heart be pumped-it full-tilt the pissed offishness and distilled white vinegar! My Babygirl' be t-totally pissed yet it be herns own fine-assed fault though she won't nor would any knowingly at faulted totally in the wrong woman *Medgar Evers* be to done admitted-it that factual real truth, Ruth that it be she the one who be totally in the wrong big-*selfish*-butts my Babygirl' she be wrong thus dat be why I be gots wronged! My Babygirl be *to the left-to the left* plainly there be nuttin absolutely nuttin right about herns evil jealousy fueled thought process! What had happened, I hadda gone fo' a little swim bouts an hour or so earlier doing *easy like a Sundae moaning* laps in the apartment's pool when I had gotten this big assed cramp in my upper-inner left-thigh muscle. A peculiar ting musta happened-it to done caused-it the Universe to done slipped-it whilst shifting thems synchronized gears and the whole of our done knowed-it reality just got bent to some sorta obscured angle fo' my Babygirl as she stood a'front the picture window yet she hadn't knowed-it that the Universe done spun itself awry therefo' when she observed dis beautiful buxom blonde neighboring woman ergo dat distilled white vinegar yet it be just so innocent that Swedish woman done justa innocently massaged-it my severely cramped-it upper-inner left-thigh B*aby, I'm for real* muscle all innocently whilst my helpless injured selfie done gingerly leaned-it back against the pool's entry gate! I had much needed-it and medically required-it dat innocent massage from our Swedish Angel of the *Lord have Mercy* big-*big ems'*-butts could I helped-it that onliest the slightest minuscule of a gander dat *Swedish Angel of Kindness* it be to done seed herns magnificently endowed *blessed be the child that has herns own* bountiful mounds of the *jo' lady, please feed yo' baby* nourishment! My Shorty, my Babygirl be an RN, a'nuttier one of them damned psycho registered nurses why must life be so cyclical, my sweet little RN chocolate-bunny done hauled-it from herns window perch to done sneaky-sneak stepped-it up to me and the sweet little Angel of Kindness on the sneak-thief thus it be dat all my painful troubles curled-it up on our Love Grotto floor be all my Babygirl's own damned jealous fine-assed fault!

My Babygirl be the *Sneaky-Pete who'dat* done runned-it down the flight of stairs to done sho'nuff played me *Bo-Bo* the clown bye-bye an act of feigned kindness. The firstest ting first my Babygirl done helped me to hobble-it back into our *aint' life wonderful* Love Garden where the dark and lovely Merciless perpetrated herns evil intent to done did me wrong by giving me some little white potassium pills *"Here Zeke, com' on beau take these, they'll help to reduce the swelling in your thigh and ease that cramp"* big-*lying*-butts in less than 10-minutes after ingesting thems white sucker pills there I be all knotted-it with the fricking raw-dawg gastronomical pain of biblical proportions that I'll be damned iffn I hadn't begun to done thunk-it that those little white pills might not have been that what my sweet little RN Black be beautiful my Babygirl done purported theys be! "*I asked her for water and she gave me gasoline*" Howling Wolf done sang dat blues song, *Chess* records done recorded-it, I done heard the song since I be justa jitterbug big-*diaper dandy*-butts I done never knowed-it the meaning *Emmett Till* that there very moment all curled-it up in the fetal positioned befo' the Angel of Death suffering a'nuttier RN's inflicted humongous *death unto yo' black ass* defying pain! *"Potassium, potassium, I'll show you potassium! I gave your dumb butt poison, cyanide poison, Hemlock! Oh, God! What's the use, you're so dumb, you don't even know what I'm talking about!"* My sweet little Black Angel showed-it me supreme love *"I poisoned your butt, you dumb Duf' don't mess with me, walk on my love, will you? I don't think so! No way! I'll kill you first! How could you have done that to me? In front of God and everybody! Why? Do you think I'm a fool? And if you mistakenly do just happen to wrongly think that I'm a fool then I for sure, am not now nor never will I ever be your fool that you can bet on, damn you Zeke!"*

The *Luv Goddess* done gave Word-up! It be over an hour dat I be wrestled-it up into one gigantic gastronomic intestinal knot and it done felt like I'd swallowed a baby elephant and baby elephant's long ass trunk be stuck way the too fricking sway too deep double-Dutch deep down inside my brownie! I'd always done heard-it that your life done flashed-it lightning be quick befo' your eyes when death came a'knock-it yo' iron grated door big-*no tanks*-butts as I laid all curled-it up and twisted-it upon the *Grim Reaper's* knob, I could only remember the day that I done firstest met-it up with that wonderful *Heaven helps me* chocolate Wonder-Woman as swell herns beautiful *Russell's* milk-chocolate semi-sweet kisses and Good Lawdy, what a day, ands *Oh, what a night* holla@ya'Boy dat day be rootin' tootin blastin' black cherry *Kool-Aid* kool, Babycakes! It had been so-so-so magical, musical and justa maybe a mite too unto the mystical slice of the *ain't it a wonderful life*! I had been driving south along a redneck hillbilly *Arrr-kin-saw* hims hillbilly ass justa' doing hisns babysis mis-State interstate 30 south as I twas justa bout to put Little Rock, the *Arky-saw* in my rearview mirror when it all went down!

Chapter 49

78' I BE BOUND FOR Altus, *Oak-lee-homie* by-way of Dallas, *Taxdatass* all dressed-it up in the camouflage USMC utility-uniform caused it made dat life or death situation fo' any a Black man DWB*DrivingWhileBlack* along a racist America bible-thumping interstate be justa bit mo' on the easier side then with me being camouflaged I done past-it all thems damned po'dunk racist *po-po* bastard mofos because theys dumb redneck asses thunk-it the car be driving itselfie! I had started-it late fo' that journey and I done knowed-it that I'd have to *keep-on trucking* petal to the metal non-stop to done picked-it up the love-struck *Who-BC, check-it* my Boy' done fallen-it tree-cliffs deep in love with a Navy wave reservist, a fine-assed Puerto Rican babe who be kicking-it on the out-skirts Dallas *how bout dem Cowboys*! I done left the home front *Oh Snaps* I be *winner-winner chicken dinner* cause Rosie-*growed-it all up tits till Tuesday*-tripleG done tripped-up to done let Zeke knock-it outta the park a straight-up 4-bagger *run dem bases at jo' leisure* thus I be cruising I-30 still wrapped-it up to be warped-it up all cozy and comfy liked a motherfucker within them warm kinda friendly *fuzzy-wussy was a bear* feelings! I done just picked-it up I-30 south on the other side of that Little-*I can't stand*-Rock when it all done happened-it outta a fucking *SPOOF* there-it-be WTF da' *spook done sat by the door*! Time ceased-it liked a motherfucker and I perchanced-it upon a heavenly vision seed them Universal time differential plates on a relative plane done shifted to done glitched-it a wee-bit to done bumped me a sampling of the future. I peeped-it across that 4-lane inter-state *Peace be* still all giddy the fuck thems after glows when some kinda super imposed somewhere somehow outta the fricking nowhere *BOOM CHAKKA-LA-KA* I managed-it to peer with my big brown lying-eyes directly inside a north-east bound 77' light-blue/grey Thunderbird anda chocolate love-child be sitting upon the comfy cushiony driver's seat justa lovely fat-free toffee crunch-cake singing alongside *Aretha* bouts *a do-right woman in need of a do-right man*! I flipped-it a bitch then to be there done caught-it up to that *T-Bird*' which I followed-it to within a few hundred clicks of a Veteran Administration hospital entrance just a bite the outta-sides the Little-*you aints gots to*-Rock me cause I done knowed-it straight-up what dat hillbilly Arky-saw! Happy Halloweenies, *no tricks all treats* and a Merry-cherry Christmas my Brotha!

The Aretha, Queen of Soul mimicking gingerbread cinnamon toasted heavenly vision Black be sooooo beautiful songbird *Sooners* to straight-up gonna be my one and be onliest my Babygirl stopped to done eased-it herns bucket to the side of the entry road then she done strutted-it herns Superfly fine-ass outta dat 77' hoop-tee with TLC*TenderLovingCare*! She be wrapped-it super-tight in an immaculate nurse's white uniform, an Angel so unique and *Medgar Evers* so dusky be the beauty of herns loveliness! She stepped-it a subtle grace yet the kicker be she done sported-it an authentic *Angela Davis* Black Panther Party clenched raised *Right-on* fist solid like a mofo afro that done bounced-it to done sprung-it on the ups followed swiftly bye-bye the downs each and every perfectly timed long-stride of herns fully developed muscled-up gams *check dems nasty thoughts*, baby! Babygirl's fro' be justa spongy scintillating scintilla of sensual sexual potency dat sho'nuff done shimmered-it deep within that afro's halo dat done held balls-tight unto a little RN's cap as iffn that little white split-in the back wannabe pillbox be the Miss Universe diamond studded tiara! *Hey-eh-hey, Virginia, there do be a Shanty Claus*! Her walk be all business herns hefty succulent scrumptious yips moved-it from the on-point, locked and ready front to the gots Good n' Plenty gear in the rear there be certified junk in her trunk big-*struttin*-butts herns honey-dripped chocolate chips hadn't swayed-it a'tall herns gait be sexy as all Hell! Babygirl be da' shit and she done fo' sho'nuff be done knowed-it up-front dat she be the one lovely *PHATT* paragon, Soul-Sista Emperoress she be all dat and a bag of fiddy-dollar poker chips! Babygirl be an elegant ebony Love Goddess, a lofty voluptuous chocolate Easter bunny *I be po-leeza to bite-off thems ears* beauty that had been fully *naked as a jaybird* body dunked-it in *Lady Godiva* justa love-bite on the shady-side of the street semi-sweet hot-chocolate yet the ebony Goddess hadn't stopped her stride *Emmett Till* she done towered-it befo' me seated inside my bucket. Deeply embedded within them sparkling bright *yappy to see ya' Baby-browns* of herns be herns mostest recently of the moment bio and it done read sumptin-sump'n liked just that Blessed-it morning *Her Majesty* herns high-stepping hip-swinging caramel-fudge *Shortie* be fine-assed self be justa chunk of the silky sweet cuddle-me up swell placed kiss across herns luscious *ruby-Tuesday* painted-on lips! The Heavenly Black Power dish hadda just dat morning dew done awaken-it mere *time being a relative ting* hours afore upon a fluffy tender cosmic cloud when herns Superfly bump-dat ass bounced-it across thems upper-sky Heavens in'a Grecian bucket driven by Eros hisns own-damned-self then herns magnificent *bustin-it loose* booty-bump hadda vividly enraged a green-eyed sho'nuff needed-it to be jealous monster rage within *Isis* to the point that the great Goddess of the Morning star done thumped-it the Babygirl's Black be beautiful caramel-nougat body up and outta that *bucket of the Gods* past thems pearly-white gates sway passed-it all thems fluffy clouds to come nigh a honey drizzled fudged-it kiss upon my *been awaiting all theys life* kiss me *po'leesa, kissa me* lips!

Babygirl done oracled a torrid riff across my attentive eardrums *"Hel-lo, solider boy!"* I done heard-it *rat-a-tat-tat come they told me a-rumpa-pump-pump* seed the Babygirl done seed it the all of me the each to every bite *a'nuttin be camouflage fo' the lovely one* ahh the Soulful strut of music within her voice be da' shit, Baby! My Babygirl's voice be the *Peace be* still hushed over with a velvety smoothness sooo feminine yet so authoritative my Babygirl's vocals be justa wet-willy crescendo with a sly sensual ease done caressed my earholes! *"Hey, Cro-Magnon man, Neanderthal! Hello! Yo' anybody home? Just what the heck, were you following me for?"* A choco-holic love-shake, form-fitted breastestes be extra-large with some helpings on the way-side justa coke-bottled stand-out dark and lovely beauty stood before me! My Babygirl be tall, college educated-it female University of Texass basketball playa elegant tall! A brazen bronzed over free-falling from the on high earthbound Angel done bumped-it unto me a slattered-it up gourmet semi-sweet milk-chocolate bundle of the everlasting the goodie-stuff Blessedness' all of it every bite be the mostest exquisite *good Lord hava Mercy* on my soul fo'reallies herns enchanting brown-eyes, there justa be sump-sumptin' special about a brown-eyed girl and them two wide-open peepers, thems two fierce ravishing beauties done blazed-it a hot torrid fiery trail of the loveliness along the empty be void corridors dems lonely vacated chambers of my cold loveless be lovelorn heart *hell yeah* I done up-chucked dat lonely heart a *do as you please, my Goddess* gift! The then to be there I done snatched that lonely heart outta my hairless chest this stone-pit be yourns, Babygirl!

A heady erotic splendor engulfed her there be a pinch of the pearl, a potpourri of crushed roses *Black American beauties*, cinnamon spice and that one to onliest explicit fragrance witch I would come to love fo' *Medgar Evers* justa cool charming spritz of the *Coty*! *Good Lord*, the scent of that woman! My sensory system be full alert status *Danger Danger Danger Jolly Rodgers* My eyes done heard the beauty, my ears seed the harmony, my lips tripped the light fantastic, my hands whiffed the copper-toned curves concealed-it beneath herns skin-tight freshly ironed RN uniform that busted-it my nose a taste of the wonderful! Awed, thunder-struck, I had lost all rational as well physical control, I couldn't move nor speak on the reals I damned near passed-it the fuck out *"Breathe*!*"* She'd ordered! "*Uh, uh, uh, uh, uh"* be my onliest reply of the day in herns eloquent presence fuck I'd become one of thems bitch ass crippled-it up po'dunk returds *ugh ugaa uh guh*! Yes Lordy that be why I done believed-it be some kinda mystical dream shit a fleeting moment within a moment, I be lost and t-bird RN done totally stupefied my dumbass to cripple-it up status.

Chapter 50

IT HADDA HAPPENED SOME FIVE-YEARS earlier big-*bedazzled*-butts on the floor of the Love Grotto it be *oh good God the pain, oh Lordy* I be in agony all curled-it up on the shaggy! *"Who was she? Just who the heck was that European witch?"* My Babygirl shattered-it my moist wonderfully deliciously backwards daydream to the reality and that horrific *helps me oh Lord, po-lease helps yo' baby-boy* stomach pain *"You want that old crone? Go get her*! *I hate you*! *Zeke, I hate you with every bone in my body. Why did you, how could you do that* *to me?"* Say whattay, a European witch? Crone? It had all been so innocent thus it had to be something else *oh shit* my Babygirl had herns lovely be sooooo lovely chocolate drop self an altered ego seed it be a fo' sho'nuff that my Babygirl had herns fine-assed angelic self an altered-evil twin, the *Twisted-Sista'* and it be that dat *beyotch* come to play!

"Oh *God, the pain, oh please, Lord helps me*! *Let me buzz the frick'n tower, just once, please dear God*!" I remembered-it that my Babygirl's evil assed twin be Michael *sorry Miss* Jackson, *Off the wall,* crazy-fucking eights! Could it be that mayhaps the *Twisted-Sista'* done stepped-it out that insane lunatic no longer be strapped in a straight-jacket locked and loaded inside the closed *out-fo'-the holidays* closets of my Babygirl's mind or had that damned pussy prayer swung-it full circle and done come to roost! I'd done met-it herns alter-ego the *Twisted-Sista* up-close and on the very personal flashed-it a'plenty times these past 5 years big-*awful*-butts never so un/not expected the *Twisted-Sista'* onliest reared herns ugliness come sum special occasion a birthday, X-mass, Valentine's day, our anniversary or any-kinda *come what may* holiday special be the day I done perchanced-it the precious opportunity to done gifted-it my Babygirl the gift of all gifts thus on thems such daze it be mostest likely that the Twisted-Sista stepped-it offa herns evil *the horses on the merry-go round-go round* demented carousel! Generally, the Twisted-Sista be a little sumptin something *"You cheap S-O-B"* my Babygirl rarely cussed-it a ting witch she done forced fed-it unto my *cuss CC-minute* ass be trying da bestest dat I couldn't to manage-it to just stop big-*what the fuck*-butts it be justa work in progress!

"Damn you, Zeke! You cheap, cheap, cheap bonehead, Duf! Why do you do this to me? Why? You know I hate it when you give me this cheap two-dollar whore's minstrel crap!" My main reply *"But you wore it the day we had done firstest met-it up!"* then the Twisted-Sista would've justa frick'n lost it! *"You Duf' I was going to work, no woman ever wears her good perfume to work! Why, why, why can't you get that through your thick skull? Why can't you buy me something that smells good something erstwhile like Coco Chanel"* my thoughtless reply *"My Moms wears that you wanna smell like my Moms?"* the Twisted-Sista counter-spin "O*k, Anis-Anis*" she hadn't really meant-it big-*kindly*-butts it had been herns own little special way to gift the fool in me the chance to done stepped-it up to done kinda rethunk-it big-*kindly*-butts not for my dumb-ass to actually ventured the weak-assed *"You wanna smell like anus-anus"* a chance to stop the non-sense *"That ain't funny, White Diamonds, even Liz Arden, better yet White Shoulders"* yet times be when a

man justa gotta strap-on a pair! Holding double-fisted tight onto my clip-on balls be my finale bow-wow *"My sisters wear those!"* busted, game to be over *"Stop your lying, Zeke! You don't have any sisters!"* True, I would be lying cause since that first day that I'd done met-it up with herns fine-assed chocolate-*drop the mike*-self just one whiff of my Babygirl caressed by a mist of *the Coty* woulda done set my cannon to motion seed on the reals that smell done pickled my brains then scrambled my hormones *Coty* musk done brought-it out and it be the done dat done brought-it on, my Babygirl done put it *the Coty* jump-started the Cro' in my magnum! Thems late 70s, early 80s *Coty* musk for the majority of American workforce females be just an ordinary everyday everywoman cheap generic perfume an on the reals fricking Jew-boy steal the pennies offa dead man's eyes cheap thus my Babygirl hadn't lied two George *wooden teeth* Washington dollars bought-it a bottle of the *goodie-stuff* at any *Walgreens/Rexall. The Coty* be my *Jello* Mr. Viagra 20-odd years befo' thems little blue pills done gotz theys *call to duty,* Baby! *"You want that tawdry trollop? Just carry your dufus butt back down to that pool and fetch that white trash! I don't need your ignoramus butt in my life!"* the Twisted-Sista tormented *"I hate you, Zeke! Your butt is just too much of a duf' to know just how much I really do hate you!"*

I be *"Oh, God, po'lease save Della Mae's bubbling brown bouncing baby boy! Please God, just ease Your Holy Finger up my Holy of Holies and jerk loose a fatty justa one to be the onliest great big fatty fart! Purdy please God! I'll never steal outta the collection plate a'gin-n-juice no mo' dropping a fiver to be palm sweating a twenty! So helps me, Lawd!"* the Twisted-Sista strutted on full display *"Momma was right about your no-good dumb dufus butt!"* The Momma' now that be a piece of work! Lord iffn You be and iffn You be a'listening Big Guy that the Momma be NOT and I fo'reallies mean NOT any parts near Your bestest of work! "*...I love you too, Duf*"

Me and my Babygirl lived-it the goodie-stuff kinda life in OKC, *Okla-homies* she had transferred to its VA hospital because I be at the flyboy base near *Whiskey Faults,* Taxdatass some 70 miles away and dat might just have been the reason why TOP got me assigned the training at that flyboy school. Thems fools TOP and the boys usta holler-it on the regular how fricking pussy-whipped I be abouts my Babygirl and thems *hard to theys* Corps clowns done placed-it thems 22-inch big floppies on my feets with the nerved to say *ah shucky-shuck heck* dat my whipped big-*hopeless*-butt wouldn't even cuss around her, go figure! Then theys done meet-it up to her and then them bums be whupped-it up too thus theys done found-it out the easy way why I'd been so damned retrained-it not whipped-it bouts my Babygirl a chocolate nougat Goddess *who'dat* be so lovely a Wonder-Woman dropped-it down from the Heavens!

A crazy unwanted side effect to OKC, it be sway too super fricking close to the home of the big-*grits and bacon eating*-butt the Momma *who'dat* be the leastest piece of the Big Guy in the sky's Hisns unholy work outta-progress: the Momma *"Now baby-child looks ain't important but his ugly ass just way too damned dumb to be a dufus but since you seem to like him, I'll have to call that one Duf' Now, honey-child, do yourself a big ol' favor, before you get attached and just throw that ugly-ass runt right back into the litter box!"* It had been just after my initial meeting with the Momma when the evil one, the Devil's personal old assed handmaid herself done made sho'nuff I be swell within ear-shot of that little snippet of ill-belched from the bowels of Hell advice witch the big bad boo-witch outta Whiskey Faults the malcontent done gladly yet maliciously given to her youngest and *Yes Lord* beautiful daughter. How outta all *Hell's screaming southern belles* could sumptin so evil be done birthed such a lovable girl-child? No doubt about it, the Momma gave birth to the Twisted-Sista, fo' sure! The Momma be one mean spirited spiteful sack of shhh "… *say it, I double-dog dare ya duf' ass to say it* …"! I had been living in the Love Grotto with my Babygirl for mostest unto two-years still the Momma had thems Greek boys those Phi Kappa whatever the frick boys thems usta bees my Babygirl's ex-boyfriends and ex-classmates drive the Momma's big old sausage and biscuit eating big-*bumpy face*-butt to the OKC fo' one of the Momma's unannounced and definitely unwelcomed-it *Mary pop-ins* weekend *Surprise Surprize Surprise Sgt. Carter* visits! The Momma done wanted-it an educated professional, a doctor, a lawyer even a dentist to be the man fo' herns youngest and brightest not an once a'month weekend ghost-turd disguised as a computer technician wearing a *boy-George* suit! Short pause fo' a'nuttier cause justa a lil' ole classic lesson, the Pullman company in theys racist beginnings all porters had to wear navy blue pants and navy blue suit coats, white shirts with navy blue ties then all thems Colored porters had to *step-n-fletch* to the name *boy-George* then dat derogatory term became a staple of the American racist shit pie ergo the Momma be no fool big-*frumpy*-butts I worked-it IBM and I had to dress blue suit, white shirt and tie thus dat frumpy bacon, eggs, biscuit and a slice of fried green tomato eating big-*flabby*-butt be pure buttocks kicking witty!

"Now, Son, don't fret none about some silly old motel. I know you can afford it but you can just stay here with us. You already know my baby and Duf' he won't mind. Besides, I'm going to need you to chauffeur me around this big city come the morrow" the Momma would tell the geek-boy then old fatty-butt extended her invite to the geek *"Son, just relax and enjoy yourself, you are to home!"* I done seed-it enough warfare not to give a frick'n *titi* to that green-eyed monster the weak man's master *Sir Jealousy* so them weekends/week daze crappy-stuff be done bye-bye the Momma went down then I justa chilled *Ice-Ice baby* do yo' thang frat' boy! The harder someone attempts to take something away from a'nuttier somebody seems the harder that a'holding-it onto dat thang somebody done tried-it most harder to cling even tighter. The Momma be Hell-bent on taking herns fine assed *chocolate chip* fudged dipped daughter away from me big-*dummy*-butts a fool don't need no help in losing hisns paradise fo' me it be a fat fact, Jack dat I and my Babygirl be living in a *tank-you God fo' this* Paradise witch that slimy snake the Momma done slithered-it back to fro' into my little Garden of *Yes, Lawd everytings perfect* Eden with a different rotten apple-headed geek bastard on the regular! *"Oh, Rhonda remember blah-blah-blah he's a doctor, a dentist, an accountant…blah-blah-blah just opened his own practice"* Hell, I had my own darn practice and it be opened 24/7 seed I'd done practiced my *tank-ya Big Guy* b-ball skills at the flyboy base gym or YMCA everyday on the daily-double! *"…Yes you did Duf' and that was just one of your many and numerous faults"*…ole woman get outta my head!

Big-*fatty*-butts the one thing the Momma never done correctively factored-it into herns personal evil begets evil theory of separation be the raw-dawg power of mule-headed passion because just liked the *Beast*, I be unto my *Beauty* fo' the long haul! I hadda truly done appreciated-it all the time spent with my Shorty. Them daze and nites being held surrounded by and all up and inside my Babygirl's *squeeze-me-tight-its-all-right* arms had been the bestest of the bestest and I be grateful to both the Big Guy rolling Black thunder in the upper-sky and my Babygirl for them times of sublime joy that she done brung-it to the table bumping a daily-double tri-fecta the goodie-stuff my mental, spiritual and physical worlds! Besides iffn my Babygirl hadda done wanted-it anyone of them *Greek* boys then any to one of thems educated/professional whores with theys big old college degrees, licenses and practices would have been there in the *Land of Chocolate Milk and my Honey'* then I'd have been out praying fo' pussy in some 3rd world mud hole! About 20-minutes into that abdominal pain then I hit the wall the worstest of all that pain the crossover point, No, I didn't see no damned halos nor the light nor had thems fiery fires of Hell bellowed to done scorched my black ass! The Twisted-Sista had been enunciating herns evil dat baby she-devil be on the good foot *"Nobody, and I mean nobody plays me the fool! I am not a fool and I refuse to become a folly. I will not be anyone's fluff and to become a foolish woman to and for your dumb-butt! Never, why I..."*

The Twisted-Sista done raged-on when one heck-of-a shultz-storm lightning done struck unadulterated raw-dawg awful pain danced-it sear agony big-*oh frick*-butts dat huge bolt be the worstest fricking pain that I'd *Medgar Evers* done felt-it usually *brotha pain* be justa number yet that fricking gastric spasm done stabbed-it *straight the frick* into then through my dumb-butt, *frick me* I'd done thunk-it *good-bye sweet world of mine*! Up to that point, I hadn't frick'n prayed-it not the one plea, I'd done thunk-it that fricking pain be sumptin outta the damned walking dead so I done flipped-it that little threshold switch to the auto-pilot of acceptance liked always either I would live through it or I be gonna die. Hecks be Huckleberry, that one frick'n bolt of mega-gastric agony be soooo bad it fo'reallies changed my shit to *hey Mr. Universe let my black ass live or pronounce me dead, jo' iffns youse be a God get the frick-up offa ya' once dead been nailed-it yo' Holy-shits ass atop a fricking cross! Come-on Holy Mofo bump dat Holy ass up and offa the fricking post and take a fricking stance*! That fricking pain zapped-it clear the fuck through my dumb-ass and I done felt dems lying-eyes of mines began to be rolled-it to the backsides of my nappy-head, fuck it! I be like on the fucking reals Zeke jo' fucking shit be over! The horrific gastric pain done cut-it-loose the raw-dawg then all thems fucking *cussed yo' ass* words that I hadda had justa been a'sitting on thems sidelines theys be liked *say it motherfucker justa say it to dat bitch* the dawg in me be liked *fuck this shit* yo' Babyg' done gone and she done straight-up kilt yo' dumb love-struck ass without a fight therefore I done let my ball-sack be dropped-it there be no need be to a'hold back thems star-list *cuss like a man mofo* words big-*lucky*-butts it be then inside dat exactamente *I be fucked* moment that it all hadda done played itself the fuck out, WTF!

Yowl-Sir, I'd done fo' sho'nuff done seeded-it that little lifesaving *hey-hey-hey Mr. life guard on duty* it be just a Biggy-smalls fucking flicker seed it had been so subtle so fucking unbelievably brief a flash of the black ass saving all so *Medgar Evers* lightening quick to done played itself out such dat iffn my numb-nuts hadda done blinked-it either the one to the both thems lying-eyes of mine then I woulda done totally missed-it all big-*ups to me*-butts fo' just that instant grits time be immortal when I done glimpsed-it it be justa lookey-look, a brief glanced big-*all seeing*-butts *Yes, Lord* I done seed it the total fucking terror that had fo' the briefest of a nano-second spanned-it across the Twisted-Sista's flawlessly beautiful ebony she be evil-assed big-*in luv*-butts she Peace be still my Babygirl's beautiful flawless face! The Twisted-Sista's dementia had given fucking sway seed in that momentary monumental moment dat bad-assed be-yotch done ducked dat bitch done tooken herns selfie a dip to done bounced-it the fuck outta there! *Good Lawd,* tank-ya Big Guy the twisted-the-fuck outta herns rightful mind dat baby wicked witch of the Whiskey Faults done packed herns shit then dat she-devil done fucking fled the scene! Right be might, I done seed it all with my big baby brown love-soaked pain drenched orbs I done seed it my Babygirl done stepped-it up to be on the reals too close and my Babygirl done leaned-it in very death defying close almost too damned fucking close seed my *killing me softly* Babygirl hadda bumped-it near e'nuff to my meat hooks that iffn I be gonna fo'reallies be to done died then I could have done grabbed-it herns chocolate sweet fine-ass to shot-gun the hearse dat gonna be to carry my dead dumb luv-struck whupped-it ass away!

Chapter 51

My Babygirl done bended-it sway low to done gazed most intently at me, yes I 'm talking intensely a *Yowls Sir,* fo'reallies intense eye-fucking eyeballing just an amazingly eyeball-to-eyeballs fucking intensity! To dis day, I still gets me a solid fucking woody just from the remembrance, my Babygirls shit be lit! The RN thang in her be the shit dat done stepped-it up full frontal locked-n-loaded on-point at the ready! Maybe, she'd done seed-it exactamently the moment when my baby-brown suck-ers done officially accepted-it theys buzzard-luck fate to done rolled-it theys lying-asses from the front and centered to the backsides of my big nappy! *Tank God* thems brown-orbed bitches somewhere along theys backwards trek done got themselves resurrected then it be *Gotcha* dems baby-browns done seed-it my Babygirl done grabbed-it a'hold of that Twisted heifer like a Boss to done ordered *step the fuck back, beyotch! You* *fucking with my man*! My Babygirl stepped-it up to the plate to peep into my baby-browns with a look of total terror on herns cinnamon spiced café-latte face followed-it up quickly with a look of t-total concern from a woman peering into the rolling backwards lying-eyes of the man that she loved! My Babygirl examined then reexamined my dumb-ass for all thems important vital signs of life! My Babygirl done gots it all caught-it up in that sickness and health thang and I had to admit even from death's shagged-carpeted floor holla@ya'Boy my chocolate love-bunny looked-it extremely scrumptious whilst herns fine-ass selfie be all caught-it up into the throes of murder one! My Babygirl's big brown *Bambi should have been a doe eyes* squinted as herns arched eyebrows done simultaneously bunched-it upwards to be giving me a quizzical yet perplexed WTF *please don't die, I luv you, Zeke*! My Babygirl's lovely countenance beheld a comical expression big-*a'scard*-butts herns bunched-it up brows in combination with herns perfectly red *kiss me kiss me quick before you die* painted-on mouth witch had justa outta the blue went abruptly silent hadda slackened to done formed the perfect *Oh shit*!

Oh, my God, WTF*WhatTheFrick* my Babygirl rarely cussed *I've really killed him*! *Zeke is going to die and I'm going to rot in prison*!" that shit be softly chiseled in brownstone all across herns dark yet lovely Angelic face instant grits became an all endearingly precious CC moment! My Babygirl's face be lit up with the *Guilty pleasures* thems feelings of you done knowed-it all to damned swell not to do a certain ting big-*can't helps me self*-butts it just felts soooo good to done just said *fuck-it* then to done went ahead and just done the shit any fucking way! That odd combination of emotions, *guilty pleasures* had a'scared da' fucking shit outta the Twisted-Sista to done on the Superfly put that beyotch in-check, to done back jumped-it a step or two onto her broom-stick then jackrabbit flash dat twisted beyotch be gone the way of the good *Toto there's no place like home* bye-bye! My Babygirl's guilty fucking pleasures witch momentarily baffled herns lovely semi-dark chocolate impeccable *Yes, Sir my brotha* beauty has a face which hadda just been *girl interrupted* bye-bye a *what the fuck have I done, Oh shit*! Armed with the this newly founded-it information the dumb-ass in me be *I'll be damned ain't I da' shit* that one lookey-look from my Babygirl's blazing baby-browns hadda assured-it to done re-assured-it dat I be *not so much* the dumb-ass them little white pills brought-it on by herns own selfish little green-eyed passion monster had not been meant to actually kill my dumb-ass theys onliest JOB be to done caused-it me excruciating pain and agony. Good Laud, those two motherfucking little white What-TheFuck ever deys be pills hadda done did exactamente dat Lord knows thems two little white bitch pills did done *Semper fi*!

In the aftermath of all dat shit the Twisted-Sista had officially backed the fuck *all hands down* and my Babygirl be back and ready to take care of her business and herns business be me, the love-struck twisted innards numb-nuts! The real strength of the Twisted-Sista's tirade done clearly abated *"Er, you're, you're going to die, Duf! The groundhog's gonna be your next fucking mailman*!" Dat be straight-up *Bullshit* about a funky assed hedge-hog done officially sealed the deal! My Babygirl be frick'n real proud of her education thus she'd hardly *Medgar Evers* to never cussed-it not even when the *Twisted-Sista* be done showed face-time big-*twisted*-butts she never uttered-it the colloquial and fo' her to done spoke-it that ghetto slang big-*all chips in*-butts she be holding duces bluff swells I'm just not as stupid as I done looked-it like! "*Yes, you are, Duf'...*" Yes, Sirrreee *Bobs mi uncle* that there *Shakeyspear* hadda gotten it all to the right when he done wrote that *the world is a masquerade...* and my dumb-ass hadda had gotten-it all caught-it up in the Twisted-Sista's grand entrance into the ballroom witch be masked by the pain that I had damned near missed my chance to dance, Babycakes! Self-assured that I would live, it be then I done began to waltz-it with all thems frick'n off the wall odd-ball array of the *me-me-me* prayers anew loud, Black and proud! *"Please God, just let me have just one big old school' fart! Please God, Please, let me fart! Po'lease Big Daddy in the sky hear my humbled cry*!"

The day had been great, the apartment pool had been t-totally empty when I went for that ill-fated swim. In the midst of all thems laps, I had gotten a *charlie-horse* cramp in my inner-upper left-thigh muscle then just as I hadda eased-it my body ups from outta the pool that Swedish neigh-bor, she and her young'em justa little tyke of blondie curls preschooler entered *"Hi" "Hello" Hi-ya, what's the matter*?" It had all been so innocent, I explained-it my ache thus my predicament to the all-natural Swedish bombshell *momma said these knockers gonna knock you out* it be then Swed-ish-mom hadda all natural-liked innocently begun to lightly tap-rub my inner thigh at the point of the cramped and swollen muscle *"Here? Oh, my*! *You need to add more potassium to your diet, like bananas, it will help your body to relax"* all the while we had rapped-it out in the fishbowl, out-front in the open and it be all so innocent and as the Angel of Mercy continued to light as a feather tap-rub at my cramp the pain had slowly begun to dissipate and be replaced-it by itty-bitty *bubbled-it* up tickles! About the time, I recognized dems familiar musical octaves of my Babygirl's velvety hushed voice, how long she hadda been standing behind me and the Angel of Mercy I hadn't knowed-it big-*beautiful*-butts it had all been all so innocent straight-up Word, it be all about the cramp! My Babygirl be relaxed with the pearly whites wrapped within an *easy as a Sundae moaning* smile which she'd flashed-it to me along with a well-rested coy grin that be consumed with an unspoken promise that she be *fired up* just about to spritz on *the Coty* and she be a'wondering iffn *anybody here be looking for passion*? Instant grits, I'd forgotten all about big breasted ofay Angel of Mercy and herns medically approved innocent massage when my Babygirl said-it *"Hey beau, I've got some potassium pills up-stairs. Come-on, let's go home, babe! I'll give you a couple"* to the smiling mom she'd simply said *"hi!"* witch the mom followed *"hiya, yes, potassium will help his cramp!"* then the follow-it up *"Thanks!" "Tanks! "You're both welcomed I'm sure"*

Every bite all innocent then me and my Babygirl be *Up, up and away* to the Love Grotto where I done those little white pills witch been offered to me by my Babygirl the RN. *Oh, God this aints rights* I had fallen-it to the floor with the worst stomach-cramps of my entire *get ya' war on* life! I had been consumed with the most un-imaginable and the most un-believable gut-wrenched pain *"Those were gas pills that I gave you. They're for surgery they produce and trap gas inside your intestines"* I done knowed-it them words be of the Twisted-Sista there be no-way my Babygirl could of nor would of have boasted-it abouts such an ill-conceived dirty deed then to done trash talked-it *"I gave you way too much and your guts are going to produce gas til they explode! You're dead meat, Mister! Buzzard bait! Casper! You're going to be the ghost of Christmas past, Zeke! Tell me because I'm curious just what did you think you were doing?"*

"Good Lawd, I knew I had too fart! Please God, iffn you're listening, help a Brother out! I won't call any religious nutcase a pew-boy, choir-chickee-chick nor gospel gooney goo-goo for most parts to a year! Yet the Twisted-Sista persisted *"Why the Hell, was that old hag rubbing on my stuff? Tell me, Zeke just when did you get blonde ambition?"* rubbing on *her stuff*? Had I heard it rights? I be Babygirl's on the personal *Stuff*? Could my Babygirl have fo'reallies said-it out loud fo' my big ears to done heard-it that I be her *stuff*? I had to be delirious

thems little white gas producing twin bitches done gone and done made my imagination run amok big-*happy nappy*-butts iffn my Babygirl done said it then I'll be damned, I be her *stuff*!

Brrrup *hey hey its happening, oh Hell, yeah baby I be da' shit* brrrrrrruuup RRRRRRRRRRRRRRRRRRRRRRUUUUUUUUUUUUPP! BB-Brrrrruper, Brrruuper! Brrrrrrrrrrrrrrrruuuuuuuuuper! GoodLawd!! BBrrrrrrrruuuper! uuuuuuuper! There dew Be a God! Brrrruuuuuuper Brrrrruuuuppppperer brrruupper! Yo', Big Guy, You duh Man! Ahhhh BBBBBBBBrruuuupper !Brrrrupper! Rupp rupper Brrruupper! Brrr-ruppppers rrrrruuppers! Oh Happy Daze! Brrrrrrrupppers! brrrruuup-pers! bbbbruppper! I'm singing to the Choir! Brrruppers! brruuper! Let a brotha say, Amen! Brruupth! Tankz Big Guy, Tank-ya tank-ya berry berry mucho-much" Brruupth! Good God me tinks dat be da' last one!

After the gas company bankrupted-it then my Babygirl unleashed the water works just a torrid of concentrated tears as she simultaneously as-serted-it herns unalienable rights to my Temple simply because she done said it, I be her *stuff,* Yes Sir! Distracted by the cloudburst, the passion and her admittance that I be her stuff, I had given-in all too quickly and my numbskull totally whupped-it ass done begged-it herns forgiveness *"I got a sweet little Black Angel and I just love the way she spreads her wings*!" Muddy Waters, a'gin-n-juice Chess records classic RB cut outta thems early 60s! I had gotten so tangled-it up and within herns frumpled feathers that I had forgotten to question her about the whys and the hows that she had those damned gas pills in our *haus of luv* in the first place! Big-*mystery*-butts that painful gastric experience of a lifetime I done learnt-it what the ancients writ ...*through great pain there must come great wisdom* thus from the Gods I had been given the answer to the question that's done con-fused mankind *Medgar Evers* since them days of *Paradise Lost* just *WTF* had convinced Adam to bite that Eve done offered-it apple thens to get hisns dumb-ass tossed outta the garden? *Aha,* Na'Eve subtly done let it be knowed-it befo' God, all Angels and all thems newly named creatures and critters that Adam just so happened-it to be Na'Eve's *stuff*!

Chapter 52

I BE ONE DONE BEEN whupped-it no-cussing mofo ass for sure big-*nerdy*-butts in my defense I be one clueless mofo! My whole life be all about the fighting, be it other kids, big-*growed it up kid ass kicking older sadistic*-butts Mr. Bobby's older brothers, combat and my onliest womenfolk be of the *loved you long time* poontang variety. It taints no National security secret that a young finger-popping *shore leave* GI with cash in hisns hip-pockets and a beautiful babe on hisns arm be a KISS Universal Law dat GI buster *Sooners* gonna be one silly happy skinning-grinning broke-down empty-pockets, Mofo! I held meself a super-imposed mis-understanding of the hows, whats and wiles it be to the confusing world of thems womanfolk seed titi be my knowledge of womankind! Shakespeare said it bestest…*the whole world is a stage… everybody has his entrance and exit…* iffn I had wanted-it to done entered-it dat there stage the fool then I could've justa heaped-it my piles of *I gots women* troubles upon thems firstest tree brown-suga cooties Thelma, Geraldine and Rosie-tripleG because I done growed-it up with thems honey-dripped chocolate dipped *sexy mamas* and fo' years them royal triplets of ebony Queens and I done managed-it to somehow a'nuttier nighttime be the right time stayed-it the bestest of the big-*friends with benefits*-butts it had always been friends firstest thus we tree done shared-it a love with no real deep committed feelings justa you be and I be then we be our *all hands on deck* the love boat theme! That had been the difference with my Babygirl and all thems on the fly or on the sly other womankinds in that my Babygirl be the one that I done caught-it thems *hang on in there, baby* fo'reallies feelings! My Babygirl somehow let it be knowed-it that she indeed held such on the reals feelings for me and that conveyance alone be all that it done tooken to kept-it me a'wearing the dunce-cap to be bumping thems floppy-red clown shoes in herns *Amen* corner! Everyday be a brand new day fo' me with my Babygirl cause we be on the reals plus it be justa us two lovey-doveys pigeon holed-it up in our Love Grotto justa *honeymooning-it* up! Not to come down hard on my Babygirl big-*beautiful*-butts it wasn't herns fault a'tall seed I survived thems crazy-eight *on to be off to the on to again* years with my caped-crusader chocolate shak'em up *Wonder Woman* and that rapscallion the Twisted-Sista plus the both thems beauties be presided over *bye-bye* the fiendish Devil's own personal old be old assed handmaid *the opera aint over til the fat-lady sing* the Momma! Maybe it hadda been sump-tin so simple as the KISS*KeepItSimpleStupid* factor in-that one kiss from my Babygirl and I became both the simple and the stupid!

Mayhaps, I had just needed-it that trio of my beautiful Babygirl plus thems two knuckle-head wayward beyotches outta Whiskey Faults on the everyday 24/7 to be real live replacements for thems two original life-changing lunatic hard to the Corps clowns TOP and Trips. At one point me and my Babygirl done gotten-it married even psycho-assed tar-baby black Mexican wannabe Trips done made it to the wedding skinny-*po'dunk*-butt TOP had a family tragedy and couldn't done made it or instinctively TOP probably done knowed-it butter than my big-*whupped*-butts he'd been too wise to give-it a voice and a presence to such a sacrilegious thought of the inconceivable in dat me not marry my Babygirl, *All Hell to the Nawl!* There had been high winds with tornado sightings all through-out that blessed wedded day and then the unfucking unbelievable happened-it for a firstest and onliest time *Medgar Evers* it be that me and the Momma done actually spoken on one accord "...*Yes, we had Duf' it's a fact that my baby should've never married yo' dumb dufus ass!...*" STF old lady big-*tatter teller*-butts this all be true seed because of that brewing tornado then me and the Momma wanted-it to called-it off the nuptials with differ reasoning me fo' dat day onliest for old fatty-butt entirely! My Babygirl be having none of that *don't be afraid of a little wind* shit! You gotta done knowed-it fo' sho'nuff ya' whupped sumptin good iffn Ma' Nature herself come down outta the Cosmos to done tugged-it on your coattail during our rite of passage there be a thunderous ass rip-roaring 70+mph wind, golf-ball sized hail plus thems big assed oak trees be exploded by the lightening-strikes looked-it like *war-zone* shit be happening outside the building yet I had not listened-it to the resounding roar of Ma' Nature's thunderous *wake the fuck-up stupid* shout-out thus life and the Universe done said *Fuck-it, you fucking idiot you done gets what you gots!*

The highs with my Babygirl had been stratospheric and aside from the gas pills episode mostest of thems low-balled jack-assed stunts staged bye-bye thems two lunatic witches the baby witch be the Twisted-Sista and the big bad ugly wicked-witch of the southwest the Momma be more hilarious than painful! The Thanksgiving of our firstest year living-it up in the Love Grotto the Momma had personally invited-it me to herns formal turkey-day dinner party to done set me at the head of her extra-long dining room table! *Wow*, I thought hot-damn, finally the Momma gets it now I be da' shit! The Momma then done placed-it my lovely Babygirl at the opposite end of the same extra-long assed table where she be sandwiched between two Greeks and 'nuttier 4 thems geek-boys *Whoops there it is!*

The Thanksgiving past our blessed union, my Babygirl and her co-workers had staged an *after the Turkey-day* party with a twist being that one of thems lovely co-worker ladies who be not the wife, girlfriend nor any kinda kin had to call a'nuttier lady's husband/boy-friend then sexily invite the unsuspecting to the hotel room where theys *after the turkey-day party* a *Surprise Surprize Surprise Sergeant Carter* be held then all thems fools cept'n my big-*dumb*-butt done bursted-it theys leftover turkey nuts to done be a'coming on the dead run to dat there hotel room! A couple of thems lady folks had called me and I done promised-it them lovelies to get my black ass over to that hotel room big-*dumb*-butts after some two plus hours of interspersed-it calls by them lovelies and repeatedly broken promises by me the numbskull then my Babygirl had taken the hook outta the hands of thems two lovelies to done told-it to me straight-up that I bestest to get my big-*dufus'*-butt over to that hotel room because she and them ladies wassa putting-it down a straight-up past the turkey-day after *part-Tay*! I arrived-it theys party then some of them other lovelies started to play, tease and flirt with me about my being all lovely-dovey honeymooning with me new wifey big-*green eyes*-butts my Babygirl be having no parts that flirty shit because she done knowed-it exactly what be the real truth, Ruth! It be Friday evening and a new up-start cable-TV channel *ESPN* be showing the #8 Oklahoma State *Cowboys* live football game against my #3 *Sooner Nation*! My Babygirl knowed-it fo' a fat fact, Jack that both my sports first nuts be *Mr. Happy's* main boo-coos dem two swinging odd balls ruled-it equally within my dumb-ass and that the tree-selfish bastards would have joined-it forces and justa said *bump dat* to all the bullshit thems nutz be like fucks dem bitches and fucks theys *no-tell* hotel room service! *Sooner* football, be the shit, Babycakes! Miss da' game fuck, Nawl! Bros befo' hoes! Once a'gin-n-juice I be completely innocent no matter the reason!

My Babygirl's force fed invite big-*First Sgt*-butts she hadn't officially issued thems Orders to report *Emmett Till* she done knowed-it the game be justa bouts over then she done soured-it that minor incident into a major mistrusted be misunderstanding into the lead blocker to the start of our final pick-six touchdown run separation cause our marriage shit be a one and done da' shit be over, baby! Four days after that there partay wiles my happy as all fuck crazy-bouts my Babyg' dumb-ass be to work the Twisted-Sista and the Momma done rented-it two twenty-four foot U-Haul trucks then with a'heaping handful thems geek-boys theys done completely stripped-it bare our refurnished Love Shack stark naked even the kitchen theys done tooken-it all the appliances big-*stupid*-butts not the dishwasher cause in the Love Shack dat dishwasher aints white nor stain-less steel the Love Shack dishwasher be Black justa my scrape, rinse and wash big black ass which theys done on a purpose left behind!

Chapter 53

The grand finale to theys mad exodus them two cronked-it Whiskey Faults clowns on crack backed-it thems over-stuffed U-Haul trucks into then over my B-ball backboard *Emmett Till* both the backboard and pole be as I had come home to find thems broken and smashed-it bye-bye two 24-foot U-Haul trucks rear-tires ruts deep into the front lawn! Finally, as all thems white laughing theys non-po'dunk asses-off neighbors whom had watched it all proudly and happily reported-it to my deliriously stunned-it black ass, the Momma and the Twisted-Sista hadda tooken-it theyselves a good and a'plenty happy-assed *you go, I go* turns pummeling my 1981 midnight blue tan leather seats Nissan 280-ZX thems two done used-it my personal silver and black aluminum baseball bat witch theys dumb-asses done left-it my bat laying across the windshield as some veiled-it threat! I hates me some baseball! The grandest to beat all thems other grandest of the grand witch became the end finales fo' me hadda reared its ugly ass justa tree nights after my Babygirl's impromptu she done moved-it the fuck out! I be a'sleep on a borrowed army cot big-*grateful*-butts the much appreciated cot be in front of the curtain-less picture window of the *no love for you Blackie-boy* shack's living room where the outside street lamp made the living room the only lighted room in the house because the Twisted-Sista done turned-it off all the house utilities to done left me in the cold and waterless dark dat weekend! I had awoken-it hearing the squealing and peeling 85' *T-bird* rear tires as theys done screamed-it the get-away bye-bye dat bedlamite the Twisted-Sista because her crazy-ass done tossed-it a lit kerosene filled *Boone's Farm* the wino's choice bottle against the outside wall of the garage in some sorta mad-assed attempt to done set my world afire! Luckily fo' herns demented fine-ass she'd done won the daily-double *winner winner chicken dinner* after the small explosion against the garage sidewall witch was all brick a'nuttier *good fo'* *her* fine-assed selfie the little fire ball had only charred the wall justa bite befo' I extinguished it with a previously borrowed blanket. The little act of kindness bye-bye thems whitefolk lending me the cot and blanket had proven-it to be far more than luckier fo' the Twisted-Sista because I had extinguished that fire completely out justa moments befo' the *what the hell* the loco po'dunk fire department arrived wanting entry unto my property seed even though the fire had been completely extinguished thems all whiteys hose-jockey whores had tried using all kinda lies be theys excuses to take a step onto my property under the guise of they needed to do a fire safety inspection. The local *BarneyFife* po-po placed second in the race to fuck with my shit! A little TV aside *Barney Fife* be that rail thin deputy only allowed to carry one bullet fo' hisns gun and that bullet be buttoned-it up inside hisns front shirt-pocket. *Barney* be the skinny-assed whiteboy deputy from the 60s TV sit-com the *Andy Griffith Show,* "*An-deeeeee*!" Thems *BarneyFife* po-po done arrived-it on scene the curbside to be standing po'dunk shoulder to shoulder them assed-out fire-bugs and whom I done also solemnly denied all thems mofos entrance unto my property lessen theys po'dunk asses held a search warrant because all them white po'dunk whores be the one to theys all be the same just out to *get a rope* to done run a Brotha's black ass up a tree! My Moms hadn't birth-it no idiot and my daddy raised country Hell but not a black assed fool!

The Twisted-Sista's idiotic fired-up popping-it off the garage dat shit be my cue to pack what little of my shit that there be left inside a house that just aint no home without my Babygirl thens to done exited staged right big-*beautiful*-butts even though I be the mad lonely broken hearted yet I be not a fucking WOP sad-eye Mofo! The exodus done tooken-it almost a'nuttier year bye-bye my dragging me wussed-it footsies and thems divorce proceedings initiated bye-bye her just daze after she'd done moved-it the fuck out! I got this cheap-ass lawyer hisns office and home be this single-wide trailer big-*delusional*-butts my stupidity and grand illusions of the *I be in loves* allowed me to continue with that po'white trash lawyer big-*skank*-butts tank-God the Universal Benefactor takes care to both the babe and the fool alike when we arrived-it Court side the Judge be an older kindly fair-to-midland man whom didn't put up with po'dunk legal shits strutting theys chicken-shit inside hisns courtroom! The Judge done let *Sooners* to be ex-Babygirl's high priced-it lawyer and my cheap-assed bastard skank-hoe lawyer wannabe go about their co-opted shenanigans every bite of witch I had been entirely clueless to big-*scandalous*-butts that Judge done knowed-it exactamente what thems to *shylocks* be up to! The Judge told me that because I nor my *brilliant lawyer* had not contested any issues in answering the divorce compliant then he couldn't grant me nonya the stuffs that ex-Babyg' done took big-*naked*-butts my clothes, photos, trophies and plaques he told her that she will give them back to me within two days. The Judge then asked-it me why I wanted the divorce because it seemed to him that I might still be wanting to stay the marriage. I told-it the Judge justa wee bite bouts *Sooners* to be ex-Babygirl's failed attempt to done burned-it down the love shack with me inside asleep on a borrowed army cot. The Judge done sly smiled it my way to done made me tinks that old fool of a kindly Judge believed me to be some kinda *bare-footed Pilgrim* been taken to the wood shed! The Judge asked-it ex-Babygirl iffn she done wanted-it any alimony then befo' herns *yes, your honor I surely would* finished caressing my *Good Lawd I miss that woman* ears the Judge chuckled-it hard then he done denied forever any kinda form of all-*he*-money! The Judge even made ex-Babygirl give back my money just how she'd done gotten-it ahold of all that money of mines would onliest serve to make me to be mo' wussified then its already been told yet the thumbnail: *Sooners* to be ex-Babyg' had bout $6,000+ dollars of my money in 86' she be a rich bitch! The Judge told-it to a *Surprise Surprize Surprise ex-Sergeant Carter* ex-Babyg' to done walk-it offa that stand and to personally hand thems VA checks to me because that money be my money and that ex-Babyg' would not get one penny of that money! The Judge berated me in a legalese way in that I be a truly sorry kinda dumb-ass fo' not axing him to grant me back my money then he done an oater high-noon stare-down to both thems agaped-mouth shylocks! The Judge seemed-it to done thunk-it himself to be mo' wiser than bud and greater than King Solomon big-*dummy*-butts what that whitey robed in black old kindly judicious man too dumb for hisns own judicial po'dunk ass hadn't done knowed-it hadda been the fat fact, Jack be that money no matter the amount don't mean *shee-it* to a lonely man holding desperately onto a broken dream and a broken heart! The Judge also done told-it to ex-Babyg' that she had to pay her own lawyer fees, all thems court cost and all thems other fees that her-*ravishing*-self done in writ requested-it be paid by yours truly! Outside the courthouse atop them steps in front of thems two evil imps old ass the Momma and the Twisted-Sista, I shattered-it my Muddy Waters' *Sweet Little Black Angel* album then showed-it thems cold-heartless she-devils my newly purchased-it BB King' *The Thrill Is Gone* cause it be a brand new day, a brand new song and in the Queen's words a *brand new me* sing-it Aretha!

God looks after both thems suckling offa the tit as swell thems sho'nuff be growed-it up fools dat do anything and all tings fo' da' woman with big tits! *Tank-ya tank-ya berry mucho* Big Guy fo' giving me the Sampson liked strength to have done just moved-it me love-starved dumb-ass the fuck on! In retrospect, Adam bit-it that damn rotten Na'Eve offered-it apple because Na'Eve be the onliest woman in Paradise thus it had mattered *titi* to Adam that Eve done befriended the snake because that giver of all the creatures on earth a name be a name hisns own damned selfie that once the Garden of Eden tenant be justa straight-up *wuss* and it be a fat fact, Jack dat apple eating Adam be just liked me a Na'Eve done straight-up pussy whupped-it firstest man ever dumb-ass! My life amidst those two schizoid psychopaths the Twisted-Sista and that ghoul the Momma "*...you got lucky that Judge was an old assed fool just like your dumb-ass duf*" In reality my *Paradise* be mo' liked a *Pair-of-dice*, *Sooners* be dems big old shitty brown snakes-eyes of the Momma gonna roll! Toothbrush, washcloth, tree-neckties, navy blue suit, half a duffle bag of gym clothes, full duffle bag of brand new unopened-it gift wrapped bottles of *the Coty*, BB King album *The Thrill Is Gone*, aluminum baseball bat decorated 81' Nissan mid-knight blue 280ZX, two small cardboard boxes with two certified certificates box 1 read: This box of shredded materials contains all the childhood and prior to the marriage photographs and clothing of one dumb dufus. Box 2 Certified certificate read: This box of sawdust mixed plastic/metal/pewter flakes contains the trophies, medals and plaques of one Duf'!

Chapter 54

I BE PISSED-IT THE FUCK-OFF as *all Hell to southern redneck belles* after the deal went down! I'd done dropped-it the Corps reserves by that divorce time so I couldn't justa done runned-it to done shook-it off in some 3rd-world mudhole thumping them babygirls instead I done taken on a part-time weekend job that paid *onions n' taters* witch be an unlivable bullshit minimum wage I be a *nickel and dime* rent-a-cop where I on paper hadda onliest made enough monies to cover my shake-em up tab in thems Gentleman's *sto-bought titties* clubs of the OKC. What done happened-it be that rent-a-cop shit be a straight-up fucking Blessing in disguise seed thems po'dunks assigned me to work the weekends at a big Holiday Inn downtown OKC witch already the done started-it theys X-mass banquets and all thems other end of the year office parties. The hotel's season of the office parties arrived a couple weeks prior Halloween then sprinted through Valentines-day to done staggered-it across the finish-line comes *May-day* firstest day of May like a Mofo! My supervisor be this small raghead Iranian, a mad at the world holdover outta dems Prez Jimmy-*soggy peanuts*-Carter daze and that little bastard be a *Billy-bad-ass* raggamuffin sans the rag Mofo and just the man that I needed-it to done side-kicked-it to! Hell, I'd spent a life time of being *Tonto*stupid to a'many *Quien-no-sabe hewhoknowsnothing* big-*lonely ranger*-butts Boss'man be da' Rag-headed shit! Boss'man done carried-it in hisns skinny assed hip-pocket when retracted a 6-inch steel telescopic nightstick that extended to about 14-inches with a tree-quarta inch steel ball at the end of that steel rod then it be *nite-nite* mofo with justa the snap of hisns righthand at the flick of his right wrist! The hotel booked most them banquets and office parties within the its tree big ballrooms and two smaller banquet rooms plus a *high-n-tight* VIP lounge at them parties theys done sold or doled-it out big *Texass-sized* alcoholic drinks thus mostest thems banquet *party-party we gonna part-Tay* goers gots theys dead skunk-on to be drunker than a mofo! My Iranian boss be justa the sorta big Billy-bad-ass Mofo exactamente that I'd done needed-it during them nightmarish times of my dumb-wussed-ass pent-up bluzing daze cause my wussed-it ass be Biggy-smalls time missing ex-Babyg'! The good news be I done re-growed-it thems hairy-assed coconut balls of mine so I coulda out-right no-holds barred cuss a'gin-n-juice *fuckin' A-bitches*! Boss'man raghead light in the pants ass would've done rolled-it up on thems drunken cowpokes, oil-riggers and just any plain assed-out Oklahoma red neckbone when theys done gotten-it outta line then without blinking an eye he'd axed-it thems drunken shit-kicking ruff-necks *"you wanna fuck with a raghead"* next he'd flicked-it hisns damned nightstick opened as he'd done called-it me over hisns way via the radio, Good *Lord* thens and onliest then the shit be on and da' shit be *Right-on* my brotha! My anger be unmanaged as swell the shit be unchecked justa raging like a mofo then coupled-it up with Boss'man own ill brew conjured-up willingness to *fuck thems cowboys* it seemed to me dat Boss'man hadda fo'reallies liken unto my selfie done needed-it badly to fight some rednecks thus us two rent-a-cops with a crazed thirst fo' blood and fist fighting be the perfecto match lit inside a kerosene tinderbox ballroom! *Hell's southern belles* the two of us peace keepers done made-it a name for ourselves our firstest knight amongst thems late night hotel mostly female staff, party hosts and DeeJays for effectively and efficiently handling our business and it be our business to be bringing the umbrella of *Peace be still* wherever drunken roughneck chaos done fucking reigned in thems ballrooms! That pertinent information got worded-it up to all thems DJs and party hosts who had on the sly be done hit-us-up sumptin-sumpting byway of *trickled-down Reaganomics* thems under the table extra bonus funds *jello-Benjamins* just fo' us two mad-at-the-world the *sand-nigger* and hisns *nigger* to be dishing-it out the peace be quick and easy or the rough and tumble "*rumble young man rumble*"-Bundini, Mohammad Ali's trainer and corner man- to the tune of a *Hondo* plus odd bones each from each and every DJ/host at each and every one thems party-party get jo' party-on come the Friday and Saturday nights and even some Sunday nights just fo' doing our job to done walked-it security each host done slipped-it us two raw dogs a hondo each to provide the surveillance as swell control the drunkards at theys party *yes Lord* it be a mad-dash for the cash-money thus jo' boy became a po' man's buzzard-breath, Babycakes! Thems Benjamins added-it up quite nicely and we hadda made close to or over a grand a piece to be kicking all dat redneck drunken ass on the fly to be making thems drunken cowpokes honest Injuns each and all them rent-a-cop *I gots paid* weekend knights! Truth be told, I would have been whupping-it up on all dat drunken redneck ass fo' free big-*bucks*-butts my Boy' Boss'man pulled-it me by the short-ones that first knight right after my very firstest drunken cowpoke fight done ended. The happy-ass raghead done knowed-it sho'nuff that hisns raggamuffin ass be in the company of a real *blood moon mad ass-kicking* mofo to done backed-it hisns *I just loves to kick drunken cowpokes in their redneck asses* selfie! It went down, me and Boss'man onliest after both our palms be greased a hondo per then we'd done walked-it that firstest walk-through together them parties early-on and often big-*peaceful*-butts during thems firstest few walked-it throughs we'd look for the rowdy and iffn dat frog done leapt then we'd go over and bump its wart-toting-ass right-on up to be fucking offa dat lily-pad and out them banquet/ballroom doors and that *no bullshit* reaction to theys actions done usually kept mostest of the rest thems bitch-ass bullfrogs at bay and justa anchored-it to theys damned padded stools through-out the night and dat shit be the easy money, baby! Big-*cheap*-butts iffn a DJ or party host hadn't done paid-it us when the rowdy shit done started-it in on theys non-payment party then we two would go near enough to watch the *brew-ha* justa make sure it didn't get too far outta hand and thems drunken sod-buster/rough necks causing the display hadn't done brung-it theys rough and tumble hayseed shit our way big-*dumb*-butts there had been those chosen few, *tank God* fo' the chosen ones!

Some of thems cheap-ass non-paying assholes DJ/party hosts would rat us out to management big-*snitches get even bigger stitches*-butts that hadn't worked-it out so swell because the hotel nightshift consisted mainly an all-female staff be working-it the front-desk reception and emergency room/housekeeping services and thems smart working ladies of the nightshift done let management be to done knowed-it very quickly that theys done felt-it very safe and secure when me and Boss'man be on the watch as well thems cheap-assed DJs and hosts to be done knowed-it that theys didn't give a trailer rat's scurry-ass to how me and Boss'man done laced-it up our boots because iffn trouble arose witch seemed to have happened quite a bit fo' thems ladies yet iffn either myself or the Boss'man got called-it to a bad situation then peace ensued and that peace had usually ensued very quickly and that theys be very happy with the service that us two *gotta get paid* knuckles done provided! The hotel management liked-it that the staff be pleased as apple-cider punch plus Boss'man and me be cheap labor without benefits thus it be a no-brainer dat management done sided-it with hotel staff and thems paying DJs/hosts because bye-bye all theys accounts Boss'man and me be the triple-crown of security in-that we be effective, efficient and cheap-assed labor therefore thems cheap-asshole DJs/hosts either had to pay-it up or suck the fuck-up!

The onliest thang I done knowed-it that I be one mad-assed unhappy day-camper big-*confessional*-butts I be an angry mofo on the insides I be justa one big-*mad at the world*-butts my anger hadn't stepped-it up to done paraded itself down front-street big-*mad*-butts I done knowed-it the rent-a-cop ting would never be anything more than a temporary excursion down an one-way *ass-kicking* lane yet unhappy-assed and getting paid-it liked a mad mofo, I done just loved-it me the *com'on Boss'man lets us two fuck thems roughneck fools up* journey! The angry shit be all about and onliest about ex-Babyg' it be a self-inflicted inner wuss-assed turmoil therefore when dat shit done absconded-it my numb-skull and I be no mo' mad then fo' sho'nuff my black ass be quick to be its a *bye-bye rent-a-cop*!

My dumb-ass losing ex-Babyg' thang done left-it meself without my happy-nappy dugout big-*feelings*-butts justa large and empty hole to fill when Boss'man bumped that itch to done whacked-it dems rowdies thus us two-knuckles made fo' a bad keg of the dynamite! I needed-it bad fo' somebody justa anybody to done step-it the fuck up then to justa hauled-it sledge hammer *momma said to knock yo' ass out* punched the fuck outta my dumb-ass! I needed-it me a punch hard enough to make the blood to run hot and sticky-sweet down the back of my throat because the anger that I be toting had itself an on the reals desire to done tasted the bad moon rising flavor to feel the heat and to hear the faint sound of a bone crackling fist smacking hard against my wussed-out ass! It be the sight of an *In-coming* WTF *its gonna be yo' ass nigger-boy* punch dat be the onliest times that I could chill the fuck e'nuff down to take a respite of the inner *Peace be* still! My inner-turmoil anger shit dat done rolled-it up to done overpowered and numb-nutted my physical pain sensors big-*painless*-butts being rocked bye-bye a hard hitting punch be the onliest ting what to done eased my mind, yeah Trips be not the onliest psycho mofo from the unit!

I done believed-it that thems drunken *yo' nigger-boy let's dance* hayseeds done seed-it, felt-it and or sensed-it that need to be hit be justa bubbling-it up inside my wussed-out ass besides I hadn't given a shit about taking an ass whupping iffn theys redneck ass could *pony the fuck-up*! Yes, Lord, *Tank-ya sweet-tea baby Jesus* a'many tried yet justa few dems fools done *shattered the fucking lights*! Hell, boxing be my ghetto pass back the CC then thems two psychotics war dawgs TOP and Trips loved-it nuttin mo' butter than rolling-it into an unknowed-it *turn-off the fucking lights* barroom fo' some bare knuckled *git jo' numb-nuts in there its a free for all* fisticuffs! The problem fo' my masochistic wussified ass be with justa bare minimum glance at that *oh my God he handsome* mug of mine to be done told-it all seed it been hammer punched-it all over my beautiful Black face that I be sway too young to done lost-it mostest my eyebrows the natural way and dat flip scar above my right eye and a few other nicks dat be notches adorned my *rich-lady boy-toy* the money-maker face done told-it thems drunken fools a real truth, Ruth that iffn you came, you'd best to have done brung-it alls youse gots! Thems two meat hooks had theys own story the knuckles on the backsides of both hands be tripled calloused dat stood out like big black booty-bumps Hell, I'd done caught a'many everyday peoples justa straight-out starring at thems bumps like WTF! I walked-it straight-up, head-up, standing tall and my feet never *Medgar Evers* got close to being parallel seed I stepped-it with a rigid yet thoroughly disciplined purpose a cantered gait in-that I never placed-it that second foot beside the first foot stride be a beacon *tell the tell* to all thems drunken rednecked *Superman* wannabees that theys would not become a hero dat night by fucking with the likes of me! It be a Hollywood oater somber like a mofo because my two lonesome baby-browns be a'looking-it fo' all the troubles thems drunken whores be a'seeking and all that shit be on the reals, Babycakes!

I didn't get many takers big-*tank-ya*-butts when I did we done danced the whole song and it hadn't mattered-it one damned bite iffn that ditty be the tango or the *cotton-eyed joke* justa lined-it up come the one or comes them yalls! The onliest bad thing be I had so much hurt and anger inside that I be collard-greens stoopid because it hadda felt-it butter to done taken-it dat firstest punch of the night thus I'd on a purpose to done *put a glitch in my hitch* justa mite justa taste the blood running down the backside of my nose befo' lightening quick I done struck-it upon them drunken assholes with a flurry of fisted sometimes kicked-it combinations to be reigning down all that *rent-a-cop be in the house* peace on theys drunken rowdy redneck asses! The physical final exam happened-it sum 6 rent-a-cop months into the fray seed Boss'man and me done always runned-it security fo' a young black teenaged dance hosted by a kool ass all Hell get-the-fuck outta here strawberry *Kool-Aid* kool as all fuck DJ witch he'd done held-it in the largest ballroom that particular Sat-night I'd done a'sumpting so crazy-ass chilling to be frightening that even meselfie had to step the fuck back! Brotha DJ found-it out fast on the furious that Boss'man and me could control hisns crowd both inside the ballroom then outside in them parking lots when the party be over seed teenagers aint gots much to do 'cept hanging-it out in p-lots after hours and blasting rap-music fo' hours on end. Swells, Boss'man and me usually cleared-it them young mannish whores outta them p-lots bordering on the *no shit* furious without frills plus Boss'man and me had never had to call the southern white boy *BarneyFife* po-po on them young Black teenaged asses thus things be going super blue berry hill *Kool-Aid* kool with thems Black teenagers, Brotha DJ and hotel management.

Chapter 55

It be a quarta-moon night, I personally just loved-it meself a quarta-moon and that peculiar night wassa soft springy time knight so Boss'man and I cleared-it thems big parking lots while Bro DJ watched-it all befo' we split-it up then I stepped-it alone to the back and furtherest away smaller p-lot. It be there that I done runned-it upon two big-*dumb*-butts in reality thems two fools be justa two empty-headed chicken shits wannabe gangbangers and each of them numb-nuts dip-shits done held a pepper-pot witch be a small .22, a double-duce caliber ghetto bird *no name* pistol in hisns dumb-fuck meat-beater and thems two wishful fucks be a'standing less than 10-feet apart munching hard thems wolf cookies! Without fucking thinking witch had always been a major *pro-blame-o numero uno* for my dumb-ass! Nawl, it wasn't even that I didn't always think befo' I done acted-it, I swear it be a real truth, Ruth that in any emergency situation I'd always done stopped-it to just briefly intake my environment to done thunk-it out and formulated-it a plan of action iffn any that shit be about to happen onto my black ass! The problameo be that it be all on the instant grits *Superfly* thus fo' me it be *Due the due, Son* time and once I'd done thought-it and made-it the plan of action then I done executed-it that plan without question nary a second guess nor a guest opinion! I hadda taken-it my Dad and dem Unks lessons about kicking dat raunchy *brotha fear* in the ass to a'nuttier insane level! It didn't matter one damned bite whether the thought be good or be bad, be it right or be it wrong seed I had no time fo' dat kinda judgment day shit fo' brains tinkering a thought through because I be *the man* armed with a plan! My firstest thought-it be that those two ass-bite fucking wuss-monkey gangsta wannabe mofos a'standing there munching on wolf biscuits just wanted-it fo' a'somebody justa any damned some-fucking-body po'leesa to done stepped-it up to done stopped theys shit befo' da' shit got sway too far outta hand! Thems two braying jackasses both wanted-it someone to done stopped-it theys dumb-asses from what be about to go down and that's just exactamente what I done did!

My foolish emotionally pained-it I be pining fo' ex-Babyg numb-nuts be unawares of the reality of the real live death threat that accompanied my *Son, just do the do* shit because it be such a dumb-fucked WTF *were you thinking* action ergo my pained-it dumb-ass just kept-it non-stop to taking thems long-assed stepped to done strutted strides of mines *Emmett Till* I done stepped-it just liked I done thunk-it straight the fuck *where I be* right-on up then in-between thems two dumb pistol toting fucks! Befo' I done knowed-it I'd done grabbed-it the firstest skinny assed teenaged fool by bunching the front collar of hisns purple WTF I *plum hates me the color purple* shirt thens I done brunged-it that collar with hisns po' *how the fuck that skinny assed* neck done supported hisns big elongated peanut head to hisns thin assed chest in my left hand as I dragged-it hisns still gun toting skinny ass thems few fucking feet witch done separated-it thems two fool-asses over to the other WTF stunned-it wide-eyed skinny as all fuck-boy bastard-ass to done grabbed-it the front of hisns red shirt in my right hand then I shouted-it at both thems juvenile numb-nuts "WHAT THE FUCK, Motherfuckers!"

I let loose them shirt collars just long e'nuff to take theys pea-shooters, dem tinhorn pistols outta each of theys a'trembling hands. The fact be that both thems a'scared assed dick-heads hadda almost pissed-it theys pants as both jug-heads practically shoved-it theys cheap-assed pistols into my awaiting opened palms-up hands! I swear to God the All Be Mighty God that thems two still stroking theys dead meat on a nightly basis teenaged mofos hadn't done wanted-it any gun play to go down! I confirmed-it my exactamente and *corecta amundo* summation of theys fucked situation seconds later because of thems overhead parking-lot street lamps when I done locked-it firstest the one thens the other of thems two dumb-lucky ass fools in theys shitty-brown wide-the-fuck opened eyeballs to done seed-it in the each a small yet definitely flicker of a *brotha fear* be bye-bye *Jello* Sista-relief in the one then the other's *please God don't let me die tonight* buck-wild orbs! I didn't even stopped-it to check the safeties on them two cheap-assed pepper-pots, I just put them two fucking *mid-night special ghetto-birdshots* one each in one each rear hip-pocket of my rent-a-cop uniform *Dickies* black pants. I done kept thems two firing-pin removed pepper-pots hanging on my walls fo' years as a reminder to never ever do that kinda unthinkable suicidal shit never to *Medgar Evers* again! I then re-grabbed-it them two skinny Black-ass mid-nite bastard-boy mofos by theys scruffs to done spun-it theys punk-assed

Tank You God I'm still alive big-*pooping*-butts around befo' I done shoved-it firstest the one numbskull then the other dip-shit towards theys separate parties and separate cars then I told-it to every-*fucking*-body in that p-lot to "GET THE FUCK OUTTA HERE, YOUNG ASS MOTHERFUCKERS!"

In an eerie wordless silence, all thems teenaged young-guns collectively done jumped-it theys what a gift *to be young Black and foolish* asses into theys buckets chucked anchor then broke shore without blaring horns, squealing tires nor talking any parts shit! It be all on the quiet-like that all thems foolish onlookers done gots theys young buck Black asses the fuck gone! Later that night when I done retraced-it all in my mind's inner-eye it be then I done seed the foolishness of my error along with the *whats sup* behind the weird silence seed all thems other fools done looked-it stunned with theys mouths opened and that be when I done realized-it just what the fuck had actually went down! I done runned-it upon thems two pistol toting dumb-fucks at exactamente the moment thems two knuckles done run outta theys wolf-cookies and theys dumb-assed teenaged pride hadda just fucking kicked-in deys dumb-asses and thems two knuckles be bouts to done throwed-it all down big-*dummy*-butts fo' dat dumb-ass inter-turmoil emotionally pained-it dumb-fuck missing hisns ex-Babyg' to done stepped-it the fuck betwixt theys on the verge of death fuck-heads! Thems two clowns and all thems other teen fucks done knowed-it dat shit thus I be the onliest clueless fuck that parking-lot howling-it out worthless orders, Fuck! That shit there be da' *Whadd-up* that done given-it to me thems funky shaky-shakes then I'd done had e'nuff dat shit *fuck you ex-Babyg' and yo' Momma, Elvis done left the building*! *I'm alive and bouts to git grits*! Justa tinkering bouts dat shit in an alternant Universe gave and still does gives me thems damned the hopping junkie eerie assed skin-crawling *willies*! All my *WTF* adult life to dat point be all about the killings in-that either I done runned-it away from or done runned-it upon some kinda 3rd world killing field! Da' shit be bad e'nuff to done died-it swinging my monkey-ass anyone of them fucking jungles either fighting over a can of *Pepe DuPont's* matte one-coat yella-assed pinko-commie-red paint or a buzzard breath ambush fo' a single-line of uncut cocaine big-*stoopid*-butts to done died-it as a dumb-assed numbnuts decked *Dickies* black pant with light-blue shirt *rent-a-cop* suit and it don't be Halloween po'leeese Angel of Death *Get the Fuck Outta Here*!

chapter 56

I DIDN'T LEAVE THE COMPANY right then nor straight-up quit that night nor that weekend 'cept physically big-*shaky*-butts on the reals I done *check please* mentally knowed-it that night be the toast of my rent-a-cop daze and dat toast be burnt! Tree-weeks later, I bursted-it the fuck completely loose from the rent-a-cop business because the very next Sat-nite err *easy liked a Sundae* moaning I'd done given Boss'man my two weeks-notice bouts thems walking papers big-*toasted*-butts da' shit hadda happened-it in one big swelled swoop on the following weekend justa one fucking week straight-up after thems foolish teens and theys pistolero bullshit then came the big she-banged! I knowed-it taint right to find sublime joy in the misery of a'nutter cause my Moms done raised-it me to be butter than that anyways big-*happy*-butts *Good Lawd,* Sat-night following thems two knuckles when I be a happy-ass walking-it in fo' the rent-a-cop duty swells Boss'man be out front them hotel entry doors and be all casual liked when he'd done queried my clueless ass iffn I wassa gonna be Ok? *What the fuck you talking about, Boss'man*? The VA Hospital Black Employees had months back rented-it the VIP lounge fo' theys annual sweethearts couples only dance witch happened-it every first April Saturday seed I'd done forgotten thems VA employee fools be a chunk of the God damned gotta be April fools! Boss'man hadn't never to done seed ex-Babyg' big-*nosey*-butts he knowed-it from some our *OnTheJobTraining* rap-sessions that she be Black and that she done nursed-it for the VA hospital so he had put thems two be a fat fact, Jack assumptions together befo' he done stepped-it over just to done chased my squirrel-ass outta the tree! Boss'man be liked *what's up, with you*? *Girl gonna be here*? Now up and *Emmett Till* then I be *one happy-yappy nappy day-camper* I be a'sitting by the fireside justa roasting thems marshmallows awaiting the nighttime be the right time to be telling dems scary ass fireside ghost stories! Hells-a' fire Boss'man yapping bouts dat there sweetheart dance shit done pulled-it my black ass up then straight outta that *happy-nappy* campgrounds, fuck! The VIP lounge held about 200+ nappy-heads and it be up-front near the front desk also it be the only party room in the *hotel, motel, Holiday Inn* that be a contractual part of our duties to patrol. The VIP crowd usually be older and pina-pineapple *Kool-Aid* kool the peeps partying in the VIP had never made any kinda problems excepting maybe asking a rent-a-cop mofo to call theys drunken-ass a cab *Ok, you be a taxi motherfucker*! Big-*on point*-butts Boss'man be T-totally correct though I'd never admitted-it to him dat just the fucking thought ex-Babyg' done showed-it face with a'nuttier nappy-headed mofo in that hotel and on that nite then I might not just be a *pro-blame-o* big-*tripping*-butts a shoot a Black mofo in the ass psycho wannabe a Messykin Trips kinda problem!

I didn't tink-it ex-Babyg' would attend such an event knowing full and well that I worked-it thems weekends yet I hadn't wasted-it no time to brake stride I'd kept thems twinkling toes to stepping full gait as I done hauled-it my k-kool mofo cause I be the calmed befo' the storming on the insides k-kool ass over to that VIP lounge fo' justa little look-ey-look the place over *Surprize Surprise Surprize Sgt. Carter*! I turned the corner to the lounge area when *WTF* there thems whores be, ex-Babyg' hugged-it up high-n-tight on the arm of herns newest victim, the geek and the Momma, fuck! The good, the bad and the ugly *…watch-it Duf'* the thing be that somethings never to *Medgar Evers* done changed thus my eyeballing the geek had kinda done made me to wanna chill the fuck down and smile justa bite such that when thems *WTF are youse doing here* fools peeped-it me swells geekboy stepped-it over to make conversation big-*nerdy*-butts I really wasn't feeling him *what-up my brotha how ya' been* a few kindly Word-ups! I eased-it on the bye-bye thems other tree fools without words nor gestures big-*whoa Nelly*-butts something about that whole scene yeah both thems Whiskey Faults witches and I say witch-es with big time love hadda rolled-it theys big ol' cow eyes, ex-Babyg' *Peace be* still big beautiful *I love you so mucho-much baby-browns* then dat *imp* the Momma done rolled-it thems shitty-brown raw-dog turd fo' orbs of herns *...don't be getting ugly, Duf'* fuck!

I left-it thems fools at the scene of the crime because heart-break be felonious! *Oh to be still my achey-breaky heart*! Ex-Babyg' had herns fine-ass self a pair to done sho'nuff showed-it up to fuck with my head on a purpose herns exquisite beautiful sepia self be stroked in an whol-ly edible spaghetti strapped tight-assed black evening gown stretched it hardtack across herns gum-drop nipples and she be splattered-it with *the Coty* plus she'd brunged-it that particular geek on a purpose because outta all thems *I want ya' woman fools* that one and me hadda always gotten along fair-to-mid-land dat boy could sho'nuff hoop-it up then on hisns weekend runs we two would run down to the flyboy base and take on all comers! Ex-babyg' done knowed-it I be patrolling them hotel hallways thus dat geekboy be herns fair warning *I hates yo' ass Zeke* nuttin personal though she be guilty as all *Hell's southern belles* just cause herns fine *the Coty* spritzed ass done got me charged! *Houston we'z done gots ourselves a problem*!

A couple of hours into the VIP dance I gots me an itch to done set about fucking-up that trio of assholes and theys *dance with me sweetheart* night. I done knowed-it my ass be seething with an intense disco inferno of *po'lease justa somebody anybody come and punch me in the fucking face* it be dat kinda knight big-*seething*-butts jo' Bro man done gots hisns rage full the fuck on! The party had been tight as a motherfucker thems peeps be jamming deys shit, theys had the comedy with both the funny men and laughable women up on the stage rolling pure hilarious Superfly shit and a bad ass DJ done lit-it up in-between the sets big-git ya' *party on*-butts theys done justa fucking bumped dat shit! Thems tree scumbags ex-Babyg' the Momma and the *Hell, nawl* replacement fools done needed-it theys dumb-asses an up-close *Hell yes*, it be on the personal lesson in knuckle-headed *welcome to my world* rent-a-cop hospitality! I done tooken-it the simple ordinary itty-bitty a little paper-clip then whilst patrolling inside the lounge I done all quiet like stepped-it near bye-bye the all steel lounge emergency exit door then I inserted that paper-clip inside the alarm box attached to the door when that little itty-bitty paper-clip with purely an evil-assed intended purpose made contact with the alarm's off/turn-on terminals withouts my having to pull the handle that fucking alarm done broke the fuck loose and blared the fuck-off-the hook, baby that shit be wicked-ass loud as all fuck! The good news be that that alarm was onliest set fo' that particular door to witch it be attached therefore it hadn't set off any other emergency alarms yet did I give a flying fuck at a rolling hot outta the oven *Krispy Cream* doughnut! Bump dat shit! The onliest problem be that young ass hotel manager hadda come a'running-it down the hallway into the lounge then once he'd seed-it that it be only that door alarm gone awry and not any real emergency that dumb-fuck had tried to *here I come to save the day* all the while Boss'man be justa straight-up eyeballing me, yeah big-*smarty pant*-butts can you prove-it, mofo! I only tooken-it my good eye offa that hotel manager fo' a nano-second to deal with Boss'man's when the fool assed whiteboy went and grabbed-it the fire axe with on the plus-side of some seven boney-armed full swings of the axe that fool managed to done chop knocked-it dat damned alarm box still fucking blaring completely offa the emergency door. I runned-it over there and grabbed-it the loud-ass fuck alarm box away from the manager and on the way to the rear of the hotel, I done shook-it loose the simple itty-bitty paper clip witch done started-it all then without fail exactamente when that paper-clip fell offa thems terminals still inside the box and the fire-alarm stopped blaring then fucking Boss'man jumped-it the fuck outta thin air with hisns *"I fucking knew it!"* Anytowho, me and Boss'man dumped the box in a storage room to done hustled-it back to the lounge where thems tree assholes be with the geekboy still lined-it up in the hallway awaiting to get back inside the party and that's when Good *God Amighty*, there fo'reallies do be a God because the shit had fo'reallies done happened-it! No, I hadn't crossed over that hallway to done right-crossed to done upper-cut thems tree fool asses, No! What happened be front street and center-court the newest victim, the educated certificate toting replacement, ex-babyg's new big professional man though it had been slight a very *Medgar Evers* so on the sly it be big-*hooked on mo' than phonics*-butts I done caught-it fo' sho'nuff that mofo' be a straight-up junkie that bitch-hoe bastard professional whatever the fuck he and hisns junkie-ass practice be swells dat dirty-dog bastard hanging tight unto my ex-woman's arm be justa a straight-up *Sooners* to be living in thems mean assed streets of the Whiskey Faults junkie! Dat mofo had been ever so slightly scratching hisns-self on the Sly *aint no family* stoned big-dummy-butts hisns slick junkie-ass be sneak-thief scratching at all thems imaginary heroin bugs witch be all to fo'reallies reals to hisns junkie ass and thems *smack* bugs be crawling theys imaginary asses all over hisns *hooked on heroin* junkie monkey ass!

Big-*Yes Lord*-butts stills that shit hadn't even been *da' shit* what done fo'reallies happened-it, the Momma old crusty sausage crunching evil ass be the real shit that night in the exacto momento that I had just figured-it the replacement be a fucking straight-up junkie fuck-shit swells the Momma that old bag of the bad breath be both barrels of herns beady black snake-eyes aimed and locked onto my beautiful baby-brown orbs thus she done knowed-it that I'd done knowed-it sho'nuff dat ex-babyg' new victim be a straight-up junkie, WTF! I be across and down a bite dat hallway big-*funky*-butts it done lookey-looked to me liked the Momma's beady snake-eyes teared-it the fuck-up big-*Hells belles*-butts most likely herns older brother the Devil himself hadda done spit in thems shitty-browns "...*don't you dare Duf'* they say shit happens swells Sir *da' shit* done happened-it, Babycakes! That split second be *da' shit* that done truly set my sweet sweetback Black ass to be free! The Momma teary-eyed big-*brisket*-butt sad-eye like a mofo old frumpy butt done looked-it so damned sad thems snake-eyes be holla@ya'Boy *I broke you and my baby up for this*! I knowed-it be the real truth, Ruth because I done felt-it that shit, Yes, Sir *Bobs me uncle* that shit hadda been *da' shit* what done happened-it! The Momma be a *Baby, I'm for real* sad-eye beady snake-eyed mofo and witness to my grand revelation that herns youngest girl child be a justa a *lost cause* professional junkie's girl fine-assed *who'dat* done chosen the perfecto *nurse ratchet* profession because ex-babyg' needed-it thems broken mens to be done fixed-it up and herns newest one needed-it a fix justa get hisns brokedown junkie ass up so my happy-nappy black ass be *fucks thems tree whores*!

I'd done bounced-it *Disneyland* because I be the happiest ass on Mother Earth! Motherfucker, that knight that moment you couldn't have chiseled the *I'm a happy ass motherfucker* stoned-cold smile offa my skinning and grinning *dat Black man be handsome* face with a jack-hammer cause my shit be lit, Babycakes! I had let Boss'man, Brotha DJ and the hotel manager all tree to be done knowed-it that I be bounced-it the fuck outta the rent-a-cop game big-*tank ya*-butts I done respected thems tree as straight-up *honest Injuns* that be why it be thems tree mo' weeks after thems two pistol banging teenagers done punked-it my dumb-ass to done played me the suicidal fool, Word! I spent less than a'nuttier year in the backdrop of OKC working them computers when serendipity caused-it my Good *Lord, good gots damned-it I be a happy-ass* to done unpacked all my leftover baggage then to done set all that emotional *I be in need of a good ass whooping* bullshit on ex-babyg' outside porch steps fo' the replacement's junkie monkey ass to done picked-it up! The mad exodus happened in an outta sorts odd-ball kinda way seed I hadda been on the removal then installation team helping this insurance company move theys computer shit from Tulsa, OK to Dallas big-*gotta go*-butts some 2-months laters thems insurance fools still be experiencing problems with theys junk mail printers let ya know dat karma be a bitch, baby!

Chapter 57

THE IBM 1403 CHAIN-PRINTER HAD become my on the J-O-B specialty. The main power and the mechanical heart of that printer be a hydraulic pump witch drove the print-chain as well all the other mechanical movable parts. One of the main reasons that I had been hired by the company be that I had over 9-years the experienced jet engine technician and during my interview the regional manager and the OKC branch manager had somehow gotten-it the grandest idea that I done knowed-it a Hell-of-a-lot bouts the ins and outs workings of hydraulic power units. I'd truly done knowed-it all about the inner mechanical workings of a hydraulic pump witch got proven quickly during my firstest month on the job seed thems other IBM technicians for the 1403 printer had to order anuttier expensive hydraulic pump or an equally just expensive print-chain when there be pump and or print-quality problems. It had happened-it during my non-stop chip fucking paint-chipping time on that navy tub seed I had volunteered-it extra-duty time in the ship's hydraulic shop to build-up and breakdown hydraulic turbine pumps just fo' a little sump'n sumptin to do on that boring ass floating shit-bucket of hard-legs that be why I could teardown then rebuild that pump with cheap-ass anywhere hardware store bought parts. I had also been mentored-it by an old head IBM tech that always be done pissed-it hisns pants because he didn't wanna stop working a task just to drain the lizard dat be why thems other techs done shied-it away from hisns piss-soaked white ass thems big-*dummies*-butts dat old pissy-ass po'dunk straight-up done knowed-it how to sync any given print-chain to its particular pump witch he done learnt-it to me firsthand just how to accurately sync the print-chain to its pump for damn near perfecto printing thus dat shit be my technical niche and kitchen pass into the world of IBM.

Anytowho, I hadda been in Dallas for about two-weeks synchronizing them print-chains to theys pump because I didn't work-it them weekends and that insurance company had about fiddy thems junkmail printers. I parked-it my car in the insurance company's parking garage big-*unlucky*-butts that last day the infamous fo' me onliest *I done finished-it up* Friday the insurance company done held a regional meeting then all thems free insurance company garage parking spots had been tooken by my arrival. I be on the CP clock, *Colored Peoples* time and our clock don't go tic-tock our clock goes tickety-*what's up my brotha come holla@ya'Boy*-tocks thus I had done parked-it my mid-night blue baseball bat pummeled 280-ZX in the garage of the adjacent building across the street big-*unsure*-butts my babyZ done got towed-it the fuck away bouts as *Sooners* I'd done jumped-it my Black ass up and offa thems tan leather seats then my unknowing dumb-ass spent mostest of that last day finished-it up Friday knight a'hopping-it from the one downtown building's parking garage to the next parking garage with the dire hope of finding a mid-night blue baseball bat pummeled 280-ZX no avail. Fuck the dumb-shit, it had never dawned on my dumb-ass mind that my babyZ be stolen nor towed. I had since the finished-it up bouts sixteen-thirty hundred hours *Emmett Till* round mid-night I be justa walking thems muggy ass African hot downtown streets of Dallas all confused and perplexed about the situation and headed-it to yet a'nuttier building's parking garage when Wham-Bam WTF I done jumped-it back about five-feet *air-borne ranger* to have kept from getting runned-it over by a *Greyhound* bus, WTF! The driver, a rail-assed kindly mofo opened-it the door of that bus to done hollered-it at me *You ok* then I had axed him where he be going in such a fucking hurry and he told me Phoenix then I axed-it him iffn I had time to get a ticket to ride then he done told me No! Skinny-*ass hauling*-butts he said that I could jump on board cause the next stop be Fort Worth witch be *just across the street fo' any born and raised-it Taxdatass* about sum forty minutes away then once there I could purchase dat ticket.

The following Monday morning my *babyZ-less* black ass be in Tempe home to the Arizona State *Sun Devils* the Momma's *baby-brother be theys mascot* and also it be a suburb of Phoenix and I be explaining to my ex-supervisor on a pay-phone collect-call that my black ass be lone on the fucking gone! The *Soup* had been kool as fuck, *cool hand Luke* lemon-lime *Kool-Aid* kool then we had laughed-it liked a mofo and even joked about my crazy-ass and my impromptu vacation time. He done told me that my baby-Z had gotten towed-it then he hipped me to the whole pay by-the-space garage scenario in that you parked-it yo' bucket, go find the central self-pay station then pay fo' the stall yo' bucket be kicking-it in yet I need not fret because he'd call and take care of finding my baby-Z onliest ting it would be up to me to go and retrieve it plus ex-soup told me that the job be still mine justa get my dumb-ass back when I could and that be straight-up Word from the good book man, a Mormon bye-bye religious trait and he done held unto hisns word and unto that job fo' me up-mostest over 7-years that I knowed-it of though I never went back to work-in nor lived-it in the OKC. Ex-Soup be good peoples and good peoples be good people even iffn theys be ex-Navy scrub and full-time thems damned jello eating *russellites* door-knocking moronic dumb dim-witted asses whom be done believed-it that bullshit dat Black folks aint got no Soul! Hell to thems dumb-asses, I done knowed-it full fucking swell theys *jello-shitting* funky-white asses don't take a fucking bath big-*stinky*-butts once every tree-weeks and thems butt-head fools onliest reason being so' theys funky asses can smell like God, who the fuck wanna God dats smells liked he fucking aints bathed hisns rusty-musty ass in weeks dat funky shit be justa shitty Mormon moron stoopid! Anywho aints thems M&M's dems Mormon Morons gots TV so how-it-be dat theys dumb-asses ain't to never done seed *Soul Train*! Me and ex-soup done been skin-tight water-tight as bullfrog pussy and not because ex-soup done told me mo' than once dat hisns sect of thems Mormons felt everybody hadda Soul and he had on a'many occasion invited my heathen ass to Saturday Temple though I done told-it to hisns Tabernacle choir wannabe no-singing ass dat Sat-nite be Sat-nite and lessen youse some kinda faggot Sat-nite aints no time fo' a man be on hisns knees!

Chapter 58

TEMPE BE DA' SHIT, I be liked a straight-outta Iowa corn fed Sooners to be a Hollywood star-struck spread-eagled casting couch whore cause I done felled-it non-fucking stop straight the fuck-up in love with Phoenix go fucking figure! I be loving a city named after a bird risen from the ashes WTF big-*thunder struck*-butts it be love, sight on scene, baby! Bouncing-it down to the desserts of Arizona hadn't been a big ass fucking deal for me admittedly I done always wanted-it to work IBM computers since my black ass had been a teen-*in the hood*-ager IBM be a top-shelf goal of mine thus it done tooken-it some sumptin sumpting to done just ups the fuck to done walked-it away from that OKC job! Back in the daze of thems late 60s, I had done met-it up with one of my Windy City cousins and Windy City cousin be a straight-up whitegirl brown hair, brown-eyes and the whitest to be white skin *Medgar Evers* I done seed-it up-close at the ready personal and backs then she be a front-runner to our family/neighborhood gatherings! The thing be Windy City cuz be borne of those usta be called-it uppity Negroes thems *we done flung off the hood* rare populace of the *don't yo' black hoodrat ass even dare to call me Black*! *Oh hell, to the yeah* it hadda been thems *gots airs* damned BUMPY*BlackUpwardMobilePeepsYoung* to done paved-it the way!

One thems we be family gatherings Windy City cuz be madder than a wet hen passing brown eggs because folks done hipped-it her that mostest the shit she did/had/was/ be all fucked-up and she be never gonna quit that passing shit and get it real! *Fuck dat* be the word mostest peeps done slung herns way thems peeps be liked *gurl fuck dat getting it real shit you best to keep what youse gots*! Hippy-white gurl cousin learnt-it that herns bug-eyed hooptee had been a main profit source to done funded all thems Jew-boy killing nazi motherfuckers and theys motto *das boots* be gibberish speak *fun driving dems Jews to the gas chamber* and that she be planting herns passing pleasingly plump ass-cheeks on tanned-it seats made from the thin sliced skins of dead Jew peoples. A'nuttier ting be hippy *get yo' freak-on* cousin worked-it for IBM gurl made $35 an hour over tree-hundred dollars a day Hell the mostest us peeps be welfare, factory or steel-mill workers that didn't make tree-hundred dollars a year big-*po' assed out*-butts hearing word of that IBM payday be *da' shit* I done learnt-it hippie white cousin gurl be not onliest passing big-*ofay*-butts she be big banking *das boots*! The peeps told-it Windy City cuz how it be Mr. Fucking IBM and hisns fucking gazillion numbers crunching computers shit hadda done allowed-it them bitch assed nazi racist mofos to number, rounded-it up, kept track of and eventually kill dems Jews. Hippy freak cuz be soaking herns beautiful brown orbs in theys keeping it real salty tears justa blabbering bouts quitting her job, dumping her bug as swell all herns other dumb-ass get it real whitegurl shit big-*banking*-butts I hadn't done felt-it no kinda sorry for Windy City cousin big-*nuttin personal*-butts the Word of day be that IBM Corporation done paid $35 an hour iffn my b-ball thang didn't pan out the way I wanted-it to then I couldn't wait to go and work fo' Mr. *sorry Jew-boy gotz to make dat paper* IBM!

TOP be the one mofo dat hadda actually done helped-it to take my IBM from a dream to reality then success, *Yeah baby*! TOP the po'dunk mofo peckerwood be one genuine reads hisns skinny white ass off mofo big-*schooling*-butts that redneck be mostest about the teachings thus hisns *got schooled* ass be a self-made teacher of all sorts and hisns super natural talent came about in the showing a mofo just how to snatch to done touched-it up an enemy's *done been snatched* ass! TOP hadda knack to done taught-it best a body exactamente what that body's own damned personal philosophy of life be hisns the real truth, Ruth the po'dunk had the ability to done showed-it to a dumb-ass just how to grab it then to hold balls tight unto the whatever that dumb-ass done wanted-it this life! The question be, iffn TOP be so damned good and wise then why I be calling the racist bastard a po'dunk redneck peckerwood and all kinda shit-fo' brains names cause dat mofo be a straight-outta *Missy-sip-pee* po'dunk and iffn tings be reverse engineered dat fool be calling me similar iffn not worstest names taint no disrespect its all love, Babycakes! We done earned-it the right call each other them names and also the right to kick-it into all a'nuttier asses dat hadn't earn that right whom dared to sling such foul assed racist shit our sway because TOP, Trips, me and the boys be *Word-up*, mofo! Anytawho, professor TOP done did hisns teaching on the sly seed early on he'd put thems certain books with a certain purpose that certainly be compatible to your personal mental aptitude and dis shit be no shit because I done seed-it fo' me own damned selfie with me own damned lying-eyes some them Bros be a'toting *Curious George'* monkey-assed shenanigan pubs and comic books, no shit! TOP didn't query a body none bouts them books theys done toted-it lessen dat body wanted-it to debate with him bouts the contents then the shit be on liked *poppy-t-pop* pop-corn! TOP done knowed-it that during thems tree-weeks to a few plus months with yo' ass-cheeks split and justa shiting in the bush alone to this world awaiting or searching-out a raunchy *targeted* ass then fo'sure the dumb-ass woulda done read-it them damned books over and over again justa keep on the normal side of all tings sanity. Mr. Allen's *As A Man Think it* done tuned-in, tapped-in to done turned-on my world up the one side then fucking down the other all *Hell southern belles* comes around that went around big-*guru*-butts that venture be my very firstest foray into the forest of TOP's gifted knowledge and *Hell yes* thems picked-it berries be fresh, sweet and easy as fried-*watermelon*-pie!

TOP be mo' cantered to the sleight suave side dat mofo be a slick-Willy sophisticated magician thoroughly complicated not that *I see the* hidden card up yo' sleeve mofo. TOP's preplanned-it from the jump specialized tree of the knowledge witch be subtle so fucking subtle that you hadn't even done knowed-it that you be being taught-it that shit be pimping 501 graduate schooling! TOP the teaching mofo be *Get yo' ass up and out into them streets to go and take whatever the fuck you wanna get! You be number one! You be yo' TOP priority! Fuck any to everybody else! Go get your desire! Get off your ass and just go get it! No fucking obstacles, go around the barriers or if all else fails then just go fucking through the barriers, snatch that ass, mofo and be damned quick about It!* He'd always surmised "*You be TOP priority!*"

The redneck po'dunk mofo straight-up sho'nuff pimped-it Biggy-smalls my black ass for my complete loyalty and it done happened-it thissa way, a'gin-n-juice we be out to sea on the flathead and that mofo rear Admiral lower-half be still rolling that bucket. The *I be God* Admiral wanted-it sum *git-back* so the fool in that ass done put word out that he gonna take hisns flathead because it be hisns flathead then he gonna step-it over towards the Korea way befo' he done dropped our unit off at the Cambodia way, big fucking mistake! TOP done tooken-it me, Trips and a couple of thems collards to done had ourselves a meet-it up on the Captain's deck with lower-half asshole. The Admiral gave us hisns official spiel about bumping Korea befo' dropping us off and TOP listened patiently to the Admiral's shit then outta the fucking blue TOP roared at the stunned *deer caught-it up in dems headlights* mofo "*Listen the fuck up, you scallywag bastard*" we be *at-ease solider* facing the Admiral and hisns seconds in command then the fucking mofo deliberately done eyeballed my black ass befo' relocking-it eyeball to eyeball with Admiral dip-shit "*I'm gonna have my nigger slap the shit out of your scumbag ass, you know him and he's done it before! Now get your scum bucket ass up and into the crow's nest and take this floating bucket of bolts and turds to where I gotta be and you better best to get me there on fucking time*! That shit be the bold assed wicked like a motherfucker, I aint gonna lie fucking TOP done did some bad assed git-back shit and my dumb-ass be poker-face *Semper fi* to done toed the line! I admit-it that I be not the brightest light in the fucking kitchen big-*dumb ass*-butts I be the biggest bull in the china shop besides *fuck it* I be not mad at TOP the cold-blooded redneck though he done straight-up called-it my black ass his nigger! My dumb ig'nant ass be proud like a mofo that po'dunk be swinging a pair! Looking back at it all, aints it funny just the what a fool will do for acceptance seed it be a real truth, Ruth dat TOP's *nigger* shit be liked ex-Babyg' *her stuff* bullshit theys the both be the wagered price of my living in a fucked-up *I'm a'gonna go fuck-up somebody justa any fucking somebody's* world!

Chapter 59

Now-a-days, I'm what one would call an educated egg-head a double-dome wordsmitty whore besides I yam an educated Black wordsmith thus the problem be there aren't enough Black male voices in the literary world to done bounced-it with I gotta search high and low for a corrective voice and they say pimping ain't easy try finding a Black male voice that be off the fucking chain of the common-placed man loves hisns common woman and woman loves herns man *Soul Train* of provocative thought though kicking much love to the pioneers of Black American literature Baldwin, Gaines, Zora be my bit@# and the Harlem Renaissance. There be a time south Florida way when we be kicking a little training at Homestead, AFB just south aways of Miami we'd been sky jacking and jumping the ocean outta them Herks to be fucking with them Cubans out for a little twenty-mile swim it be no fucking bullshit thems *latrinos* done *crossed the fucking ocean on a wheel-less skateboard* dat shit done gave just call fo' thems Mexican-American ex-reservists fools to be like yalls redneck fucks gots nerve to call us wet-backs! It had been a range day and we bumped-it a shit-load of #4-buck twenty-gauge shotgun shells big-*shots*-butts I had gotten bored with the scene because within justa few days we gonna be heading to Egypt for a multi-international thing with other friendly forces big-*talk da' talk*-butts thems diplomats didn't done knowed-it some things needed to be cleared-it out firstest hand by hand then round bye-bye mofo round so that sand-pit gonna be our next playground. I had started-it a cache of my own books big-*reader*-butts the books that I wanted-it to read came to be few and even most harder to find than a handful of Hell's southern debutant South Florida redneck belles evil redneck asses sporting a Heavenly halo! I desired books voiced-it by thems new wave authors that done tagged themselves *niggas, bucks, Black bitches, hoes and hoodrats* to done *bump dat ass* I needed-it justa little sump'n sumptin along thems fo' *Medgar Evers* generational life times jumped outta the harden harsh reality mofos dat done comed-it bye-bye sway thems skank-hoe inner-city ghettoes like my hoodrat ass done fought hardtack and clawed-it dat black ass up and offa thems mean ass ghetto streets thus my wont of the communal Black self-love be my on the personal predicament!

TOP big-*pimping*-butts still be justa po'dunk whitebread mofo done missed hisns damned calling anywho the backwoods *Swami* stepped-it over to where I be sitting and mulling my problem to trick with my head "*Jigga-boo don't-cha know that thinking aint good for a spook-ass the likes of you! Yo' numb-nuts jigga-boo ass might come to the fucking wrong conclusion in-that your black ass be free but you aint free mofo because I own yo' ass, Semper Fi!*" TOP done mustered-it outta my dumb-ass my predicament then he done straight the fuck-up *Semper Fi* done runned-it my ass over to the base library thems flyboy putas had theys own real time stocked-it assholes to teacups libraries on theys fly bye-bye bases. TOP showed-it to me how to work that *Dewey* decimal system witch be the library code used nationwide to done stocked and shelved theys books in a unified pecking order next he showed-it me a'nuttier systematic stored collective of thems Black writers dem anthologies witch contained the names as swell information about thems Black raw-dawg authors and a snippet of theys material *Hell yeah baby* thems anthologies be da' shit! TOP be one proud as all Hell po'dunk white-boy mofo teaching-it my dumb-ass the shit that I shoulda done learnt-it in grade iffn not high school big-*dummy*-butts thems CC public school administrative po'dunk whores had been too fucking busy force feeding me theys bullshit unschooling for the Negro only! A'nuttier TOP tier ting dat po'dunk done did to keep hisns peoples tight, on edge and of one accord be to have dat psychotic Trips lead this fucking dumb-assed *jodie* witch had originally been a *Skippy* peanut butter commercial in thems 60s and 70s where this cartoon character decked-out in Hawaiian shirt done sang-it out "Peeeeea-nut---peeeeea-nut---peanut butter" anyway Camp Pendleton Cali, Subic Bay Japan plus there be a few other choice places around this world hadda *Mt. Kilimanjaro* witch be any big fucking hill where we spent at least halfa-day to justa done runned-it up just to done runned-it down chanting that damn *jodie* every fucking step of the way dat shit be *we be a'coming hear us roar* every fucking jump befo' gangbanging into the back of them fairy Herks dat damned *Peanut Butter* jodie be on! Trips would get dat jodie a'started-it and it be a round trip going outta country thens a'coming back in-country "*Peeeeea-nut peeeeea-nutt peanut butter, gonna kill both yo' fucking daddy and yo' fucking brother, gonna ass-fuck yo' sister then throat-fuck yo' mother, Peeeeea-nut peeeeea-nutt peanut butter and jelly, jelly, jelly roll slo ya' roll the fuck over and die Motherfuckers*!"

TOP used that fucked-up ditty to psychologically plant-it a single seed of thought into our communal simplistic simple assed-minds the KISS factor because believe it or not America be the only place this world to make or to get made just fo' yo' lazy sorry-ass selfie a peanut butter-n-jelly *san-mitch*! Nobody done said-it a fucking word big-*dumb*-butts once we be back States-side or on an American military installation you coulda done walked-it yo' ass into any billeting barracks or a star-lite camp site to done found-it a jar of the damned *Skippy*, jelly and a loaf of white bread without fucking fail! All that shit be justa wee-bit part of TOP's scheme to have a communal tink-tank in that everyone of us done thunk alike, talked alike and damned well done fought-it liked Hell alike!

That po'dunk white-bread double-domed done pimp walked our dumb *hard to the Corps* asses to a way of life that be hisns *how much wood can the woodchuck chuck* way of life and dat be Word-up, Babycakes! *Yowls'er*, dat be the pimp-daddy extraordinaire Professor of *bump dat ass* philosophies of one platoon Commander all-time po'dunk TOP!

Chapter 60

My Loveland the OKC life, the ting that I hadn't done told-it about ex-babyg' fine-assed chocolate love drop be *da' shit* dat fo'reallies on the reals shit fo' my dumb-ass ex-Babyg' be the total package fine as all *Hell's jangling belles get the fuck outta here* be herns packaged shit plus ex-babyg' be the firstest woman that I hadda *Medgar Evers* met-it up who'd loved-it Aretha more than my Moms and me done did loved-it ourselves some of the Queen! My Babygirl be knot hipped-it to all the Queen's songs that my Moms had done hollered-it all over my pooh-butt to done growed-it up years seed my Moms sang them older when Aretha be younger songs dat be mo' about the blues the Queen sung thems down on the delta cotton-picking banjo tree-string guitar blues songs with a gospel-slant that stirred the blood and moved the human *Spirit* dat be why *We the Peoples* done dubbed-it Aretha Franklin *The Queen of Soul* and the Queen be herns bestest outta the gate from the git-go! When we firstest done met-it up my Babygirl sang the Queen's mid to late 70s RB with justa *riding in a Pink Cadillac* disco bite in the mix *Hell's southern belles* ex-Babyg' hadn't even heard the Queen's bestest album *Medgar Evers* the gospel one *Amazing Grace*! That be a'nuttier thang bouts ex-Babyg' that I sincerely loved-it with all my heart and Soul be that ex-Babyg' had fo'reallies hated-it the damned lying spying on a Black man scoundrel the po'assed-out country-preacher and hisns Gawd damned church filled-it with all thems damned a'scared theys own shadow church mice! I loved-it herns *No church No way* of living mo' than the fat fact, Jack that ex-Babyg' didn't cuss big-*unholy*-butts iffn and when she did cuss then you could bet jo' sweet Black ass dat some churchyfied folk be on the other-side herns *done made me go there* tirade.

The Momma didn't relent *Emmett Till* I done bought-it a house in an all-whitefolk *non*-po'dunks neighborhood and the Momma hadn't given a funky hillbilly road-kill eating shit it be a fat fact, Jack dat house be center-court a whitebread non-klan community bumping a welcomed wagon of the *Angelie Jollie* wide-opened *come to me my big black babies* arms! The one be onliest critical point to any and all real estate transactions be *location location location* and the house be not onliest in a whitefolk suburb *A-Ok* big-*fair housing*-butts our *Sooners* to be Love Shack be directly behind an acre of farm land to witch that acre done held-it virgin-girl *doubled fisted-tight onto herns never been dropped-it drawls* the OKC biggest fucking dead whitefolk cemetery witch be a square-mile of *Marble City* it be the fo'ever *bye-bye* fo' alls thems dead on arrival southern white bitches only justa haunted *the spot* of the spooky sho'nuff dead be theys white asses! Why the fuck would a brother wannabe living-it up within a turd's toss of a Whites only boneyard? I duly informed both the ex-Babyg' and old uppity-assed the Momma that living bye-bye that cemetery gonna be bad-assed buzzard-luck then theys the both my Babygirl and herns ugly-ass "*watch yo' mouth duf*"...the Momma done called-it me a fricking scared outta my black ass mind superstitious country-bumpkin dumb-ass *Duf'* dat aints got common sense to come in outta the rain! The problem be that common sense amongst the commoners never be on par to theys vaulted scholarly college education big-*news*-butts common sense must not be confused with horse sense cause most folks claiming theys got horse sense be a chunk of jackasses braying befo' a mirror all the whilst kicking up shit in theys own stalls! Common sense be thems habits performed by a man on the daily-double thus it be a fat fact, Jack that any given man be just the sum total of all hisns daily choices! Fuck, within a year and a half after moving into that gawd-damned *too near a fucking Whites only* boneyard me and my Babygirl had been done married, split apart to done re-hooked-it befo' she and an old haggardly happy-ass the Devil's handmaiden, the Momma done filed-it for and be on the tippy-tip verge of being granted that there filed-it *why are you leaving me babyg'* country-bumkin divorce!

The Love Shack be not totally bad after our done moved-it this sundae skool church bus started-it on the regular droved-it up and made big noise turning around in our drive way come the one Sunday moaning next I be laid-it back on the couch afront of the picture window preparing to be watching *dem Boys* when ex-Babyg' come a bursting-it through damned Skippy she be out the front door to done torn *faggot fucking sway* *too deep* into that perplexed-it stunned liked a mofo church-bus driver's po'dunk white asshole and that shit be live after that Sundae *tires on the bus go round and round* done to never crossed-it our driveway again, baby! I relayed-it that shit about the church-bus to *G-ma* and she'd damned near shit her granny panties that be a'nuttier ting in-that my whole *damned Skippy* family done loved-it theys belly be satisfied *dat fool-assed boy done founded-it hisns-self a good woman*! My Moms done straight-up loved-it that my Babygirl *be knot like all thems heifers running wild the streets* cause she could cook, cleaned the house and even done made me help to done both the cooking and the cleaning of the house and that my Babygirl sang Aretha close to big-*never gonna happen*-butts not even nears to almost be liked-it my Moms *who'dat* done throwed-it down herns moms-self some *Aretha*, baby! I could tell that my Moms be justa little bit slightly amused that I had founded-it a younger woman that had like herns my Moms-self born country yet lived city. The firstest family meet-it up Dad be all business-liked inside the house shaking hands with my Babygirl and asking her questions all polite-like then he had me walk him to the one-car garage out-back in the alleyway that be when he'd done bear-hugged-it my ass then whooped-it and hollered-it *You done good, son*! *You done real good*! Dems Unks throwed-it a party in her honor on the spot and that be the firstest time I done seed my knuckle-headed Unks *Medgar Evers* to do a sump'n sumptin without a pre-drawn 30-year mortgaged thought-it out plan! Calvin couldn't stop grinning all week and I done thought that I'd have to pop him one justa to take that shit-eating grin offa hisns face! Mr. Bobby and Gettis done told-it straight-up to my Babygirl to dump my ugly ass and mix-it up with a couple of real handsome men liken theys two po'assed-out selves on the up and *Sooners* to be coming! The family peeps done fo'sure loved-it that woman and I could feel it that my peeps be more than happy for me having the pleasure to done found-it meself a sho'nuff good woman plus she didn't have any thems high-brow college educated impishness ways afforded the uppity-Negro *putting on the airs* be the sole property of old brisket-butt the Momma and herns two older sisters. My Babygirl had a natural heaping helping of likable grace and enough charms fo' everybody dat be a body my Babygirl had thems *lucky charms* fo' yo' black ass kinda charms!

Hell yeah, my Babygirl done made-it a place for herns-self amongst TOP, Trips and the boys seed theys hadda all liked her plus theys wives and theys girlfriends done stepped-it to her too though them military folks and theys peeps had behind herns *baby got back* thems military folks done call-signed-it her the *First Sergeant*! TOP on the occasional called *family-time* witch be an un-officially family meet-it ups in either Houston or Miami during an official training session seed TOP done had Uncle Sammy fly our asses outta thems jungles back States-side for training daze or you could take leave *vacation days* mostly to get with any loved ones who wanted to join-in and my Babygirl usually done showed-it up just to done showed-it off! Babygirl had this thing about not wanting any of thems hotel maids in her room because they might go through herns personal shit so when she'd go to lunch, shopping or whatever with them other wives and gurlfriends then she'd tell-it to me befo' hand to clean the room and make the bed all-dat-kinda gurly-gurly stuff such that I be occupied and inside the room dems firstest few times my dumb-ass done thunk-it *girl be crazy* big-*I aints no Nancy pants*-butts iffn I hadn't done that cleaning kinda stuff by the time she'd gotten-it back or God forbid iffn thems maids done entered our room then my Babygirl hadn't trucked-it nary a trouble nor qualm seed she done had not a care to my world nonya where I be nor the whoms I would be with because she'd justa two-stepped-it up to my *Baby, please don't do this shit in-front of all my peoples* dumb-ass to done straight-up commenced-it to bite my damned ears off ...*Zeke didn't I tell you to clean the room, change the sheets, make the bed...etc.* then she'd grab my ass rights there in front of God and every other nosey done lookey-looked ass to done marched me backs to TLC that damned room! Thems military peeps done on the reals loved-it dat shit when theys hadda heard-it my Babygirl laying down the law unto my whipped-it dumb-ass thems fools just roared cause theys all done knowed-it that I be one *room cleaning sheet changing* whipped-it wussy-assed mofo! TOP, Trips and the boys had even started-it to calling me *Chavalo*! *Oh Hell to the nawls,* that bastard *Chavalo* be dat latrino championship heavy-weight fighter whom had taken a dumb-fucked stance and refused to call Muhammad Ali by hisns Muslim name big-*dummy*-butts that two-bits of broken English to be uttered *Chavalo* fucking ig'nant latrino be just a'nuttier Trips Mofo mostest likely hisns dumb-ass be a Mexican *in-passing* bastard gibberish speak wannabe Latino! The mofo didn't speak English thus calling a man the English name that man wanted-it to be called please pray tell what the fuck difference would it have made? Oh, big-*grassy ass*-butts that shit made a difference especially in the lives of the ghetto trio of *bad-news* fo' yo' ass that be me, Mr. Bobby and Gettis plus probably thousands upon thousands of other Black men a'coming up young gifted and Black men because during the fight Ali had punched-it that latrino fuck harder than all Hell big-*punchy*-butts not hard e'nuff to done knocked-it the taco shitting beaner *passing for a Latino* cement pouring beaner-ass the fuck-out! Everytime Ali done punched-it dat beaner's ass then to be there Ali would ax the fuck "What's my name?" That shit had been on the fucking reals to be off the fucking rails!

Ali done it firstest with a purpose and a flourish that will never be equaled-it seed it be broadcast-it on the tele then us hoodrats done copied-it that *real as all real gets* shit big-*Ali Ali boom ba yah*-butts when anyone be kicking some po' kids ass inside of that make-shift ghetto-assed ring or outside on thems mean-ass streets we done shouted-it "what's my name, motherfucker?" Anytowho Ali counterpunched-it that Latrino fuck weeks befo' the fight bye-bye renaming the punk ass Chavalo *the washer-woman* that be why dems assholes done tagged me *Chavalo*! I be still theys boy so theys hadn't clowned-it me front-street the women/ family folk big-*tanks*-butts all and everywhere else be open range on my pussy-whupped ass! I don't wannabe dat super anti-Mexican racist mofo big-*gibberish speak*-butts thems Mexican peoples be the only fucking ig'nant peoples populated this ball of dirt that I done knowed-it fo' a fat fact, Jack do dis fucked-it up bullshit as a peoples and its not because of theys gibberish speak thems Parakeets, Dominicans, Cubans, Columbians nonya theys asses do it big-*stupid*-butts it be a fo' Messkins onliest shit! A'nuttier of them Mexican-American usta be reservist Rodolfo *A-Rod* Rodriguez and me be cleaning personal weapons at hisns house in Tucson tug on ya' good ear and get this truth from the firstest day that I had to *Medgar Evers* done seed her, A-Rod's wife be wider than she be tall and the lady stood bouts five-foots two-inches yet she onliest be 25-years young then what happened be I done fucked-it up Biggy-smalls I admit it, the shit be *my Bad* and *my Bad* alone seed there be lots of 8 by 10 and larger pictures of a very skinny beautiful Mexican woman on the coffee table and hanging on them living room walls thems pics be justa spreaded-it out all over to be around the room and this be my done fucked-it up shit seed instead of whispering to A-Rod *who that woman be*? I axed it aloud then it be fucking buzzard-luck that I done axed-it exactamente the moment that A-Rod's little wifey just entered into the living room then hisns little tree-hundred pound trophy wife answered-it with a Coke and a smile "*Oh, that's me*" yet instead of my dumb-ass justa nodding my head politely and going with the flow bye-bye *STF mofo* my dumb-ass foolishly axed-it a'nuttier question "what happened?" Little *wifey* done kicked my ass outta the house, to the curb! That there be *the shit* thems married Mexican ladies be skinny and fine-ass all fuck befo' yet on the wedding day right after thems *I do* the bullshit be started-it thems fucking Messykins *let's us just make little wifey a fat-ass* shit begins then on the QT fine-assed little wifey be hundreds of *refried beans and taco* farts heavier whilst the men Messkins done stayed-it slim and healthy, WTF be up with thems fools!

My Babygirl be telling thems Messykin fools how theys be ruining their wife's health and bodies due to that stupid Messkin onliest macho *make your young skinny beautiful wife a whale of a fat-ass just so other men won't want her* shit! Babygirl done *news flashed-it* thems all *Hello, men love to do fat women too*! *Girl, go get yourself a Sancho*! Babygirl told them wives *fuck the kind polite mind yo' own fucking business* to make theys own food lots veggies, don't eat any damned food provided bye-bye family, drink plenty of water and to start-it walking slowly about an hour a'day to lose all that damned fat-assed weight and dat be a'nuttier reason why thems fools tagged-it her *First Sergeant*! Nobody got even slightly mad at my Babygirl when she done *schooled dem fools* big-*diet*-butts when the womenfolk done left the building then my Boy's come hardtack at my ass then I'd axed them mad-assed beaner mofos why they hadn't voiced that shit to the *first sergeant*? My Babygirl be one charming fine-ass mofo with boss people skills!

Chapter 61

Sunday mornings the Love Grotto or Love Shack the wake-it up be Aretha's *Amazing Grace* tight-ass gospel music dat album be the onliest Christian ting in the house *Hells, to all racist southern belles* Palm Sunday meant that my Babygirl be on her period! Thems cursed 7-daze be a major problem for her and tortuous fo' my pussy-whupped ass because I taints nobody's vampire *don't want yo' blood* and not that she would have let me big-*bumping*-butts neither does I *park my junk in a nobody's trunk* though neither one of us be Christian-fucks big-*pagan*-butts from the jump it be missionary, woof-woof, cowgirl rodeo or burst! You wanted-it yo' ass eaten justa shake yo' monkey ass ova' to the jungle and find yo' freaky-deaky self a cannibal, baby! During all Hell week my Babygirl done Pavlov's dog me horny ass on-point seed she'd put the Queen on the stereo and *Tanks-ya tank-ya berry much* iffn *there justa gotta be a God*, *the Coty* and the *Frederick of Hollywood* lingerie bumped-it herns bodacious body wanna holla injustice seed it takes a mean assed evil woman to tempt a man dats got no religion to go at odds with hisns one be onliest sacred sacrifice big-*horny*-butts I done passed-it the mostest of 8-years no mud, no blood and no spit on my shit! My Babygirl done on the sho'nuff knowed-it my ass fo' the good, the bad-ass and the *just what* to done did me the ugly! She tested-it my ass aplenty and abouts every damned ting big-*test dummy*-butts alla time and on the regular especially befo' we lived-it together always she'd axed-it about my j-o-b and I be *I'm a jet engine mechanic* and she'd be *I talked to the wives* then I be *I don't care iffn ya' talked to the animals Nurse Doolittle, I'm a shock-jock* Beatles *let it be*! Mostest thems test be so that she be assured-it I don't be nobody's bar-fly, didn't truck them drugs and the worstest fo' sho'nuff I didn't have that violence streak against women-folk disease stalking-it the insides of me then it hadda been *skool be fo' fools* fuck all dat testing shit and we done hooched-it-up from the Love Grotto to the Love Shack big-*horny*-butts she'd be just like the National Broadcast System cause she'd done runned-it a test pattern *every now thru the thens* just so I be a'standing me twinkling toes! One Fri-nite she hadn't come to home and that Saturday afternoon she'd done called-it my ass pissed to done questioned-it as to why I hadn't called around for her and I'd been *who would I call* then she'd be *I left my phone book on the breakfast counter* big-*nosey*-butts I'd countered *I ain't the nosey one* then she be *what if it had been an emergency* swells then thems *BarneyFife po-po gonna called me* the killer *why hadn't I called the Momma* we'd uncontrollably laughed-it our black asses off *Emmett Till* she'd done ordered-it me to make the dinner cause she be leaving the Momma's house fo' the homecoming!

An Easter weekend and we two be headed-it to the dreaded-it Whiskey Faults fo' a'nuttier the Momma's big assed formal dinner parties and my Babygirl be Hell-bent cause I'd done chanced-it to give her a gift-wrapped bottle of *the Coty* everybody done knowed-it that women-folk just loved-it theyselves a *surprised surprize surprized* store-bought pre-wrapped-it gift! She hadn't looked-it that horse's ass in the gifted mouth she'd knowed-it all to damned swell what be under them wrapping papers. I be driving along the Interstate dems double-nickels *stay alive 55* because my Babygirl done worked-it a one be too many accident victims to be speeding and or toting shot-gun fo' anytowho soons to be dead *Speedy*

Gonzalez driving ass! My Babygirl started-it in on me bouts how I'd have to be a real dumb monkey to think that things didn't change and that to expect our life together to always be liked dat firstest day that crappy thinking just be bananas big-*change gonna come*-butts she justa kept to harkening-it thems changes that she done made to keep our relationship on par befo' axing me what changes that I had made or planned to make. I should have justa remained STF because I hadn't a clue as to what she be talking about seed I be driving dat slow snail's poop speed limit and there be nuttin along that highway to entertain a body so I be listening to herns rant with halfa closed-it ear and the other ear done gone fishing!

I started-it to explain to her that changed the oil in my mid-knight blue tan leather seats pre-baseball bat pummeled 280-ZX and that I changed my gym clothes to don a done growed-it up man suit and tie just fo' the trip to done seed the Momma, BFM*BigFuckingMistake*! Fuck, the Babygirl express done jumped-it off theys rails to done bumped-it up a notch all demonic like on my selfish *don't care about her feelings* ass worstest yet I pulled-it over to the side of the turnpike just to calm her shit down then when I started-it back the drive she'd reached-it over and snatched Aretha right outta the cassette player, opened the glovebox and center console to done tossed-it all the Queen's music outta my babyZ passenger side window, *Good Lord baby, baby please* be mad-assed at me big-*sacrilegious*-butts to be dis-respectful to the Queen to justa done bounced-it all that soulful music unto that filthy roadside like the Queen be some kinda buster seed it be *dat there kinda foolish shit just mighta been the why she done awoke one wintery morn to done founded-it herns hot fine-assed selfie to be the ex-Babyg'* nobody dis-RESPECT the Queen! My Babygirl done lost herns mind she'd told-it to me to justa *close ya mouth, your Duf' ass catching flies* then added that from that day forward there won't be any mo' *Aretha*, no damned *the Coty* and no mo' fricking early moaning sunshine, fuck! We sometohow done muddled-it through them sociables dat bunny be not hip-hop awful weekend at the Momma's big-*funky*-butts *last supper* party with e'nuff pleasantries to suffice them geeks and family folks big-*tank ya*-butts on the ride backside to the *mi casa no es su casa* my Babygirl done tugged-it Pavlov's coattail justa *Sooners* I done turned-it onto the freeway.

My Babygirl dropped-it the Queen into the cassette-player *Giving him something he can feel* then as *Aretha* crooned-it softly she undid her seat-belt then snuggled-it up Easter bunny on the real close to be biting my earlobes then she stopped-it all dat *the goodie-stuff* just long enough to reach inside the glovebox to done unwrapped-it the *gift of gifts* and instant grits spritzed-it *the Coty* on them heavenly breastestes of herns, Good Lord! That ensuing Tuesday morning round zero-four hundred thirty hours as I reached-it into the fridge for my befo' breaking gym morning orange-juice and raw egg ritual justa little sumptin sump'n learnt-it from thems country-strong assed *Sampson* collard-greens there be a enrollment form to a local JUCCO attached to the bottle. Ex-Babyg' done realized-it butter than me over the course of dat resurrected weekend at the Momma's house of *ill begots* that I hadn't any real clue as to all the changes crap she'd been muttering-it about during our the drive to *flap-jacks and halfa hog eating* big-*funky*-butts Easter din-din party. My Babygirl knowed-it that I wasn't about the talking and that my ass be mo' into the doings witch I done that day right after work seed I drove to that JUCCO school then enrolled into its business administrations courses. My Babygirl be not a dumb-shit nor the fool seed she understood me in that I needed that one clear voice for guidance and not the bitching curmudgeon shit justa kvetching to be heard that a majority them womenfolk would have done because she'd seed it all up-close how my *duf* ass truly be the dumb-ass seed ex-Babyg' been there to done that thus she knowed-it firsthand that me, Trips and the boys had that one clear voice in our rank and file and fo' a *ja'rene* that one voice thing be da' shit cause it saved men lives as swell it got things done! Ex-Babyg' had the *burning bush* the goodie stuff on my black ass and at some point into the wonderful journey called *Us* she done finally got-it drilled into my numbskull that what I had needed-it mostest be herns onliest one woman voice to move my ass forward the journey of life! My Babygirl done the right and onliest thing fo' my *Sooners* to be away from the military ass when she done stepped-it up the *First Sergeant*!

Chapter 62

My Babygirl handed-it to me them awaking orders to report ASAP to dat JUCCO community college! A man's pride may swell then tell him that he needs two or mo' women and that he gotta be a playa' *pimping* fo' life big-*dumb*-butts that shit just be pride, check-it! Po'leesa to step the fuck up to Zeke's newest best laid plan hisns *One Woman-One Voice* philosophy and in-accordance to the thesis it don't matter who the woman be, what she be that kinda useless informational shit didn't matter one wit whether dat one woman could read or write, speaked-it yo' language or the gibberish shit because the any *one* given woman can read the any one given man then write herns own personal writ bylaws all over hisns *Shit* and that be Word-up, baby! You best to believe that shit! A woman any woman, as a force of nature can attune her-*fine funky fresh*-self to a man's Soul then writ her freewill all over hisns all-encompassing being witch be hisns onliest Soul, brotha! The major ting be dat there aint no written words for communicating with the Soul because the Soul that mofo bastard child vibrates thus the Language of the Soul be vibrational and even the mostest dumb-assed flat-footed shoe-less assed-out woman given the time and I aints talking bouts some long winded lengthy time big-*knowing*-butts a woman can bye-bye just vibrating attune herself with an any man's Soul given the least bit of time cause time be a relative and not jo' assed-out Unk Ike begging thems ends!

The bestest times for a woman to done *tuned-it up* a man's Soul be in thems wee-wee be done did it hours justa right after she done giveth it up dat wild thang, the dirty-deed, dat mantra ode to the mattress mambo been danced then it be the man all happy-assed relaxed in slumber time and dat be why iffn a man don't want the *Midas* touch he bestest to done shaken-it dat ass and runned-it the fuck-off unto them far away hills sway over the rainbow just offa the yawls yonder! Big-*a'scared*-butts iffn a man wannabe someting in this life then he gots to take the time to find hisns-self a good for hisns own good and on the personal a woman with thems good vibrations witch be herns own positive happy feel-good thoughts abouts hisns *far away to dreamland* ass to justa let her vibrate hisns ass to the successful life and all the fo'reallies happiness dat be hisns! My Baby-girl did exactamente that shit for me seed she'd sho'nuff done shook-it my ass, I aint shamed to admit the fat fact, Jack them youngsters be on the holla my Babygirl done *rocked my world*! There don't be many songs that be originally song buy-buy the straight-up long-haired hippy-freak *whiteboy* bands cause the mostest done stole the Black man's songs and put it on a platter of the pity-patter turned-it sing-song bullshit liked that sad-eye mofo Priest, he'd only do Catholic gurls *may he rest in peace* always a'bumping hisns *Best of Bread* tracks witch on the reals be just shit fo' yo' ears!

Listen up and hear Word iffn there truly be an original put down by a whiteboy band that a *Baby, I'm for real* Black man truly can enjoy it be

Katie bar the door get the wax outta yo' big ears there be a sho'nuff Universal cut a WTF dope-ass track thems *surf's up* whores the Beach Boys done cut a track, Baby! The tune be a straight-up happening regardless of color iffn youse got a healthy pair swinging-low thems straight-up musical sneak-thiefs the *Beach Boys* done sung-it theys song of the songs thems white *surfer boy* asses done clowned-it the world with theys genuine perfection titled *Good Vibrations* that song gots the perfect name, the perfect-o rhythm and the perfect sound dat be Universal the real truth, Ruth acknowledged by the fat fact, Jack that all American men be theys Black, Red, White, Brown, Yellow or any thems gibberish speaks swinging a hairy pair on the down-low did, do and will continue to be-bop even *hip-hop* to that perfect song of the songs, baby! This be the ugly test go listen to the *Beach boys* *Good Vibrations* and even iffn you don't done knowed-it nor never to *Medgar Evers* remembered having to have done heard-it cause believed-it me iffn youse gots older male relatives borne of thems fiddies through 70s dems *bye-bye Miss American pie* era then yo' ass done heard-it and done heard-it a'plenty next go and find fo' yo'self a brotha or a po'dunk of the previously mentioned era and start humming that tune then check-it a lookey-look justa *Sneaky-Pete* to done seed iffn hisns ass don't be head nodding-it to the beat and quiet mouthing them lyrics!

Truth can't be hidden under a babbling bush for *Medgar Evers* justa glimmer of a spark thens dat rosebush gonna blush and its gonna fire-it up to speak-it the real truth, Ruth once a startled-it ass done *busta move* to the wildfire of thems *good vibrations* of a good woman onto the Soul of a hisns raw dog ass it be straight-up Word! That shit be biblical go-git yo'self a *King James* flip-it through thems pages of the old testaments to the Book of Ruth seed Ruth be that gentile-girl *who'dat* be a straight-up truth on Jew-boy Prince *Boaz* she be the epitome of what it be when a man finds hisns-self a sho'nuff good woman! The lesson be *Hell bent* to be learnt-it or there gonna be Hell to be paid and the paycheck aints a'coming outta no bank account it's a'gonna be snatched-it outta yo' dumb-ass! A woman attunes herself to a slumbering man's one and hisns onliest Soul that inner being that man's *I AM* hisns onliest shit hisns been given *a ticket to ride* this roller-coaster world! A'nuttier ting liked unto all contracts that be in this life tis good to done read-it or at least to done knowed-it the fine print befo' youse done signed-it on the bottom-line! Don't be to ever to catch yo'self a'standing tall befo' *the man* the Captains deck with yo' balls hanging low not knowing what you don't know!

There be a tricky part to that synchronization of the woman to the man's Soul and that be in the Biggy-smalls print why a smart man don't be a'letting just any given woman vibrate hisns raw dawg ass! Shake that ass, Hell to the yeah big-*horny*-butts vibrates-it Fuck, No! Thems womenfolks done knowed-it exactamente *what I'm about to put it down* fo' all them ages past then some mo' ages a'coming on yonder horizon dems womenfolk sits-it on theys fine-asses onliest to done stepped-it the one to a'nuttier amongst themselves abouts the all of *It*! Womenfolk haves thems ladies onliest little *get-it-togethers* where buy-n-buy them babes done hollered-it the one to a'nuttier about how theys done shook a man's ass then that ass done jumped-it up outta that bed, outta dat backseat or outta dat *no-tell* motel to done runned-it home liked a'scared jackrabbit! Ladies, the reason menfolk do such a thing be because there be a tricky part Biggy-smalls print bouts a woman vibrating herns PHATT self unto the Soul of a man's raw dawg ass. The tricky be that the woman uses herns gut feelings to attune herns fine assed selfie to the man's Soul while theys both be relaxed-it and justa slumbering! The woman does not nor cannot attune to hisns heart and for damn sure not to hisns intellect be that he gots any of that intellectual shit! Womens done knowed-it that gut-feelings shit to be a true fat fact, Jack from many moons yonder big-*spirited*-butts men have done learnt-it or been trained-it to dismiss even to dispel the witch's brew that be anything sensed-it or felt-it witch can't be touched, hit and or cut then it be nonya to all that unseen shit because menfolks be *bump dat shit* the unseen be feelings thus men be *Fuck* them feelings, be a man, Mofo! *Man the fuck up*!

Thems winged-it butterflies in the stomach be justa gut feeling therefore dat feelings shit must be rebuffed at all costs because us be the all-knowing man and we done learnt-it that the guts be shit sausages thus gut feelings for a man be not to be relied-it upon even the most dumbest of dumb-assed man done learnt-it dat hard edged factual never ever to put a trust to hisns fucking gut feelings because using *shit for brains* evens the worstest situation just gonna gotta get fucking mo' worstest, baby!

The womenfolk on the nuttier hand theys gut-feelings be knot just the tried-it to be true scientific factuals big-*premonition*-butts also an inherent vibration that be, hipping her-*fine assed*-self to exactly what be the real deal bouts them facts of her life about to go down! Thems sacred trusted gut feeling of the woman about a man coupled-it up with herns innate ability to attune to a man's raw-dawg ass whether she wants to attune to it or not be why them professional whores be theys coiffed blonde and or coco-puffed high-classed escorts of the high-rise penthouse for a knight and even thems bleached-it stringy-haired crack-head walkers of them mean assed inner-city streets those professional whores be womens firstest thus thems ladies of the *you ain't gotta be lonely* knights thems *gots to gets paid* strumpets don't be kissing and cuddling with no mofo after, before nor during the *let's get down-n-dirty* deed because them whores done knowed-it be a fat fact, Jack that iffn the eyes be the windows of the Soul then thems kisses be the doorway when added to the cuddling all dat mixed-it together kissy-cuddly shakey-puddin be a super-sonic portal to the *fuck the bullshit* eternity! The professional whore be liked lookey-here Mofo *"you done rented this here good pussy knots me! Pay-it up, get-it up, nutt-it up then get the fuck up and outta here, trick* and that shit be Word!

Parts two of the tricky be that befo' a man's ass done after the act cuddled-it up with a woman hisns happy ass bestest to done knowed-it that the woman somewhat happened-it to done liked-it hisns ass in the least little bit because then he gonna receive-it no less than door number-two *Howdy-do partner* relaxed and peaceful slumber! The tricky part of the part-two be in just how the woman accomplishes the feat of attuning to a man's Soul it's simple all too damned simple that be why time don't be taint never to ever gonna be a factor in the equation because the woman vibrates herns own on the personal gut feelings about that particular man liked theys some kinda mystical enhanced tuning-fork unto that man's slumbering liked a Mofo one be only hisns Soul for as long as she and only she wants to tune-*a man's slumbering ass*-in! A'gin-n-juicy Lucy *its* the woman *who* attunes her-*fine assed*-selfie to the man's Soul and it be Universal Law that the woman's gut feelings don't lie not the bold faced *No, baby I won't come in yo' mouth* nor the *that's the biggest dick I done ever seed* neither thems *No, baby I likes them little titties* nor the *Yes'um, big daddy I came* little white-only lies. The attunement of a woman's gut feeling to a man be slumbering Soul be the straight-up uncoerced co-mingling of that woman's inner on the reals truth raw-dog gut-feelings concerning that particular man thus that woman's straight-up no Bullshit gut-feelings that she has to that slumbering man gonna be writ all over and onto that man's Soul! A'nuttier factual, there can be no Bullshit by either party because it alls done happened-it within each theys separate yet equal subconscious justa slumbering liked a mofo minds. Big-*dumb*-butts the problem occurs when the woman don't like the man and *Lord helps* that man iffn that woman despises hisns dumb-ass either ways that man's Soul be welcomed to door number-tree the *Zonk!*

The problem be iffn the woman that man done cradled-it up to for any reason does not like hisns ass then dat a'slumbering ass gonna gets the *nightmare* and not just any old fucking nightmare liked the bad dreams of the regular sleeping it all off *Mister Sandman bring me a dream* fuck No! The woman cannot attune to a man's heart nor unto hisns intellectual mind *hang-on to ya' shitty drawls* because the nightmare from a *I don't like yo' ass* woman gonna shake, rattle then roll that man's slumbering Soul fo' eternity! The *crazy-ass eight* woman, first tings firstest iffn a woman don't like the man then by all logic she gotta be a *crazy-ass* then the *eight* be the symbol of infinity thus she be a crazy-ass forever! Them nightmares from the crazy-ass eight woman dat done written-it all herns truth be told *I don't like yo' ass* gut-feelings witch be all herns *crazy-ass* nightmarish pent-up unleashed, unchecked and unfiltered crazed shit onto a slumbering man's raw dog Soul then dat fool assed man be *straight-outta Hell's belles* fucked! That fucked man's shit be gonna be ghetto like a motherfucker! The crazy-ass eight woman done spent all herns slumbering time to just done writ the straight-up bylaws of herns mostest be personal *hates hisns ass* dislikes unto that man's Soul swells that shit be psychotic and mentally painful as all Hell and thems crazy-ass things gonna *ride til he die* dat man's Soul the infinity! The shit be knot just mental big-*slumbering*-butts that bullshit be a fo'reallies psychological torture on the physicality because that mofo won't be able to sleep, shit nor eat and he gonna be *a'pissing in hisns own boots* just a'scared shitless of hisns own damned shadow WTF! Moving forward that man gonna be like *I gotta gets me some pussy* big-*a'scared*-butts *I gotta gets me that pussy then gets the fuck gone*! After the *Zonk* nightmare be unleashed by a crazy-ass eight woman done sprung upon a man's Soul then dat there man don't be shut-eying it with nobody's woman *Medgar Evers* a'gin-n-juice! Hell nawl, don't get the shit twisted the man don't be done runned-it the faggotry way and done switched-it thems horses up in the middle of hisns forever nightmarish screams, fuck the fuck, No dat man will lay hisns a'scared rabbit ass down and fake sleep *all the knight that be forever long* with the next woman trust-it the one ting dat Bro taints bout to do be to never *risk-it fuck the brisket* ever slumber with a'nuttier woman because of the possibility of having hisns one be onliest Soul to be done Miss *Crazy-ass eight* shaken again! The Soul don't be playing dat shit neither because the Soul has an unblockable passageway to the Brotha's inner-ear the Ego that be where the Soul captures the man's subconscious by hawking-it straight-up into hisns inner-ear ego then the Soul be serious *"Yo' Mofo, check dis shit out you lay yo' monkey ass down iffn ya' has too big-*wussy-*butts don't you dare sleep with this bitch! Jo' punk-ass won't be to ever gonna take me through them fucking nightmarish vibrations ever to never again, stupid motherfucker yo' dumb ass be trying to kill us both*!"

A'nuttier tip my Brotha be the nightmare of the Soul only happens with a woman who just slightly dislikes-it dat ass so listen to hear and be done heard-it so as to don't fuck-it-up! *NEVER TO FUCKING NEVER EVER SLEEP WITH A BITCH WHO STRAIGHT-UP HATES YO' DUMB-ASS*! That shit be the fucking *Prozac* time on the daily-double reality time! That shit be the what done happened-it to them addicts and thems always drunken alcoholics seed theys ig'nant dumb-asses done fucking gots high as a *kiki* then had the misfortuned-it buzzard-luck to done slumbered-it off with the *Hateful crazy-eight* bitch witch hisns higher than high a'slumbering ass done knowed-it a fat fact, Jack dat bitch just straight-up hated-it hisns raw-dog ass! Check-it the everybody and hisns fucking momma have/had/do/done/did at the one to a'nuttier done gots sway too high to done tooken-it dat extra drank, nose-capped a'nuttier line and theys be k-kool mofo the hang-over be a bitch big-*chilled*-butts I made it, its all good! It's the mofo dat done hit dat shit then cuddled-it up hisns dumb-ass with a bitch whom he'd done knowed-it afore hand fo' a fat fact, Jack on the fucking reals that dat *beyotch* done straight-up hated hisns skank-hoe ass big-*hateful*-butts it taints to never gonna be no help fo' that fuck because he justa gonna be fo'ever a lost cause! The hateful crazy-eight bitch will straight-up bitch-blast to done crazy-eight bug-out hisns Soul and once the Soul done hollered-it *ta-ta baby, adios mofo, arrivederci, goodbye-bye* hisns dumb-ass be fo'ever lost to this world!

Chapter 63

The main essence of the One Woman-One Voice ism be to live life to the fullest rewards a man gotta bump-it dat Door number-One Woman-One Voice reserved-it fo' dat lucky raw-dog mofo dat done laid-it-down with a woman that in any kinda way fo' any kinda reason(s) done liked-it to done loved-it hisns raw dawg ass then fo' dat luckiest of the lucky mofos of this world it be the *song of the songs* it be thems *Surfing USA* time *surf's up, mofo* dat one woman-one voice babygurl gonna be bringing-it on all dems *Good Vibrations*! That woman gonna be the real truth, Ruth and she gonna *Boaz* hisns lucky ass seed my Babygirl done held thems *good vibrations* fo' my big-*dumb ass*-butts she done with purpose slow cooked resonated-it my cuddled-it up *I be honeymooning* slumbering black ass alls thems years its all good *Emmett Till* the turning of that final page done gots itself turned-it on thems cold-hearted assed-out stone cold steps of the OKC Superior Courthouse big-*learnt it*-butts I hadn't done knowed-it backs then whats I done knowed-it now!

I had just been justa straight-up pussy whupped by the numbers bye-bye an ebony Queen's 100% *pure prune juice* standing tall at attention all dems early moaning roll-calls *back dat ass up* and all dems *as we lay* knightly Good Vibrations through-out the knight time be the right time fo' my Babygirl to done sho'nuff vibrated the Soul of my wussy whupped-it raw dog ass! My Babygirl done sho'nuff be the real truth, Ruth to done a *Boaz* to my lucky liked a mofo dumb black ass the goodie-stuff! Reason numero-*Uno* why I done eaten-it hardtack the welcome banquet of low-down and dirty blues at the all you can eat buffet table whence ex-babyg' done dipped, dumped then divorced my dumb puppy-love pussy-whupped one-woman be my one-voice crazed ass big-*Tank ya*-butts *Tank God* iffn there indeed do be a God then an added special Tanks to the Devil hisns-own damned-self *tank-ya tank-ya berry kindly* fo' spitting all Hell's afire the purest of the conjured-it up misery into thems shitty brown orbs of dat old assed reprobate, the Momma …*watch it sucka*! Thems beady black snake-shit fo' eyes of the Momma had been the *Hot Damned* what that done made-it all worth my ex-babyg' wiles because the Momma's turded-it up orbs had been the saddest shit dat I'd ever to have ever done lived-it *can I get a witness* to done seed-it that VIP lounge April fools sweet-hearts dance night fo' *Medgar Evers*!

Good Lawdy Miss Claudie it be thems sad-sack shitty-assed spheres of the Momma's pure misery that hadda been the perfect *shit-storm* to done officially released-it me from the misery for both my dumb-ass and my soulful Soul strut to recoup the glory daze because I'd done heard em' *damned Skippy* the *be happy don't worry* gooney-goo-goo gospel choir singing to the raw-dawg in me! *Hell yes*, I be back, baby nonya dat *Mr. Numbnuts* because my pussy-whupped dumb-ass be Mr. Happy-nappy …*free at last, free at last Thank God All-Mighty...* I's be free at last dat be the gospel Word-up from the good doctor King, Babycakes!

Check-it I had been sooo internally pissed bouts losing ex-babyg' and the subsequent divorce plus I be engulfed-it in thems pent-up brooding emotions cause I'd been forced stepped-it to be divorced-it a sway from the goodie-stuff my Babygirl! I'd been so whupped-it and damned to be collard-greens stupid iffn wisdom be a cunt-hair then I'd been one bald-headed pussy-whupped Mofo! It be a fort-night hence she'd done moved-it the *fuck out* night when I'd done returned-it to dat stripped-it fucking bare bones to the house without my Babygirl *ain't a home* then alls thems be laughing theys white asses off neighbors be across the street justa *hee-hee-hee* laughing-it up since ex-babyg' done *moved-it the fuck out* thems fools had a common joke in dat my black ass be living *Splitsville, say it aints so, Joe* the mostest thems non-po'dunks done waved-it a *howdy-do lonely Black ass neighbor* as I'd done drove-it pass so that the second-time around herns reversed engineered shit be the fucking blindside a'gin-n-juice my perplexed-it ass be t-totally dumbfound-it when ex-Babyg' done *burst dat move*!

The Corps had done forced learnt-it me the self-discipline and once I'd done developed a routine set of the daily habits theys simply be auto-pilot theretofore my particular routine befo' be the same after ex-babyg's grand public spectacle of it be personal *go to Hell, Zeke,* I done *moved-it the frick out* exodus my daily-double went unhampered. The onliest thing mucho much to be missing from my daily routine some 13+ daze of the 200 fiddy-tree hours, 30-tree minutes justa fuck thems sloppy-seconds hence my chocolate drop Goddess, *why-why-why* the madding exodus big-*gone*-butts I gots-it up all the same 0415 hours washed, drank the OJ with raw egg a solid tribute to them collard-greens then bounced-it my lonely feeling sorry fo' myself down in the dumps ass in my newly decorated by baseball bat pummeled mid-knight blue babyZ smoldered in the *shit for brains* syndrome of thems emotional *feelings* sitting them tan leather seats cept' I be MDGV *missing dems good vibrations* on the daily-double firstest up YMCA b-ball, work the IBM then hitting the JUCCO be the finished-it off. The knight of the second coming I'd brake parked-it the driveway runned-it through the front door on the fast be furious to take the just arrived-it to my *house ain't no home* fo' the this race horse gotta piss! I'd opened-it the front door still on the dead runned-it through an empty house with a curtain-less picture frame front window when BLAM, bam, wham, no thank-ya Ma'am! Fuck, I'd done slammed-it my fucking po' sore ass aching left shin hardtack into ex-coffee table then flipped a bitch over the *fucking where the fuck did that wood and bevel edged glassed topped* table come the fuck from felled-it straight onto my wussified ass on the other side that living room floor, fuck! I damned near force pissed-it my khaki-pants! *Hallelujah*, I be da' shit, Babycakes! My Babygirl done moved-it mostest to all the shit she and the deranged the Momma hadda done taken-it *instant grits* I be home on the range once a'gin-n-juicy Lucy *Hells belles* I admit-it, I'd been physically, mentally then sexually floored yes *Virginia, there do indeed be a Shanty Claus* cause my Babygirl done spritz-it *the Coty* then she done *this is where I live* backed-it dat smoking hot fine PHATT ass up! My Babygirl's coming home as swell to her damned good senses had fo' sure stomped-it hard to done pleasured-it up all to be over my whupped-it wussy ass big-*naked*-butts in thems almost two separate yet not quite so equal weeks, I'd must have done growed-it up a hairy pair big-*on the reals*-butts the real truth, Ruth my mind justa couldn't forgets-it just how much evilness it musta tooken-it to set a man's house afire be firstest ting first big-*tinkering*-butts dat number-two thing bouts my *love lost love found* situation be that I hadda been dat house owing man justa *Rip Van Wrinkling*-it liked a mofo inside my house atop a borrowed-it Army cot *Oh, Hell nawl,* Babycakes!

It hurt like Hell big-*emotional*-butts within a week of ex-Babyg's return I packed-it what be my shit then bounced-it the fuck out! Yeah baby, I done slow dragged-it cause thems itty-bitty nuts fo' sho'nuff done fought-it the good fight big-*babysteps*-butts I'd done growed-it a pair, a big hairy pair thems man-sized extra-large coconut-*get jo' black ass up Mofo, jo' ass asleep at the wheel in a house afire*-balls! That be how ex-Babyg' had come to have possession of my money in that OKC courtroom, my six-thousand plus unaxed for yet kindly Judge ordered returned to me mere seconds befo' the divorce be a one and done thems checks had amounted to damn near a whole year of my VA monthly checks for attending dat JUCCO school seed the VA mailed them checks to my house witch *Sooners* to be ex-Babyg' lived-it in after *Elvis done left* the building. She done kept-it thems VA checks un-cashed probably just some good ole' boy advice from herns expensive *as all Hell, get the fuck outta here* lawyer plus that legal mouth-piece whore told-it to ex-Babyg' to back dat fine *good God she be fine* ass back to home. The house I'd done *purchased-it* befo' thems nuptials that be within pissing distance of a Whites only Marble City, in'a non-po'dunk white suburbia and in my name onliest therefore herns only iffn any entitlement to any proceeds from the sell or escrow could only be gained bye-bye herns beautiful fine-ass physically living in the *house aint a home without her Hersey kissed drop-dead gorgeous justa somebody po'leeese helps this wussified wuss* dwelling thus dat be the onliest reason that she hadda *Oh Happy day* done backed-it easy like Sundae moaning herns sweet so fine ass *honey I'm home* to roost! I would had never knowed-it a ting bouts that little itty-bitty bite of misinformation a'tall 'cepting fo' the big-*braying*-butts thems two jack-asses done needed-it something awful to say abouts my lucky ass doing herns firstest official duty as ex-babyg' when she done cussed-it my ass out big Taxdatass style on thems stone cold OKC courthouse steps where bye-bye she and the Momma done hee-hawed and belched-it all kind tidbits to all thems *happy listening* big assed ears standing around us tree on thems steps plus she done added to that shit just how happy theys two be to be to finally be a rid of a *dumb dufus country bumpkin* rube the likes of me! Ex-babyg' done fo'reallies iffn you hadda axed-it of her and the Momma theys version of the events the final week preceding the we be divorced as to what done played-it out justa bouts a week earlier bye-bye the *happy to tell it all* ex-babyg' as she'd done bumped-it herns gums on thems *why Lordy, tell me just why did she divorce my black ass* courthouse steps!

Chapter 64

I PERSONALLY HADN'T THUNK-IT THAT she hadda planned-it the shit hadda went that way of its own damned accord and herns cinnamon nutmeg brown fine ass justa be as lucky assed she be Superfly fine! Da' shit happened serendipitously justa quirk of the luck being a fickled fat-ed chocolate fine ass muse dat hadda stepped-it in on our once we be love-birds then we be love-torn parted-it bye-buy the wayside legally split asunder asses *Emmett Till* the final bite atop thems courthouse steps yet it hadda been the *luck of the draw* dat a small financial boon bumped-it ex-babyg's flavor! What hadda happened-it, *Sooners* to be ex-Babyg' had lived-it in the house, Hell, yeah she done paid the monthly mortgage I maybe a dumb-assed wussy big-*wuss*-butts I aints stoopid yet her paying the mortgage may have also been on the advisory board of herns *wind in* *cheeks* lawyer to keep things on the legit big-*wussy*-butts some 10-months passed befo' I done officially sold that wood and drywall dwelling back to thems whitefolks community committee for a hefty profit. The same day I closed on the property *Sooners* to be ex-Babyg' had gotten-it all sweet liked and done runned-it up on my not getting-it big-wussy-butts stillz a well whupped-it ass besides ex-Babyg' be drizzling to be sizzling spritzed *the Coty* then she be *"Zeke, you know beau, we didn't really have a honeymoon just that one weekend get-away so instead of letting the courts decide about the money from the sale of the house why don't you and I just go to Vegas and spend it all that way neither of us will have any regrets about the money nor our last days together which I promise, you'll never forget!"*

Hot to be fucking hot-nuts be damned, it be a sho'nuff factual my done growed-it up man-sized hairy assed coconut balls done gots themselves a good very firstest sensational whiffed-it up whiff of *the Coty* cause thems two nutty-buddy whores done STFS*andTheFuckdown* to let a brotha be! Yeah, I knowed-it that she be playing the temptress trying to Pavlov's raw-dawg my just got paid-it dumb horny-toad pussy-whupped wussified black ass big-*beautiful*-butts the twinkling bell in herns tender slow-hand hadn't been ringing-it to thems big wide the fuck opened earholes of mines that bell be heard-it exclusively bye-bye thems branded-it *slapped the baby on its newborn ass* never suspected a ting dems big done growed-it up hairy assed coconut sized balls of mines then thems two swing nuts be hearing *the Coty's* spritzed heated peal *ahhh, shookie-shookie* thus the chocolate Goddess's thundering be all too appealing! Re-whupped-it a'gin-n-juicy Lucy, OK I'd never really fo'reallies done gotten-it unwhupped-it big-*wussy*-butts hot gots damn I'm a gonna be in it up to my eyeballs, Babycakes! I no longer be anybody's fool, I be an officially *cowtech Jr.* educated-it egghead to quote that Beverly Hillbilly TV show Jethro Bodine *I done grad-u-ated the sixth-grade* straight the fuck-up, us tree me and thems two newly educated big hairy-assed coconut balls done hollered-it "*Hell to the yeah, let's rock, Babygirl!*"

It be a freaked-it Friday evening me and Sooners to be ex-Babyg' packed our shit into herns 85' light grey T-bird then good to herns *Word* ex-Babyg' locked the T-bird as she'd taken my thunder-struck hand to done stepped-it me inside her new house *Good Lordy justa be there* then herns spritz of *the Coty* chocolate nougat selfie done put it all down like a Boss! *Heaven helps the one that helps himself* Sooners to be ex-Babyg' grooved thems good vibrations all over my *aints life wonderful* nappy done slapped dat ass happy numb-nuts befo' we bounced-it south Interstate fo'dee witch be a straight two to tree-day bump dat ass to Vegas, baby! We each had two-weeks off the tickety-tock thus father time be not crucial for our torrential rain be tornado warning be damned delayed honeymooning and my 11+ thousand duqats yet according to herns testament on thems OKC courthouse steps fo' ex-Babyg' it be all about dat straight-up cash money, baby! I be one rich *Bitch*, gots money in the bank, my shit dew stank, Babycakes! Anywho at near bouts to Amarillo, Taxdatass some five hours two-hondo-fiddy miles south the OKC I'd done told-it to Babygirl dat I be a tired mofo then done axed-it of her iffn she wanted to rent a room *please, please, please* or did she wanna drive? Big-*mistaken*-butts because I'd been sleepy-tired whupped-it and full all thems warm and fuzzies aftermaths I'd done forgotten-it all about the *it* witch be a'nuttier big bad news problem-o cause ex-Babyg' hadda quirkish kinda thang an *I don't believe dis shit* problem witch be dat she done refused-it to drive over a bridge with water under it, WTF! Thus early Saturday-morn when I hadda sleepy-eyed to awoken-it to done seed-it all that flat brown and grassy grazelands and a two-laned concrete highway dat not to nowhere be looking anything liked an I-40 black-top rolling westward-ho because the onliest tings that be in my vision be thems two retro-active little baby green soggy-*soul satisfied*-nuts of mine thus I done lookey-looked it at all the flat-iron prairie wheat grass surroundings then I be *Baby*, w*hat happened?* Ex-Babyg' started-it up with a little sumptin about this river just outside Amarillo and that she had changed roads big-*its all good*-butts don't worry because we be still headed to Vegas, baby that be when I done also remembered-it that ex-Babyg' didn't read road maps she'd done all herns interstate driving by rote seed all of that shit occurred-it mere moments befo' I'd peeped thems little black letters on a stark white placard road sign that read Wichita, Kansas 45 miles, fuck! Babygirl had simply *flipped a bitch* to done drove them two-hondo-fiddy miles north on an Oklahoma state highway without bridges that didn't done crossed-it over any parts water! Right to the then we just chuckled-it like a couple of teenaged first-loves because that be just the purpose of a previous knight-before the drive to Vegas, baby throwdown on a wussed its been mo' than 10-months missing thems *good vibrations* done to a man-wuss rolling baby green horny-toad nuts thus be the moment that we two re-awaking lovebirds done just chunked-it all thems Vegas, baby plans to be *I'm going to Kansas City, Kansas City here we come,* baby!

Sooners to be lessen tree-hours we done got there to done lived-it up high offa the hog! We got a room at the Hyatt that be the sky-scraping hotel with the rotating top-floor restaurant and bar overlooking all of the KC then we proceeded to done partied liked the *Richey-rich*, Baby! I had two suits tailored for about a grand total just fo' the to done stepped-it out with herns fine strutting selfie to be all over dat one-hayseed town! Stillz mine, my Babygirl bought six dresses each a thousand plus dollars big-*fancy*-butts here be the rub according to her she hadn't actually bought-it them expensive assed gowns that I'd done watched her model ala years befo' dat pic *Pretty woman*! Stillz my Babygirl said she'd tipped-it the saleslady then tipped sista-girl done wrapped-it empty store boxes witch I hadn't opened to peep inside because of my all trusting one-voice one-woman stillz mine, my Babygirl! *Hells a fire*, thems two demonic knuckles the Momma and the Twisted-Sista atop thems cold ass OKC courthouse steps swells thems two clowns put on a show to be seed theys done spoken *crazy-eight* Word! Big-*ig'nant*-butts I hadn't cared-it one shit about the money then why knot now my dumb tricked ass held no regrets, baby! All thems times with my Babygirl, I done lived-it the daze of my life and she done taught me swell just how good living thems daze be then comes the knight-times *Good Laud* she'd done vibrated-it my ass through the sho'nuff Door number-one filled-it top to bottom withs nuttin big-*lucky me*-butts the *goodie-stuff*! What be important to me thems two-weeks of *Oh, Toto we be* in *Kan-an-ass* daze be that I be a rich bitch with the cash to spend on my ebony Queen justa enjoy herns elegant smile because I be handling our business with nonya thems cash restraints thus them lucky 13 daze be some of the riches and the fondest daze of my life besides *Sooners* to be ex-Babyg' done rocked-it then re-rocked my world, moanings, nooners and always comed the Black Knight! News flash, the monkey be no longer in hisns tree! Yeah, I knowed-it I be whupped-it big-*wussy*-butts the real truth, Ruth for once in my life to done lived-it large with that woman *who'dat* brung-it me the joyfulness thats I'd onliest *Medgar Evers* done read about or done heard-it lied about yet me and *Sooners* to be ex-Babyg' done lived-it our buck-wild *Richey-rich* asses the goodie-stuff because she'd held fo' me thems Good Vibrations! The fat fact, Jack be just as *Sooners* my bighead crossed-it over that new house threshold of herns to done bumped-it unto thems fluffy *new house* pillows back the OKC all that money became herns money *instant grits* so all that ex-love shack money be monies well spent not a penny lost and iffn she hadda actually done planned-it all then good for ex-Babyg' *God Bless her* because the real joke be on her in that she'd onliest succeeded into having conned the fuck-outta of herns own-*fine assed*-selfie them Benjamins be herns befo' we'd ever gotten-it Kandatass City!

The divorce date be set in wet-back poured-it cement lessen a week back the OKC thus we hadn't been justa fooling each other either fo'reallies we both done knowed-it that the party be over just neither one of us had been in any madding bum-rush dash to done turned-out them lights! The mo' I done thunk-it ex-Babyg be the mo' I sho'nuff seed the hows and the whys I be plum crazy-assed about her, everybody my peeps, Dad and especially my Moms loved that girl. My Moms of her own done gave-it to my Babygirl herns real cooked-it from the scratched soulfood recipes and thems two had cooked-it thems *scratched* recipes together plus my Moms done turned my Babygirl on to thems original songs by the Queen, Aretha so that my Babygirl could learn to ad-lib them words in a more enriched tone such it be pure and from the heart! My Moms be *No, baby, sing it from yo' chest* whilst theys done rehearsed-it theys own renditions of the songs of '*Retha*! My Moms didn't want any thems foolish amongst the womenfolk to be *cuttin-heads* with my Babygirl. Back in the daze, in the blackfolk clubs thems club bouncing ladies could holla cause theys all done growed-it up banging thems gospel gooney-goo-goo choirs so when a female super-star entertainer performed live the smartest ones changed theys words justa little sump'n-sumptin from the vinyl and radio versions because thems once church egotistical ladies would stand-up inside the club to done cut-loose the song to out sing thems stars then thems heifers be *I sung it butter* those womens dubbed dat shit cuttin-heads witch be challenging a body at the thing witch that somebody supposed to have been fo'reallies professionally good at doing thus theys foolishly done challenged the star though the singer be on the stage with herns band and back-ups whilst thems fools be a'standing out in the audience with theys *brunged-it from thems cottonfields* foolishness!

chapter 65

My Moms showed my Babygirl how to get a an honest on the reals feel for changing up them words to a song and adding herns own personal spice seed my Moms hadda chunk of them on the reals feelings fo' my Babygirl to done taught-it her how to karaoke long befo' thems karaoke machines came along! Dad and dem Unks everytime theys done seed my Babygirl and me thems old men be a'punching me in the shoulder *you done good son, you done real good. You done done us proud*! Laters, my peeps though theys had never axed-it of my dumb-ass yet theys be nobody's country *tears of thee* bumpkins so theys hadda done knowed-it a straight-up that it had to have been justa sump-tin something awful specially bad-assed fo' me to have gone and done given-it-up on my Babygirl then when I finally done told-it to dems bouts her setting the garage on fire with my ass asleep inside the house be the WTF! Dad, Calvin and dem Unks justa all thems menfolks had all the same punched me in the shoulder *you done good son, you done real good. You done us proud*! *No matter how fine or good a woman be you can't let her burn yo' black ass up nor yo' house down! And never evers the two of thems bad-assed motherfuckers together! Ya' gots to hat-up, bottle-up and go! You dones good, Son, ya' dones us real proud!*

The Momma big-*funky*-butts that woman without a doubt had been a pure *Hell toted in a hand basket* on my ass, Word! The question be why pray tell had she been so hellaciously Hell-cat bent swells I suspected-it that *bye-bye* old woman any minimal terms of decency the Momma fo' surely had done knowed-it to be a fat fact, Jack that I *scout's honor* truly loved, respected herns youngest daughter and had never to *Medgar Evers* meant my Babygirl no harm then why the miscarriage of justice? I believed-it in the little cold ass ice stonepit of my heart of hearts that it had been my man, my mentor *who'dat* just so happened-it to be an ex-pilot, a Korean war veteran, war on China flyboy mercenary and my Babygirl's very own the Step-dad big-*heroic*-butts by default dat made him the husband of dat *Minnie the Moocha* the Momma! Step-Dad had not only loved, big-*blessed*-butts done openly encouraged the union of meself and my Babygirl that be my cow tech JUCCO educated opinion and self-manufactured *not my fault* theory of separation. The Momma had not onliest been dirt poor big-*squash eating*-butts she and thems underfoot-kiddies of herns be of the rural southern country dirt poor variety to the point that my po'assed rags-to-tattered rags up-bringings would have been considered a glorious done stepped-it up Biggy-smalls putting on the *Ritz* bye-bye theys pre-the Step-Dad standard of living! I hadn't gone to church because of our family folks done truly believed-it that them jack-legged preachers be justa scum-buckets and low-down dirty Uncle Tom spies for thems po'dunk evil assed redneck soda-crackers and that all dems black preachers been trained and hired by thems po'dunk fools to spread thin slices of the Lord's prayer from theys bad bag of bull-manure theys *lord's turds* witch we as a family be having nonya of that pre-ordained-it country preacher Bullshit! My Babygirl's lack of church up-bringing hadda been a different cup of piss poured over a well-used teabag because she, herns tree other siblings and the Momma be too damned raggedy-Ann fricking poor to attend any church even iffn theys done held-it a warped mind to wanna attend a first *bap-the-piss* house of lies coupled-it up to the fat fact, Jack theys be living in a one acre cabbage-patch small *bump dat ass* town the likes of Wichita Falls just intensified the poverty of theys *it aints inflation* situation seed all them country-bumpkin peeps the Negro as thems mean assed po'dunk rednecks done knowed-it all dat be abouts theys potential in life and financial score be a futuristic *Dunkin Doughnut* big fat zero! Under any a'nuttier circumstances then the Momma would have hugged and Blessed herns own assessment of me with opened-it *welcome son come to momma* big smelly-flabby arms to done on the fricking quick doubled-armed shoved-it me into my Babygirls arms as swell theys family in a CC moment big-*richy rich*-butts with Step-Dad's coin tucked-it deeply within herns once empty-*Hell even dust mites wouldn't settle into*-purse then I became in the Momma's beady snake-eyes justa a'nuttier dumb country-bumpkin ass bumping buzzard-luck, Duf'!

Word-up, ex-Babygirl been spared the dreaded curse of living dirt assed-out poor in southern poverty in a one-hitch po'dunk redneck town. Step-Dad be one K-kool kool as blastin' black cherry Kool-Aid he had flown sorties over Korean afterwards my man done flown flyby sorties over China to done filled hisns coffers seed my man the Step-Dad had real coin in hisns hip-pockets come the one sunny day the Momma be out and about thems hills and byways of the Whiskey Faults flyboy training base panning fo' gold! Step-Dad be a good man, he be good to the Momma and herns ready-made family besides he had whole heartedly approved-it of my young thoroughly whupped-ass! My theory of separation be Step-Dad must have repeatedly told-it to the Momma what a great thing it be that me and ex-Babyg' to done found-it in each the other and that had been the major problem big-*git yo' grits on*-butts the Momma unbeknownest to Step-Dad as swell to any man thems womenfolks possess an innate inbred chromosome for survival of the *me me me* and theys family. Step-Dad couldn't have and didn't have any kids excepting thems already-mades of the living incubus the Momma thus the devil's old handmaid had been trying to ensure herns four once be poor assed-out chillens theys financially secured future buy-bye any to all means with all things being natural *dog eat dog* the Momma just had to kick my interloping pussy-whupped ass to the curb! Admittedly that be a done covered my ass reasonable done thunk-it kinda self-actualizational glorified theory because I may never gonna knowed-it the real truth, Ruth maybe dat old frumpy biddy just hated my black ass on sight! Step-dad owned-it hisns own single-wing four passenger plane witch a'many times he'd flown-it with my dumb-ass alongside to the mostest of hisns capital investment/holdings meetings and nuttier business ventures therefore the Momma's survival chromosome thing musta been kicking-it hard in thems fatty pork-belly ass-cheeks of herns "*watch it duf'* ..." ergo for the Momma the only reasonable course of action be to separate my dumb po'assed-out outsider lookey-looking to be the insider ass from crowding in on herns hard earned-it when she had done most desperately needed-it riches! Once I left-it the OKC in the dust I've never ventured-it to done returned, never a'gin-n-juice seed ex-Babyg' nor *tank God* the Momma big-*see ya*-butts fo' *Medgar Evers* the Momma's pure assed-out unadulterated misery bumped-it herns snake-bit beady eyes that April fools party be my take-it to the grave-digger eternal *I be one happy-assed man* experience!

Why the fuck had I done put up with that demonic the Momma be the KISS because jo' boy had been mayhaps still just be a bit whupped-it by the Momma's lovely chocolate drop dead gorgeous youngest daughter thus the whupped-it part in me done always on the Superfly be in it fo' the long haul *Memorexed* idealized versions of all the idyllic wiles of joy bustin loose thems blissful *good vibrations* put-it down bye-bye ex-Babyg'! I swear it hadn't been just all about the pussy seed me and ex-Babyg' done gots along just fine when left to our lonesome lovey-dovey selves where-ever we be iffn one thems hotels/motels then I be herns personal happy ass *sheet changing handimaid*, the *Love Grotto* or the *Love Shack* we be just fine k-kool get jo' luv on fine, baby!

chapter 66

CHECK-IT, AFTER THE 77' MET-IT-UP some 6 to 8-months later I be doing make-it up flyby drills for my flight pay *baby need a new pair of combat boots* witch be extra monies fo' always going up to be jumping *Semper Fi, motherfucker* outta the thems Herks besides every little bite helps to done stuffed-it thems empty ass-cheek pockets of mines big-*dummy*-butts you had to maintain a monthly average of flight-time hours to keeps getting paid thems extra pesos so after most missions the unit be riding the belly of thems war-birds fo' the hours justa keep getting thems extra monies! It be all about the money, baby! It be one of them *give me the money* flights where I done *Hello my friend* a meet-it up with a top-notched flyboy *who'dat* be a loadmaster whom dems the flight whores be done actually runned-it the plane's day to day mundane operations seed theys the peeps dat keeps it light and tight for the flight big-*loaded*-butts anytowho me and dis flyboy got to rapping life's up-sides fucks them downs and I done told-it flyboy bouts my new justa met-it up my Babygirl in how *my soul be Satisfied* we loved-it ourselves the Queen *aint dat da' shit,* baby! Brotha flyboy hustled-it them sidelines a DJ rolling outta Mildenhall, England and he'd let me to done knowed-it fo' a *Hamilton* plus a few *Jacksons* he'd make me two seven inch-reels with nuttin big-*say what Tay*-butts Aretha's songs on thems reels and iffn I tossed a'nuttier *Jackson* then he'd give me two each all the cassettes and eight-tracks that it took to record all the Queen's albums! Flyboy DJ sales pitch be that having thems twin sets of the same music when I gots my girl on the hook then we could both play the same songs/albums at the same time whilst we done made the chit-chat he said *ya' gurl gonna love dat shit* then I be Hell, yeah K-kool Mofo!

I be *right-on, mah brotha* just don't record any gospel especially the gospel album *Amazing Grace* though it be one of my fav big-*unHoly*-butts I hadn't knowed-it then that ex-Babyg' didn't do the church scene big-*unHoly roller*-butts the reals be the gospel and all dat shit be churchyfied and thems churches hold thems weddings and I'd justa done met-it-up with herns fine chocolate ass seed I hadn't wanted-it fo' her to be farming any thems *jump the broom* ideas! Anytowho flyboy done made more than just good on hisns end of the deal plus he done even given me two computer print-outs with all the albums and songs that he'd recorded chronologically listed by year and the individual tracks seed all that *intel* shit be da' shit, baby! Comes September on ex-Babyg's b-daze yeah, she be Libra good golly Ms. Molly I hadda unknowingly done given herns Superfly fine chocolate ass the perfect second bestest ever gift one-set each of all thems cassettes and eight tracks of all the Queen's recordings sans the gospel along with a copy of the computer print-out and *Hell say yeah* the *perfecto* gift #1 *Medgar Evers* a gift wrapped-it bottle of *the Coty*, yeah baby! Jo' boy don't just be anytobody's fool! Next, I'd taken DJ flyboy advice about chit-chatting a *bump dat shit* one two-step further to done taught-it to my Babygirl how to arrange, list and speak in 6-figured coordinates to be our own little love language that we'z two *getting it on the good foot* love-bird knuckles done tagged the Queen's English!

The Queen's English worked-it thissa way them firstest two numbers be the chronological listed album's number as per each our exactamente same computerized list thus the first album on the print-out be *zero-one.* The next two numbers represented-it witch side of the album the song be located thems two numbers be either zero-one side-A, zero-two side-B or fo' multi-set albums zero-tree side-C or zero-fo' side-D. The last two numbers of the six numbered-it coordinated the Queen's English be the track itself as in zero-one be the first track or say one-two be the twelfth track's name as specified by our computer print-out. Those last two numbers of the 6-figured code be the mostest important thing to interpreting the code because the name of that track be the actual words that we'z be done communicated-it to each other. My Babygirl done taken to that like a fly to shit paper Biggy-smalls time seed she done loved-it that shit probably because of its simplicity plus we tossed-it in some off-shoots variety of the add-ons to be quick up-front and to the point references liked-it we'd say sumptin sump'n liked *ten–cover* witch meant-it album #10 and the album's cover title be the words then fo' us according to the computerized printed-out album-10 be titled *I Never Loved a Man the Way I Love* You! I just loved-it me sum my Babygirl when she done *hit me up* with the shout-out *Ten-cover*! A'nuttier example *zero-six-cover* my git back when ex-Babyg' be tossing too much shit my way seed album-6 be titled *You Running Out of Fools*! Fo' my dumb-ass learning that shit be easy as *I scream ice-cream* on thems far and away missions I be liked *fuck dis shit* the Queen be calling then I'd done picked-it up my hand-copied copy of the print-out to get my *skooling-on* to done memorized-it the Queen's English big-*tank ya*-butts the *Surprise Surprize Surprise Sergeant Carter* be all mines because ex-Babyg' thunk-it that secret language shit be too skool fo' kool cause she'd tooken-it the time to done put it to memory herns copy of the print-out! I'd been too much of a knuckle-head to done knowed-it that the #1 love of any woman with all tings being equal in this life be to have a starring role in sumptin secretive and the bigger the secret the bigger the *loving* thus our secret an easy done learnt-it language code *yeah, baby* big-*cryptic*-butts that da' shit done propelled my dumb-ass from the dunce-corner directly to the head of my Babygirl's *I do declare, I love that dumb-ass* class! All the *King's horses and all the King's men* fo' thems a'sniffing and a'whiffing boys gots theys degrees big-*educated*-butts it be factual *Heaven may have but God Bless the child that's got hisns own* Ja'rene bastard ass an *I'll be damned* a secretive language *das boots* the Queen, Aretha Franklin English!

All our peeps knowed-it we'z be up to shit with thems numbers TOP and the boys recognized the coordinated big-*knowing*-butts theys thunk-it we be hollering bouts places to hook-up and family peeps thunk-it we be playing *the numbers* thems *who'dats* done knowed-it that we two be rapping big-*games people play*-butts theys had to clue as to what the Hell we be rapping about all thems nuttier nosey-Rosies be just *what the Hell yall two lovie-dovies be speaking abouts?* Thens me and my Babygirl be liked thems Siamese cats that done swallowed dat yella-canary when we be as one with the done holla back *Nuttin, we only speaking the Queen's English*! That doubled-it up Jack-fiddy to DJ flyboy be liked that eleven grand money *Hell yes, Miss Dorothy we be in Kansas* as swell all the duqats and boo-coo ends from the one-buck to the *Bennies* theys all be the same because any monies spent on my Babygirl be Biggy-smalls money swell spent!

Chapter 67

"This fucking zoo had a female gorilla in heat and they needed somebody to fuck the bitch, see so three men put in for the job; a cracker, a chink and LeRoy. The redneck gets first crack, see he being a cracker and all, dumb-fuck Bubba enters the cage with the gorilla chained spread eagled liked a motherfucker all muzzled and shit. Soon the peckerwood's screaming at the top of his lungs "Guards, guards, guards!" the guards come running and the peckerwood demands to be let out. The Chinaman, nemba One-Son, goes in the cage next and pretty soon one-tongue soup be screaming at the top of his lungs "Guards, guards, guards!" the guards come running and the chink demands to be let out. The Brotha struts into that cage then pretty soon LeRoy be screaming at the top of his lungs "Guards, guards, guards!" the guards come a'running and they say "we suppose, you want out, to!" the Brotha shouts "Hell, Nawl, mother-fucka take the muzzle offa this bitch, I gotta kiss her!" hey-heh-hey *"Niggas, you know niggas gotta have passion when they be fucking!"* dat joke I done remembered-it having firstest heard-it live and in-person by a pencil-thin comedian whom I done always believed-it to be dat skinny-*funny*-butt Rich *da' shit* Pryor whilst I be laying belly-side down hidden alongside the both Gettis and Mr. Bobby because we tree be camped-out under thems floor boards of the Chocolate City's copy-cat Apollo nite-club. Just liked Pavlov's dog on cue whenever I heard, thunk-it or even per chanced-it to eat a slice of passion fruit that joke done on the always flavored warm be thems fuzzies within my lucid mind. Big-*star*-butts I ain't a trying to name drop this here be a jive-assed rap about the passion that everyday common man seeking a common woman passion purely for the sake of bumping dems uglies! This also be about how TOP would flip the script on the anyone in the unit all by hisns lonesome situated in some 3rd world jungle awaiting an assignee with a'nuttin big-*lone ranger*-butts one or two of TOP's good books nonya hisns gonna *burn dat ass* done fucked with me now I gonna fuck with you, the po'dunk spared no quarters to done packed-it thems military brochures of the bullshit *hoo-rah* propaganda. I'm gonna bump gums *Oh, what a night* bouts a *Yes big Daddy* I'm a for real Chinese Shorty *[Yuppies:* nemba one Golden girl-child be an attractive Asian woman*]* whom I had unsuccessfully attempted to seduce at a now defunct Tucson RB oldies club. My freed of ex-Babyg' black ass done bounced-it the OKC to done moved-it to Phoenix big-*wandering*-butts summertime later I'd done managed-it to meander meself passed the valley then beyond to the Tucson ex-home on the range to mostest thems ex-reservist Mexican-Americans. 95' *Baby Boomers* be an old skool disco backed *rhythm done jaw-jacked them blues* genre bar with good and plenty DJ music stomping *dyke-ville* tongue-n-groove a tight assed wooden dance floor *Disco be back, baby* the spot be old skool *Sugar Hill*, the Tucson the 70s era Black side of thems railroad tracks inside a strip-mall where it be *bye-bye* see ya' hip-hop because *Baby Boomers* had jammed that Old Skool that 70s and 80s disco dance it be time-out to the Busta Rhymes, MC

Hammer and Sugarhill gang bumping it a hardy *Jello* Ohio Players, Barclays and the P-funk!

What attracted me to the she who be from the *land-of-chinks* Shorty be the obvious: BAM! *Bangkok Shorty* stepped-it some 5-foot 2-inches by two of the biggest nature's own self-grown twin-peaked titties *Bangkok Shorty* justa itty-bitty piece of raw-hide tanned leather big-*nip nipples*-butts swell put together! [Cowboy junkies: *such a tiny spool the little lady be sport'n ah mighty heap of thread*] *Bangkok Shorty* be a world class beauty far beyond her years and her magnificent breastestes be a step-above and a far superior cut than our LBFMs in all those southeast Asia brothels, bath-houses and *massage you long time* GI *sex just aints on the beach* parlors on the personal I do miss you ladies *Tank-ya* to all thems little oriental-rentals much respect for all thems *LBFM* dats done rocked my world with the *she bang she bang* back thems Pacific rim jobs nawl Shorty bedazzled with a straight-outta the Bangkok softly baby-dolled face, tea rose dusky cinnamon complexion, jet black brows arched over two on the semi-slanted huge melt-in yo' heart never-in yo' hands dare to peep deeply into *needs to be kissed* bedazzling eyes and the both be thems opened wide windows to herns *baby gots* Soule, a snuggle-it up to me button-bunny nose, ever so slightly parted blushed rose painted on kissable lips, two pleased-to-be-nibbled sapphire studded lobes and the thinnest curvature of a delicate throat encased by a string of oriental egg-shell pearls with an attached sapphire teardrop that sat atop that bountiful endowment of the succulent we be *made in Taiwan* huge be we breast-estes! [my Brothas*: Bunz Baby, we luvz da boo-Tay! Duzzda' Bangkok fly babyg gotz back?* Tucson-Spaniards: *la chi-chona-Big Tittied Woman*; Yuppies: *buxom bosom;* Trailer-trash: *Big'ums;* Eastside Player-haters: *SVG silicon valley-girl, we all know them chinks aint gots no for real tits;* Southside Player-haters: *hoochie-momma;* Cowboy junkies: *the filly got spurs dat jingled-jangled-dangled;* Religious Reich: *Hell hounds on all you heathens*] No! It had been the KISS principal at work again the simplest of the simple, Bangkok-babygirl wore an elegant navy blue soft satin silky smooth glittered to be sparkling evening gown but that little black loop of thread witch usually clasped such an elegant evening to be dressed-it up gown at the small of the back and just above the zipper well that little loop had dared to supple a wee bit of herns Bangkok tenderness to done pressed itself unto the sweetest spot of the lovely *muneca's* [Tucson-Spaniards: *Babydoll*] slightly sweated blush rose upper back, the Utopia! That

PHATT' [my Brothas: *PrettyHotAssTotallyTempting*] part of a woman's upper back where no matter the arm's length alone it can't possibly be accessed as in an attempt to lick one's elbow utterly impossible because arms be knot meant to bend that way unless my halfa-Windy City cousin *Guido* outta the southside been paid ta give ya' a personal *it aint personal* visit! She be the real *4-1-1* living large proof dat Big Daddy in the Sky had saideth unto Adam *lie down and I shall make you a helpmate* [Religious Reich: *WWJD: What Would Jesus Do*] The same damned thing dat Zeke wanted to do, get biblical with dat fine assed Bangkok-Babyg' Shorty! That little loop blazed a fo'dee foot neon sign *Yo'! Zeke, Word-up! Shorty don't break no man intimately enough to allow him the ecstasy of hooking me up*! *You best to break yo' self, Mofo*!

I cast my fears upon them never to be forgotten disco *Evelyn Champagne King* waters reeled in my courage, sauntered over to that little black loop and introduced meself and the Biggy-smalls talk the tête-à-tête, justa bite of the repartee, the lover's spar, Bangkok-babygirl jabbed justa bit of herns bio *"I'm outcast Chinese because I'm parts Black and Spanish"* back-a-step the fuck-up *Say What-tay*! *Whooooa da fuck, Nellie* that's a sump'n sumptin special ting, now check this fucking, fo' reals *no shit* check this shit out! I'd been all over this funky ball of dirt bursting chops with both the bestest and worstest of thems all kinda peeps yet and it be a fat fact, Jack that I'd only experienced this peculiar *Yo', mofo you can't guess it so I'm gonna tell ya' what my Nationality be* quirky assed-out shit in Tucson, *fucking dry-heat my Black-ass* a ting onliest and I taint just ah a'shitting thems sandy candied-ass pebbles be that Tucson peoples thems real live Mexican straight-outta the Mexico *splash down* peoples especially thems recently arrived folks via the Rio Grande over to the El Paso way thems authentic *May-he-co* peeps that be legally and or illegally living-it up in that patch of the world's *this here desert aints no dessert* its justa gotta musta be the heat that done overly cooked theys *re-fried beans fo' brains* dumb-fuck asses because thems beaner mofos always be to fucking talking bouts theys damned Spanish ancestry WTF liked that bullshit European po'dunk gibberish speak wannabe shit fo' DNA be some kinda *I be royalty*! Bangkok-Babyg' be the firstest *Medgar Evers* and she be *damned Skippy* the onliest person to date ever whether male or female possibly a combo that I done a meet-it up with in a Tucson bar to done mentioned any parts that their personal ancestry be Black thus Bangkok-Babyg mayhaps had a self-propelled herns personally own set of the *how to plan* fo' herns fine-assed Oriental selfie to go *Stella* on my dumb-ass and gets herns *groove back*!

I'd yet to meet a Mexican male or female in a Tucson bar whose grandfather wasn't a gibberish speak Spaniard within *dos cevesas within dos horas* that be two beers or two hours of conversing the damned DNA braggart *puta puto* gibberish speak mofo be on the holla dat a fucking Spaniard be hisns/herns bastard ass grand-daddy! Not to be *the* racist damned Skippy not to demean a race of peoples as a collective big-*not apologizing*-butts what my *I yam Black* ghetto ashy assed big lipped *Whats happening, baby* outta the hood inner-city *ghetto fabulous Black* be Black from the balding pate atop my shaven head to the hawk like talons attached to my baby Black toes taints No mix and even iffn there be some sorta combination of an inter-*helps me Lawd*-racial hereditary mix that I hadda knowed-it of or supposed-it of then most definitely I be knot the dumb-assed *duf'* to tempt to brag about that shit over a beer or two in a barroom full of illegal *Messykins*! [Tucson Spaniards: *pinche puto Negro! You fucking Black ass whore*] Big-*holla@yaBoy*-butts iffn you ever for WTF be ever the reason just happened to done found-it a reason to land yo' dumb-ass cheeks on a barroom seat in any Tucson, Arizona bar to be busting brews or being served brews for the to be busting and yo' ass be in the company of a Tucson *Messkin* bye-bye round #2 then fo' a fat fact, Jack jo' ass gonna be hipped to the gist of the matter of that bold faced lie *my grandfather came from Spain* WTF be this bullshit *caca del toro*!

Chapter 68

THEMS IG'NANT FUCKS THEMS TUCSON Messykins theys own damned selves don't wannabe no fucking Messkin thems drunk or sober dumbasses always be claiming theys got a fucking Spanish grandfather in other words thems whores be hollering *I aints no fucking Messkin look at me when I'm talking to ya' my grand-dey-Papi be from Spain therefore I be Spanish*! Every damned Skippy Messykin in America holla *la raza, I'm Messkin*! Thems Tucson fools be eyeball to eyeballing-it locked and loaded on-point steely eye when theys fool asses be *fuck chew logic, gringo Mofo* theys continued with the straight-up it all be bullshit *its been some 800+ plus years since the fucking Spaniards done left this continent buttz I'm here in this barroom to tell'ya* *my grand-dey-Papi be a Spaniard. Nana gots his Methuselah ancient ass locked balls tight downstairs in a barrel of Jose Cuervo where chew tink the fucking worm comes from?* That be the a'nuttier ting bouts dat psychotic assed Trips he the onliest fool this fucking world that I done knowed-it to fo' reallies wannabe a Messkin WTF yet hisns black psycho wannabe a Messykin ass best to never be done ventured-it into a fucking Tucson barroom or its gonna be Surprise Surprize Surprise Sgt. Carter fo' hisns too black to be a Messykin ass! *All our grand-dey-Pappies done came from Spain therefore we'z be knot the fucking Messykins we'z all be Spaniards, drink ya' fucking beer*!

Big-*stacked*-butts Bangkok-Babyg Shorty be a sho'nuff *Shawtee*, she be a late fo'dee something going on an early twenty something a sultry fine assed Oriental temptress [my Brothas: *Asian honeys age with an elegant inherent grace such that beauty haz no age nor limitations on satin dolls, da' Chinese honeybee an Oriental Barbie*!] I had the better parts of two hours to get my *woo-woo-woo* on, in between the *Electric slide*, the *Hustle*, the *New Jack Swing*, the *Macarena* and a *Good n' Plenty* champagne toasts I gleamed the key elements of Bangkok-Babyg's recent descent into demonic decadence. Shorty and herns *party motherfucker, let's get this party-On* Hawaiian hula-hula gingered-snapped girlfriend be out bumping the town because theys both celebrated their ass-spankling brand newly founded and richly funded divorcee decrees witch had been issued earlier that very day bye-bye the Sovereign State of *WTF* it's a fat fact, Jack dat we be residing in the racist mis-State of *how the fuck did that wet-back git in here* Arizona and thems two party-gurlz each held within theys soft be delicate hand witch be held on high a legal and legit edict that had rendered unto each *party like you mean it gurl* herns own *thank God we bye-bye* done earned-it each their respected marriage *no mas* shit to be legally State sanctioned asunder! The two celebrators had rented unto theys *partying cause we still be fine assed rich beyotches* selves a stretch limo on theys from this lucky day forward ex-hubby's dollar thus the two Pacific Islander lovelies done purposefully drank the expensive *bubblies* then club hopped-it with the joyous glee of a new world justice league benefiting unto each a great financial boon and the legal status of a renewed lease on an un-tethered *Cameo* holla the *Single life* cause theys be ...*free at last, free at last*... from an old and frizzled yet rich as all Hell living on a golf-course boney white skeleton's ass thus theys gots the freedom, baby as swell theys good to be young and richy-rich life! Bangkok Shorty' thems fucking *chinks be damned* done boasted-it a Moorish big-*bootylicious*-butts fo' meselfie I justa loved-it me herns Black parts specially dat tight little booty bump!

Mi-Linda [Tucson-Spaniards: *My Pretty*] had been duly married to a good man big-*impo'tant*-butts hubby whom be some 20+ odd years herns senior be an executive Chairman to the Board Chase Bank and the breaking news be since year two of theys blessed union that po'dunk executive had been not only important big-*can't get it up*-butts impotent [my Brothas: SNAPS! Dat shit be the fucking **NIGHTMARE!**] not onliest had *the man* ran a bank but he had by hisns own *sad-n-the-sack* self done also ran a bodacious tight parts Black Bangkok-Babyg' into the arms of a'many pre-paid Cali-fornicating lover the past 13+ years of theys nuptials' and actually that last little fat fact, Jack had been the thing that for reallies had helped Mi-Linda to organize her life to get herns shit together baby, here in the land of the happy-shopping grounds.

Mi-Linda and her impo'tant hubby Mr. Big-*monies*-bags had lived-it up in suburbia *La-La land* home to the *Mickey* mouse club and Bangkok-Babyg' maintained tastefully discreet yet severely needed booty-call pre-paid sexual rendezvous with thems iffn you paying never a word we be saying boytoys to the rich living fabulously females married to impo'tant husbands witch the fine ass *bump dat* Spanish-Moor had intermixed with her Rodeo Drive shopping sprees to slacken then quaken herns *OMG* [mall-rats: *Oh, my God!*] *please to send me some Hollywood nemba eight-inch dick to ride-out these* powerful yearnings! The rub, some two years prior the richly living and loving dysfunctional couple had been transferred from their castled estate *City of Angels* to a townhouse on the greens of Green Valley bouts 30+ miles south the Tucson an expensive as all Hell golfing resort exclusive to the rich and only the richest you can keep yo' fucking famous! [Gold-diggers: *you gotta have MO'NEY, lots of Mo'Nay iffn you wannabe with me!*] "*UGH! Old, wizened wrinkled white skeletons!*" be how she depicted the white male only populace that kicked-it home on a golf course *Senior Citizenville* thems upper 2% the richest motherfuckers on earth justa living-it up their dry white skeletonized asses on the inner edges of a golf course "Damn, I hate those boney-assed impotent bastards!" Mi-Linda affirmed.

"Footsteps guided by demonic power whose pastime it is to trample on human reason and dignity..." Thomas Mann *Oh Hell, Nawl Please God, fuck No,* not that old rottening in his centuries old grave-site dead assed fossilized

European broke-down whore of a sage, please to let him just to bounce outta the same whatever fucking door that he justa bumped hisns ghostly be fucking white ass in from! Now, don't bust my chomps, it be knot that I have anything against buried old white guys because dead presidents stuffed in my wallet and stashed into my bank accounts done as a whole suited me just to be fine. It be the timing, there I had sat justa gazing into two perfectly drunken wine soaked Chink-Moorish orbs in a disco where it be a known fact that the Messykin barkeep gots fo' hisns ass an authentic gibberish speak straight outta Spain grandpappy, sipping champagne to be dumb found-it starring into two of the most beautifully Richey-rich brown champagne drenched orbs of a gushingly new *money just broke the fucking bank Geisha girl*, a sho'nuff *Baby I'm for real* Bangkok-Babyg' and good Gawd All-Mighty herns bestest parts be Black! Mi-Linda had begun to spew forth the lusty details of an intimate self-actuated sexual rumpus caught awry a fo'reallies *Dear Penthouse* moment thus T-Mann WTF *bump dat shit* yo' old sage ass be the last ting I done needed-it! What I needed at the time be that BT Express thems *blue thunder* pills or justa whiff of *the Coty* not a virtuoso for the passionate tempestuous! Thomas *da'* Mann's novel A Death in Venice, be one of them books TOP done once given me during a 4+ months hiatus witch that fucking geek novel my alone ass done times over read then its over the top valued wisdom became my ultimate technical manual of the passioned fruit witch done gone the way of the unrighteously rotten dead fucking wrong!

Mr. Allen did a re-arrangement to the furniture in my mind big-*stupid*-butts onliest the divan of the man cave gots moved back aways seed that dead bitch ghostly white bastard da' Mann only pushed-it my loveseat outta the corner to be lo and behold center front big-*weakling*-butts Rich *da' shit* done layed a firm foundation on the business end of *what passion be* that be Pryor's wit be foremost subjective anyting passion and its interlockings within the psyche of this black man. *Da' Mann* novel deconstructed the intricate steps of the mind's innate ability to self-rationalize the pursuit of an obsession beyond the acts necessary in the sustaining of life's physical self! Do not weep for me *Oh, Susanna* seed Pryor just skimmed mayhaps shifted the mansion's curtains KISS [Ja'renes: *Yo Mofo, Keep It Simple Stupid*] witch meant iffn you're lucky enough to run upon a babe in heat, strut into that cage, my brotha, be brave, do yo' thang just don't kiss da' bitch! The desire to kiss and to be kissed shit be passion fumbling with yo' mind and passion be a 500-pound ape bitch chomping at the bit to rip yo' dumb ass asunder! Pryor's logic be my ig'nant bliss a blessed virtue throughout the honey-butter come on a square paddy lustful daze of my youth befo' *Da'* Mann complicated thems safe-guards to done dis-assembled thems previous passionate thoughts and ideals with such diabolical minute details *OMG* yet that Black knight in *Baby Boomers* bumping-it up with Bangkok-shortie *the shit done got real* such that I recognized dat my very own baby-browns be turned-it inwards whilst the hushed velvet soft voice of Bangkok Babyg' done caressed to done mesmerized my earholes the proof positive reconstruction parallelism contained in herns ominous bumping hot revelation bouts herns 10-month sensational a'sway too brief jump-off!

That be TOP's teachings hisns undetectable subtle philosophical sessions in life's needed to be done learned-it lessons seed I'd read that damn novel sum 20-years befo' that reality clock struck the mid-knight at the dawn of dat new day! Gustave be an intellectual, a master craftsman took a vacation to Venice to be *"startled at the godlike beauty … his mind and heart were drunk with passion"* that he felt *"…almost an hallucination"* from the brief moment he first sighted the *"half-grown lad"* Gustave mildly stalked the *"pure perfection"* now pause yo' ass fo' the cause justa give me a CC moment and be assured that the novel be knot a lustful deviant of the iffn Anita Bryant's Godly world where *Steve never gonna met-it up with Bruce* homosexual repast nor an epic saga bouts a perverted pedophile stalking his prey it be a tale of woe, a passage through the valley of self-inflicted regrets where bye-bye an old ass sage's passion becomes an obsession down the straight and narrow path to be hisns untimely death. Bangkok-babyg' had thems first few months living on the hills boasted how self-satisfied she be that she'd managed to stave-off a craving to *jimmy-jam* Tucson in quest of a young jump-off tryst to quench her *I needs me a young man with a hard dick* to get herns thrust-on! May the mid-way point of their first year she had her first panic attack *why the fuck did I leave Rodeo Drive* and all that good pre-paid *mums the word* dick in addition the *is this shit for reals*? Yes, baby, it be for reals the Arizona desert bumped-it up to done ushered in its most searing heat onto the newly arrivals OMG *whooo-wee Virginia there is a God* and that God mofo be living-it up in the Hell fires of the Arizona heat!

The dawn of one mid-May early-morn it be *Surprize Surprise Surprize Sergeant Carter* Mi-Linda's first thunk-it the heat and it be just a fleeting flickering mirage yet on the reals her God-like be standing tall as swell walking in the vivid lustful flesh in the perfect form of a young flaxen curly headed Adonis, a full-time University of Arizona *bear-down* hockey-player student-athlete big-*brawny*-butts also a parttime summertime pure fresh water deliveryman fated to deliver her that babyboy' goodie-stuff! Mi-Linda espied the *godlike* be toting *Arrowhead* water bottles to the neighboring townhomes along the course a 5-gallon jug heft atop each muscled, broad and beefy shoulder and when she ogled the unsurpassed beauty she done lost all track of time, bathes over-flowed, dinners burnt and she fluxed in then out of an odd but glorious stupor [Brothers: *homegirl got sprung*] herns predilection fo' the *come to me stud-boy* beef-cake had cracked the door to an even darker unbeknownest to her world because in the beginning she'd merely watched for the golden hair fair-skinned splendor through a kitchen crystal, sneaked-a-peek at the Heavenly sent hunk from behind a curtain, glimpsed the *oooooOOH he make my quim quake* with herns dare to be bare PHATT Bangkok body tightly pressed against a barely opened-it hand-carved mahogany front door then driven by her incessantly torrid, the bum-rush on-set of an *In-coming* obsession she'd paraded even times done the unimaginable Bangkok babyg' found-it hernself jogging along them gilded streets to *Sneaky-Pete* yet a'nuttier friendly *he smiled at me* gander at the comely one to gets herns growing increasingly hornier selfie an eyefull, she be eyeballing a taste of the desirous muscled male candy striding hard on and throughout thems golf course hills! E'nuff the summertime mildly stalking the playful prey she placed the order hey big-*splendor*-butts just *Sooners* received-it she'd uncapped-it to done rolled the jug spewing the fresh clear sparkling waters onto the surrounding desert landscape a process repeated almost daily interspersed with *upper valley-gurl* slight of mind stalking herns *boytoy* nigh onward the approach of autumn *Emmett Till* the fall of one schemed and deigned Saturday morning while impo'tant *Skeletor* hubby be sent to a far outta town destination then at the firstest opportunity Mi-Linda stationed herns petite oriental hottie self behind the partially closed all mahogany door to done leapt-it a *Surprize Surprise Surprize Sergeant Carter* upon the just stepped inside the foray hunk's firm muscled youthful body finally she'd thunk-it a worthy jump-off as she done enwrapped herns naked *can't stop the tingling tenderoni* thighs around hisns thin yet muscled waist-line. She kicked-it closed the slightly opened door then to her enchanted delight the heart-throb had been just as eager to frolic the *river aint dry* long-time forgotten waters that over-flowed then flooded from her too long deserted dessert oasis herns Word-up! *Tarzan* swung-it through the tree-less jungle straight-up Mi-Linda's agape oasis to the wonderful! "Thank God, I waited!" she gasped "OMG, Zeke, he was sooo-oooOOH marvelous his—" Bangkok-babyg's spring hadda done gotz sprung! *"Passion is like crime ..."* da' Mann, baby! Mi-Linda been there to done that big-*I be in luv*-butts OMG she done did that much mucho-much the *Moor* for she had experienced "*the rapture of his blood, the poignant pleasure of*"... da' Mann and she'd became infused by the constant steady strokes of the god-like to done felt-it hernself one lucky babe, sexually Bangkok-babyg' soared! [my Brothers: *Shorty's fear of flying got jacked*!; Eastside Player-haters: *Tramp*!; Southside Player-haters: *Skeeze skank*!; Trailer-trash: *git in da truck, Sis*! Po'dunks: *Fuck dat chop-stick stank cheating chink whore*!] Driven by her insatiable lust Mi-Linda had repeatedly correlated for herns unsuspecting and impo'tant banker man husband just an array of the business dates, golf trips mingled within a slewful of the whatevers whenevers wherevers just to get no lubby-dubby hubby outta the townhouse and onto a'nuttier it is what it is course of action witch be to put po'assed-out hubby on the gotta *run-run-run* be it the Tucson, Rio Rico, Phoenix, Tubac, Nogales justa anywhere outside of those Green Valley city limits for the few precious hours that the two secret yet ardent lovers desired fo' theys shared hushed whisper that only true lovers experienced!

Mi-Linda with hubby safely furloughed out of town, out of sight and most definitely outta her *need that Nordic dick* mind invited her new found love the awesome hunk out of the northern horizon full-time student-athlete always on time stud-muffin cause herns anytime be the right time *gotta have it* lover seed Mi-Linda had acquired for herns selfie a total body-ache for the ex-*Minnie-ha-ha* hockey playa/lover-boy to fluff and throwdown thems bed-pillows in the each *let's do it in* every bedroom of the grand hacienda [Tucson-Spaniards: *townhouse on the hills of a golf course for Spaniards-only*!] to thoroughly sate her uncontrollable desires to ruminate upon the magnificence, to languish in the powerful yet loving arms and to tend to the secretive affairs of lust on the golf *how many licks to the center of the lollipop* course of love! [Southside Player-haters: *straight-up Richy-rich booty-call! You go rich-bitch get yo' swerve-On*!; Trailer-trash: *baby-Sis is us's and uncle-daddy's fluff only*!] *So, Mi-Linda* after a'nuttier tour of the dance floor cause jo' Brotha won't never ever *electric slide*, I'd queried her, *y'all bumped-it them uglies, 60-by-60!* [Yuppies: *sweaty sex every hour on the hour*;

Religious Reich: *God don't like ugly! Ugly is ugly, whether you bumped it or not!*] "We did no such vulgar thing, you bug-eyed creep! His kisses were like the morning dew upon the rose and that cherished moisture caused my petals to spread and my awakened bud sought comfort cradled in the curl of his tantalizing tongue!" [my Brothas: *homie don't play dat shit!*] then as iffn on cue, Mi-Linda leaned inwards just a little closer unto me in-such that our noses had momentarily touched and I'd perceived to have felt them lustful yet deadly daggers in her beautiful baby-Bangkok browns protruded beneath herns semi-closed lids, her nostrils flared slightly and the left corner of her mouth raised a skosh when Bangkok-Babyg' spoke-it a heated rush "he not only penetrated my belly with the stamina of the tiger big-*long stroking*-butts he possessed the tongue of the prophet to fire-up my very soul. Now, that my little wild-eyed fiend is passion." She'd readily admitted he be addicting then after nearly 10-months of the sublime and extreme bliss she'd gotten careless and in one exhilarating moment the screams of herns joyous pleasures done completely silenced the soft footsteps of a *Surprize, Surprise Surprize Sergeant Carter* herns early arrival *honey, I'm home* hubby done limped *silent night* along the deep plush carpeted halls thus herns dear softly sweet hubby done stepped into a buena vista [Tucson-Spaniards: *a Spectacular view*] of her and the Adonis tightly interlaced in a complicated yet absolutely joyous intricate love knot! The lover cursed, chased, fired, kicked-off the hockey team had eventually with stout and strong stick returned to the land of the Minnie-ha-ha lakes!

Here, Zeke, my chocolate-man she handed me a flue of the bubbly *tip a toast to both my consummated lust and freedom"* Clinky-Clink-Clink---Clinky-Clink-Clink da' freaks come out at night and it be on, Baby! [my Brothas joined-it bye-bye hula-hula *get jo' party-on* gurlfriend: *the roof, da' roof, the roof is on fire, we don't need no water, let the motherfucker burn! Burn-Motherfucker-Burn!*] Bangkok-Babyg's hula-hula gets jo' party-on gurlfriend be working-it a righteous groove unto a Mexican-American whom had right-on time after we fo' done sipped-it thems firstest two cheap-assed overly charged-card theraputive champagne-filled flues hisns Messykin ass done bumped-it ugly the fat fact, Jack that hisns G-daddy be from of all the fucking places this fucking world, ya' knowed-it, Spain! [Tucson Spaniards: *El tiene mucha suerte! The lucky man. Because his grandfather like ours came from Spain*] Mi-Linda be knot just a'nuttier set of the pretty legs big-*so-*

phisticated-butts she be quite the intelligent, urbane and new-money rich *who'dat* be the sole-proprietor of a golf course townhome plus the fine-ass *abouts to be knocking them boots* Bangkok-babyg' gots a natural free-flowing sense of humor big-*wonderful*-butts she be super *Medgar Evers easy on the eyes* Mi-Linda be *da' shit* and she'd just done rolled-it hardtack life's fleeting and glorious *hot-damn, Its good to be me* punches! Da' Mann's as well Rich da' shit Pryor's characters had not flared nowhere near as swell Mi-Linda whom merely lost both an impotent husband and a young virile stud-muffin yet she retained her sense of humor, custody of the hacienda on the golf course and most importantly her gilded life-style [my Brothas: *Babygurl banged-cock gots paid! Yo' you still gotz dem digits?;* Gold-diggers: *ALI-MO'-NEE you go Bank-cock-gurl! Git that paper*!; South-side playa haters: *Bangkok-Shorty broke the bank, Holla!;* Tucson Spaniards: *just another proven fact just how easy it be for us Spaniards to find then keep the gold*!; kkk po'dunks: *Get a rope*!] The Brotha Leroy of Pryor's joke by all logic bro' man done gotten-it mortally maimed and or gravely bitten attempting to kiss that gorilla once that muzzle be removed then Gustave forced-fed by his own obsession over-stayed his welcome in Venice to done contacted *"the city's evil secret ...Asiatic cholera"* fo' sho'nuff da' Mann's Gustave paid passion's ultimate price, death to an old assed European *this be love* soda-cracker!

Tanks to Professor TOP breaking out the knowledge that Black knight at the disco became an on the personal passion filled virtuoso because thems tree tenors: Pryor, *da' Mann* and Mi-Linda done resonated a novel concerto in the inner chambers of my mind to be bumping the ego that concluded with a great crescendo of thought that unbridled, passion be a moment of total madness when reason vacates logic and rationale expands itself into a self-inflicted perpetual abyss of gleeful joy thus passion then becomes as endangering as it be endearing to the beholder! [Tucson-Spaniards: *estas loco mi burro, tu abrelo es un culo de negro no es de Espana! You crazy ass! Yo' Black ass grandfather didn't come from Spain*!] My wee-wee be hours of the woo woo-woo be whittled to just a few we-wee be minutes walking from the dance floor hand in hand with Mi-Linda the DJ announced *last call* and played the late great Marvin Gaye melody *"Let's get it on"* as both Pryor and da' Mann wrestled for control of a mind gone berserk the vividly lustful heated hush of Bangkok-Shortie's obsessive tale plus all the lovely hushed-it feathery sweet flickering kisses from a lovely Spanish-Moor! Mi-Linda had definitely dubiously decided to very subtly yet seductively have re-aligned once and again our noses to touch and caress continuously as Bangkok-Shorty delivered our finale converse

"Zeke, mi Negron guapo [Tucson-Spaniards: *WTF no way puto negro*!- Do the dew, mofos just do yo' job and interpret - *my big Black handsome buck*!] *I tell you these intimate secrets because you have the look of a lost and starved coyote wandering aimlessly through-out the hot and arid Arizona desert feeding off jackrabbits and cholla*! Thems damned Arizona jackrabbits be long-eared rats onliest mucho-much bigger and cholla be prickly burr encased cactus-weeds!" [my Brothas: *dat buster be bump'n skank hoes*!] Mi-Linda dwelled deadly deep down into the cellar of my glazed sparkling wine champagne soaked baby-browns then leaned much the Moor intimately closer unto my ruby-red smoke-free lips so close that each of her slovenly slowly whisked whispered words instant-grits became the most softest moistest flatteringly fluttered sweet kisses sans ex-Babyg' to *Medgar Evers* pressed my stealthily surprisingly silent lips *"I however, am choice Adam's rib, luxuriously primed and precious. I do not bump the uglies nor do I nosh the nasties! However I do make love with a passion! Mon Cheri, can you say the same?"*

Good Lawd, Hells afire! Good God damned, my surprised, stunted and warped dumb-fucked mind be t-totally blown the fuck away! To such that be that I hadda shouldda knot done did that witch my dumb-ass hadda done did because right then to be there I done shouted-it loud and clear *guards, guards, guards* big-*dummy*-butts thems po'dunk guards done come fast be furious on the run-run-run up and unto dat cage when theys done arrived thems skinny assed BarneyFife po-po guards stopped-it in theys redneck tracks to done looky-looked-it over firstest at the centuries old dead assed ghostly-white European sage dat maddening interloper mofo *da' Mann*, thems guards done peeked-it hisns as equally ghostly white-assed dead character *Gustave* befo' thems po'dunk po-po wannabe guards hadda seed me sitting-it all up and kissy-kissy face with the beautiful Bangkok-Babyg' anda her justa flutter kissing my non-Spanish *never done smoked-it* ruby-red lips with herns own blushed-it red sweet super-sweet sultry plush elegantly she be a rich-bitch lips justa feathery light fluttery butterfly Superfly all powerfully sweet kissing whilst delivering to me herns speech. Thems befuddled BarneyFife po'dunk axed-it my dumb hot-nuts ass the million dollar question of the Black Knight *"Yo' Bro, you want us to put the muzzle back on?* I be like *"Hell, No, motherfuckers*! *Get me da' fuck outta here*! *I just wanted a booty-call!"*

chapter 69

A'NUTTIER LESSON OF AND THROUGH that psychotic Black ass wannabe a fucking Messykin Trips be there will always be a logical and acceptable reason for everything performed under the sun yet always there be the real truth, Ruth why that shit done gots done liked its been done! Unlike *Windy City cuz* I'm gonna git it real to keep it on the reals seed my *KISS* version be that on the subconscious level I musta sensed-it that my Babygirl had come-down *Wonder Woman* strong hand in-order to done saved my *where be the war* because I gotta *kill kill kill fo' every meal* Black ass! My Babygirl had with the help of her evil twin *beyotch* the Twisted-Sista jumped-it down from atop the pedestal into the rabbit's hole abject abyss of my darkness then pulled my *screaming please don't do this shit* whupped-it-ass up and into the light and that be an on the reals fo' sho'nuff fat fact, Jack! I hadda done felt-it justa real and cloudy overcast after leaving behind thems VC tunnels back Saigon way that a dark presence had exited alongside me big-*darken*-butts that dark presence done dwelled handsomely unfettered all to its lonesome within my subconscious *how you doing* thus its dark presence became a welcomed habit dat eventually evolved itself into a lifesaving presence witch presided over all my immediate *give em' Georgia Hell then charge em' the price of Texas* In-coming endeavors! My Babygirl done bounced-it strong hand into my darken life with herns all healthy sunshiny bright countenance thus My Babygirl's joyful glee and love of life be the sunshine that had let in the light to done pierced-it my darken presence.

My darkness be an acceptance that done proven *its* worth fortified in the solid 24-carat gold on a'many *Good n' Plenty* deadly encounters along a path shrouded with onliest the two deadly options: death and destruction and dat shit be on the daily-double up-front ready on the personal then my darkness done looked-it at death's a'coming face to face, locked and loaded at the ready on-point then we done lived to done tasted its sweet unforgiving *Oh Lord, Death* done passed me bye-bye! The dark presence had been my survival mode *flip of the switch* instinctive acts of the *get yo' shit together* it be hammer-time, fight or flight, Mofo! Always there be no answering witch went without saying because there be no questioning liked the po'dunk TOP that darkness be just a calm and commanding *fucking do as I say do, mofo* presence that on many a dangerous *death be on jo' black ass* encounter I done relied upon, expected and knowed it to be always alive, ready and deadly on-point! The darkness done showed *its* presence and command by orchestrating all the actions that had proven-it to be instrumental in the sparing of my life at all cost seed my darkness gots a *me, me, me* complex an I come firstest, mofo over all else as it done scrolled the mantra rolling hardtack my skull that my life mattered-it over any and all other lives witch begot my personal thesis of the *bump dat ass Mofo* get in there and *get ya' fight-on*! My darkness had a desire to live bye-bye defeating death with death to be delivering-it *death to yo' dumb-ass* to all beings that done confronted me with a fucking its my life or theys death choice!

Mr. D done made *itself* to home in the *not for sale* open-house of my subconsciousness and *it* had started on the tub whilst I be idlily chipping paint when its dark ass be getting busy building hardwood shutters over the windows of my Soul to keep-out the any to all sunshine that be the light witch be the knowledge because fighting aints about the knowing nor the learning seed fighting be all about the doing witch be the fighting 101 dat be *Son, do the do*! *Now's not the time fo' the tinkering*! Fighting be all about instinctive actions and re-actions there gonna be a'nuttier as well a mostest favorable time for the planning and the thinking! On the reals dat darken Mr. D mofo been within me fo' the long haul ways back in the daze of rolling Unk' Zeke's pond it had been that mofo that done commanded-it my *knee-high to a cricket tater-tot* ass to done low-crawled-it through thems scraggly bushes and tall weeds when da' *Dirty Dozens* be a'popping! The dark mofo been inside that legendary make-shift ghetto-ass boxing ring when Mr. Bobby's grown-assed little kid ass kicking brothers be a'whupping-it up on my black ass *duck, left-hook, right-cross* it be justa calling-it out a series of the on-point self-defense instructions *Emmett Till* the mofo kid-ass kicking growed-it up grown-assed man done straight-up *Momma said to knock you* the fuck out! Assurdidly that dark Mofo be stumping *high-n-tight* when I done rolled-it up a dumb-ass with a useless weapon slung diagonally across and down my skinny-ass back onto a skank-ass fully armed locked and loaded slant-eye zipper-head then the darken one be liked *drop to the ground, motherfucker, crab-crawl yo' ass backwards, now forward to the left to the right, zig-zag our monkey ass the fuck outta here*! There be a time in the Gaza, I be fully dressed-it up pot on my big empty nappy, flax-jacketed with a cache of weapons strapped and walking a second-story hallway when outta the nowhere da' darken Mofo done commanded *jump the fuck outta that window on the left* then I be Blam the fuck bam airborne! No fucking pre-flight check nonya just mere seconds after I be up and outta that window on the dark command instant grits that fucking building gots mortared then chunk after chunks of concrete and rebar be raining all-around to be upon my ass on the down-*Swoop there it is*-fall! My Bros done looked-it me bug-eyed fucking *Zeke dawg be a ghost-turd* my arrival that safe-house!

There be no Psychic Hot-line to holla@ya'Boy nonya that *Ms. Cleo, hey* Dionne *that what friends are for* Warrick shit seed caught-up in a fix it onliest be me and *my Boy'* the darkness cause we be the onliest the bestest of friends to the *kiss my sweet black ass* it be the goodbye-bye end! We'z onliest done had peeps liked mah brotha Rich *da' shit* Pryor earlier comedy album *Is it something I said* where buy-n-buy he done introduced the world to a sidekick of hisns named *Mudbone* and the crazy-eight psychic *Miss Rudolf* to thumbnail-it seed Mudbone done visited-it dat psychic Miss Rudolf whom as she done offered-it up herns cure through the intervening of the metaphysical in the chaos of it all be happening a gigantic tarantula spider had come from out of the nowhere to done run up Pryor's leg and arm then down hisns backside before disappearing later when Pryor axed her what had happened to the tarantula Miss Rudolf referred him a reminder of her expected payment for having provided Mudbone her psychic service in that theys bring her either a goose or a turkey come next Thanksgiving day! Miss Rudolf done told Pryor not to worry about the tarantula big-*a'scard*-butts come next Thanksgiving day ...*iffn he don't bring that bitch a goose or a turkey, he gonna see that tarantula again*!

My Babygirl taught-it me that same Universal law and a proven straight-up fo'reallies reality in-that when the student be ready then the teacher shall come and my Babygirl with a great delight and a beacon of the sunshiny rays done burst forth knowledge unto my world because I had done come then herns PHATT ass be the teacher dat done sho'nuff bursted-it loose hardtack my dumb-ass! To my self-imposed darkness my Babygirl simply done shouted-it out *let there be light* when she went about herns business on the daily-double of opening them wooden shutters previously built within my subconscious by the lifesaving darkness under the guise of survival fo' the fittest witch hadda let it be done sho'nuff knowed-it to all thems comers dat I be the fittest! My Babygirl's alter-ego the Twisted-Sista's demonic actions had been a necessary evil in-that my

Babygirl's *Oh happy day* rays of the goodness could onliest open them shutters big-*Hells afire*-butts the Hell bent twist of the Twisted-Sista done burn-baby-burn thems opened-it shutters such dat theys became piles of the forgotten burnt ashes dat done dust dance along the winds of time. My Babygirl had trampled upon all that darkness bullshit utilizing my own KISS principal witch my dumb-ass had fully learnt-it to understand her utterance *let there Be Light* she had been determined to done reeducated-it my dumbness to the knowledge that everything done in this life has a consequence Biggy-smalls witch shall be proportionally repaid in-accordance yet not necessarily equal equity referenced against any a thought or performed action!

My Babygirl burst forth-it herns one-voice one-woman lessons unto my dumb-ass with a vengeance and my Babygirl done taught-it all slowly and gentle-like all the while she done on the itty-bitty baby-step walked-it me safely back to be away then completely off the ledge! My Babygurl done talked softly sweet unto my Soul in Blessed slumber all the wonderfully wonderful whilst she done vibrated my Black ass through Door numba-One the *Goodie-Stuff*! My Babygirl taught-it to me that once a lesson be learnt-it in the light then I could for *Medgar Evers* be to done walked-it back and forth in the enjoyment gleamed from the experienced and *Heaven helps me* it be not just the *one night stand* big-*lucky*-butts everytime forevers time I be enabled-it to done walked in the hardedge of that done learned-it light! *Yeah, dat shit be heavy*, baby! The darkness had instinctually stepped-it to my conscious ass to done commanded actions that had ultimately saved my life yet *its* darken quest of payment be … *come Thanksgiving* that Mr. I.B da' Darkness be exactly liked the psychic *Miss Rudolf …I had bestest to bring that bitch a goose or a turkey or I'm gonna see that tarantula again*!

The darkness demanded compensation in a forever series of lifetime installments in-that I become its unwavering servant with an unequivocal adherence to its rules and its by-laws as swell its sway of life! My Babygirl done learnt-it me to answer the darkness and its request of my total loyalty, compliance and obedience as its demanded payment thus it be then that my Babygirl done the KISS factor! My Babygurl simply grabbed ahold to done shook my wussified ass then as we lay all cuddled-it up with herns good vibrations she done taught-it me to done answered my darkness just tell dat mofo, *Fuck that shit,* Zeke! That ice-breaker had been even more provocative for me because it be a straight-up rarity iffn my

Babygirl had *Medgar Evers* done straight-up cussed-it thus the strength of her answer to my darkness *Fuck that shit,* Zeke be a major instrument utilized within herns gotta reeducate this dumb-ass to the facts that be life, baby! My Babygirl done taught-it to me that life be lived within the moment, the here and the right the fuck now because the past dat bitch ain't a never coming back be gone and the future witch may be or not be a question of destiny may or not be a'coming outta the horizon over on the yonder that quick be furious fast approaching light you see might be a 200mph freight train bouts to done run jo' dumb ass over! She done taught-it to me that being beholden to actions done in the past be illogical and just plain assed sharecropper mentality stupid ergo by herns KISS teachings and persistence be da' shit therefore I done felt-it deep within the little stoned-pit that be my itty-bitty iced-over heart of hearts that I done owed an immense raft of gratitude and a 10-fold forever a chunk of the gratefulness unto my Babygirl for having the fortified fortitude and courage to done shaken my slumbering like a mofo cuddled-it up black ass to be bustin-loose from the darken grip thus it be herns *good vibrations* dat done sho'nuff saved-it my ass from dat dip into the darkness!

Chapter 70

The awful true fo'reallies reason be that although my Babygirl done saved-it my ass from that dip into the darkness be the no macho-bullshit real truth, Ruth big-*confessional*-butts the illogical legit what be the on the reals be that my sorry ass could not, would not nor didn't even try to do the very same for her most lovely of the lovelies fine brown-suga PHATT ass. The Momma in her zeal to see all tree of her girls get the bestest that life had to offer had done placed-it sway too much pressure on theys slender shoulders to do good, be good to almostest be Heavenly perfect *fuck, theys silky fine asses didn't even tank Gawd attend nonya a'nobody's damned church*! I'd done seed-it and yes, I'd even done heard-it all the pressurized bullshit because the Momma had on the constantly berated herns tree girl-chillens straight-up and all in theys grilles and it be a self-evident fat fact, Jack that thems tree babygirls had done good even mos' butter than good because thems tree ebony Queens done great and theys all done it great the right-way there be no backsliding sassy-hussy sneak-thiefs amongst them! Theys all the tree be college graduated professionals, the oldest one be an accountant, the middle lovely be a high school teacher and ex-Babyg' c*razy-eights* ass be a Registered Nurse theys all gots good as swell legit careers. The Momma big-*sourdough*-butts she hadn't challenged theys straight-up impeccable merits seed the evil bag of rottening *get along evil doggie* turds done crab-walked down on the personal egos of each them tree beauties! The Momma chose to straight-up out in the fucking open air theater *snatch thems tree lovelies bald* bye-bye way of badmouthing each theys personal choices outta the mens department store seed nonyas them tree girlchilds could even come a bite close to choosing the right man-sized apparel to suit the *now that I've gots money I can be an uppity ass* Momma.

The thing that nonya thems babygirls especially my Babygirl never done learnt-it be that it didn't matter *WTF* the Momma done wanted-it in theys choice of a man to done hit theys shit because thems mens be theys men besides thems other two hubbys be college educated professionals thus theys be nobody's fools! In this life it be easy to done seed-it what be the *pain in the ass* problems of others yet we individually be t-totally fucking clueless about the shit that be fucking-it all up our own damned personal lives! Thems tree dumb-assed girlchilds response to the Momma's nick-picking hardtack gum-flapping to the each abouts theys of theys own self personally chosen man should have been big-*funky*-butts *Momma he's my man*! I done mixed-it up with thems nuttier two uppity drunken knuckles because the Momma always gots herns evil assed frumpy self some kinda dinner party invite for her to be trucking out the parade of just how *no good yo' dumb-ass husband be* to us tree *a'scardy-ass* fools front-street our lovely wives, all thems geeks and any-to-all peeps in attendance herns shit be straight-outta the mouth of the uppity shameful! The Momma dat fool didn't spare no-quarters thems two fools be lazy-assed drunkards big-*flabby biscuits*-butts I'd done represented-it *Boo-Boo the clown* in dress *Ja'renes* blues and 22-inch big red floppies taint no wonder as to just why thems two other *good fo' nuttin never do wells* addictive alcoholic shits had been the in the flesh and the obvious answer to the firstest WTF question as to why my Babygirl had been all Hell-bent demonic like constantly on the search for drugs and alcohol throughout the both my mental as swell physical closets! Thems two older husbands instead of fighting the Momma abouts herns incessant *fucking with theys wife's head* thems two fools had done looked-it one to the other and to all thems other ways whilst the Momma and theys wives done *cut theys balls off* at the nubs! My dumb-ass done nearly the same damned ting to done toed the Momma's hardline then all tree us hubbys be just a sack of the big-*a'scared*-butts instead of us tree been whipped wussies *getting our shit together* to be a'fighting the Momma the dog in me had just liked thems nuttier two done rolled-it over to done tucked its tail between its legs liked-it be justa little wuss-puppy answering to the call of *duf'* to done runned-it to the local YMCA, the park or the gym to done played *fetch* the b-ball then mo' *Sooners* to be dumped-it I'd done gotten-it into sum the evil ass Momma *said to knock you out* fisticuffs with drunken rednecks justa to fucking avoid waking-up the dawg then doing the *Right ting* witch be stepping-it up like a grown-ass man *swinging a hairy pair* and protecting my Babygirl from the demonic wiles of the *ugly ass* Momma! "*Your duf' ass was scared shit-less*"

In my hour of need unselfishly my Babygirl hadda on herns own accord done stepped-it up to done fought-it the hard and righteously good fight fo' to done saved-it my dumb-ass from the front-street my Babygirl bumped-it hardtack against all comers as she be battling the likes of TOP, Trips, the boys and especially my darkness *tank God* fo' my Babygirl cause she be *winner-winner* no chicken dinner done won! Babygirl done kicked-it mucho culo as she done stepped-it two tits deep into all theys asses then stood proudly looking-it back my way over herns succulent shoulders. In payment my raw-dawg ass turned tail to done left-it herns sweet sexy selfie drown-it in thems nasty assed tar-pits of the Momma's shitty-ass sorrows without even the whimper of a there be a dog in me fight! In my onliest defense I hadn't figured-it nonya all that psychological family verses family narcissistic shit out *Emmett Till* many moons done passed-it the bye-bye keeping it real I'd done sensed-it that evil shit dat the Momma couldn't stand to done seed-it any of herns young girlchilds married, happy and enjoying the fruits of theys labor witch the big-*old biscuit and sausages slamming*-butt hadn't garnered until later in herns despicable life!

Ex-Babyg' spending all that house aint a home sale money be a cover story because behind the green curtains that little piddling sack of the mo' than I'd done *Medgar Evers* seed monies be justa half-assed half-hearted down payment on the how comes I didn't have the heart to *stand by my woman's* side to *battle mofo* harder to done freed herns fine-ass from the lurking evil ass heavy-handed demanding, demeaning and nasty assed-out tricks used-it bye-bye the Momma to command ex-Babyg's total servitude, obedience and loyalty under the guise of survival because *we be family*! It be a Universal fat fact, Jack that ignorance of the Law aint no excuse! My selfish clueless ass hadn't done a'nuttin about all dat Cinderella syndrome psycho momma bullshit! Iffn I'd done sported-it a hairy pair I woulda done told-it ex-Babyg' to go tell herns crazy-eights the Momma to just *Fuck that shit, Momma!*

Chapter 71

THE TING I DID DONE learnt-it witch I perceived to be a major problem amongst womankind that onliest occurs when thems womenfolks done formed-it of themselves some sorta momma/daughter, teacher/student justa any kinda dems woman to woman no-*dyking* tings! The problem be that thems womenfolks can't and must at all cost never *Medgar Evers* be done trusted-it the each to the other any given female's requested and or unsolicited advice concerning any to all of theys on the personal male to female relationship problems. In any male to female relationship the womens are far mo' superior and sway ahead the game such that thems womenfolks be justa sitting on deys rumps clipping, chipping and trimming theys fingernails and or toenails outta relationship boredom! Mostest dem womenfolks already have all theys male-relationships figured-it from dat unsuspecting mofo's very firstest wink *Whats sup* to the naming of all theys chillens! Theys pre-planned done thunk-it shit be to the lady *cat's in the bag* that be why thems womenfolk be *BORING*! The fat fact, Jack be that for any woman to woman on the personal *pinky-swear* solemn male-female relationship advice it be legally writ that for both the giver and the receiver of such bullshit advice the both theys talkative asses done knowed-it at the time of the giving that she the giver as swell she the receiver did done knowed-it be the real truth, Ruth that some to all parts of herns given advice to be pure assed unadulterated BULLSHIT! The law further states that iffn the receiver woman of the given BULLSHIT advice be to confronted-it the woman that done up-chucked all that bullshit given as good advice when confronted the giver of the bullshit woman shall forever plus a day be *Bitch don't listen to me, I just told you what be on my mind* and that there bullshit answer will forever suffice to be the end of all said bullshit because woman to woman dat shit be legit!

The bullshit advice concerning any male-female relationship given of one woman to a'nuttier woman be justa *bitch, you gotta done learnt-it* process to a woman's rite of passage into womanhood that dat dumb-bitch won't forever forget because that dumb-bitch just gots *SKOOLED*! It's the same thing for the man because the dumb-ass in man has to done self-taught it himself to done learnt-it that acting on hisns gut-feelings be having *shit for brains* soons hisns dumb-ass about to be SKOOLED thus when it all be sad to be done in both case scenarios for both the dumb-ass man as equally the dumb-ass woman it be in all reality knot a Prozac moment big-*shouldda known better*-butts an unpleasant yet life necessity for theys adult maturation *it be what it be* sometimes a dumb-bunny gots to be skooled!

That woman to woman advice bullshit don't be *no excuse me Miss* I knowed that I'd still done ex-Babyg' wrong, keeping on the reals the onliest reason that I hadda gotten them hairy assed coconut balls with the courage to leave the *Love Shack* to done it on the good foot, hauled-it asshole over dems teacups a sway from herns PHATT *Hersey's* kissed ass had been that damned the Twisted-Sista crazy-eights forever chocolate bombshell ass failed-it tank Gwad attempt to done set my house afire with my dumb-ass inside bumping-it a blissful *Peace be still* asleep to this world! The Twisted-Sista done hi-jacked to done straight-up crazy-eight fucked-it up my darkness from afar! The mofo became a'scard ass thus I could not nor would not shut-eye with my Babygirl after dat nightmarish shit! Hell, yeah it mattered not one spit the Devil's wit even iffn she be drenched in *the Coty*!

The real truth, Ruth be that my Babygirl hadda babystepped-it to done walked-it my raw-dog ass from outta them fucking shadows and into the light thus my darkness had done not onliest learnt-it to love the PHATT chocolate Wonder Woman big-*in luv*-butts dat dark Mofo be all chips in because *In my Babygirl* fo' us two it be Biggy-smalls *trust* seed me and my darkness did done trusted herns most beautiful cinnamon nutmeg brown sexy ass to the fullest big-*dummy*-butts the Twisted-Sista's fucking fire-bombing of the garage hadda serious as a heart-attack grip unto the darkness cause that shit done singed hisns darken ass thus the mofo *Billy-bad-ass* Mr. I.B. da' Darkness became a'scared ass because fo' hisns raw-dog ass there be not any altered ego the Twisted-Sista theys both be the one beauty as swell theys PHATT ass be the same beauty witch be my Babygirl. When my Babygirl done moved-it back into the *Love Shack* and I be the one happy-nappy black ass then after the good deed be done did and my Babygirl liked times past be done cuddled-it up to done bringed-it on the Goodie-Stuff with all herns good vibrations *let the Good Times roll* daze of yore swells *Sir* it hadda been in that exact-amente CC moment that the darkness done grabbed-it up hisns hat and hadda been liked *Yo' Zeke, I gotta step around the corner and see a man about a dog*! Dat bad-assed mofo done left-it me to sleep-it one eye-opened all the *I be sleepless in the OKC* night long cuddled-it up beside my Babygirl then after tree to four daze of no fucking sleep it be not the usual flare of thems warm and fuzzies big-*itchings*-butts it be thems fucking crazy-eights willies dat be a'creeping-it up to be a'crawling-it all to be over my dumb-ass because I'd done given-it in to the nightmare done *bursted-it loose* then moved-it to that apartment!

My Babygirl done crazy-eight bitch slapped-it to done fo'reallies a'scared the shit outta the one Mofo dat I hadda on the reals fo' a fat fact, Jack done straight-up knowed-it be not afraid of anyting nor anybody this world! That mofo, my Mr. I.B. da' Darkness hadda been through it all because dat mofo always hadda plan! Hisns darken ass done seed the many be theys a'plenty ways *Brotha Death* be *In-coming* to done stood tall his ground to been stabbed, cut and shot-it up then went the fuck back fo' mo' the same old shit big-*a'scaredy cat*-butts when my Babygirl tempted to put afire to hisns sound asleep darkened ass and hims be a *she be my girl* trusting ass with all hisns little peach-pit of a heart plus all hisns Soul thens that darkened Mofo be liked damned *Skippy* bump dat shit thus that mofo hadda hatted-it up and done took-it my horny-toad ass along fo' the ride! Thems few daze after my Babygirl done moved-it back to the Love Shack *good Lord* with all herns sweet this be what I be missing the goodie-stuff I be justa happy-ass big ole' black bug-eyed lovebug, baby! Big-*a'scared*-butts my darkness dat mofo be the one a'scared of hisns own jackass shadow to done grabbed-it hisns skycap and go around the corner and done seed a man about a dog and pony show! Ergo when it came time to cuddle-it up fo' all thems *good vibrations* to be writ all over my one be my onliest Soul bye-bye my Babygirl then in thems exactamente moments Mr. I.B. da' Darkness the done planned-it all to done saved-it my black ass forever and a daze strong-arm like a motherfucker done told-it me straight-up *Zeke, Fuck that shit!*

Made in the USA
Las Vegas, NV
31 July 2023

75479326R00166